THE
WINNER

The Winner

David Baldacci

Thorndike Press • Chivers Press
Thorndike, Maine, USA   Bath, England

This Large Print edition is published by Thorndike Press, USA and by Chivers Press, England.

Published in 1998 in the U.S. by arrangement with Warner Books, Inc.

Published in 1998 in the U.K. by arrangement with Simon & Schuster Ltd.

U.S.   Hardcover 0-7862-1281-0 (Basic Series Edition)
U.K.   Hardcover 0-7540-1144-5 (Windsor Large Print)

The text of this Large Print edition is unabaridged.
Other aspects of the book may vary from the original edition.

Set in 16 pt. Plantin.

Printed in the United States on permanent paper.

British Library Cataloguing in Publication Data available

Library of Congress Cataloging in Publication Data

Baldacci, David.
    The winner / David Baldacci.
      p. cm.
     ISBN 0-7862-1281-0 (large print : hc : alk. paper)
     1. Large type books. I. Title.
   [PS3552.A446W56 1998]
    813'.54—dc21
                                      97-32306

To Collin,
my buddy, my boy, my son

Acknowledgments

To Michelle, for keeping everything going while I'm off in my dream world.

To Jennifer Steinberg, for superb research, as always.

To Catherine Broome, M.D., for taking the time from a very busy schedule to talk poisons with me over lunch.

To Steve Jennings, for his always sharp editorial eye.

To Carl Patton, my favorite accountant, and Tom DePont of NationsBank, for much needed help on complex tax issues.

To Larry Kirshbaum, Maureen Egen, and the rest of the Warner crew, for being so supportive and just plain, good people.

To Aaron Priest, for being my sage, my mentor, and, most important, my friend.

To Frances Jalet-Miller, for once again making the story immeasurably better.

To the rest of my family and friends, for their continued love and support.

PART ONE

Chapter One

Jackson studied the shopping mall's long corridor, noting haggard mothers piloting loaded strollers and the senior citizens group walking the mall both for exercise and conversation. Dressed in a gray pinstriped suit, the stocky Jackson stared intently at the north entrance to the shopping mall. That would no doubt be the one she would use since the bus stop was right in front. She had, Jackson knew, no other form of transportation. Her live-in boyfriend's truck was in the impoundment lot, the fourth time in as many months. It must be getting a little tedious for her, he thought. The bus stop was on the main road. She would have to walk about a mile to get there, but she often did that. What other choice did she have? The baby would be with her. She would never leave it with the boyfriend, Jackson was certain of that.

While his name always remained Jackson for all of his business endeavors, next month his appearance would change dramatically from the hefty middle-aged man he was currently. Facial features of course would again be altered; weight would probably be lost; height added or taken away, along with hair. Male or female? Aged or youthful? Often, the persona would be taken from people whom he knew, either wholly or bits of thread from different ones, sewn together until the delicate quilt of fabrication was complete. In school, biology had been a favorite subject. Specimens belonging to that rarest of all classes, the hermaphrodite, had never ceased to fascinate him. He smiled as he dwelled for a moment on this greatest of all physical duplicities.

Jackson had received a first-rate education from a prestigious Eastern school. Combining his love of acting with his natural acumen for science and chemistry, he had achieved a rare double major in drama and chemical engineering. Mornings would find him hunched over pages of complex equations or malodorous concoctions in the university's chemistry lab, while the evenings would have him energetically embroiled in the production of a Tennessee Williams or Arthur Miller classic.

Those accomplishments were serving him very well. Indeed, if his classmates could only see him now.

In keeping with today's character — a middle-aged male, overweight and out of shape from leading a sedentary lifestyle — a bead of perspiration suddenly sprouted on Jackson's forehead. His lips curled into a smile. This physical reaction pleased him immensely, aided as it was by the insulation of the padding he was wearing to provide bulky proportions and to conceal his own wiry frame. But it was something more than that too: He took pride in the fact that he became the person totally, as though different chemical reactions took place within him depending on who and what he was pretending to be.

He didn't normally inhabit shopping malls; his personal tastes were far more sophisticated. However, his clientele were most comfortable in these types of surroundings, and comfort was an important consideration in his line of work. His meetings tended to make people quite excited, sometimes in negative ways. Several interviews had become extremely animated, compelling him to think on his feet. These reminiscences brought another smile to Jackson's lips. You couldn't argue with success, though. He was batting a thousand. However, it only took one to spoil his perfect record. His smile quickly faded. Killing someone was never a pleasant experience. Rarely was it justified, but when it was, one simply had to do it and move on. For several reasons he hoped the meeting today would not precipitate such an outcome.

He carefully dabbed his forehead with his pocket handkerchief and adjusted his shirt cuffs. He smoothed down a barely visible tangle in the synthetic fibers of his neatly groomed wig. His real hair was compressed under a latex skullcap.

He pulled open the door to the space he had

11

rented in the mall and went inside. The area was clean and orderly — in fact too much so, he thought suddenly as he slowly surveyed the interior. It lacked the look of a true working space.

The receptionist seated behind the cheap metal desk in the foyer looked up at him. In accordance with his earlier instructions, she didn't attempt to speak. She had no idea who he was or why she was here. As soon as Jackson's appointment showed up, the receptionist had been instructed to leave. Very soon she would be on a bus out of town, her purse a little fatter for her minimal troubles. Jackson never looked at her; she was a simple prop in his latest stage production.

The phone beside her sat silent, the typewriter next to that, unused. Yes, absolutely, too well organized, Jackson decided with a frown. He eyed the stack of paper on the receptionist's desk. With a sudden motion he spread some of the papers around the desk's surface. He then cocked the phone around just so and put a piece of paper in the typewriter, winding it through with several quick spins of the platen knob.

Jackson looked around at his handiwork and sighed. You couldn't think of everything all at once.

Jackson walked past the small reception area, quickly hitting the end of the shallow space, and then turned right. He opened the door to the tiny interior office, slipped across the room, and sat down behind the scuffed wooden desk. A small TV sat in one corner of the room, its blank screen staring back at him. He pulled a cigarette from his pocket, lit it, and leaned far back in the chair, trying his best to relax despite the constant flow of adrenaline. He stroked his thin, dark mustache. It too was made of synthetic fiber ventilated on a lace foundation and attached to his skin with spirit gum. His nose had been changed considerably as well: a putty base highlighted and shadowed, to make his nose's actual delicate and straight appearance bulky and slightly crooked. The small mole resting next to the altered bridge of his nose was also fake: a concoction of gelatin and alfalfa seeds mixed in hot water. His straight teeth were covered with acrylic caps to give them an uneven and unhealthy appearance. All of these illusions would be remembered by even the most casual observer. Thus when they were removed, he, in essence, disappeared. What more could someone wholeheartedly engaged in illegal activities want?

Soon, if things went according to plan, it would all begin again. Each time was a little different, but that was the exciting part: the not knowing. He checked his watch again. Yes, very soon. He expected to have an extremely productive meeting with her; more to the point, a mutually beneficial meeting.

He only had one question to ask LuAnn Tyler, one simple question that carried the potential for very complex repercussions. Based upon his experience, he was reasonably certain of her answer, but one just never knew. He dearly hoped, for her sake, that she would give the right one. For there was only one "right" answer. If she said no? Well, the baby would never have the opportunity to know its mother, because the baby would be an orphan. He smacked the desktop with the palm of his hand. She would say yes. All the others had. Jackson shook his head vigorously as he thought it through. He would make her see, convince her of the inescapable logic of joining with him. How it would change everything for her. More than she could ever imagine. More than she could ever hope for. How could she say no? It was an offer that simply no one could refuse.

If she came. Jackson rubbed his cheek with the back of his hand, took a long, slow drag on the cigarette, and stared absently at a nail pop in the wall. But, truth be known, how could she not come?

Chapter Two

The brisk wind sailed straight down the narrow dirt road between the compression of thick woods on either side. Suddenly the road curved north and then just as abruptly dipped to the east. Over a slight rise the view yielded still more trees, some dying, bent into what seemed painful shapes by wind, disease, and weather; but the majority were ramrod straight, with thickening girths and soaring, leafy branches. On the left side of the road, the more diligent eye could discern a half circle of open space consisting of mud interspersed with patches of new spring grass. Also nestled with nature into this clearing were rusted engine blocks, piles of trash, a small mountain of bone-dry beer cans, discarded furniture, and a litany of other debris that served as visual art objects when covered with snow, and as home to snakes and other creatures when the mercury made its way north. Smack in the middle of that semicircular island rested a short, squat mobile trailer atop a crumbling cinder block foundation. Seemingly its only touch with the rest of the world were the electrical and telephone lines that ran down from the thick, leaning poles along the road and collided with one side of the trailer. The trailer was a decided eyesore in the middle of nowhere. Its occupants would have agreed with that description: The middle of nowhere was aptly applied to themselves as well.

Inside the trailer, LuAnn Tyler looked at herself in the small mirror perched atop the leaning chest of drawers. She held her face at an unusual angle, not only because the battered piece of furniture listed to one side with a broken leg, but also because the mirror was shattered. Meandering lines grew outward on the surface of the glass like the slender branches of a sapling such that if LuAnn had looked head-on into the mirror she would have seen not one but three faces in the reflection.

LuAnn didn't smile as she studied herself; she could never really remember smiling at her appearance. Her looks were her only asset — that had been beaten into her head ever since she could remember — although she could have used some dental work. Growing up on unfluoridated well water and never stepping foot inside a dentist's office had contributed to that situation.

No smarts, of course, her father had said over and over. No smarts, or no opportunity to use them? She had never broached the subject with Benny Tyler, dead now these past five years. Her mother, Joy, who had passed away almost three years ago, had never been happier than after her husband died. That should have completely dispelled Benny Tyler's opinions of her mental ability, but little girls believed what their daddy told them, mostly unconditionally.

She looked over to the wall where the clock hung. It was the only thing she had of her mother's; a family heirloom of sorts, as it had been given to Joy Tyler by her own mother on the day she married Benny. It had no intrinsic value; you could buy one in any pawnshop for ten bucks. Yet LuAnn treasured it. As a little girl LuAnn had listened to the slow, methodical ticks of that clock far into the night. Knowing that in the middle of all the darkness it would always be there, it would always soothe her into sleep and greet her in the morning. Throughout her growing up it had been one of her few anchoring points. It had a connection, too, in that it went back to her grandmother, a woman LuAnn had adored. Having that clock around was like having her grandmother around forever. As the years had gone by, its inner workings had worn down considerably so that it produced unique sounds. It had carried LuAnn through more bad times than good, and right before Joy died she had told LuAnn to take it, to take good care of it. And now LuAnn would keep it for her daughter.

She pulled her thick auburn hair straight back, tried a bun, and then dexterously knotted a French braid. Not satisfied with either of these looks, she finally piled her thick tresses on top and secured them with a legion of bobby pins, frequently cocking her head to test the effect. At five feet ten inches tall, she also had to stoop to see herself in the mirror.

Every few seconds she looked over at the small bundle on the chair next to her. She smiled as she took in the droopy eyes, the curved mouth, the chipmunk cheeks, and doughy fists. Eight months and growing up fast. Her daughter had already started to crawl with the funny, back-and-forth gyrations of infancy. Walking would soon replace that. LuAnn stopped smiling as she looked around. It would not take Lisa long to navigate the boundaries of this place. The interior, despite LuAnn's diligent efforts to keep it clean, resembled the exterior largely due to the temperamental outbursts of the man sprawled on the bed. Duane Harvey had twitched once or twice since staggering into the house at four A.M., throwing off his clothes, and climbing into bed, but otherwise he had remained motionless. She recalled fondly that on one night early in their relationship, Duane had not come home drunk: Lisa had been the result. Tears glimmered for the briefest time in LuAnn's hazel eyes. She hadn't much time or sympathy for tears, particularly her own. At twenty years of age she had already cried enough of them to last her until the end of her days, she figured.

She turned back to the mirror. While one of her hands played with Lisa's tiny fist, LuAnn used the other to pull out all the bobby pins. She swept her hair back and then let her bangs fall naturally forward over her high forehead. It was a style she had worn in school, at least through the seventh grade, when she had joined many of her friends in the rural county in dropping out and seeking work and the paycheck that came with it. They had all thought, wrongly as it turned out, that a regular paycheck beat the hell out of an education any day of the week. For LuAnn, there hadn't been much choice. Half her wages went to help her chronically unemployed parents. The other half went to pay for things her parents couldn't afford to give her, such as food and clothes.

She eyed Duane carefully as she undid her tattered robe, revealing her naked body. Seeing no sign of life from him, she swiftly pulled on her underwear. As she grew up, her blossoming figure had been a true eye-opener for the local boys, making them press for manhood even before the natural order of things would allow them official entry.

LuAnn Tyler, the movie-star-slash-supermodel-to-be. Many of the residents of Rikersville County, Georgia, had thoroughly considered the issue of LuAnn and bestowed upon her that title, weighted down as it was with the highest of expectations. She was not

19

long for their way of life, it was plain to see, proclaimed the wrinkled, thick local women holding court on their broad, decaying porches, and no one disagreed with them. The natural beauty she possessed would hold out for nothing less than the glossiest of all brass rings. She was the vicarious hope for the locals. New York or maybe Los Angeles would beckon to *their* LuAnn, it was only a matter of time. Only she was still here, still in the very same county where she had lived all her life. She was a disappointment of sorts without ever — despite being barely out of her teens — having had the opportunity to realize any of her goals. She knew the townsfolk would have been surprised to realize that her ambitions did not include lying naked in bed next to Hollywood's hunk of the month or treading the models' catwalk wearing the latest creations of the haute couture crowd. Although, as she slipped into her bra, it occurred to her that, right about now, sliding into the latest fashions in exchange for ten thousand dollars a day was not such a bad deal.

Her face. And her body. Her father had often commented on that attribute too. Voluptuous, full-figured, he had described it, as though it were an entity distinct from her. Weak mind, dazzling body. Thankfully, he had never gone beyond those verbalizations. Late at night she sometimes wondered if he had ever wanted to but simply lacked the courage or the opportunity. Sometimes the way he would look at her. On rare occasions, she would venture into the deepest parts of her subconscious and sense, like the sudden, scary prick of a needle, the disjointed pieces of a memory that made her wonder if the opportunity maybe had presented itself. At that point she would always shudder and tell herself that thinking such evil of the dead was not a good thing.

She studied the contents of the small closet. Really, she owned only one dress that would be appropriate for her appointment. The short-sleeve, navy blue with white trim around the collar and hemline. She remembered the day she bought it. A whole paycheck blown. *Sixty-five entire dollars.* That was two years ago and she had never repeated that insane extravagance, in fact it was the last dress she had bought. The garment was a little frayed now, but she had done a nice touch-up job with needle and thread. A strand of small, fake pearls, a birthday gift from a former admirer, encircled her long neck. She had stayed up late methodically coloring in the nicks on her only pair of high heels. They were dark brown and didn't match the dress but they would have to do. Flip-flops or sneakers, her only other two choices, were not going to cut it today, although she would wear the sneakers on the mile-long trek to the bus stop. Today could be the start of something new, or at least different. Who knew? It could lead to some-where, anywhere. It could carry her and Lisa away to something other than the Duanes of the world.

LuAnn took a deep breath, opened up the zippered interior pocket of her purse, and care-fully unfolded the piece of paper. She had written down the address and other informa-tion from the phone call from someone who had identified himself as a Mr. Jackson, a call she had almost not answered after pulling the midnight to seven shift as a waitress at the Number One Truck Stop.

When the phone call came LuAnn's eyes had been welded shut as she sat on the kitchen floor breast-feeding Lisa. The little girl's teeth were coming in and LuAnn's nipples felt like they were on fire, but the baby formula was too damn expensive and they were out of milk. At first, LuAnn had no desire to answer the phone. Her job at the popular truck stop right off the interstate kept her running nonstop, with Lisa meanwhile tucked safely under the counter in her baby seat. Luckily, the little girl could hold a bottle and the diner's manager liked LuAnn enough that the arrangement hadn't jeopardized her position. They didn't get many calls. Mostly Duane's buddy looking for him to go drinking or strip a few cars that had broken down on the highway. Their Bud and Babe money they called it, and often right to her face. No, it was not Duane's boys calling

22

this early. Seven A.M. would find them three hours into the deep sleep of another drinking binge.

After the third ring, for some reason, her hand had reached out and plucked up the phone. The man's voice was crisp and professional. He had sounded as though he were reading from a script and her sleep-clouded mind had pretty much reasoned that he was trying to sell her something. That was a joke! No charge cards, no checking account, just the little bit of cash hung in a plastic bag inside the hamper she used for Lisa's dirty diapers. It was the only place Duane would never search. Go ahead, mister, you just try to sell me something. Credit card number? Well let me just make one up right now. Visa? MasterCard? AmEx? Platinum. I've got 'em all, at least in my dreams. But the man had asked for her by name. And then he had mentioned the work. He wasn't selling her anything. He, essentially, was offering her employment. *How did you get my phone number?* she had asked him. The information was readily available, he had replied, so authoritatively that she instantly believed him. But she already had a job, she had told him. He asked what her salary was. She refused to answer at first and then, opening her eyes while Lisa suckled contentedly, she told him. She wasn't sure why. Later, she would think that it was a premonition of things to come.

Because that's when he had mentioned the pay.

One hundred dollars per weekday for a guaranteed two weeks. She had quickly done the arithmetic in her head. A total of one thousand dollars with the very real possibility of more work to come at those same rates. And they weren't full days. The man had said four hours tops, per day. That wouldn't affect her job at the truck stop at all. That came to twenty-five dollars per hour. No one she knew had ever earned such money. Why, at a full year that was twenty-five thousand dollars! And really, she would only be working half-time. So the rate was more like fifty thousand dollars per year! Doctors, lawyers, and movie stars earned such gigantic sums, not a high school dropout mother residing in the hopeless grip of poverty with someone called Duane. As if responding to her unspoken thoughts, Duane stirred for an instant, looking at her through brick-red eyes.

"Where the hell you going?" Duane's voice was thick with the drawl of the area. It seemed that she had heard those same words, that same tone, all her life from a variety of men. In response she picked up an empty beer can off the chest of drawers.

"How 'bout another beer, bay-bee?" She smiled coyly and arched her eyebrows wickedly. Her thick lips dangled each syllable seductively. It had the desired effect. Duane

24

groaned at the sight of his malt and aluminum God and slumped back into the grip of his coming hangover. Despite his frequent drinking binges, he never could hold his liquor. In another minute he was asleep once more. The baby-doll smile instantly faded and LuAnn looked at the note again. The work, the man had said, involved trying new products, listening to some ads, getting her opinion on things. Sort of like a survey. Demographic analysis, he had termed it, whatever the hell that was. They did it all the time. It was connected to advertising rates, and television commercials, things like that. A hundred dollars a day for just giving her opinion, something she did for free just about every minute of her life.

Too good to be true, really. She had thought that a number of times since his phone call. She was not nearly as dumb as her father had thought. In fact, housed behind her comely face was an intellect far more powerful than the late Benny Tyler could have imagined, and it was coupled with a shrewdness that had allowed her to live by her wits for years now. However, only rarely did anyone go beyond her looks. She often dreamed of an existence where her boobs and butt weren't the first, last, and only thing anyone ever noticed about her, ever commented on.

She looked over at Lisa. The little girl was awake now, her eyes darting around the bedroom until they came to rest with much glee upon her mother's face. LuAnn's eyes crinkled back at her little girl. After all, could it be worse than her and Lisa's present reality? She normally held a job for a couple of months or, if she was really lucky, half a year, and then a layoff came with the promise of a rehire when times got better, which they never seemed to do. Without a high school diploma she was immediately categorized as stupid. By virtue of living with Duane, she had long ago decided she deserved that label. But he was Lisa's father even if he had no intention of marrying LuAnn, not that she had pushed him on that. She was not overeager to take Duane's last name or the man-child that came with it. However, having grown up in something less than the embrace of a happy, caring household, LuAnn was firmly convinced that the family unit was vitally important to a child's well-being. She had read all the magazines and watched numerous talk shows on the subject. In Rikersville, LuAnn was one step ahead of the welfare rolls most of the time; there were about twenty people for every lousy job. Lisa could and would do far better than her mother — LuAnn had dedicated her life to making that a reality. But with a thousand dollars, perhaps LuAnn would do all right for herself. A bus ticket to somewhere else. Some money to live off until she could find a job; the little nest egg she had so desperately wanted over the years but had never been able to accumulate.

Rikersville was dying. The trailer was Duane's unofficial sepulcher. He would never have it any better and probably would have it much worse before the ground swallowed him up. It could be her crypt too, LuAnn realized, only it wouldn't be. Not after today. Not after she kept her appointment. She folded up the piece of paper and put it back in her purse. Sliding a small box out of one of the drawers, she found enough change for bus fare. She finished with her hair, buttoned her dress, swooped up Lisa, and quietly left the trailer, and Duane, behind.

Chapter Three

There was a sharp knock on the door. The man quickly stood up from behind the desk, adjusted his tie, and opened a file folder lying in front of him. In the ashtray next to him were the remains of three cigarettes.

"Come in," he said, his voice firm and clear.

The door opened and LuAnn stepped into the room and looked around. Her left hand clutched the handle of the baby carrier where Lisa lay, her eyes looking around the room with obvious curiosity. Over LuAnn's right shoulder hung a large bag. The man observed the vein plunging down LuAnn's long, sinewy biceps until it connected with a maze of others in her muscular forearm. The woman was obviously strong, physically. What about her character? Was it as strong?

"Are you Mr. Jackson?" LuAnn asked. She looked directly at him as she spoke, waiting for his eyes to take the inevitable inventory of her face, bosom, hips, and so on. It didn't matter from what walk of life they came, in that regard men were all the same. She was thus very surprised when his gaze did not leave her face. He held out his hand and she shook it firmly.

"I am. Please sit down, Ms. Tyler. Thank you for coming. Your daughter is quite beautiful. Would you care to put her down over here?" He pointed to a corner of the room.

"She just woke up. The walk and the bus ride makes her go to sleep every time. I'll just keep her beside me, if that's okay." As if in agreement, Lisa began to jabber and point.

He nodded his assent and then sat back down and took a moment to peruse the file.

LuAnn put Lisa and the large bag down next to her, pulled out a set of plastic keys, and handed them to her daughter to play with. LuAnn straightened back up and studied Jackson with considerable interest. He was dressed expensively. A line of perspiration was strung across his forehead like a miniature set of pearls and he appeared a little nervous. She ordinarily would put that down to her looks. Most of the men she encountered either acted like fools in attempts to impress her or shut down within themselves like wounded animals. Something told her that neither was the case with this man.

"I didn't see a sign over your office. People might not know you're even here." She looked at him curiously.

Jackson smiled tightly at her. "In our business we don't cater to foot traffic. It doesn't matter to us if people in the mall know we're here or not. All of our business is conducted via appointments, phone calls, that sort of thing."

"I must be the only appointment right now then. Y'all's waiting room is empty."

Jackson's cheek twitched as he formed a steeple with his hands. "We stagger our appointments so as not to keep people waiting. I'm the only member of the firm at this location."

"So you got other places of business?"

He nodded absently. "Would you mind filling out this information sheet for me? Take your time." He slid a piece of paper and pen over to her. LuAnn quickly filled out the form, making short, tight motions with the pen. Jackson watched as she did so. He reviewed her information after she finished. He already knew everything on it.

LuAnn looked around the place. She had always been observant. Being the object of many males' desires, she typically studied the configuration of every place she was in, if only to determine the fastest exit.

When he looked up he noted her scrutinizing the office surroundings. "Something wrong?" he asked.

"It's kinda funny."

"I'm afraid I don't understand."

"You got a funny office, is all."

"How do you mean?"

"Well, there's no clock anywhere, no trash can, no calendar, and no phone. Now, I ain't

worked in any places where people wear neck-
ties on the job, but even Red over at the truck
stop keeps a calendar, and he's on the phone
more than he's not. And the lady out front,
she don't got a clue as to what's going on.
Hell, with those three-inch nails, using that
typewriter would be mighty hard anyway."
LuAnn caught the stunned look on his face
and quickly bit her lip. Her mouth had gotten
her in trouble before, and this was one job
interview she couldn't afford to blow. "I don't
mean nothing by it," she said quickly. "Just
talking. Guess I'm a little nervous, is all."

Jackson's lips moved for an instant and then
he smiled grimly. "You're very observant."

"Got two eyes like everybody else." LuAnn
smiled prettily, falling back on the old reliable.

Jackson ignored her look and rustled his
papers. "You recall the terms of employment
I gave to you over the phone?"

She snapped back to business. "One hundred dollars per day for two weeks, with maybe
some more weeks at that same pay. I work
until seven in the morning right now. If it's all
right I'd like to come and do this job in the
early afternoon. Around about two? And is it
okay if I bring my little girl? She takes her big
nap around then, she won't be no trouble at
all. Cross my heart." With an automatic motion LuAnn reached down and picked up the
toy keys from the floor where the little girl had
flung them and handed them back to Lisa.

Lisa thanked her mother with a loud grunt.

Jackson stood up and put his hands in his pockets. "That's fine. It's all fine. You're an only child and your parents are dead, correct?"

LuAnn jerked at the abrupt change in subject. She hesitated and then nodded, her eyes narrowing.

"And for the better part of two years you have lived with one Duane Harvey, an unskilled laborer of sorts, currently unemployed, in a trailer in the western part of Rikersville." He looked at her as he recounted this information. He was not waiting for affirmation now. LuAnn sensed that and merely stared back at him. "Duane Harvey is the father of your daughter, Lisa, age eight months. You quit school in the seventh grade and have held numerous low-paying jobs since that time; all of them I think would be accurately summed up as dead-ends. You are uncommonly bright and possess admirable survival skills. Nothing is more important to you than your daughter's well-being. You are desperate to change the circumstances of your life and you are just as desperate to leave Mr. Harvey far behind. Right now you are wondering how to accomplish any of this when you lack the financial means to do so and likely always will. You feel trapped, and well you should. You are most assuredly trapped, Ms. Tyler." He stared across the desk at her.

LuAnn's face was flushed as she stood up.

32

"What the hell's going on here? What right do you have —"

He impatiently broke in. "You came here because I offered you more money than you've ever earned before. Isn't that right?"

"How come you know all those things 'bout me?" she demanded.

He crossed his arms and studied her intently before answering. "It's in my best interests to know everything I can about someone with whom I'm about to do business."

"What does knowing about me have to do with my opinions and surveys and such?"

"Very simple, Ms. Tyler. To know how to evaluate your opinion on things I need to know intimate details about the opinion maker. Who you are, what you want, what you know. And don't know. The things you like, dislike, your prejudices, your strengths, and weaknesses. We all have them, in varying degrees. In sum, if I don't know all about you, I haven't done my job." He came around the corner of the desk and perched on the edge. "I'm sorry if I offended you. I can be rather blunt; however, I didn't want to waste your time."

Finally the anger in LuAnn's eyes passed away. "Well, I guess if you put it that way —"

"I do, Ms. Tyler. May I call you LuAnn?"

"That's my name," she said brusquely. She sat back down. "Well, I don't want to waste your time either, so what about the hours? Is the afternoon okay?"

Jackson abruptly returned to his seat and looked down at the desk, rubbing his hands slowly over its cracked surface. When he looked back up at her, his countenance was even more serious than it had been seconds before.

"Have you ever dreamed of being rich, LuAnn? I mean rich beyond all your wildest fantasies. So wealthy in fact that you and your daughter could literally do anything in the world you wanted to do, when you wanted to do it? Have you ever had that dream?"

LuAnn started to laugh until she caught the look in his eyes. There was no humor, no diffidence, no sympathy in their depths, merely an intense desire to hear her answer.

"Hell, yes. Who hasn't had that dream?"

"Well, those who are already filthy rich rarely do, I can tell you that. However, you're right, most other people, at some point in their lives, have that fantasy. Yet virtually no one ever makes that fantasy a reality. The reason is simple: They can't."

LuAnn smiled disarmingly. "But a hundred bucks a day ain't bad either."

Jackson stroked his chin for several seconds, coughed to clear his throat, and then asked a question. "LuAnn, do you ever play the lottery?"

She was surprised by the inquiry but readily replied. "Now and then. Everybody around here does. It can get expensive, though. Duane plays every week, sometimes half his paycheck — that is when he pulls a paycheck, which ain't usually the case. He's all-fired certain he's going to win. Plays the same numbers every time. Says he saw them in a dream. I say he's just dumber than dirt. Why?"

"Have you ever played the national Lotto?"

"You mean the one for the whole country?"

Jackson nodded, his eyes fixed on her. "Yes," he said slowly, "that's exactly the one I mean."

"Once in a while. But the odds are so big I got a better chance of going for a stroll on the moon than I do of winning that thing."

"You're absolutely right. In fact, the odds this month are approximately one in thirty million."

"That's what I mean. I'd rather go for the dollar scratch-offs. At least then you got a chance to make a quick twenty bucks. No sense throwing good money after bad, I always say, particularly when you don't got none to speak of."

Jackson licked his lips and leaned his elbows on the desk as he looked at her. "What would you say if I told you I could drastically better your chances of winning the lottery?" He kept his eyes trained resolutely on her.

"Excuse me?" Jackson said nothing. LuAnn looked around the room as if expecting to see a surveillance camera somewhere. "What's this got to do with the job? I didn't come here to play no games, mister."

"In fact," Jackson continued, ignoring her queries, "what if I could lower your odds to one in one? Would you do it?"

LuAnn exploded. "Is this some kind of big joke? If I didn't know better I'd think maybe Duane was behind this. You better tell me what the hell's going on before I really get mad."

"This is no joke, LuAnn."

LuAnn rose out of the chair. "You durn sure got something else on the burner and I don't want no parts of it. No parts! Hundred bucks a day or not," she said with deep disgust, mingled with deeper disappointment as her plans for the thousand-dollar payday rapidly faded away. She picked up Lisa and her bag and turned to leave.

The quiet tones of Jackson's voice rippled across her back. "I am guaranteeing that you will win the lottery, LuAnn. I am guaranteeing that you will win, *at minimum,* fifty million dollars."

She stopped. Despite her brain's telling her to run as fast as she could out of the place, she found herself slowly turning to face him.

Jackson had not moved. He still sat behind the desk, his hands clasped in front of him. "No more Duanes, no more graveyard shifts at the truck diner, no more worrying about having food and clean clothes for your daughter. Anything you want, you can have. Anywhere you want to go, you can go. Anyone you want to become, you can." His tone remained quiet and steady.

"You mind telling me how can you do that?" *Had he said fifty million dollars? Lord Almighty!* She placed one hand against the door to steady herself.

"I need an answer to my question."

"What question?"

Jackson spread his hands. "Do you want to be rich?"

"Are you a crazy man or what? I'm strong as all get out so if you try anything I'll kick your little butt all the way down the street and leave you with half the brains you started the day with."

"Do I take that as a no?" he said.

LuAnn tossed her hair to one side and switched Lisa's carrier from her right to her left hand. The little girl was looking back and forth at them, as though absorbed in the heated conversation. "Look, there is no way in hell that you can guarantee me something like that. So I'm just gonna walk on out of here and call the nut house to come get you."

In response, Jackson looked at his watch and walked over to the TV and turned it on.

"In one minute the national daily drawing will be held. It's *only* a one million dollar pay-off; however, it will serve to illustrate a point nonetheless. Understand, I do not profit from this, it's used only for demonstration purposes, to quell your quite understandable skepticism."

LuAnn turned to look at the screen. She watched as the lottery drawing began and the ball machines fired up.

Jackson glanced over at her. "The winning numbers will be eight, four, seven, eleven, nine, and six, in that order." He pulled a pen and paper from his pocket and wrote the numbers down. He handed the paper to LuAnn.

She almost laughed and a loud snort did escape her mouth. It stopped just as quickly when the first number announced was eight. In rapid succession the four, seven, eleven, nine, and six balls were kicked out and announced as the winning combination. Her face pale, LuAnn stared down at the paper and then at the winning numbers on the screen.

Jackson turned off the TV. "I trust that your doubts about my abilities are now satisfied. Perhaps we can get back to my offer."

LuAnn leaned back against the wall. Her skin seemed to be humming against her bones, as though a million bees had plunged into her body. She looked at the TV. She saw no special wires or contraptions that could have aided him in predicting the outcome. No VCR. It was just plugged into the wall. She swallowed hard and looked back at him.

"How the hell did you do that?" The words came out in a hushed, fearful tone.

"You have no possible need to know that

information. Just answer my question, please."
His voice rose slightly.

She took a deep breath, tried to calm her twitching nerves. "You're asking me if I want to do something wrong. Then I'm telling you flat-out that I won't. I ain't got much, but I'm no criminal."

"Who says it's anything wrong?"

"Excuse me, but are you saying that guaranteeing to win the lottery ain't wrong? Sure as hell sounds like a fix to me. You think just because I work crap jobs I'm stupid?"

"I actually have a high opinion of your intelligence. That's why you're here. However, someone has to win that money, LuAnn. Why not you?"

"Because it's wrong, that's why."

"And who exactly are you hurting? Besides, it's not wrong, technically, if no one ever finds out."

"I'd know."

Jackson sighed. "That's very noble. However, do you really want to spend the rest of your life with Duane?"

"He has his good points."

"Really? Would you care to enumerate them?"

"Why don't you go straight on to hell! I think my next stop's gonna be at the police station. I got a friend who's a cop. I betcha he'll be real interested to hear about all this." LuAnn turned and gripped the doorknob.

This was the moment Jackson had been waiting for. His voice continued to rise. "So Lisa grows up in a filthy trailer in the woods. Your little girl will be extraordinarily beautiful if she takes after her mother. She reaches a certain age, the young men start to get interested, she drops out of school, a baby perhaps comes along, the cycle starts anew. Like your mother?" He paused. "Like you?" Jackson added very quietly.

LuAnn turned slowly around, her eyes wide and glimmering.

Jackson eyed her sympathetically. "It's inevitable, LuAnn. I'm speaking the truth, you know I am. What future do you and Lisa have with him? And if not him, another Duane and then another and another. You'll live in poverty and you'll die in poverty and your little girl will do the same. There's no changing that. It's not fair of course, but that doesn't make it any less certain. Oh, people who have never been in your situation would say that you should just pack up and go. Take your daughter and just leave. Only they never tell you how you're supposed to do that. Where will the money for bus fare and motel rooms and food come from? Who'll watch your child, first while you look for work, and then when you find it, if you ever do." Jackson shook his head in sympathy and slid the back of one hand under his chin as he eyed her. "Of course, you can go to the police if you want. But by the time you get back, there will be no one here. And do you think they'll really believe you?" An expression of condescension played across his features. "And then what will you have accomplished? You'll have missed the opportunity of a lifetime. Your only shot at getting out. Gone." He shook his head sadly at her, as if to say, "Please don't be that stupid."

LuAnn tightened her grip on the baby carrier. An agitated Lisa was starting to struggle to get out and her mother automatically started rocking the little girl back and forth. "You talking about dreams, Mr. Jackson, I got me my own dreams. Big ones. Damn big ones." Her voice was trembling though. LuAnn Tyler had a very tough exterior built up over long, hard years of scrapping for an existence and never getting anywhere; however, Jackson's words had hurt LuAnn, or rather the truth in those words.

"I know you do. I said you were bright and you've done nothing at this meeting but reinforce that opinion. You deserve far better than what you have now. However, rarely do people get what they deserve in life. I'm offering you a way to achieve your big dreams." He abruptly snapped his fingers for effect. "Like that."

She suddenly looked wary. "How do I know you're not the police trying to set me up? I ain't going to no prison over money."

41

"Because it would be a clear case of entrapment, that's why. It would never hold up in court. And why in the world would the police target *you* for such an elaborate scheme?"

LuAnn leaned up against the door. Under her dress she felt her heart beating erratically between her breasts.

Jackson stood up. "I know you don't know me, but I take my business very, very seriously. I never do anything without a very good reason. I would not be here wasting your time with some joke, and I most certainly never waste my time." Jackson's voice carried an unmistakable ring of authority and his eyes bored into LuAnn with an intensity that was impossible to ignore.

"Why me? Out of all the people in the whole friggin' world, why'd you come knocking on my door?" She was almost pleading.

"Fair question; however, it's not one I'm prepared to answer, nor is it particularly pertinent."

"How can you know I'm going to win?"

He looked at the TV. "Unless you think I was incredibly lucky with that drawing, then you shouldn't doubt the outcome."

"Huh! Right now, I doubt everything I'm hearing. So what if I play along and I still don't win?"

"Then what have you lost?"

"The two bucks it costs to play, that's what! It might not sound like much money to you, but that's bus fare for almost a whole week!"

Jackson pulled four singles from his pocket and handed them to her. "Then consider that risk eliminated and a hundred percent return on top of it."

She rubbed the money between her fingers. "I wanta know what's in it for you. I'm a little too old to believe in good fairies and wishes on a star." LuAnn's eyes were clear and focused now.

"Again, a good question, but one that only becomes applicable if and when you agree to participate. You're right, however: I'm not doing this out of the goodness of my heart." A tiny smile escaped his lips. "It's a business transaction. And in all good business transactions, both sides benefit. However, I think you'll be pleased at how generous the terms will be."

LuAnn slid the money into her bag. "If you need my answer right this very minute, it's going to be a big, fat no."

"I realize that my proposition has certain complexities. Therefore, I will give you some time to think about it." He wrote a toll-free phone number down on a piece of paper and held it out to her. "But not too much time. The monthly lottery drawing takes place in four days. I have to have your answer by ten A.M. the day after tomorrow. This number will reach me anywhere."

She looked at the paper in his hand. "And

if I still say no in two days, which I probably will?"

Jackson shrugged. "Then someone else will win the lottery, LuAnn. Someone else will be at least fifty million dollars richer and they certainly won't waste any time feeling guilty about it, I can assure you." He smiled pleasantly. "Believe me when I tell you that a lot of people would gladly take your place. *Gladly.*" He put the paper in her hand and closed her fist around it. "Remember, one minute past ten A.M. and the offer to you is gone. Forever." Jackson of course did not mention the fact that if LuAnn said no, he would have her immediately killed. His tone was almost harsh, but then he quickly smiled again and opened the door for her, glancing at Lisa as he did so. The little girl stopped thrashing and stared wide-eyed at him. "She looks just like you. I hope she got your brains as well." As she passed through the doorway, he added, "Thank you for coming, LuAnn. And have a nice day."

"What makes me think your name ain't Jackson?" she said, giving him a piercing stare.

"I sincerely hope to hear from you soon, LuAnn. I like to see good things happen to deserving people. Don't you?" He shut the door softly behind her.

Chapter Four

On the bus ride home, LuAnn clutched both Lisa and the piece of paper bearing the phone number with equal tenacity. She had the very uncomfortable feeling that everyone on the bus was acutely aware of what had just happened to her and was judging her harshly as a result. An old woman wearing a battered coat and droopy, torn knee-high stockings gripped her plastic shopping bags and glared at LuAnn. Whether she was really privy to LuAnn's interview or simply resented her youth, looks, and beautiful baby girl, LuAnn couldn't be sure.

She sat back in her seat and let her mind race ahead to examine her life if she said yes or no to the proposal. While declining the offer seemed to carry with it certain consequences, all of them emblazoned with Duane-like features, acceptance seemed to bear its own problems. If she actually won the lottery and came into incalculable wealth, the man had said she could have anything she wanted. Anything! Go anywhere. Do anything. God! The thought of such unbridled freedom only a phone call and four days away made her want to run screaming with joy through the bus's narrow aisle. She had put aside the notion that it was all a hoax or some bizarre scheme. Jackson had asked for no money, not that she had any to give. He had also given no indication that he desired any sexual favors from her, although the full terms had not, as yet, been disclosed. However, Jackson did not strike her as being interested in her sexually. He had not tried to touch her, had not commented on her features, at least not directly, and seemed, in every way, professional and sincere. He could be a nut, but if he was he certainly had done an admirable job of feigning sanity in front of her. Plus, it had cost money to rent the space, hire the receptionist, and so forth. If Jackson was certifiable, he definitely had his normal moments. She shook her head. And he had called every number correctly on the daily drawing, before the damn machines had even kicked them out. She couldn't deny that. So if he was telling the truth, then the only catch was that his business proposal resonated with illegality, with fraud, with more bad things than she cared to think about. That was a big catch. And what if she went along and then was caught somehow, the whole truth coming out? She could go to prison, maybe for the rest of her life. What would happen to Lisa? She suddenly felt miserable. Like most people, she had dreamt often of the pot of gold. It was a vision that had carried her through many a hopeless time when self-pity threatened to overtake her. In her dreams, though, the pot of gold had not been attached to a ball and chain. "Damn," she said under her breath. A clear choice between heaven and hell? And what were Jackson's conditions? She was sure the man would exact a very high price in exchange for transforming her from penniless to a princess.

So if she accepted and actually won, what would she do? The potential of such freedom was easy to see, taste, hear, feel. The actual implementation of it was something altogether different. Travel the world? She had never been outside Rikersville, which was best known for its annual fair and reeking slaughterhouses. She could count the times on one hand that she had ridden in an elevator. She had never owned a house or a car; in fact, she had never really owned anything. No bank account had ever borne her name. She could read, write, and speak the king's English passably, but she clearly wasn't Social Register material. Jackson said she could have anything. But could she really? Could you really pluck a toad from the mud in some backwater and deposit it in a castle in France and really believe it could actually work? But she didn't need to do it all, change her life so dramatically, become something and someone that she decidedly wasn't. She shuddered.

That was the thing, though. She flipped her long hair out of her face, leaned against Lisa, and played her fingers over her daughter's forehead where the golden hairs drifted across. LuAnn took a deep breath, filling her lungs with the sweet spring air from the open bus window. The thing was, she wanted desperately to be someone else, anyone other than who she was. Most of her life she had felt, believed, and hoped that one day she would do something about it. With each passing year, however, that hope grew more and more hollow, more and more like a dream that one day would break completely free from her and drift away until finally, when she was the shrunken, wrinkled owner of a quickly fading, unremarkable life, she would no longer remember she had ever possessed such dreams. Every day her bleak future became more and more graphic, like a TV with an antenna finally attached.

Now things had abruptly changed. She stared down at the phone number as the bus rolled down the bumpy street, carrying her and Lisa back to the dirt road that would lead to the dirtier trailer, where Duane Harvey lurked, awaiting their return in what she was certain would be a foul temper. He would want beer money. But she brightened as she recalled she had two extra singles riding in her pocket. Mr. Jackson had already provided her with some benefit. Having Duane out of the way so she could think things through would be a start. Tonight was dollar pitcher night at the Squat and Gobble, his favorite hangout. With two bucks, Duane would happily drink himself into oblivion. She looked out the window at the world awakening from winter. Spring was here. A new beginning. Perhaps for her as well? To occur at or before ten A.M., two days from now. She and Lisa locked eyes for a long moment and then mother and daughter exchanged tender smiles. She laid her head gently down on Lisa's chest not knowing whether to laugh or cry and yet wanting very much to do both.

Chapter Five

The busted screen door creaked open and LuAnn passed through carrying Lisa. The trailer was dark, cool, and quiet. Duane might still be asleep. However, as she navigated through the narrow passageway, she kept her eyes and ears on high alert for movement or sound. She wasn't anything close to being afraid of Duane unless he got the drop on her. In a fair fight, she could more than hold her own. She had kicked the crap out of him on more than one occasion when he had been particularly drunk. He normally didn't try anything too outrageous when he was sober, which he would be now, or as close to it as he usually got. It was a strange relationship to have with someone who could be categorized as her significant other. However, she could name ten other women she knew who had similar arrangements, based more on pure economics, limited options, and in essence, inertia, than on anything approaching tender emotions. She had had other offers; but rarely was the grass greener elsewhere, she knew that firsthand. She picked up her pace as she heard the snores coming from the bedroom and leaned her head in the small room. She sucked in her breath as she eyed the twin figures lying under the sheets. Duane's head was visible on the right. The other person was completely covered by the sheet; however, the twin humps in the chest region suggested it was not one of Duane's male drinking buddies sleeping it off.

LuAnn quietly stepped down the hallway and placed an anxious-looking Lisa and her carrier down in the bathroom, then closed the door. LuAnn didn't want her little girl to be disturbed by what was about to happen. When she again opened the bedroom door, Duane was still snoring loudly; however, the body beside him had moved, and the dark red hair was clearly visible now. It only took a second for LuAnn to clamp a hand around the thick mane, and then she pulled with all her immense strength and the unfortunate owner of those long locks was hauled out of the bed to crash buck-naked against the far wall.

"Shit!" the woman bellowed as she landed on her butt and was immediately pulled across the rough, ragged carpet by a grim-looking LuAnn. "Dammit, LuAnn, let go."

LuAnn looked back at her for a split second. "Shirley, you slut around here again, and I swear to God I'll break your neck."

"Duane! Help me for chrissakes! She's crazy!" Shirley wailed, pulling and clawing at her hair in a futile effort to make LuAnn let go. Shirley was short and about twenty pounds

51

overweight. Her chubby legs and full, wobbly breasts slapped back and forth against each other as the two women made their way to the bedroom door.

Duane stirred as LuAnn passed by. "What's going on here?" he said sleepily.

"Shut up," LuAnn snapped back.

As his eyes focused on the situation, Duane reached across to the nightstand and pulled out a pack of Marlboros from the drawer. He grinned at Shirley as he lit up.

"Going home so soon, Shirl?" He wiped his droopy hair out of his face as he sucked contentedly on his cigarette.

Facing to the rear as she was, Shirley glared at him, her fat cheeks a deep burgundy. "You're a piece of crap."

Duane blew her an imaginary kiss. "I love you too, Shirl. Thanks for the visit. Made my morning." He belly-laughed and slapped his thigh as he propped himself up on the pillow. Then LuAnn and Shirley disappeared through the doorway.

After depositing Shirley next to a rusted-out Ford engine block in the front yard, LuAnn turned back to the trailer.

Shirley stood up and shrieked, "You pulled half my hair out, you bitch." LuAnn kept walking, not looking back. "I want my clothes. Give me my damned clothes, LuAnn."

LuAnn turned around. "You didn't need 'em while you were here, so I can't see no reason why you'd need 'em now."

"I can't go home like this."

"Then don't go home." LuAnn went up the cinder block steps to the trailer and slammed the door behind her.

Duane met her in the hallway, dressed in his boxers, an unlit Marlboro dangling from his mouth. "Does a man good to have two alleycats fighting over him. Got my blood going, LuAnn. How 'bout you stepping up to the plate? Come on, baby, give me a kiss." He grinned at her and tried to slide an arm around her long neck. His next breath was a tortured one as her right fist smashed into his mouth, loosening a couple of his teeth. As painful as that blow was, it did not come close on the hurt scale to the knee that planted itself violently between his legs. Duane dropped heavily to the floor.

LuAnn hovered over him. "If you pull that crap again, Duane Harvey, so help me God, I'll rip it right off and flush it down the toilet."

"Crazy-ass woman," he half-sputtered, half-whimpered, clutching at his groin; blood seeped through his lips.

She reached down and clamped an iron grip across his cheeks. "No, *you're* crazy if you think for one second I'm gonna put up with that shit."

"We ain't married."

"That's right, but we live together. We got a kid together. And this place is as much mine as it is yours."

"Shirl don't mean nothing to me. What do you care?" He stared up at her, small tears gathering in the corners of his eyes as he continued to clutch his privates.

"Because that little fat piece of bacon is gonna waddle on down to the IGA and the beauty parlor and the damned Squat and Gobble and tell everybody that will listen all about it and I'm gonna look like the biggest piece of trash in the world."

"You shouldn't have left me this morning." He struggled up off the floor. "See, this here's all your fault. She came by to see you about something. What was I supposed to do?"

"I don't know, Duane, how about giving her a cup of coffee instead of your dick?"

"I don't feel so good, babe. I really don't." He leaned up against the wall.

She roughly pushed past him on her way to check on Lisa. "Best news I've heard all day."

A minute later she marched past him again and entered the bedroom, where she proceeded to rip the sheets off the bed.

Duane sulkily watched her from the doorway. "Go ahead and throw 'em away. I don't give a crap, you bought 'em."

She didn't look at him as she answered. "I'm taking 'em over to Wanda's to wash. If you're gonna sleep around with sluts, it ain't gonna cost me nothing."

As she lifted the mattress, a flash of green

54

caught her eye. She shoved the mattress off the bed frame and then looked over at Duane. "What the hell is this?" she demanded.

Duane looked at her coldly. He sauntered into the room, scooped up the piles of cash, and stuffed them in a paper bag that had been sitting on the table beside the bed. He continued to eye her as he closed up the bag. "Let's just say I won the lottery," he said arrogantly.

She perceptibly stiffened at his words as though she'd been slapped flush in the face. For a moment she felt as though she would topple right over in a dead faint. Had Duane actually been behind all of this? Were he and Jackson in this together? She could not have envisioned a more unlikely pair. It couldn't possibly be. She quickly recovered and crossed her arms. "Bull. Where'd you get it, Duane?"

"Let's just say it's a real good reason to be nice to me and to keep your mouth shut."

Angrily pushing him from the room, she locked the door. She changed into jeans, sneakers, and a sweatshirt and then quickly packed an overnight bag. When she unlocked and threw open the door, Duane hadn't budged; the bag was still clutched in his hand. She moved quickly past him, opened the door to the bathroom, and scooped up a wriggling Lisa in one arm; the dirty linen and overnight bag in her other hand, she headed for the front door.

"Where you going, LuAnn?"

"None of your damned business."

"How long you gonna be pissed about this? I didn't get mad at you for kicking me in the balls, did I? I done already forgot about it, in fact."

She whirled around for a second. "Duane, you have got to be the dumbest person on the face of this earth."

"Is that right? Well who do you think you are? Why, if it weren't for me, you and Lisa wouldn't even have a damned place to stay. I took you in or you wouldn't have nothing." He lit up another cigarette but warily kept out of range of her fist. He scrunched the match out on the tattered carpet. "So maybe instead of bitching all the time, you oughta try being nice to me." He held up the paper bag stuffed with cash. "There's plenty more where this came from, too, little girl. I ain't gonna be living in this craphole much longer. You best think about it. You best think real good about that. I ain't taking crap from you or anybody else anymore. You hear me?"

She opened the front door. "Duane, I'll start being nice to you right now. You know how? I'm gonna leave before I kill you!" Lisa started to cry at her mother's angry tones as though she thought they were directed at her. LuAnn kissed the little girl and cooed in her ear to calm her down.

Duane watched LuAnn march across the muddy yard, admiring her soft behind in the tight jeans. For a moment he looked around for Shirley, but she had evidently already made a run for it, naked and all.

"I love you, babe," he yelled after LuAnn, grinning.

"Go to hell, Duane."

Chapter Six

The mall was far busier than it had been during her visit the day before. LuAnn was grateful for the crowds as she made a wide berth around the office she had visited earlier, though she did glance in its direction as she passed by. Through the glass panes on either side of the door it seemed dark inside. She supposed if she tried the door, it would be locked. She didn't imagine that Jackson would have hung around long after she had left, and she assumed she had been his sole "client."

She had called in sick to work and spent a sleepless night at a friend's house alternating between staring at a full moon and Lisa's tiny mouth as it randomly produced smiles, grimaces, and every expression in between while the little girl slept heavily. She had finally decided not to make a decision on Jackson's proposal until she had some more information. One conclusion had come fairly rapidly: She would not go to the police. She could prove nothing, and who would believe her? There was no upside potential to such a move and at least fifty million reasons against it. For all her sense of right and wrong, she could not get past that one inescapable temptation: Incredible, sudden wealth was perhaps staring her in the face. She felt guilty that the decision wasn't more black and white. However, her latest episode with Duane had only reinforced to her that Lisa could not be allowed to grow up in such an environment. Something had to give.

The mall office was at the end of a corridor on the south side of the building. LuAnn swung open the door and went in.

"LuAnn?"

LuAnn stared at the source of this exclamation. Behind the counter, the young man was dressed neatly in a short-sleeve shirt, necktie, and black slacks. In his excitement, he repeatedly clicked a pen in his right hand. LuAnn stared at him, but no recognition was forthcoming.

The young man almost vaulted over the counter. "I didn't expect you to remember me. Johnny Jarvis. I go by John now." He extended a hand in a professional manner and then, grinning, he gave her a solid hug and spent a full minute cooing over Lisa. LuAnn pulled out a small blanket from her bag, set her daughter down on it, and gave her a stuffed animal.

"I can't believe it's you, Johnny. I haven't seen you since, what, the sixth grade?"

"You were in the seventh, I was in the ninth."

"You look good. Real good. How long you

been working here?"

Jarvis grinned proudly. "After high school I went on to the community college and got my A.S. That stands for associate degree in science. Been at the mall for two years now. Started out as a data inputter but now I've moved up to sort of the assistant manager of mall operations."

"Congratulations. That's wonderful, Johnny — I mean John."

"Oh hell, you can call me Johnny. I can't believe you just walked on in that door. When I saw you, I thought I was gonna fall over and die. I never thought I'd see you again. I supposed you'd just gone on to New York City or something."

"Nope, still here," she said quickly.

"I'm kinda surprised I've never seen you around the mall before then."

"I don't get up here much. It's a pretty long way from where I live now."

"Have a seat and tell me what you been up to. I didn't know you had a baby. Didn't even know you were married."

"I'm not married."

"Oh." Jarvis's face reddened slightly. "Uh, you want some coffee or something? I just put on a fresh pot."

"I'm kind of in a hurry, Johnny."

"Oh, well, what can I do for you?" He suddenly looked surprised. "You aren't looking for a job, are you?"

60

She looked pointedly at him. "What if I was? Something wrong with that?"

"No, I mean, course not. I just meant, you know, I never expected you to hang around here, working in no mall, that's all." He smiled.

"A job's a job, ain't it? *You* work here. And while we're talking about it, exactly what am I supposed to be doing with my life?"

Jarvis's smile quickly faded and he rubbed his hands nervously down the legs of his pants. "I didn't mean nothing by it, LuAnn. I just always thought of you living in some castle somewhere wearing fancy clothes and driving fancy cars. I'm sorry."

LuAnn's anger faded as she thought back to Jackson's proposition. Castles might be within her reach now. "It's okay, Johnny, it's been a long week, you know what I mean? I'm not looking for a job. What I'm looking for is a little information about one of your renters here."

Jarvis glanced over his shoulder at the rear office area where the sounds of phones and clattering keyboards could be heard mixed with short bursts of conversation, and then he turned back to her. "Information?"

"Yeah. I came by here yesterday morning. Had an appointment."

"With who?"

"That's what I want you to tell me. It was that business on the right as you come in the mall next to the bus stop. It ain't got no sign or anything, but it's next to the ice cream place."

Jarvis looked puzzled for a second. "I thought that space was still vacant. We got a lot of that. This mall isn't exactly in the middle of a booming area."

"Well, it wasn't vacant yesterday."

Jarvis walked over to the computer on the counter and started punching buttons. "What was the appointment for?"

LuAnn's reply was immediate. "Oh, it was a sales job, you know. Pushing products door-to-door."

"Yeah, we've had some people like that come in on a temporary basis. More like an interview room than anything else. If we have the space, which we usually do, we rent it out, sometimes just for the day. Especially if it's already been built out, you know, ready-made office space."

He pulled up a screen and studied it. As voices continued to filter in from the back office he went over and shut the door. He looked a little apprehensively at LuAnn. "So what'd you want to know?"

She noted his concerned look and glanced in the direction of the door he had just shut. "You're not going to get in trouble over this, are you, Johnny?"

He waved his hand dismissively. "Hell, no. Remember, I'm the assistant manager here," he said importantly.

"Well, just tell me whatever you can. Who the people are. What the business is. An address somewhere. Stuff like that."

Jarvis looked confused. "Well, didn't they tell you that during the interview?"

"Some of it," she said slowly. "But I just want to make sure it's all legit, you know. Before I accept or not. I got to buy some nicer clothes and maybe get me a car. I don't want to do that if it's not on the up-and-up."

Jarvis snorted. "Well, you're smart to do that. I mean just because we rent space to these people, it don't mean they're shooting straight with you." He added anxiously, "They didn't ask for money from you, did they?"

"No, as a matter of fact, the money they were talking about me getting was pretty unbelievable."

"Probably too good to be true then."

"That's what I'm afraid of." She watched his fingers sail across the computer keyboard. "Where'd you learn to do that stuff?" she said with admiration.

"What, this? That's when I was at the community college. They got programs over there that teach you just about anything. Computers are cool."

"I wouldn't mind going back to school one day."

"You were always real smart in school,

LuAnn. I bet you'd pick it up like nobody's business."

She gave him a pretty look. "Maybe one day. Now what'cha got for me?"

Jarvis studied the screen again. "Company's name is Associates, Inc. At least that's what they put on the rental agreement. They leased for a week, starting yesterday in fact. Paid in cash. Didn't give any other address. When they pay in cash we don't really care."

"They ain't nobody there now."

Jarvis nodded absently as he tabbed down the screen. "Guy named Jackson signed the lease agreement," he said.

"About my height with black hair, sort of fat?"

"That's right. I remember him now. He seemed very professional. Anything out of the way happen during your interview?"

"Depends on what you call out of the way. But he was real professional to me, too. Anything else you can tell me?"

Jarvis studied the screen again, hoping to find a few more kernels of information with which to entice LuAnn. Finally, strong disappointment etched across his features, he looked at her and sighed. "Not really, I guess."

LuAnn hoisted up Lisa and then eyed a stack of steno pads and a cup of pens on the counter. "Could I have one of those pads and a pen, Johnny? I could pay you something for them."

"You kidding? Good golly, take all you want."

"One of each is all I need. Thanks." She put the pad and pen in her handbag.

"No problem at all, we got tons of that stuff."

"Well, I appreciate what you told me. I really do. And it was real nice seeing you, Johnny."

"Hell, you made my whole year walking in the door like that." He took a peek at his watch. "I take my lunch break in about ten minutes. They got a nice Chinese place down at the food court. You have time? My treat. We could talk some more, catch up."

"Maybe another time. Like I said, I'm kind of in a hurry."

LuAnn observed Jarvis's disappointment and felt a little guilty. She put Lisa down and gave him a big hug. She smiled as she listened to him breathe deeply into her freshly washed hair. As he pressed his hands against the small of her back, and the warmth and softness of her chest spread over his, Jarvis's spirits were instantly rekindled. "You've done real well for yourself, Johnny," LuAnn said as she stepped back. "Always knew you'd do just fine." Things might have been different, she thought, if she had come across Johnny a while back.

Jarvis was now treading across fine white clouds. "You did? I'm kind of surprised you even thought about me at all."

"There you go, I'm just full of surprises. Take care of yourself, maybe I'll see you around." She picked up Lisa, who was rubbing the stuffed animal against her mother's cheek and jabbering happily, and headed for the door.

"Hey, LuAnn?"

She turned back around.

"You gonna take that job?"

She considered the question for a moment. "I don't know yet. But I expect you'll probably hear about it if I do."

LuAnn's next stop was the public library, a place she had frequented when in school, but it had been years since she had last been there. The librarian was very pleasant and complimented LuAnn on her daughter. Lisa snuggled against her mother while she looked around at all the books.

"Da. Da, ooh."

"She likes books," said LuAnn. "I read to her every day."

"She's got your eyes," the woman said looking back and forth between mother and child. LuAnn's hand gently slid against Lisa's cheek.

The woman's smile faded when she saw no ring on LuAnn's finger. LuAnn noted the look. "Best thing I've ever done. I ain't got much, but this little girl's never gonna be hurting for love."

The woman smiled weakly and nodded. "My daughter is a single mother. I do what I can to help out but it's very hard. There's never enough money to go around."

"Tell me about it." LuAnn dug a bottle and a container of water out of her diaper bag, mixed some formula she had gotten from a friend together, and helped Lisa get a grip on it. "If I ever get to the end of a week with more money than I started with, I'm not going to know what to do with myself."

The woman shook her head wistfully. "I know they say that money is the root of all evil, but I often think how nice it would be not to have to worry about the bills. I can't imagine the feeling. Can you?"

"I can imagine it. I imagine it must feel pretty durn good."

The woman laughed. "Now, how can I help you?"

"You keep copies of different newspapers here on that film stuff, don't you?"

The woman nodded. "On microfilm. It's in that room." She pointed to a doorway at the far end of the library.

LuAnn hesitated.

"Do you know how to use the microfilm machine? If not, I can show you. It's not very difficult."

"That'd be real nice. Thank you."

They entered the room, which was vacant and dark. The woman turned on the overhead light, seated LuAnn at one of the terminals, and picked out a microfilm spool from one of the files. It only took a minute to insert the spool, and information appeared on the lit screen. The woman worked the controls and lines of text flashed across the screen. LuAnn watched her carefully as she removed the spool and turned the machine off. "Now, you try it," the woman said.

LuAnn expertly inserted the spool and manipulated the controls as the film advanced.

"That's very good. You learn quickly. Most people don't get the hang of it right away."

"I've always been good with my hands."

"The catalogue files are clearly marked. We carry the local paper, of course, and some of the national ones. The publication dates are printed on the outside of the file drawers."

"Thank you very much."

As soon as the woman left, LuAnn carried Lisa, who was still slurping on the bottle, and started exploring the rows of file cabinets. She set Lisa down and watched in amusement as the little girl rolled to a cabinet, put down the bottle, and tried to pull herself up. LuAnn located a major newspaper in one of the cabinets and proceeded to check the boxes housing the spools until she found the dates corresponding to the last six months. She took a minute to change and burp Lisa and then inserted the first spool into the microfilm machine. With Lisa perched on her lap and pointing excitedly and jabbering on about the sights on the screen, LuAnn's eyes scanned the front page. It didn't take long to locate the story and the accompanying two-inch headline. "Lottery Winner Nets Forty-five Million Dollars." LuAnn quickly read the story. Outside, the sound of a sudden rainstorm assailed her ears. Spring brought a lot of rain to the area, usually in the form of thunderstorms. As if in response to her thoughts, thunder boomed and the entire building seemed to shake. LuAnn glanced anxiously over at Lisa, but the little girl was oblivious to the sounds. LuAnn pulled a blanket from her bag, set it down on the floor with some toys, and put Lisa down. LuAnn turned back to the headline. She pulled the steno pad and pen out of her handbag and started scribbling notes. She flipped to the next month. The U.S. Lotto drawing was held on the fifteenth of each month. The dates she was looking at were for the sixteenth through the twentieth. Two hours later she had completed her review of the past six winners. She unwound the last spool and replaced it in the file drawer. She sat back and looked at her notes. Her head was pounding and she wanted a cup of coffee. The rain was still coming down hard. Carrying Lisa, she went back into the library, pulled some childrens' books down, and showed Lisa the pictures in them and read to the little girl. Within twenty minutes, Lisa had fallen asleep and LuAnn put her in the baby carrier and set it on the table next to her. The room was quiet and warm. As LuAnn felt herself starting to doze she put one arm protectively across Lisa and gripped the little girl's leg in a gentle squeeze. The next thing she knew she was startled awake when a hand touched her shoulder. She looked up into the eyes of the librarian.

"I'm sorry to wake you, but we're closing up."

LuAnn looked around bewildered for a moment. "Good Lord, what time is it?"

"A little after six, dear."

LuAnn quickly packed up. "I'm sorry for falling asleep in here like that."

"Didn't bother me a bit. I'm just sorry I had to wake you, you looked so peaceful there with your daughter and all."

"Thanks again for all your help." LuAnn cocked her head as she listened to the rain pounding on the roof.

The woman looked at her. "I wish I could offer you a ride somewhere, but I take the bus."

"That's okay. The bus and me know each other real good."

LuAnn draped her coat over Lisa and left. She sprinted to the bus stop and waited until the bus pulled up a half hour later with a squeal of brakes and a deep sigh of its air-powered door. She was ten cents short on the fare, but the driver, a heavyset black man whom she knew by sight, waved her on after dropping in the rest from his own pocket.

"We all of us need help every now and again," he said. She thanked him with a smile. Twenty minutes later, LuAnn walked into the Number One Truck Stop several hours before her shift.

"Hey, girl, what you doing here so soon?" asked Beth, LuAnn's fiftyish and very matronly coworker, as she wiped a wet cloth across the Formica counter.

A three-hundred-pound truck driver appraised LuAnn over the rim of his coffee cup and, even soaked as she was from her jaunt in the rain, he came away dutifully impressed. As always. "She come early so she wouldn't miss big old Frankie here," he said with a grin that threatened to swallow up his whole wide face. "She knew I got on the earlier shift and couldn't bear the thought of not seeing me no more."

"You're right, Frankie, it'd just break her heart if LuAnn didn't see your big old hairy mug on a regular basis," Beth rejoined, while prying between her teeth with a swizzle stick.

"Hi, Frankie, how you?" LuAnn said.

"Just fine, now," Frankie replied, the smile still cemented on his features.

"Beth, can you watch Lisa for a minute

while I change into my uniform?" LuAnn asked as she wiped her face and arms down with a towel. She checked Lisa and was relieved to find her dry and hungry. "I'm going to make her up a bottle in just a minute and mix up some of that oatmeal. Then she should be ready to go down for the night even though she had a pretty big nap not too long ago."

"You bet I can take that beautiful little child into my arms. Come here, darling." Beth hoisted up Lisa and settled her against her chest, where Lisa proceeded to make all manner of noises and pull at the pen stuck behind Beth's ear. "Really, now, LuAnn, you ain't got to be here for hours. What's up?"

"I got soaked and my uniform's the only clean thing I got. Besides, I felt bad about missing last night. Hey, is there anything left over from lunch? I sorta can't remember eating yet today."

Beth gave LuAnn a disapproving look and planted one hand on a very full hip. "If you took half as good care of yourself as you do this baby. My Lord, child, it is almost eight o'clock."

"Don't nag, Beth. I just forgot, that's all."

Beth grunted. "Right, Duane drank your money away again, didn't he?"

"You oughta drop that little sumbitch, LuAnn," Frankie grumbled. "But let me kick his ass first for you. You deserve better than that crap."

Beth raised an eyebrow that clearly signaled her agreement with Frankie.

LuAnn scowled at them. "Thank you both for your vote on my life, now if you'll excuse me?"

Later that evening, LuAnn sat at the far corner booth finishing a plate of food Beth had rounded up for her. She finally pushed the dinner away and sipped a cup of fresh coffee. The rain had started again and the clattering sound against the diner's tin roof was comforting. She pulled a thin sweater tighter around her shoulders and checked the clock behind the counter. She still had two hours before she went on duty. Normally, when she got to the diner early she'd try to catch a little overtime, but the manager wasn't letting her do that anymore. Hurt the bottom line, he had told LuAnn. Well, you don't want to know about my bottom line, she had told him right back, but to no avail. But that was okay, he let her bring Lisa in. Without that, there'd be no way she could work at all. And he paid her in cash. She knew he was avoiding payroll taxes that way, but she made little enough money as it was without the government taking any. She had never filed a tax return; she had lived her entire life well below the poverty line and rightly figured she didn't owe any taxes.

Lisa was in her carrier across from her. LuAnn tucked the blanket more snugly around her sleeping daughter. LuAnn had fed Lisa parts of her meal; her daughter was taking to solid food real well, but she hadn't made it through the mushed carrots before falling asleep again. LuAnn worried that her daughter wasn't getting the right kind of sleep. And she wondered, Was putting her baby under the counter of a noisy, smoky truck stop every night going to mess up Lisa's head years from now? Lower her self-esteem and do other damage LuAnn had read about in the magazines or seen on TV. That nightmarish thought had cost LuAnn more sleep than she could remember. And that wasn't all. When Lisa turned to solid food for good would there always be enough? Not having a car, always scrounging change for the bus, walking, or running through the rain. What if Lisa caught something? What if LuAnn did? What if she were laid up for a while? Who would take care of Lisa? She had no insurance. She took Lisa to the free county clinic for her shots and checkups, but LuAnn hadn't been to a doctor in over ten years. She was young, strong, and healthy, but that could change quickly. You never knew. She almost laughed when she thought of Duane trying to navigate the endless details of Lisa's daily requirements. The boy would run screaming into the woods after a few minutes. But it really wasn't a laughing matter.

While she looked at the tiny mouth opening

and closing, LuAnn's heart suddenly felt as heavy as the semis parked in the diner's parking lot. Her daughter depended on her for everything and the truth was LuAnn had nothing. One step from the edge every day of her life and getting closer all the time. A fall was inevitable; it was only a matter of time. She thought back to Jackson's words. A cycle. Her mother. Then LuAnn. Duane resembled Benny Tyler in more ways than she cared to think about. Next up was Lisa, her darling little girl for whom she would kill, or be killed, whatever it took to protect her. America was full of opportunity, everybody said. You just had to unlock it. Only they forgot to give out keys for LuAnn's kind. Or maybe they didn't forget at all. Maybe it was intentional. At least that's how she usually saw things when she was more than a little depressed, like now.

She shook her head clear and squeezed her hands together. That kind of thinking wasn't going to help her now. LuAnn pulled her handbag over and slid out the steno pad. What she had found at the library had greatly intrigued her.

Six lottery winners. She had started with the ones last fall and continued up to the present. She had written down their names and backgrounds. The articles had carried a photo of each winner; their smiles had seemed to stretch across the width of the page. In reverse order of winning they were: Judy Davis, age twenty-seven, a welfare mother with three young children; Herman Rudy, age fifty-eight, a former truck driver on disability with massive medical bills from an injury on the job; Wanda Tripp, sixty-six, widowed and subsisting on Social Security's "safety net" of four hundred dollars a month; Randy Stith, thirty-one, a recent widower with a young child, who had recently been laid off from his assembly line job; Bobbie Jo Reynolds, thirty-three, a waitress in New York who after winning the article said had given up her dream of starring on Broadway to take up painting in the south of France. Finally, there was Raymond Powell, forty-four, a recent bankrupt who had moved into a homeless shelter.

LuAnn slumped back in her seat. *And LuAnn Tyler, twenty years old, single mother, dirt poor, uneducated, no prospects, no future.* She would fit in perfectly with this desperate group.

She had only gone back six months. How many more of them were there? It made for great stories, she had to admit. People in dire straits hit the jackpot. Old people with new-found wealth. Young children with a suddenly bright future. All their dreams coming true. Jackson's face appeared in her thoughts. *Someone has to win. Why not you, LuAnn?* His calm, cool tones beckoned to her. In fact, those two sentences reverberated over and over in her head. She felt herself beginning to slide over the top of an imaginary dam. What was awaiting her in the deep waters below, she was not sure. The unknown both scared her and drew her, fiercely. She looked at Lisa. She could not shake the image of her little girl growing into a woman in a trailer with no way to escape while the young wolves circled.

"What'cha doing, sweetie?"

LuAnn jerked around and stared into Beth's face. The older woman expertly juggled plates full of food in both hands.

"Nothing much, just counting up all my fortune," LuAnn said.

Beth grinned and looked at the steno pad, which LuAnn quickly closed. "Well, don't forget the little people when you hit the big time, Miss LuAnn Tyler." Beth cackled and then carried the food orders to the waiting customers.

LuAnn smiled uneasily. "I won't, Beth. I swear," she said quietly.

Chapter Seven

It was eight o'clock in the morning on *the day*. LuAnn stepped off the bus with Lisa. This was not her usual stop, but it was close enough to the trailer that she could walk it in half an hour or so, which was nothing to her. The rain had passed and left the sky a brilliant blue and the earth a lush green. Small clusters of birds sang the praises of the changing season and the exit of another tedious winter. Everywhere LuAnn turned as she tramped along under the newly risen sun there was fresh growth. She liked this time of the day. It was calm, soothing, and she tended to feel hopeful about things.

LuAnn looked ahead to the gently rolling fields and her manner grew both somber and expectant. She walked slowly through the arched gateway and past the patinated sign proclaiming her entrance into the Heavenly Meadows Cemetery. Her long, slender feet carried her automatically to Section 14, Lot 21, Plot 6; it occupied a space on a small knoll in the shadow of a mature dogwood that would soon begin showing its unique wares. She laid Lisa's carrier down on the stone bench near her mother's grave and lifted out the little girl. Kneeling in the dewy grass, she brushed some twigs and dirt off the bronze marker. Her mother, Joy, had not lived all that long: thirty-seven years. It had seemed both brief and an eternity for Joy Tyler, that LuAnn knew. The years with Benny had not been pleasant, and had, LuAnn firmly believed now, hastened her mother's exit from the living.

"Remember? This is where your grandma is, Lisa. We haven't been for a while because the weather was so bad. But now that it's spring it's time to visit again." LuAnn held up her daughter and pointed with her finger at the recessed ground. "Right there. She's sleeping right now, but whenever we come by, she sort of wakes up. She can't really talk back to us but if you close your eyes tight as a baby bird's, and listen real, real hard, you can kinda hear her. She's letting you know what she thinks about things."

After saying this, LuAnn rose up and sat on the bench with Lisa on her lap, bundled against the chill of the early morning. Lisa was still sleepy; it usually took her a while to wake up, but once she did, the little girl wouldn't stop moving or talking for several hours. The cemetery was deserted except for a workman LuAnn could see far in the distance, cutting grass on a riding mower. The sounds of the mower's engine didn't reach her and there were few cars on the roadway. The silence was peaceful and she closed her eyes tight as a baby bird's and listened as hard as she could.

At the diner she had made up her mind to call Jackson right after she got off work. He had said anytime and she figured he would answer the phone on the first ring regardless of the time. Saying yes had seemed like the easiest thing in the world to do. And the smartest. It was her turn. After twenty years filled with grief, disappointment, and depths of despair that seemed to have endless elasticity, the gods had smiled upon her. Out of the masses of billions, LuAnn Tyler's name had turned the hat trick on the slot machine. It would never happen again, of that she was dead certain. She was also sure that the other people she had read about in the paper had made a similar phone call. She hadn't read anything about them getting in trouble. That sort of news would have been all over, certainly in as poor an area as she lived in, where everyone played the lottery in a frantic effort to throw off the bitter hopelessness of being a have-not. Somewhere between leaving the diner and stepping on the bus, however, she had felt something very deep inside of her prompting her to not pick up the phone but, instead, to seek counsel other than her own. She came here often, to talk, to lay flowers she had picked, or to spruce up her mother's final resting place. In the past, she had often thought she actually did communicate with her mother. She had never heard voices; it was more levels of feelings, of senses. Euphoria or deep sadness sometimes overtook her here, and she had finally put it down to her mother reaching out to her, letting her opinion on things having to do with LuAnn seep into her child's body, into her mind. Doctors would probably call her crazy, she knew, but that didn't take away from what she felt.

Right now she hoped for something to speak to her, to let her know what to do. Her mother had raised her right. LuAnn had never told a lie until she had started living with Duane. Then the fabrications seemed to just happen; they seemed to be an inextricable part of simply surviving. But she had never stolen anything in her life, never really done anything wrong that she knew of. She had kept her dignity and self-respect through a lot over the years and it felt good. It helped her get up and face the toil of another day when that day contained little in the way of hope that the next day and the next would be any different, any better.

But today, nothing was happening. The noisy lawn mower was drawing closer and the traffic on the road had picked up. She opened her eyes and sighed. Things were not right. Her mother apparently was not going to be available today of all days. She stood up and was preparing to leave when a feeling came over her. It was like nothing she had ever experienced before. Her eyes were automatically drawn to another section of the cemetery, to another plot that lay about five hundred yards away. Something was pulling her there, and she had no doubt what it was. Eyes wide, and her legs moving of their own accord, LuAnn made her way down the narrow, winding asphalt walkway. Something made her clutch Lisa tightly to her bosom, as though if she didn't the little girl would be snatched away by the unseen force compelling LuAnn to its epicenter. As she drew nearer to the spot, the sky seemed to turn a terrible dark. The sounds of the mowing were gone, the cars had stopped coming down the road. The only sound was the wind whistling over the flat grass and around the weathered testaments to the dead. Her hair blowing straight back, LuAnn finally stopped and looked down. The bronze marker was similar in style to her mother's, and the last name on it was identical: Benjamin Herbert Tyler. She had not been to this spot since her father had died. She had tightly clutched her mother's hand at his funeral, neither woman feeling the least bit saddened and yet having to display appropriate emotions for the many friends and family of the departed. In the strange way the world sometimes worked, Benny Tyler had been immensely popular with just about everyone except his own family because he had been generous and cordial with everyone except his own family. Seeing his formal name etched in the metal made her suck in her breath. It was as though the letters were stenciled over an office door and she would soon be ushered in to see the man himself. She started to draw back from the sunken earth, to retreat from the sharp jabs that seemed to sink in deeper with each step she had taken toward his remains. Then the intense feeling she had not realized beside her mother's grave suddenly overtook her. Of all places. She could almost see wisps of gauzy membrane swirling above the grave like a spiderweb picked up by the wind. She turned and ran. Even with Lisa, she hit an all-out sprint three steps into a run that would have made many an Olympian bristle with envy. Without missing a step and gripping Lisa to her chest, LuAnn snatched up Lisa's baby carrier and flew past the gates of the cemetery. She had not closed her eyes tight like a baby bird. She had not even been listening particularly hard. And yet the immortal speech of Benny Tyler had risen from depths so far down she could not contemplate them, and had made its way ferociously into the tender ear canals of his only child.

Take the money, little girl. Daddy says take it and damn everyone and everything else. Listen to me. Use what little brain you've got. When the body goes, you got nothing. Nothing! When did I ever lie to you, baby doll? Take it, dammit, take it, you dumb bitch! Daddy loves you. Do it for Big Daddy. You know you want to.

The man on the mower paused to watch her race away under a sky of pristine blue that begged to be photographed. The traffic on the road had picked up considerably. All the sounds of life, which had disappeared so inexplicably for LuAnn during those few moments, had once again reappeared.

The man looked over at the grave from which LuAnn had fled. Some people just got spooked in a graveyard, he figured, even in broad daylight. He went back to his mowing.

LuAnn was already out of sight.

The wind chased the pair down the long dirt road. Sweat drenched LuAnn's face as the sun bore down on her from gaps in the foliage; her long legs ate up the ground with a stride that was both machine-like in its precision and wonderfully animalistic in its grace. Growing up she had been able to outrun just about everybody in the county, including most of the varsity football team. God-given world-class speed, her seventh-grade gym teacher had told her. What exactly she was supposed to do with that gift no one ever told her. For a thirteen-year-old girl with a woman's figure it had just meant if she couldn't beat up the boy who was trying to feel her up, at least she could probably outrun him.

Now her chest was burning. For a minute she wondered if she would keel over from a heart attack, as her father had. Perhaps there was some physical flaw buried deep within all the descendants of the man, just waiting for the opportunity to cleave another Tyler from the ranks. She slowed down. Lisa was bawling now and LuAnn finally stopped running and hugged her baby hard, whispering soothing words into the little girl's small pink ear while she made slow, wide circles in the dense shadows of the forest until the cries finally stopped.

LuAnn walked the rest of the way home. The words of Benny Tyler had made up her mind. She would pack what she could from the trailer and send somebody back for the rest. She would stay with Beth for a while. Beth had offered before. She had an old ramshackle house, but it had a lot of rooms and after the death of her husband her only companions were a pair of cats that Beth swore were crazier than she was. LuAnn would take Lisa into the classroom with her if need be, but she was going to get her GED and then maybe take some classes at the community college. If Johnny Jarvis could do it then she could, too. And Mr. Jackson could find somebody else to "gladly" take her place. All these answers to her life's dilemmas had come roaring in upon her so fast she could barely keep her head from exploding off her shoulders with relief. Her mother had spoken to her, in a roundabout manner perhaps, but the magic had been worked. "Never forget about the dearly departed, Lisa," she whispered to the little girl. "You just never know."

LuAnn slowed as she neared the trailer. Duane had been rolling in money the day before. She wondered how much he had left. He was quick to buy rounds at the Squat and Gobble when he had a few bucks in his pocket. Lord only knew what he had done with the wad he had under the bed. She didn't want to know where he had gotten it. She figured it was only an additional reason to get the hell out.

As she rounded the bend, a flock of black-birds scattered from the trees overhead and scared her. She looked up at them angrily for a moment and then kept walking. As the trailer came into her line of sight, she abruptly stopped. There was a car parked out front. A convertible, big and wide, shiny black with white sidewalls, and on the hood a huge chrome ornament that from a distance looked vaguely like a woman engaged in some indecent sexual act. Duane drove a battered Ford pickup truck which had been in the impoundment lot the last LuAnn had seen it. None of Duane's cronies drove anything like this crazy machine. What in the world was going on? Had Duane gone flat-out loco and bought this boat? She stole up to the vehicle and examined it, keeping one eye on the trailer. The seats were covered in a white leather with inlays of deep burgundy. The inside of the car was spotless, the dashboard clock polished enough to hurt your eye when the sunlight hit it just so. There was nothing in the front or rear seats to identify the owner. The keys hung in the ignition, a tiny Bud can attached to the ring. A phone rested in a device built specifically to hold it and attached to the hump between the front seat and the dashboard. Maybe this thing did belong to Duane. But she figured it would've taken all the cash under his mattress and then some to buy this rig.

She moved quickly up the steps and listened for sounds from within before venturing farther. When she didn't hear anything, she decided finally to brave it. She had kicked his butt the last time, she could do it again.

"Duane?" She slammed the door loudly. "Duane, what the hell did you do? Is that thing out there yours?" There was still no answer. LuAnn put an agitated Lisa down in her baby carrier and moved through the trailer. "Duane, are you here? Come on, answer me, will you, please. I don't have time to play around."

She went into the bedroom, but he wasn't there. Her eyes were riveted by her clock on the wall. It took her an instant to stuff it in her bag. She wasn't going to leave it with Duane. She exited the bedroom and moved down the hallway, passing Lisa as she did so. She stopped to calm the little girl down and placed her bag next to the baby carrier.

She finally saw Duane, lying on the raggedy couch. The TV was on, but no sound came from the battered box. A grease-stained bucket of chicken wings was on the coffee table next to what LuAnn assumed was an empty can of beer. A mess of fries and an overturned bottle of ketchup were next to the bucket of wings. Whether this was breakfast or the remnants of dinner from last night, she didn't know.

"Hey, Duane, didn't you hear me?"

She saw him turn his head, very, very slowly, toward her. She scowled. Still drunk. "Duane, ain't you never going to grow up?" She started forward. "We got to talk. And you ain't going to like it, but that's too bad becau—" She got no further as the big hand clamped over her mouth, cutting off her scream. A thick arm encircled her waist, pinning her arms to her sides. As her panicked eyes swept the room, she noted for the first time that the front of Duane's shirt was a mass of splotchy crimson. As she watched in horror, he fell off the couch with a small groan and then didn't move again.

The hand shot up to her throat and pushed her chin up so hard she thought her neck was going to snap under the pressure. She sucked in a huge breath as she saw the other hand holding the blade that descended toward her neck.

"Sorry, lady, wrong time, wrong place."

LuAnn didn't recognize the voice. The breath was a mixture of cheap beer and spicy chicken wings. The foul odor pressed against her cheek as fiercely as the hand against her mouth. He had made a mistake, though. With one hand bracing her chin and the other holding the knife, he had left her arms free. Perhaps he thought she would be paralyzed with fear. She was far from it. Her foot crunched backward against his knee at the same moment her bony elbow sunk deep into his flabby gut, hitting right at the diaphragm.

The force of her blow caused his hand to jerk suddenly and the knife slashed her chin. She tasted blood. The man dropped to the floor, spitting and coughing. The hunting knife clattered to the bare carpet next to him. LuAnn hurtled toward the front door, but her attacker managed to snag a leg as she passed by and she tumbled to the floor a few feet from him. Despite being doubled over, he clamped thick fingers around her ankle and dragged her back toward him. Finally, she got a good look at him as she turned over on her back, kicking at him with all her might: sunburned skin, thick, caterpillar eyebrows, sweaty, matted black hair, and full, cracked lips that were at the moment grimacing in pain. She couldn't see his eyes, which were half-closed as his body shrugged off her blows. LuAnn took in those features in an instant. What was even more evident was that he was twice her size. In the grip that tightened around her leg, she knew she had no chance against him, strength-wise. However, she wasn't about to leave Lisa to face him alone; not without a lot more fight than she had already given him.

Instead of resisting further, she threw herself toward him, screaming as loudly as she could. The scream and her sudden leap startled him. Off-balance, he let go of her leg. Now she could see his eyes; they were deep brown, the color of old pennies. In another second they were shut tightly again as she planted her index fingers in both of them. Howling again, the man fell backward against the wall but then he ricocheted off like a bounced ball and slammed blindly into her. They both pitched over the couch. LuAnn's flailing hand seized an object on the way down. She couldn't see exactly what it was, but it was solid and hard and that's all she cared about as she swung with all her might and smashed it against his head right before she hit the floor, barely missing Duane's limp body, and then she slammed headfirst into the wall.

The telephone had shattered into pieces upon impact with the man's thick skull. Seemingly unconscious, her attacker lay facedown on the floor. The dark hair was now a mass of red as the blood poured from the head wound. LuAnn lay on the floor for a moment and then sat up. Her arm tingled where she had hit the coffee table, and then it went numb on her. Her buttocks ached where she had slammed into the floor. Her head pounded where it had struck the wall. "Damn," she said as she struggled to regain her equilibrium. She had to get out of here, she told herself. Grab Lisa and keep running until her legs or lungs gave out. Her vision blurred for an instant and her eyes rolled up into her head. "Oh, Lord," she moaned as she felt it coming. Her lips parted and she sank back down to the floor, unconscious.

Chapter Eight

LuAnn had no idea how long she had been out. The blood that had poured out of the wound on her chin hadn't yet hardened against her skin so it couldn't have been all that long. Her shirt was ripped and bloody; one breast hung loose from her bra. She slowly sat up and rearranged herself with her good arm. She wiped her chin and touched the cut; it was jagged and painful. She slowly lifted herself up. She could not seem to catch her breath as lingering terror and physical trauma battered her from within and without.

The two men lay side by side; the big man was clearly still breathing, the expansions and contractions of his huge gut were easy to see. LuAnn wasn't sure about Duane. She dropped to her knees and felt for his pulse, but if it was there, she couldn't find it. His face looked gray, but it was hard to tell in the darkness. She jumped up and flipped on a light, but the illumination was still poor. She knelt down beside him again and touched his chest gingerly. Then she lifted his shirt. She quickly pulled it back down, nauseated at the sight of all the blood there. "Oh, Lord, Duane, what have you gone and done?

Duane, can you hear me? Duane!" In the dim light she was able to see that no more blood was flowing from his wounds: a sign that his heart was probably no longer beating. She felt his arm; it was still warm to the touch, but she felt his fingers and they were already beginning to curl and grow cold. She eyed the remnants of the phone. There was no way to call the ambulance now, although it didn't look like Duane was going to need one. She should probably go fetch the police, though. Find out who the other man was, why he had cut up Duane and tried to kill her.

When LuAnn rose to leave, she noticed the small pile of bags that had been hidden behind the greasy bucket of chicken. They had fallen off the table in the scuffle. LuAnn stooped down and picked one up. It was clear plastic. Inside was a small amount of white powder. Drugs.

Then she heard the whimpering. Oh God, where was Lisa? But there was another sound. LuAnn sucked in her breath as she jerked around and looked down. The big man's hand was moving, he was starting to rise. He was coming for her! Oh sweet Lord, he was coming for her! She dropped the bag and raced to the hallway. Using her good arm to snatch up Lisa, who started screaming when she saw her mother, LuAnn bolted through the front door, slamming it back against the side of the trailer.

She ran past the convertible, stopped, and turned back. The massive wall of flesh she had clocked with the phone didn't explode through the door. At least not yet. Her eyes shifted slightly to the car; the dangling keys glimmered temptingly in the sunlight. She hesitated for only an instant, then she and Lisa were in the car. LuAnn gunned the motor and fishtailed out of the muck and onto the road. She took a minute to get her nerves under control before she turned onto the main highway into town.

Now Duane's sudden wealth made a lot of sense. Selling drugs was obviously far more lucrative than stripping cars for a living. Only Duane had apparently gotten greedy and kept a little too much of the drugs or green for himself. The stupid idiot! She had to call the police. Even if Duane was alive, which she doubted, she was probably only saving him for a long spell in jail. But if he was still alive, she couldn't just leave him to die. The other fellow she didn't give a damn about. She only wished she had hit him harder. As she sped up, she looked over at Lisa. The little girl sat wide-eyed in her baby carrier, the terror still clearly observable in her quivering lips and cheeks. Lisa settled her injured arm over her daughter, biting back the pain this simple movement caused her. Her neck felt as though a car had run over it. Then her eyes alighted on the cellular phone. She pulled off the road and snatched it up.

After quickly figuring out how to work it, she started to dial 911. Then she slowly put down the phone. She looked down at her fingers. They were shaking so hard she couldn't make a fist. They were also covered with blood, and probably not just her own. It was suddenly dawning on her that she could easily be implicated in all of this. Despite his starting to move, the guy could have slumped back down, dead, for all she knew. She would have killed him in self-defense, she knew that, but would anyone else? A drug dealer. She was driving his car.

This thought made her look around suddenly to see if anyone was watching. Some cars were heading toward her. The top! She had to close the ragtop. She jumped into the backseat and gripped the stiff fabric. She pulled upward, and then the big white convertible top descended down upon them like a clam closing up. She hit the ragtop's clamps, jumped back into the driver's seat, and tore down the road.

Would the police believe that she knew nothing about Duane's selling drugs? Somehow Duane had kept the truth from her, but who would accept that as the truth? She didn't believe it herself. This reality swept over her like a fire raging through a paper house; there seemed to be no escape. But maybe there was. She almost shrieked as she thought of it. For an instant her mother's face appeared in her thoughts. It was with immense difficulty that she pushed it away. "I'm sorry, Momma. I ain't got no choices left." She had to do it: the call to Jackson.

That's when her gaze came to rest on the dashboard. For several seconds she could not even manage a breath. It was like every ounce of blood had evaporated from her body as her eyes stayed locked on the shiny clock.

It was five minutes *past* ten.

Gone. Forever, Jackson had said, and she didn't doubt for an instant he had meant it. She pulled off the road and slumped over the steering wheel in her misery. What would happen to Lisa while she was in prison? Stupid, stupid Duane. Screwed her in life, and now in death.

She slowly raised her head up and looked across the street, wiping her eyes so she could make out the image: a bank branch, squat, solid, all-brick. If she had owned a gun, she would have seriously contemplated robbing it. Even that was not an option, though; it was Sunday and the bank was closed. As her eyes drifted over the front of the bank her heart started to beat rapidly again. The change in her state of mind was so sudden as to feel almost drug-induced.

The bank clock showed four minutes *before* ten.

Bankers were supposed to be steady, reliable

folk. She hoped to God their clocks were reliable as well. She snatched up the phone, at the same time digging frantically in her pocket for the slip of paper with the number on it. Her coordination seemed to have totally deserted her. She could barely force her fingers to punch in the numbers. It seemed to take forever for the line to begin ringing. Fortunately for her nerves, it rang only once before being answered.

"I was beginning to wonder about you, LuAnn," Jackson said. She could envision him checking his watch, probably marveling at how close she had cut it.

She forced herself to breathe normally. "I guess the time just got away from me. I had a lot going on."

"Your cavalier attitude is refreshing, although, quite frankly, it's a bit amazing to me."

"So what now?"

"Aren't you forgetting something?"

LuAnn looked puzzled. "What?" Her brain was near serious burnout. A series of pains shot throughout her body. *If all this turned out to be a joke . . .*

"I made you an offer, LuAnn. In order to have a legally enforceable arrangement, I need an acceptance from you. A formality, perhaps, but one on which I have to insist."

"I accept."

"Wonderful. I can tell you with complete

assurance that you will never regret that decision."

LuAnn looked nervously around. Two people walking on the other side of the highway were staring at the car. She put the vehicle in gear and headed down the road. "So now what?" she again asked Jackson.

"Where are you?"

Her tone was wary. "Why?" Then she added quickly, "I'm at home."

"Fine. You are to go to the nearest outlet selling lottery tickets. You will purchase one."

"What numbers do I play?"

"That doesn't matter. As you know, you have two options. Either accept a ticket with numbers automatically dispensed by the machine or pick whatever numbers you want. They're all fed into the same central computer system with up-to-the-second results and no duplicate combinations are allowed; that ensures only one winner. If you opt for a personalized combination and your first choice has already been taken, simply pick another combination."

"But I don't understand. I thought you were gonna tell me what numbers to play. The winning numbers."

"There is no need for you to understand anything, LuAnn." Jackson's voice had risen a notch higher. "You are simply to do what you're told. Once you have the combination, call me back and tell me what the numbers are. I'll take care of the rest."

"So when do I get the money?"

"There will be a press conference —"

"Press conference!" LuAnn almost flipped the car over. She fought to keep it under control with her good arm as she cradled the phone under her chin.

Now Jackson sounded truly exasperated. "Haven't you ever watched one of these things? The winner attends a press conference, usually in New York. It's televised across the country, the world. You'll have your photo taken holding a ceremonial check and then reporters will ask questions about your background, your child, your dreams, what you'll do with the money. Quite nauseating, but the Lottery Commission insists. It's terrific PR for them. That's why ticket sales have been doubling every year for the last five years. Everybody loves a deserving winner, if for no other reason than most people believe themselves to be quite deserving."

"Do I have to do it?"

"Excuse me?"

"I don't want to be on TV."

"Well, I'm afraid you don't have a choice. Keep in mind that you're going to be at least fifty million dollars richer, LuAnn. For that kind of money, they expect you to be able to handle one press conference. And, frankly, they are right."

"So I have to go?"

"Absolutely."

"Do I have to use my real name?"

"Why wouldn't you want to?"

"I've got my reasons, Mr. Jackson. Would I?"

"Yes! There is a certain statute, LuAnn, not that I would expect you to be aware of it, popularly termed the 'right to know' law. To put it simply, it says that the public is entitled to know the identities, the *real* identities, of all lottery winners."

LuAnn let out a deep breath filled with disappointment. "Okay, so when do I get the money?"

Now Jackson discernibly paused. The hair on the back of LuAnn's neck started to bristle. "Listen, don't try pulling no crap on me here. What about the damn money?"

"There's no cause to get testy, LuAnn. I was merely pondering how to explain it to you in the simplest terms possible. The money will be transferred into an account of your designation."

"But I don't have any account. I've never had enough money to open a damn account."

"Calm down, LuAnn, I'll take care of all of that. You don't have to worry about it. The only thing you have to do is win." Jackson's voice tried to sound upbeat. "Go to New York with Lisa, hold that big check, smile, wave, say nice, humble things, and then spend the rest of your life on the beach."

"How do I get to New York?"

"Good question; however, one for which I have already prepared. There's no airport near where you live, but there is a bus station. You'll take a bus to the train station in Atlanta. That's on Amtrak's Crescent line. The Gainsville station is closer to you, but they don't sell tickets there. It's a long ride, about eighteen hours or so with numerous stops; however, a good part of it will be while you're sleeping. It will take you to New York and you won't have to change trains. I'd put you on a plane to New York, but that's a little more complicated. You have to show identification, and, frankly, I don't want you in New York that quickly. I'll make all the arrangements. A reserved ticket will be waiting for you at each station. You can leave for New York right after the lottery drawing takes place."

The prone figures of Duane and the man who had tried his best to kill her flashed across LuAnn's mind. "I'm not sure I want to hang around here that long."

Jackson was startled. "Why not?"

"That's my business," she said sharply, then her tone softened. "It's just that if I'm gonna win this thing, I don't want to be around here when people find out, is all. It'll be like a pack of wolves on a calf, if you know what I mean."

"That won't happen. You won't be publicly identified as the winner until the press conference occurs in New York. When you arrive in the city, someone will be waiting for you and will take you to the lottery headquarters. Your winning ticket will be confirmed and then the press conference will occur the next day. It used to take weeks to verify the winning ticket. With the technology they have today, it takes hours."

"How about if I drive to Atlanta and take the train up today?"

"You have a car? My goodness, what will Duane say?" There was considerable mirth in Jackson's tone.

"Let me worry about that," LuAnn snapped.

"You know, LuAnn, you might want to act a little more grateful, unless, of course, someone makes you rich beyond your wildest dreams on a routine basis."

LuAnn swallowed hard. She was going to be rich all right. By cheating. "I am," she said slowly. "It's just now that I made up my mind, everything's going to change. My whole life. And Lisa's, too. It's a little mind-boggling."

"Well, I understand that. But keep in mind that this particular change is definitely of the positive variety. It's not like you're going to prison or anything."

LuAnn fought back the catch in her throat and clenched her bottom lip between her teeth. "Can't I please take the train up today? Please?"

"Hold on for one minute." He clicked off. LuAnn looked up ahead. A police cruiser sat on the side of the road, a radar gun perched on the door. LuAnn automatically checked her speedometer and, although she was under the speed limit, slowed down slightly. She didn't breathe again until she was several hundred yards down the road. Jackson clicked back on, his abrupt tones startling her.

"The Crescent pulls into Atlanta at seven-fifteen this evening and arrives in New York at one-thirty tomorrow afternoon. Atlanta is only a couple hours' drive from where you are." He paused for an instant. "You're going to need money for the ticket, though, and I'm assuming you'll need additional funds, perhaps for some travel-related incidentals."

LuAnn unconsciously nodded at the phone. "Yes." She suddenly felt very dirty, like a whore pleading for some extra cash after an hour's work.

"There's a Western Union office near the train station. I'll wire you five thousand dollars there." LuAnn gulped at the amount. "Remember my initial job offer? We'll just call it your salary for a job well done. You just have to show proper identification —"

"I don't have any."

"Just a driver's license or passport. That's all they need."

LuAnn almost laughed. "Passport? You don't need a passport to go from the Piggly-

Wiggly to the Wal-Mart, do you? And I don't have a driver's license either."

"But you're planning to drive a car to Atlanta." Jackson's astonished tone was even more amusing to her. Here the man was, orchestrating a multimillion-dollar scam, and he could not comprehend that LuAnn would operate an automobile without a license.

"You'd be surprised how many people ain't got a license for anything and they still do it."

"Well, you can't get the money without proper identification."

"Are you anywhere nearby?"

"LuAnn, I only came to glorious Rikersville to conduct my meeting with you. Once it was done, I didn't hang around." He paused again and LuAnn could hear the displeasure in his voice when he spoke next. "Well, we have a problem then."

"Well, how much would the train ticket be?"

"About fifteen hundred."

Remembering Duane's money hoard, a sudden thought struck LuAnn. She again pulled off the road, put down the phone, and quickly searched the car's interior. The brown leather bag she pulled from underneath the front seat didn't disappoint her. There was enough cash in there probably to buy the train.

"A woman I work with, her husband left her some money when he passed on. I can ask her for the money. A loan. I know she'll give it to me," she told Jackson. "I won't need no ID for cash, will I?" she added.

"Money is king, LuAnn. I'm sure Amtrak will accommodate you. Just don't use your real name, of course. Use something simple, but not too phony sounding. Now go buy the lottery ticket and then call me back immediately. Do you know how to get to Atlanta?"

"It's a big place, or so I've heard. I'll find it."

"Wear something to hide your face. The last thing we need is for you to be recognized."

"I understand, Mr. Jackson."

"You're almost there, LuAnn. Congratulations."

"I don't feel much like celebrating."

"Not to worry, you have the rest of your life to do that."

LuAnn put down the phone and looked around. The car windows were tinted so she didn't think anyone had actually seen her, but that could change. She had to ditch the car as fast as possible. The only question was where. She didn't want to be seen getting out of the car. It would be pretty hard to miss a tall, blood-caked woman hauling a baby out of a car with tinted windows and a chrome figure doing nasty things on the vehicle's hood. An idea finally hit her. A little dangerous perhaps, but right now she didn't have much alternative. She did a U-turn and headed in the opposite direction. Within twenty minutes she was pulling slowly down the dirt road, and straining to see ahead as she drew nearer to her destination. The trailer finally came into view. She saw no other vehicles, no movement. As she pulled in front of the trailer cold dread poured over her as she once again felt the man's hands around her throat, as she watched the blade swooping toward her. "You see that man coming out that house," LuAnn said out loud to herself, "you're gonna run right over his butt, let his lips kiss the oil pan on this thing."

She rolled down the passenger window so she could check for sounds coming from within but heard nothing. She pulled a diaper wipe out of Lisa's bag and methodically rubbed down all of the car's surfaces that she had touched. She had watched a few episodes of *America's Most Wanted*. If it hadn't been too dangerous she would have gone back inside the trailer and wiped down the telephone. But she had lived there for almost two years. Her fingerprints would be all over the place, anyway. She climbed out of the car, stuffing as much cash from the bag as she could under the liner of Lisa's baby seat. She pulled her torn shirt together as best she could. She noiselessly closed the car door and, holding Lisa with her good arm, she quickly made her way back down the dirt road.

From within the trailer, the pair of dark eyes watched LuAnn's hasty departure, taking in every detail. When she suddenly glanced around the man stepped back into the shadow of the trailer's interior. LuAnn didn't know him, but he wasn't taking any chances at being observed. His dark leather jacket was zipped halfway up the front, the butt of a 9-mm visible sticking out of the inside pocket. He stepped quickly over the two men lying on the floor, careful to avoid the pools of blood. He had happened along at an opportune time. He was left with the spoils of a battle he had not even had to fight. What could be better? He scooped the drug packets off both the coffee table and the floor and deposited them in a plastic bag that the man pulled from his jacket. After thinking about it for a moment, he put half the stash back where he had found it. No sense being greedy, and if the organization these boys worked for got wind that no drugs had been discovered by the police in the trailer they might start looking for who took it. If only part of the stash was missing they'd probably assume the cops had sticky fingers.

He eyed the fight scene and then noted the torn fabric on the floor; recognition spread across his features. It was from the woman's shirt. He put it in his pocket. She owed him now. He looked at the remnants of the phone, the position of each man's body, the knife and the dents in the wall. She must have walked right into the middle of this, he deduced. Fat man got the little man, and LuAnn somehow got the fat man. His admiration for her in-

107

creased as he noted the man's bulk.

As if he sensed this observation, the fat man started to stir again slowly. Not waiting for the fat man to recover further, the other man stooped down, used a cloth to snatch up the knife, and then plunged it repeatedly into the man's side. The dying man grew momentarily stiff, his fingers digging into the threadbare carpet, hanging on to the last seconds of his life, desperately unwilling to let go. After a few moments, though, his entire body shook for an instant and then slowly relaxed, his fingers uncurled and splayed out, his palms flush against the floor. His face was turned to the side; one lifeless, blood-filled eye stared up at his killer.

Next, he roughly flipped over Duane, squinting in the dim light as he tried to determine if the chest was moving up or down. Just to be safe he used several carefully aimed thrusts to make certain Duane Harvey joined the fat man in the hereafter. He tossed the knife down.

In another few seconds he was through the front door and around the back of the trailer where he plunged into the woods. His car was parked off a little-used dirt trail that snaked through the heavy woods. It was windy and rough, but it would deliver him onto the main road in plenty of time to take up his real task: following LuAnn Tyler. When he climbed into his car, his car phone was ringing. He picked it up.

"Your duties are at an end," Jackson said. "The hunt has officially been called off. The balance of your payment will be sent to you via the usual channels. I thank you for your work and I'll keep you in mind for future employment."

Anthony Romanello gripped the phone hard. He debated whether to tell Jackson about the two bodies in the trailer and then decided not to. He might have stumbled onto something really interesting.

"I saw the little lady tearing out of here on foot. But she doesn't look like she has the resources to go very far," Romanello said.

Jackson chuckled. "I think money will be the least of her worries." Then the line went dead.

Romanello clicked off his phone and pondered the matter for a moment. Technically, he had been called off. His work was at an end and he could just return home and wait for the rest of his money. But there was something screwy going on here. Everything about the job was somehow off. Sending him down here to the sticks to kill some hick chick. And then being told not to. And there was Jackson's passing reference to money. Dollars were something that always held Romanello's interest. He made up his mind and put the car in gear. He was going to follow LuAnn Tyler.

Chapter Nine

LuAnn stopped at a gas station rest room and cleaned up as best as she could. She cleaned the wound on her jaw, pulled a Band-Aid out of Lisa's diaper bag, and covered the cut with it. While Lisa slurped contentedly on a bottle, LuAnn bought her lottery ticket and some ointment and gauze at the local 7-Eleven. As part of the ten numbers she picked, she used her own and Lisa's birthdays.

"People been coming in here like damn cattle," said the clerk, who was a friend of hers named Bobby.

"What happened there?" he asked, pointing to the large Band-Aid on her face.

"Fell and cut myself," she said quickly. "So what's the jackpot up to?" LuAnn asked.

"A cool sixty-five mil and counting." Bobby's eyes gleamed with anticipation. "I got a dozen tickets myself. I'm feeling good about this one, LuAnn. Hey, you know that movie where the cop gives the waitress half his lottery winnings? LuAnn, tell you what, darling, I win this thing, I'll give half to you, cross my heart."

"I appreciate that, Bobby, but what exactly do I have to do for the money?"

"Why, marry me, o' course." Bobby grinned as he handed her the ticket she had purchased. "So what do you say, how about half of yours if you win? We'll still get hitched."

"I think I'll just play this one all by myself. Besides, I thought you were engaged to Mary Anne Simmons."

"I was, but that was last week." Bobby looked her up and down in obvious admiration. "Duane is dumb as dirt."

LuAnn jammed the ticket far down into her jeans. "You been seeing much of him lately?"

Bobby shook his head. "Nah, he's been keeping to himself lately. I heard he's been spending a lot of time over Gwinnett County way. Got some business over there or something."

"What kind of business?"

Bobby shrugged. "Don't know. Don't want to know. Got better things to do with my time than worry about the likes of him."

"Duane come into some money that you know of?"

"Come to think of it, he was flashing some cash around the other night. I thought maybe he won the lottery. If he did, I think I'll just go kill myself right now. Damn, she looks just like you." Bobby gave Lisa's cheek a gentle rub. "You change your mind about splitting the pot or marrying me, you just let me know, sweet cheeks. I get off at seven."

"I'll see you around, Bobby."

At a nearby pay phone, LuAnn dialed the number again and once again Jackson picked it up on the first ring. She gave him the ten digits from her ticket and she could hear him rustling paper on the other end of the line as he wrote them down.

"Read them to me once more, slowly," he said. "As you can understand, we can't have any mistakes now."

She read them again and he read them back to her.

"Good," he said. "Very good. Well, now the hard part is over. Get on the train, do your little press conference, and sail away into the sunset."

"I'm going to the train station right now."

"Someone will meet you at Penn Station and take you to your hotel."

"I thought I was going to New York."

"That's the name of the train station in New York, LuAnn," Jackson said impatiently. "The person meeting you will have a description of you and Lisa." He paused. "I'm assuming you're bringing her."

"She don't go, I don't go."

"That's not what I meant, LuAnn, of course you can bring her. However, I trust you did not include Duane in the travel plans."

LuAnn swallowed hard as she thought back to the bloodstains on Duane's shirt, how he had fallen off the couch and never moved again. "Duane won't be coming," she said.

"Excellent," Jackson said. "Enjoy your trip."

The bus dropped off LuAnn and Lisa at the train station in Atlanta. After her phone call with Jackson, she had stopped at the Wal-Mart and purchased some essentials for herself and Lisa, which were in a bag slung over her shoulder; her own torn shirt had been replaced with a new one. A cowboy hat and a pair of sunglasses hid her face. She had thoroughly cleaned and dressed the knife wound in the rest room. It felt a lot better. She went to the ticket counter to purchase her train ticket to New York. And that's when LuAnn made a big mistake.

"Name, please," the agent said.

LuAnn was fiddling with a fussing Lisa and thus answered automatically, "LuAnn Tyler." She caught her breath as soon as she said it. She looked at the clerk, who was busily typing the information into her computer. LuAnn couldn't change it now. That would obviously make the woman suspicious. She swallowed hard and hoped to God the slip would not come back to haunt her. The woman recommended the Deluxe sleeping car accommodations since LuAnn was traveling with a baby. "There's one available and it has a private shower and all," the woman said. LuAnn quickly agreed. While the ticket was being processed, the sales agent raised an eyebrow

113

when LuAnn pulled some bills from under Lisa's baby seat to pay for the ticket, stuffing the rest in her pocket.

LuAnn observed the woman's look, thought quickly, and smiled at her. "My rainy day money. Figured I might as well use it while the weather's nice. Go up to New York and see the sights."

"Well, enjoy yourself," the woman said, "but be careful. You shouldn't be carrying a lot of cash up there. My husband and I made that mistake when we went years ago. We weren't five minutes out of the train station when we got robbed. Had to call my mother to send us some money so we could come home."

"Thanks, I'll be real careful."

The woman looked behind LuAnn. "Where's your luggage?"

"Oh, I like to travel light. Besides, we got family up there. Thanks again." LuAnn turned and walked toward the departure area.

The woman stared after her and then turned back and was startled by the person who had seemingly appeared from nowhere and was now standing in front of her window. The man in the dark leather jacket put his hands on the counter. "One-way ticket to New York City, please," Anthony Romanello said politely and then stole a sideways glance in LuAnn's direction. He had watched through the plate glass of the 7-Eleven as LuAnn had purchased her lottery ticket. Next, he had observed her make the phone call from the pay phone, although he had not risked getting close enough to overhear the conversation. The fact that she was now on her way to New York had piqued his curiosity to the maximum. He had many reasons for wanting to leave the area as quickly as possible, anyway. Even though his assignment was over, finding out what LuAnn Tyler was up to and why she was going to New York was just an added inducement. It was all the more convenient because he happened to live there. It could be she was simply running from the bodies in the trailer. Or it could be more. Much more. He took the train ticket and headed toward the platform.

LuAnn stood well back from the tracks when the train came noisily into the station a bit behind schedule. With the aid of a conductor she found her compartment. The Deluxe Viewliner sleeping compartment had a lower bunk, an upper bunk, an armchair, sink, toilet, and private shower. Because of the lateness of the hour, and with LuAnn's permission, the attendant changed the compartment to its sleeping configuration. After he was finished, LuAnn closed the door to the room, sat down in the armchair, pulled out a bottle, and started feeding Lisa as the train slid smoothly out of the station half an hour later. The train gathered speed and soon LuAnn was watching the countryside sail by through the two large picture windows. She finished feeding Lisa and cradled the little girl against her chest to burp her. That accomplished, LuAnn turned Lisa around and started playing with her, doing patty cake and singing songs, which the delighted little girl joined in on in her own unique fashion. They passed an hour or so playing together until Lisa finally grew tired and LuAnn put her in the baby carrier.

LuAnn sat back and tried to relax. She had never been on a train before, and the gliding sensation and rhythmic click of the wheels was making her drowsy as well. It was hard to remember the last time she had slept, and she started to drift off. LuAnn awoke with a start several hours later. It must be nearly midnight, she thought. She suddenly recalled that she hadn't eaten all day. It hadn't seemed important with everything that had happened. She popped her head out the compartment door, spied an attendant, and asked if there was food on the train. The man looked a little surprised and glanced at his watch. "They made the last call for dinner several hours ago, ma'am. The dining car is closed now."

"Oh," LuAnn said. It wouldn't be the first time she had gone hungry. At least Lisa had eaten.

However, when the man caught sight of Lisa and then looked at how tired LuAnn seemed, he smiled kindly and told her to wait just a bit. Twenty minutes later he came back with a tray loaded with food and even set it out for her, using the lower bunk as an impromptu table. LuAnn tipped him generously from her stash of funds. After he left, she devoured her meal. She wiped off her hands and reached carefully into her pocket and pulled out the lottery ticket. She looked over at Lisa; the little girl's hands were gently swaying in her slumber, a smile played across the small features. Must be a nice dream, LuAnn thought, smiling at the precious sight.

LuAnn's features grew softer and she leaned down and spoke quietly into Lisa's tiny ear. "Momma's gonna be able to take care of you now, baby, like I should've been doing all along. The man says we can go anywhere, do anything." She stroked Lisa's chin and nuzzled her cheek with the back of her hand. "Where you wanta go, baby doll? You name it, we'll go. How's that sound? That sound good?"

LuAnn locked the door and laid Lisa down on the bed, checking to make sure the straps on the baby seat were tight. LuAnn lay back on the bed and curled her body protectively around her daughter. While the train made its way to New York City, she stared out the window into the darkness, wondering mightily about what was going to come next.

Chapter Ten

The train had been delayed at several points along the route and it was nearly three-thirty in the afternoon when LuAnn and Lisa emerged into the frenzy of Penn Station. LuAnn had never seen this many people in one place in all her life. She looked around, dazed, as people and luggage flew past her like sprays of buckshot. She tightened her grip on Lisa's carrier as the train ticket agent's warning came back to her. Her arm was still throbbing painfully, but she figured she could still deck just about anybody who tried something. She looked down at Lisa. With so many interesting things going on around her, the little girl seemed ready to explode out of her seat. LuAnn moved slowly forward, not knowing how to get out of the place. She saw a sign for Madison Square Garden and vaguely recalled that several years ago she had watched a boxing match on TV that had been telecast from there. Jackson said someone would be here, but LuAnn couldn't imagine how the person would find her in the middle of all this chaos.

She jerked slightly as the man brushed against her. LuAnn looked up into dark brown eyes with a silvery mustache resting below the broad, flattened nose. For an instant LuAnn wondered if he was the man she had seen fighting at the Garden; however, she quickly realized that he was much too old, at least in his early fifties. He had the breadth of shoulders, flattened, crusty ears, and battered face, though, that marked the man as an ex-boxer.

"Miss Tyler?" His voice was low but clear. "Mr. Jackson sent me to pick you up."

LuAnn nodded and put out her hand. "Call me LuAnn. What's your name?"

The man started for an instant. "That's not really important. Please follow me, I have a car waiting." He started to walk away.

"I really like to know people's names," LuAnn said, without budging.

He came back to her, looking slightly irritated, although somewhere in his features she thought she discerned the beginnings of a smile. "Okay, you can call me Charlie. How's that?"

"That's fine, Charlie. I guess you work for Mr. Jackson. Do you use your real names with each other?"

He didn't answer as he led her toward the exit. "You want me to carry the little girl? That thing looks heavy."

"I've got it okay." She winced as another stab of pain shot through her injured arm.

"You sure?" he asked. He eyed her bandaged jaw. "You look like you've been in a fight."

She nodded. "I'm okay."

The pair exited the train station, moved past the line of people waiting in the cab stand, and Charlie opened the door of a stretch limo for LuAnn. She gawked for a minute at the luxurious vehicle before climbing in.

Charlie sat across from her. LuAnn couldn't help staring at the vehicle's interior.

"We'll be at the hotel in about twenty minutes. You want something to eat or drink in the meantime? Train food sucks," said Charlie.

"I've had a lot worse, although I am kinda hungry. But I don't want you to have to make a special stop."

He looked at her curiously. "We don't have to stop." He reached into the refrigerator and pulled out soda, beer, and some sandwiches and snack foods. He unlocked a section of the limo's interior paneling and a table materialized. As LuAnn watched in astonishment, Charlie laid the food and drink out and completed the repast with a plate, silverware, and napkin, his big hands working quickly and methodically.

"I knew you were bringing the baby, so I had the limo stocked with milk, bottles, and stuff like that. At the hotel they'll have everything you need."

LuAnn made up a bottle for Lisa, cradled

her against one arm, and fed her with one hand while she devoured a sandwich with the other.

Charlie watched the tender way she handled her daughter. "She's cute, what's her name?"

"Lisa, Lisa Marie. You know, after Elvis's daughter."

"You look a little young to be a fan of the King."

"I wasn't — I mean, I don't really listen to that kind of music. But my momma did. She was a big fan. I did it for her."

"She appreciated it, I guess."

"I don't know, I hope she does. She died before Lisa was born."

"Oh, sorry." Charlie fell silent for a moment. "Well, what kind of music do you like?"

"Classical. I really don't know nothing about that kinda music. I just like the way it sounds. The way it makes me feel, sorta clean and graceful, like swimming in a lake somewhere up in the mountains, where you can see all the way to the bottom."

Charlie grinned. "I never thought about it that way. Jazz is my thing. I actually play a little horn myself. Outside of New Orleans, New York has some of the best jazz clubs around. Play until the sun comes up, too. A couple of them not too far from the hotel."

"Which hotel are we going to?" she asked.

"Waldorf-Astoria. The Towers. You ever

been to New York City?" Charlie took a swig of club soda and sat back against the seat, unbuttoning the front of his suit coat.

LuAnn shook her head and swallowed a bite of sandwich. "I ain't never really been anywhere."

Charlie chuckled softly. "Well then, the Big Apple is a helluva place to start."

"What's the hotel like?"

"It's real nice. First-rate, especially the Towers. Now it's not the Plaza, but then what is? Maybe you'll be staying at the Plaza one day, who knows." He laughed and wiped his mouth with a napkin. She noticed that his fingers were abnormally large and thick, the knuckles massive and knobby.

LuAnn looked at him nervously as she finished her sandwich and took a sip of Coke. "Do you know why I'm here?"

Charlie settled a keen gaze upon her. "Let's just say I know enough not to ask too many questions. Let's leave it at that." He smiled curtly.

"Have you ever met Mr. Jackson?"

Charlie's features grew grim. "Let's just leave it alone, okay?"

"Okay, just curious, is all."

"Well, you know what curiosity did to that old cat." The dark eyes glittered briefly at LuAnn as the words rolled off his tongue. "Just stay cool, do what you're told, and you and your kid have no problems, ever again.

Sound good to you?"

"Sounds good to me," LuAnn said meekly, cradling Lisa closer to her hip.

Right before they climbed out of the limo, Charlie pulled out a black leather trench coat and matching wide-brimmed hat and asked LuAnn to put them on. "For obvious reasons, we don't want you to be observed right now. You can ditch the cowboy hat."

LuAnn put on the coat and hat, cinching the belt up tight.

"I'll check you in. Your suite is under the name of Linda Freeman, an American business executive with a London-based firm traveling with her daughter on a combination of business and pleasure."

"A business executive? I hope nobody asks me no questions."

"Don't worry, nobody will."

"So that's who I'm supposed to be? Linda Freeman?"

"At least until the big event. Then you can go back to being LuAnn Tyler."

Do I have to? LuAnn wondered to herself.

The suite Charlie escorted her to after he checked her in was on the thirty-second floor and was mammoth in size. It had a large sitting room and a separate bedroom. LuAnn looked around in wonderment at the elegant furnishings, and almost fell over when she saw the opulent bathroom.

"You get to wear these robes?" She fingered the soft cotton.

"You can have it if you want. For seventy-five bucks or so a pop that is," Charlie replied.

She walked over to the window and partially drew back the curtains. A goodly slice of the New York City skyline confronted her. The sky was overcast and it was already growing dark. "I ain't never seen so many buildings in all my life. How in the world do people tell 'em apart? They all look the same to me." She looked back at him.

Charlie shook his head. "You know, you're real funny. If I didn't know better, I'd think you were the biggest hick in the world."

LuAnn looked down. "I am the biggest hick in the world. At least the biggest one you'll probably ever see."

He caught her look. "Hey, I didn't mean anything by it. You grow up here, you get an attitude about things, you know what I mean?" He paused for a minute while he watched LuAnn go over and stroke Lisa's face. "Look, here's the refreshment bar," he finally said. He showed her how it worked. Next, he opened the thick closet door. "Over here is the safe." He indicated the heavy metal door inserted into the wall. He punched in a code and the cylinders whirled into place. "It's a real good idea to keep your valuables in there."

"I don't think I have anything worth putting in there."

"How about that lottery ticket?"

LuAnn gulped, dug into her pocket, and produced the lottery ticket. "So you know that much, huh?"

Charlie didn't answer her. He took the ticket, barely glancing at it, before thrusting it in the safe. "Pick a combo — nothing obvious like birthdays or stuff like that. But choose something you'll remember off the top of your head. You don't want to be writing the numbers down anywhere. Got that?" He opened the safe again.

LuAnn nodded, and input her own code and waited until the safe was in the lock mode before shutting the closet door.

Charlie headed to the door. "I'll be back tomorrow morning about nine. In the meantime, you get hungry or anything, just order up room service. Don't let the waiter get a good look at your face, though. Put your hair up in a bun or wear the shower cap, like you're about to jump in the tub. Open the door, sign the bill as Linda Freeman, and then go into the bedroom. Leave some tip money on the table. Here." Charlie took a wad of bills from his pocket and handed them to her. "Generally, keep a low profile. Don't go walking around the hotel or stuff like that."

"Don't worry, I know I don't sound like no executive person." LuAnn pulled her hair out of her eyes and tried to sound flippant, although her low self-esteem was as plain as the hurt tones in Charlie's response.

"That's not it, LuAnn. I didn't mean . . ."
He finally shrugged. "Look, I barely finished high school. I never went to college and I did okay for myself. So neither one of us could pass as a Harvard grad, so who the hell cares?" He touched her lightly on the shoulder. "Get a good night's sleep. When I come back tomorrow, we can go out and see some of the sights and you can talk your head off, how about that?"

She brightened. "Going out would be nice."

"It's supposed to be chilly tomorrow, so dress warmly."

LuAnn suddenly looked down at her wrinkled shirt and jeans. "Uh, these are all the clothes I have. I, uh, I left home kind of quick." She looked embarrassed.

Charlie said kindly, "That's all right: No luggage, no problem." He sized her up quickly. "What, you're about five ten, right? Size eight?"

LuAnn nodded and blushed slightly. "Maybe a little bigger on top than that."

Charlie's eyes hovered over her chest area for a moment. "Right," he said. "I'll bring some clothes with me tomorrow. I'll get some things for Lisa, too. I'll need a little extra time though. I'll be here around noon."

"I can take Lisa with us, right?"

"Absolutely, the kid comes with us."

"Thanks, Charlie. I really appreciate it. I wouldn't have the nerve to go out on my own.

But I'm kind of itching to, if you know what I mean. I never seen a place this big in my whole life. I betcha there's probably more people in this one hotel than in my whole hometown."

Charlie laughed. "Yeah, I guess being from here, I kind of take it for granted. But I see what you mean. I see it exactly."

After he left, LuAnn gently lifted Lisa out of her carrier and laid her in the middle of the king-size bed, stroking her hair as she did so. She quickly undressed her, gave her a bath in the oversize tub, and dressed Lisa in her pajamas. After laying the little girl back down on the bed, covering her with a blanket, and propping big pillows on either side of her so she wouldn't roll off, LuAnn debated whether to venture into the bathroom and perhaps give the tub a try as well to work the pains out of her body. That's when the phone rang. She hesitated for an instant, feeling guilty and trapped at the same time. She picked it up. "Hello?"

"Miss Freeman?"

"Sorry, you've —" LuAnn mentally kicked herself. "Yes, this is Miss Freeman," she said quickly, trying to sound as professional as possible.

"A little faster next time, LuAnn," Jackson said. "People rarely forget their own names. How are things? Are you being taken care of?"

"Sure am. Charlie's wonderful."

"Charlie? Yes, of course. You have the lottery ticket?"

"It's in the safe."

"Good idea. Do you have pen and paper?"

LuAnn looked around the room and then pulled a sheet of paper and a pen from the drawer of the antique-looking desk against the window.

Jackson continued: "Jot down what you can. Charlie will have all the details as well. You'll be happy to know that everything is in place. At six P.M. the day after tomorrow, the winning ticket will be announced nationwide. You can watch it on TV from your hotel room; all the major networks will be carrying it. I'm afraid there won't be much drama in the proceedings for you, however." LuAnn could almost envision the tight little smile on his lips as he said this. "Then the entire country will eagerly wait for the winner to come forward. You won't do it immediately. We have to give you time, in theory of course, to calm down, start thinking clearly, perhaps get some advice from financial people, lawyers, et cetera, and then you make your joyous way up to New York. Winners aren't required to come to New York, of course. The press conference can be held anywhere, even in the winner's hometown. However, many past winners have voluntarily made the trek and the Lottery Commission likes it that way. It's far easier to hold a national press conference from here. Thus, all your activities will take a day or two. Officially, you have thirty days to claim the money, so there's no problem there. By the way, in case you haven't figured it out, that's why I wanted you to wait before coming. It would not look good if people were aware you arrived in New York *before* the winning number was announced. You'll have to remain incognito until we're ready to present you as the winner." He sounded upset that his plans had been altered.

LuAnn scribbled down notes as fast as she could. "I'm sorry, but I really couldn't wait, Mr. Jackson," LuAnn said hurriedly. "I told you what it would be like back home. It's such a small place and everything. People would know I'd got the winning ticket, they just would."

"All right, fine, there's no sense wasting time discussing it now," he said brusquely. "The point is we have to keep you under cover until a day or so after the lottery drawing. You took the bus to Atlanta, correct?"

"Yes."

"And you took suitable precautions to disguise your appearance?"

"Big hat and glasses. I didn't see anybody I knew."

"And you of course didn't use your real name when buying your ticket?"

"Of course not," LuAnn lied.

"Good. I think your tracks have been effectively erased."

"I hope so."

"It won't matter, LuAnn. It really won't. In a few days, you'll be much farther away than New York."

"Where exactly will I be?"

"As I said before, you tell me. Europe? Asia? South America? Just name it and I'll make all the arrangements."

LuAnn thought for a moment. "Do I have to decide now?"

"Of course not. But if you want to leave immediately after the press conference, the sooner you let me know the better. I've been known to work miracles with travel arrangements, but I'm not a magician, particularly since you don't have a passport or any other identification documents." He sounded incredulous as he said this. "Those will have to be prepared as well."

"Can you get them made up? Even like a Social Security card?"

"You don't have a Social Security number? That's impossible."

"It ain't if your parents never filled out the paperwork for one," she fired back.

"I thought the hospital wouldn't let a baby leave without that paperwork having been completed."

LuAnn almost laughed. "I wasn't born in no hospital, Mr. Jackson. They say the first sight I saw was the dirty laundry stacked in my momma's bedroom because that's right where my grandma delivered me."

"Yes, I suppose I can get you a Social Security number," he said huffily.

"Then could you have them put another name on the passport, I mean with my picture on it, but with a different name? And on all the other paperwork too?"

Jackson said slowly, "Why would you want that, LuAnn?"

"Well, because of Duane. I know he looks stupid and all, but when he finds out I won all this money, he's gonna do everything he can to find me. I thought it'd be best if I disappeared. Start over again. Fresh, so to speak. New name and everything."

Jackson laughed out loud. "You honestly think Duane Harvey will be able to track you down? I seriously doubt if he could find his way out of Rikersville County if he had a police escort."

"Please, Mr. Jackson, if you could do it that way, I'd really appreciate it. Of course, if it's too hard for you, I'll understand." LuAnn held her breath desperately, hoping that Jackson's ego would take the bait.

"It's not," Jackson snapped. "It's quite simple, in fact, when you have the right connections, as I do. Well, I suppose you haven't thought of the name you want to use, have you?"

She surprised him by rattling one off immediately, as well as the place where the fictitious person was from.

"It seems you've been thinking about doing this for a while. Perhaps with or without the lottery money. True?"

"You got secrets, Mr. Jackson. Why not me, too?"

She heard him sigh. "Very well, LuAnn, your request is certainly unprecedented, but I'll take care of it. I still need to know where you want to go."

"I understand. I'll think real hard about it and let you know real soon."

"Why am I suddenly worried that I will regret having selected you for this little adventure?" There was a hint of something in his tone that caused LuAnn to shudder. "I'll be in touch after the lottery drawing, to let you know the rest of the details. That's all for now. Enjoy your visit to New York. If you need anything just tell . . ."

"Charlie."

"Charlie, right." Jackson hung up.

LuAnn went immediately to the wet bar and uncapped a bottle of beer. Lisa started to make noise and LuAnn let her down on the floor. LuAnn watched with a big smile on her face as Lisa moved around the room. Just in the last few days, her little girl had started to really get the hang of crawling and now she was exploring the large dimensions of the suite with considerable energy. Finally, LuAnn got down on the floor and joined her. Mother and daughter made the circuit of the hotel room for about an hour until Lisa grew tired and LuAnn put her down for the night.

LuAnn went into the bathroom and started running water in the tub while she checked the cut on her jaw in the mirror. It was healing okay, but it would probably leave a scar. That didn't bother her; it could have been a lot worse. She got another beer from the refrigerator and walked back into the bathroom. She slid into the hot water and took a sip of the cold beer. She figured she would need plenty of both alcohol and steamy, soothing water to get through the next couple of days.

Promptly at twelve o'clock, Charlie arrived with several bags from Bloomingdale's and Baby Gap. During the next hour, LuAnn tried on several outfits that made her tingle all over.

"You certainly do those clothes justice. More than justice," Charlie said admiringly.

"Thank you. Thanks for all this stuff. You got the size just right."

"Hell, you got the height and figure of a model. They make these clothes for people like you. You ever think about doing that for a living? Modeling, that is?"

LuAnn shrugged as she put on a cream-colored jacket over a long, pleated black skirt. "Sometimes, when I was younger."

"Younger? My God, you can't be far out of your teens."

"I'm twenty, but you feel older after having a baby."

"I guess that's true."

"No, I ain't cut out for modeling."

"Why not?"

She looked at him and said simply, "I don't like getting my picture taken, and I don't like looking at myself."

Charlie just shook his head. "You are definitely one strange young woman. Most girls your age, with your looks, you couldn't drag them away from the mirror. Narcissus personified. Oh, but you need to wear those big sunglasses and keep the hat on; Jackson said to keep you under wraps. We probably shouldn't be going out, but in a city of seven million I don't think we're going to have a problem." He held up a cigarette. "You mind?"

She smiled. "Are you kidding? I work in a truck diner. They don't even let you in unless you got your smokes and plan to use 'em. Most nights the place looks like it's on fire."

"Well, no more truck diners for you."

"I guess not." She pinned a wide-brimmed, floppy hat to her hair. "How do I look?" She posed for him.

"Better than anything in *Cosmo*, that's for sure."

"You ain't seen nothing yet. You just wait till I dress my little girl," she said proudly.

134

"Now that *is* something I dream about. A lot!"

An hour later, LuAnn put Lisa, who was decked out in the latest Baby Gap fashions, in her baby carrier and hefted it. She turned to Charlie. "You ready?"

"Not just yet." He opened the door to the suite and then looked back at her. "Why don't you close your eyes. We might as well do the whole production." LuAnn looked strangely at him. "Go on, just do it," he said, grinning.

She obeyed. A few seconds later he said, "Okay, open them up." When she did, she was staring at a brand new and very expensive baby carriage. "Oh, Charlie."

"You keep lugging that thing around much longer," he said, pointing at the baby carrier, "your hands are going to scrape the ground."

LuAnn gave him a big hug, loaded Lisa in, and they were off.

Chapter Eleven

Shirley Watson was madder than hell. In seeking appropriate revenge for her humiliation at the hands of LuAnn Tyler, Shirley had taxed her ingenuity, to the extent she had any, to the maximum. She parked her pickup in an out-of-the-way spot about a quarter of a mile from the trailer and got out, a metal canister held tightly in her right hand. She looked at her watch as she made her way toward the trailer, where she was pretty certain LuAnn would be deeply sleeping after working at the diner all night. Where Duane was she didn't really care. If he was there, then she might get a piece of him too for not defending her against the Amazon-like LuAnn.

With each step, the short, squat Shirley grew even angrier. She had gone to school with LuAnn, and had also dropped out before graduating. Also like LuAnn, she had lived in Rikersville all her life. Unlike LuAnn, however, she had no desire to leave it. Which made what LuAnn had done to her even more awful. People had seen her sneaking home, completely naked. She had never been more humiliated. She had gotten more crap than she knew how to deal with. She was going to have to live with that the rest of her life. Stories would be told again and again until she would be the laughingstock of her hometown. The abuse would continue until she was dead and buried; maybe even then it wouldn't stop. LuAnn Tyler was going to pay for that. So she was screwing around with Duane, so what? Everybody knew Duane had no intention of marrying LuAnn. And everyone also knew that LuAnn would probably kill herself before she would ever walk down the aisle with that man. LuAnn stayed because she had nowhere else to go, or lacked the courage to make a change, Shirley knew that — at least she believed she did — for a fact. Everyone thought LuAnn was so beautiful, so capable. Shirley fumed and grew even more flushed in the face despite the cool breeze flickering across the road. Well, she was going to love to hear what people had to say about LuAnn's looks after she got done with her.

When she drew close to the trailer, Shirley bent low and made her way from tree to tree. The big convertible was still parked in front of the trailer. Shirley could see the tire marks in the hardened mud where something had spun out. She passed the car, taking a moment to peer inside before continuing her stealthy approach. What if somebody else was there? She suddenly smiled to herself. Maybe LuAnn was getting some on the side while Duane was away. Then she could pay LuAnn back even steven. She smiled even more broadly as she envisioned a naked LuAnn running screaming from the trailer. Suddenly, everything became very quiet, very still. As if on cue, even the breeze stopped. Shirley's smile disappeared and she looked around nervously. She gripped the canister even more firmly and reached in her jacket pocket and pulled out the hunting knife. If she missed with the battery acid she was carrying in the canister, then she most assuredly wouldn't miss with the knife. She had been cleaning game and fish most of her life and could wield a blade with the best of them. LuAnn's face would get the benefit of that expertise, at least in the areas the acid missed.

"Damn," she said as she moved up to the front steps and the smell hit her right in the face. She looked around again. She hadn't experienced such an odor even when working a brief stint at the local landfill. She slipped the knife back in her pocket, unscrewed the top to the canister, and then took a moment to cover her nose with a handkerchief. She had come too far to turn back now, smell or not. She silently moved into the trailer, and made her way down to the bedroom. Edging open the door, she looked in. Empty. She closed the door softly and turned to head down the other way. Maybe LuAnn and her beau were asleep on the couch there. The hallway was dark and she felt her way along the wall. As she drew closer, Shirley steeled herself to strike. She lurched forward and, instead, stumbled over something and fell to the floor, coming face-to-face with the decaying source of the stench. Her scream could be heard almost to the main road.

"You sure didn't buy much, LuAnn." Charlie surveyed the few bags on the chaise lounge in her hotel room.

LuAnn came out of the bathroom where she had changed into a pair of jeans and a white sweater, her hair done up in a French braid. "I just like looking. That was fun enough. Besides, I flat out can't believe the prices up here. Good God!"

"But I would've paid for it," Charlie protested. "I told you that a hundred times."

"I don't want you spending money on me, Charlie."

Charlie sat down in a chair and stared at her. "LuAnn, it's not *my* money. I told you that, too. I'm on an expense account. Whatever you wanted, you could have."

"Is that what Mr. Jackson said?"

"Something like that. Let's just call it an advance on your future winnings." He grinned.

LuAnn sat down on the bed and played with her hands, a deep frown on her face. Lisa was still in her baby carriage playing with some toys Charlie had bought her. Her happy sounds filled the room.

"Here." Charlie handed LuAnn a package of photos from their day in New York. "For the memory book."

LuAnn looked at the photos and her eyes crinkled. "I never thought I'd see a horse and buggy in this city. It was lots of fun riding around that big old park. Smack dab in the middle of all them buildings, too."

"Come on, you'd never heard of Central Park?"

"Sure I had. *Heard*, leastways. Only I just thought it was all made up." LuAnn handed him a double photo of herself that she picked out of the pack.

"Whoops, thanks for reminding me," said Charlie.

"That's for my passport?"

He nodded as he slipped the photo into his jacket pocket.

"Don't Lisa need one?"

He shook his head. "She's not old enough. She can travel under yours."

"Oh."

"So I understand you want to change your name."

LuAnn put the photos away and started fiddling with the packages. "I thought it'd be a good idea. A fresh start."

"That's what Jackson said you said. I guess if that's what you want."

LuAnn suddenly plopped down on the

chaise lounge and put her head in her hands.

Charlie looked keenly at her. "Come on, LuAnn, changing your name isn't that traumatic. What's bothering you?"

She finally looked up. "Are you sure I'm gonna win the lottery tomorrow?"

He spoke carefully. "Let's just wait until tomorrow, LuAnn, but I don't think you'll be disappointed."

"All that money, but I don't feel good about it, Charlie, not one bit."

He lit a cigarette and puffed on it as he continued to watch her. "I'm gonna order up some room service. Three courses, a bottle of wine. Some hot coffee, the works. You'll feel better after you've eaten." He opened up the hotel services book and began to peruse the menu.

"Have you done this before? I mean, looked after people that . . . Mr. Jackson has met with?"

Charlie looked up from the menu. "I've worked with him for a while, yeah. I've never met him in person. We communicate solely over the phone. He's a smart guy. A little anal for my tastes, a bit paranoid, but real sharp. He pays me well, real well. And baby-sitting people in fancy hotels and ordering room service isn't such a bad life." He added with a big smile, "I've never looked after anybody I had this much fun with, though."

She knelt down beside the baby carriage and

pulled out a gift-wrapped package from the storage bin underneath. She handed it to him.

Charlie's mouth gaped in surprise. "What's this?"

"I got you a present. Actually, it's from me and Lisa. I was looking for something for you and she started pointing and squealing at it."

"When did you do this?"

"Remember, while you were over looking at the men's clothing."

"LuAnn, you didn't have to —"

"I know that," she said quickly. "That's why it's called a gift, you're not supposed to have to." Charlie gripped the box tightly in his hands, his eyes riveted on her. "Well, go ahead and open it for gosh sakes," she said.

While Charlie carefully pulled off the wrapping paper, LuAnn heard Lisa stir. She went over and picked up the little girl. They both watched Charlie as he took off the box top.

"Damn!" He gently lifted out the dark green fedora. It had an inch-wide leather band on the outside and a ribbon of cream-colored silk lining the inside.

"I saw you trying it on at the store. I thought you looked real nice in it, real sharp. But then you put it back. I could tell you didn't want to."

"LuAnn, this thing cost a lot of money."

She waved him off. "I had some saved up. I hope you like it."

"I love it, thank you." He gave her a hug

and then took one of Lisa's dimpled fists in his. He have it a gentle, formal shake. "And thank you, little lady. Excellent taste."

"Well, try it on again. Make sure you still like it."

He slid it over his head and checked himself out in the mirror.

"Slick, Charlie, real slick."

He smiled. "Not bad, not bad." He fussed with it a little until he caught the proper angle. Then he took it off and sat back down. "I've never gotten a gift from the people I've looked after. I'm usually only with them for a couple of days anyway, then Jackson takes over."

LuAnn quickly picked up on the opening. "So how'd you come to be doing this kind of work?"

"I take it you'd like to hear my life story?"

"Sure. I've been bending your ear enough."

Charlie settled back in the chair and assumed a comfortable look. He pointed to his face. "Bet you didn't guess I used to ply my skills in the boxing ring." He grinned. "Mostly, I was a sparring partner — a punching bag for up-and-comers. I was smart enough to get out while I still had my brains, at least some of them. After that, I took up semipro football. Let me tell you, that isn't any easier on the body, but at least you get to wear helmets and pads. I'd always been athletic, though, and to tell you the truth I liked making my living that way."

"You look like you're in real good shape."

Charlie slapped his hard stomach. "Not bad for being almost fifty-four. Anyway, after football, I coached a little, got married, floated around here and there, never finding anything that fit, you know?"

LuAnn said, "I know that feeling real good."

"Then my career path took a big turn." He paused to crush out his cigarette and immediately lit another.

LuAnn took the opportunity to put Lisa back in the baby carriage. "What'd you do?"

"I spent some time as a guest of the U.S. government." LuAnn looked at him curiously, not getting his meaning. "I was in a federal prison, LuAnn."

She looked astonished. "You don't look the type, Charlie."

He laughed. "I don't know about that. Besides, there are lots of different types doing time, LuAnn, let me tell you."

"So what'd you do?"

"Income tax evasion. Or fraud I guess they'd call it, at least the prosecutor did. And he was right. I guess I just got tired of paying it. Never seemed like there was enough to live on, let alone giving a chunk to the government." He brushed his hair back. "That little mistake cost me three years and my marriage."

"I'm sorry, Charlie."

He shrugged. "Probably the best thing that ever happened to me, really. I was in a minimum security facility with a bunch of other white collar criminal types so I didn't have to worry every minute about somebody cutting my head off. I took a bunch of classes, started thinking about what I wanted to do with my life. Really only one bad thing happened to me on the inside." He held up the cigarette. "Never smoked until I got to prison. There, just about everybody did. When I got out I finally quit. For a long time. Took it back up about six months ago. What the hell. Anyway, when I got out, I went to work for my lawyer, sort of as an in-house investigator. He knew I was an honest, reliable sort, despite my little conviction. And I knew a lot of people up and down the socioeconomic scale, if you know what I mean. A lot of contacts. Plus I learned a lot while I was in the slammer. Talk about your education. I had professors in every subject from insurance scams to auto chop shops. That experience helped out a lot when I jumped to the law firm. It was a good gig, I enjoyed the work."

"So how'd you hook up with Mr. Jackson?"

Now Charlie didn't look so comfortable. "Let's just say he happened to call one day. I had gotten myself in a little bit of trouble. Nothing real serious, but I was still on parole and it could've cost me some serious time inside. He offered to help me out and I accepted that offer."

"Kind of like I did," said LuAnn, an edge

to her voice. "His offers can be kind of hard to refuse."

He glanced at her, his eyes suddenly weary. "Yeah," he said curtly.

She sat down on the edge of the bed and blurted out, "I've never cheated on anything in my whole life, Charlie."

Charlie dragged on his cigarette and then put it out. "I guess it all depends on how you look at it."

"What do you mean by that?"

"Well, if you think about it, people who are otherwise good, honest, and hardworking cheat every day of their lives. Some in big ways, most in small ones. People fudge on their taxes, or just don't pay 'em, like me. Or they don't give money back when somebody figures up a bill wrong. Little white lies, folks tell almost automatically on a daily basis, sometimes just to get through the day with their sanity. Then there's the big cheat: Men and women have affairs all the time. That one I know a lot about. I think my ex-wife majored in adultery."

"I got a little taste of that, too," LuAnn said quietly.

Charlie stared at her. "One dumb SOB is all I can say. Anyway, it all adds up over a lifetime."

"But not to no fifty million dollars' worth."

"Maybe not in dollar terms, no. But I might take one big cheat in a lifetime over a thousand little ones that eat away at you eventually, make you not like yourself too much."

LuAnn hugged herself and shivered.

He studied her for a moment and then looked once more at the room service menu. "I'm gonna order dinner. Fish okay with you?"

LuAnn nodded absently and stared down at her shoes while Charlie conveyed their dinner order over the phone.

That done, he flipped another cigarette out of the pack and lit up. "Hell, I don't know one single person who would turn down the offer you got. As far as I'm concerned you'd be stupid to." He paused and fiddled with his lighter. "And from the little I've seen of you, maybe you can redeem yourself, at least in your eyes. Not that you'd need much redeeming."

She stared up at him. "How can I do that?"

"Use some of the money to help other people," he said simply. "Maybe treat it like a public trust, or something like that. I'm not saying don't enjoy the money. I think you deserve that." He added, "I saw some background info on you. You haven't exactly had the easiest life."

LuAnn shrugged. "I got by."

Charlie sat down beside her. "That's exactly right, LuAnn, you're a survivor. You'll survive this, too." He looked at her intently. "You mind me asking a personal question now that I've spilled my guts to you?"

"Depends on the question."

"Fair enough." He nodded. "Well, like I said, I looked at some of your background stuff. I was just wondering how you ever hooked up with a guy like Duane Harvey. He has 'loser' stamped all over him."

LuAnn thought of Duane's slender body lying facedown on the dirty carpet, the small groan he had made before plummeting over, as though he were calling to her, pleading for help. But she hadn't answered that call. "Duane's not so bad. He had a bunch of bad breaks." She stood up and paced. "I was going through a real bad time. My momma had just died. I met Duane while I was thinking of what to do with my life. You either grow up in that county and die there or you get out just as fast as you can. Ain't nobody ever moved *into* Rikersville County, least not that I ever heard of." She took a deep breath and continued. "Duane had just moved into this trailer he had found. He had a job then. He treated me nice, we talked some about getting married. He was just different."

"You wanted to be one of the ones who was born and died there?"

She looked at him, shocked. "Hell, no. We were going to get out. I wanted to and that's what Duane wanted, at least that's what he said." She stopped pacing and looked over at Charlie. "Then we had Lisa," she said simply. "That kinda changed things for Duane. I don't think having a kid was part of his plan. But we did and it's the best thing that ever happened to me. But after that, I knew things weren't going to work out between us. I knew I had to leave. I was just trying to figure out how when Mr. Jackson called."

LuAnn looked out the window at the twinkling lights etched against the darkness. "Jackson said there were some conditions with all this. With the money. I know he's not doing this because he loves me." She looked over her shoulder at Charlie.

Charlie grunted. "No, you're absolutely right about that."

"You got any idea what the conditions are?"

Charlie was shaking his head before she finished asking the question. "I do know that you'll have more money than you'll know what to do with."

"And I can use that money any way I want, right?"

"That's right. It's yours, free and clear. You can clean out Saks Fifth Avenue and Tiffany. Or build a hospital in Harlem. It's up to you."

LuAnn looked back out the window and her eyes began to shine as the thoughts plowing through her head seemed to dwarf the skyline staring back at her. Right that very instant, everything seemed to click! Even the massive number of buildings in New York City seemed far too small to hold the things she wanted to do with her life. With all that money.

Chapter Twelve

"We should've just stayed at the hotel and watched it from there." Charlie looked around nervously. "Jackson would kill me if he knew we were here. I have strict orders never to take any of the 'clients' here." "Here" was the headquarters of the United States National Lottery Commission located in a brand new state-of-the-art, needle-thin skyscraper on Park Avenue. The huge auditorium was filled with people. Network news correspondents were scattered throughout, microphones clamped in their fists, as were representatives from magazines, newspapers, and cable TV.

Near the front of the stage, LuAnn cradled Lisa against her chest. She wore the glasses Charlie had bought for her and a baseball cap turned backward under which her long hair was balled up. Her memorable figure was hidden under the full-length trench coat.

"It's okay, Charlie, nobody's gonna remember me under all this stuff."

He shook his head. "I still don't like it."

"I had to come see. It just wouldn't be the same sitting in the hotel room watching on TV."

"Jackson's gonna probably call the hotel

right after the drawing," he grumbled.

"I'll just tell him I fell asleep and didn't hear the phone."

"Right!" He lowered his voice. "You're gonna win at least fifty million bucks and you fall asleep?"

"Well, if I already *know* I'm gonna win, what's so exciting about it?" she shot back.

Charlie had no ready answer for that so he clamped his mouth shut and again took up a careful scrutiny of the room and its occupants.

LuAnn looked at the stage where the lottery pinball machine was set up on a table. It was about six feet long and comprised ten large tubes, each one rising above an attached bin of Ping-Pong balls. Each ball had a number painted on it. After the machine was activated, the air would circulate the balls until one made its way through the tiny hatch, popped up into the tube, and was caught and held by a special device inside the tube. Once a ball was thus captured, the bin of balls below that tube would immediately shut down and the next bin would automatically activate. Down the line it would go, the suspense building, until all ten winning numbers were finally revealed.

People were nervously looking at their lottery tickets; many held at least a dozen in their hands. One young man had an open laptop computer in front of him. The screen was filled with hundreds of lottery combinations he had purchased as he reviewed his electronic inventory. LuAnn had no need to look at her ticket; she had memorized the numbers: 0810080521, which represented her and Lisa's birthdays, and the age LuAnn would be on her next birthday. She didn't feel any more guilt as she observed the hopeful looks on the faces surrounding her, the silently mouthed prayers as the time for the drawing drew nearer. She would be able to handle their imminent disappointment. She had made up her mind, set her plan, and that decision had bolstered her spirits incredibly and it was the reason she was standing in the middle of this sea of tense people instead of hiding under the bed back at the Waldorf.

She stirred out of her musings as a man walked onto the stage. The crowd instantly hushed. LuAnn had half-expected to see Jackson striding across the stage, but the man was younger and far better looking. LuAnn wondered for a moment if he was in on it. She and Charlie exchanged tight smiles. A blond woman in a short skirt, black nylons, and spike heels joined the man and stood next to the sophisticated-looking machine, hands clasped behind her back.

The man's announcement was brief and clear as the TV cameras focused on his handsome features. He welcomed everyone to the drawing and then he paused, stared dramatically out at the crowd, and delivered the real news of the evening: The official jackpot, based upon ticket sales up to the very last minute, was a record-setting one hundred million dollars! A collective gasp went up from the crowd at the mention of the gigantic sum. Even LuAnn's mouth dropped open. Charlie looked over at her, shook his head slightly, and a small grin escaped his lips. He playfully elbowed her, leaned close, and whispered into her ear. "Hell, you can clean out Saks and Tiffany *and* still build that hospital, just with the friggin' interest."

It was indeed the largest jackpot ever and someone, one incredibly fortunate person, was about to win it, the lottery man declared with a beaming smile and a ton of showmanship. The crowd cheered wildly. The man gestured dramatically to the woman, who hit the power switch on the side of the machine. LuAnn watched as the balls in the first bin started bouncing around. When the balls started attacking the narrow pathway into the tubes, LuAnn felt her heart race and her breathing constrict. Despite the presence of Charlie beside her, the calm, authoritative manner of Mr. Jackson, his correct predicting of the daily lottery, and all the other things she had been through in the last several days, she suddenly felt that her being here was totally crazy. How could Jackson or anyone else control what those gyrating balls would do? It occurred to her that what she was witnessing resembled sperm dive-bombing an egg, something she had seen once on a TV program. What were the chances of correctly picking the one that would break through and impregnate? Her spirits plummeted as she confronted a very distinct set of options: travel back home and somehow explain the deaths of two men in a drug-filled trailer she happened to call home; or seek the hospitality of the nearest homeless shelter here in the city and contemplate what to do with the wrecked state of her life.

She clutched Lisa even more tightly and one of her hands drifted over and clasped Charlie's thick fingers. A ball squirted through the opening and was caught in the first tube. It was the number zero. It was shown on a large screen suspended over the stage. As soon as this occurred, the second bin of balls started popping. In a few seconds, it too had produced a winner: the number eight. In quick succession, six more of the balls popped through into their respective tubes and were caught. The tally now stood as follows: 0-8-1-0-0-8-0-5. LuAnn mouthed the familiar numbers silently. Sweat appeared on her forehead and she felt her legs begin to give way. "Oh my God," she whispered to herself, "it's really gonna happen." Jackson had done it; somehow, some way, the uppity, anal little man had done it. She heard many moans and groans next to her as lottery tickets were torn up and thrown to the floor as the numbers stared back at the crowd from the stage. LuAnn watched, completely mesmerized, as the ninth bin of balls started bouncing. The entire process now seemed to be occurring in the slowest of slow motion. Finally, the number two ball kicked out and held in tube number nine. There were no hopeful faces left in the crowd. Except for one.

The last bin fired up and the number one ball quickly fought its way right against the hatch of the last tube and appeared to be ready to shoot through to victory at any moment. LuAnn's grip on Charlie's fingers began to loosen. Then, like a pricked balloon hemorrhaging air, the number one ball suddenly slid back down to the bottom and was replaced near the hatch by a suddenly energetic and determined number four ball. With sharp, jerky motions, it grew closer and closer to the open pathway leading into the number ten and final tube, although it appeared to be repeatedly repelled from the opening. The blood slowly drained from LuAnn's face and for a moment she thought she would end up on the floor. "Oh, shit," she said out loud, although not even Charlie could hear her over the crowd noise. LuAnn squeezed Charlie's fingers so tightly he almost yelled out in pain.

Charlie's own heart was racing as if in sympathy for LuAnn. He had never known Jackson to fail, but, well, you never knew. *What the hell, it couldn't hurt,* he thought. He moved his free hand up and quietly felt under his shirt for the thick, silver crucifix he had worn for as long as he could remember. He rubbed it for good luck.

Ever so slowly, even as LuAnn's heart threatened to cease beating, the two balls, as though carefully choreographed, again swapped places with each other in the swirling spray of hot air, even ricocheting off one another at one point. After this momentary collision, the number one ball, mercifully for LuAnn, finally shot through the opening and was caught in the tenth and final tube.

It was all LuAnn could do not to scream out loud from pure relief, rather than from the excitement of having just become one hundred million dollars richer. She and Charlie looked at each other, their eyes wide, both bodies shaking, faces drenched with perspiration, as though they had just finished making love. Charlie inclined his head toward her, his eyebrows arched as if to say "You won, didn't you?"

LuAnn nodded slightly, her head swaying slowly as if to the tunes of a favorite song. Lisa kicked and squirmed as though she sensed her mother's exhilaration.

"Damn," Charlie said, "I thought I was going to pee in my pants waiting for that last number to drop." He led LuAnn out of the room and in a couple of minutes they were walking slowly down the street in the direction of the hotel. It was a beautiful, brisk night; the cloudless sky housed a stretch of stars that seemingly had no end. It matched LuAnn's mood precisely. Charlie rubbed at his hand. "God, I thought you were going to snap my fingers off. What was that all about?"

"You don't wanta know," said LuAnn firmly. She smiled at him, sucked in huge amounts of the sweet, chilly air, and gave Lisa a tender kiss on the cheek. She suddenly elbowed Charlie in the side, a mischievous grin on her face. "Last one to the hotel pays for dinner." She took off like a blue streak, the trench coat billowing out like a parachute in her wake. Even as she left him in the dust, Charlie could hear her shrieks of joy flowing back to him. He grinned and then bolted after her.

Neither one would have been so happy had they seen the man who had followed them to the lottery drawing and was watching from across the street. Romanello had figured that tailing LuAnn might result in some interesting developments. But even he had to admit that his expectations had so far been exceeded.

Chapter Thirteen

"You're certain that's where you want to go, LuAnn?"

LuAnn spoke earnestly into the phone. "Yes sir, Mr. Jackson. I've always wanted to go to Sweden. My momma's people came from there, a long time ago. She always wanted to go there, but never had the chance. So I'd sort of be doing it for her. Is that much trouble?"

"Everything is trouble, LuAnn. It's just a matter of degrees."

"But you can get it done, can't you? I mean I'd like to go to other places, but I'd really like to start in Sweden."

Jackson said testily, "If I can arrange for someone like *you* to win one hundred million dollars, then I can certainly take care of travel plans."

"I appreciate it. I really do." LuAnn looked over at Charlie, who was holding Lisa and playing with her.

She smiled at him. "You look real good doing that."

"What's that?" Jackson asked.

"I'm sorry, I was talking to Charlie."

"Put him on, we need to arrange for your visit to the lottery office so they can confirm the winning ticket. The sooner that's accomplished, the sooner we can get on with the press conference and then you can be on your way."

"The conditions you talked about —" LuAnn began.

Jackson interrupted, "I'm not ready to discuss that right now. Put Charlie on, I'm in a hurry."

LuAnn swapped the phone for Lisa. She watched closely as Charlie spoke in low tones into the phone, his back to her. She saw him nod several times and then he hung up.

"Everything okay?" Her tone was anxious as she held a rambunctious Lisa.

He looked around the room for a moment before his eyes finally met hers. "Sure, everything's A-okay. You have to go over to see the lottery people this afternoon. Enough time has passed."

"Will you go with me?"

"I'll go over in the cab with you, but I won't go in the building. I'll hang around outside until you come out."

"What all do I have to do?"

"Just present the winning ticket. They'll validate it and issue you an official receipt. There'll be witnesses there and all. You'll be confirmed every which way from Sunday. They go over the ticket with a high-tech laser to verify it's authentic. They got special fiber threads in the tickets, some of them right under the row of numbers. Kind of like U.S. currency, to prevent counterfeiting. It's impossible to duplicate, especially in a short time frame. They'll call the outlet where you bought the ticket to confirm that lottery number was indeed purchased at that site. They'll ask for background info on you. Where you're from, kids, parents, that sort of thing. It takes a few hours. You don't have to wait. They'll get in touch when the process is complete. Then they'll release a statement to the press that the winner has come forward, but they won't release your name until the press conference. You know, keep the suspense building. That stuff really sells tickets for the next drawing. You don't have to hang around for that either. The actual press conference will be the next day."

"Do we come back here?"

"Actually, 'Linda Freeman' is checking out today. We'll go to another hotel where you can check in as LuAnn Tyler, one of the richest people in the country. Fresh in town and ready to take on the world."

"You ever been to one of these press conferences before?"

He nodded. "A few. They can be a little crazy. Especially when the winners bring family with them. Money can do strange things to people. But it doesn't last too long. You get asked a bunch of questions and then off you go." He paused and then added, "That's nice

160

what you're doing, going to Sweden for your mom like that."

LuAnn looked down as she played with Lisa's feet. "I hope so. It's sure gonna be different."

"Well, sounds like you can use a little different."

"I don't know how long I'll stay."

"Stay as long as you want. Hell, you can stay forever if you want to."

"I'm not sure I can do that. I don't think I'd fit in."

He gripped her shoulders and looked her in the face. "Listen, LuAnn, give yourself some credit. Okay, so you don't have a bunch of fancy degrees, but you're sharp, you take great care of your kid, and you got a good heart. In my book, that puts you ahead of about ninety-nine percent of the population."

"I don't know how good I'd be doing right now if you weren't here helping me out."

He shrugged. "Hey, like I said, it's part of the job." He let go of her shoulders and fished a cigarette out of his pack. "Why don't we have some quick lunch and then you go claim your prize? What do you say, you ready to be filthy rich, lady?"

LuAnn took a deep breath before answering. "I'm ready."

LuAnn emerged from the Lottery Commission building, walked down the street, and turned a corner, where she met Charlie at a prearranged spot. He had kept Lisa for her while she had gone in.

"She's been watching everything going by. She's a real alert kid," he said.

"Won't be long before I'm running every which way after her."

"She was doing her best to get down and crawl off, swear to God." Charlie smiled and put a very exuberant Lisa back in her carriage. "So how'd it go?"

"They were real friendly. Treated me real special. 'You want coffee, Ms. Tyler?' 'You want a phone to make calls?' One woman asked me if I wanted to hire her as my personal assistant." She laughed.

"You better get used to that. You have the receipt?"

"Yep, in my purse."

"What time's the press conference?"

"Tomorrow at six o'clock, they said." She eyed him. "What's wrong?"

As they walked, Charlie had glanced surreptitiously over his shoulder a couple of times. He looked over at her. "I don't know. When I was in prison and then doing the PI stuff I developed this kind of built-in radar that tells me when somebody's paying a little too close attention to me. My alarm's going off right now."

LuAnn started to look around, but he cut her off. "Don't do that. Just keep walking.

We're fine. I checked you in at another hotel. It's another block down. Let's get you and Lisa in okay and then I'll snoop around a little. It's probably nothing."

LuAnn looked at the worry creases around his eyes and concluded his words did not match his feelings. She gripped the baby carriage tighter as they continued down the street.

Twenty yards behind and on the other side of the street, Anthony Romanello debated whether or not he had been spotted. The streets were filled with people at this hour, but something in the sudden rigidity of the people he was tracking had set off his own warning bell. He hunkered in his jacket and dropped back another ten yards, still keeping them well in sight. He kept a constant lookout for the closest taxi in case they decided to snare one. He had the advantage though, in that it would take some time to load the baby carriage and baby in. He would have plenty of opportunity to hail a cab in that time. But they continued on foot until they reached their destination. Romanello waited outside the hotel for a moment, looked up and down the street, and then went in.

"When did you get these?" LuAnn stared at the new set of luggage stacked in a corner of the hotel suite.

Charlie grinned. "You can't go on your big

trip without the proper baggage. And this stuff is super-durable. Not that expensive crap that falls apart if you look at it wrong. One bag is already packed with things you'll need for the trip over. Things for Lisa and what-not. I had a lady friend of mine do it. We'll have to do some more shopping today to fill up the other bags, though."

"My God, I can't believe this, Charlie." She gave him a hug and a peck on the cheek.

He looked down in embarrassment, his face flushed. "It wasn't such a big deal. Here." He handed her passport to her. She solemnly looked at the name inside, as though the fact of her reincarnation were just sinking in, which it was. She closed the small blue book. It represented a gateway to another world, a world she would soon, with a little luck, be embracing.

"Fill that sucker up, LuAnn, see the whole damned planet. You and Lisa." He turned to leave. "I'm going to go check on some things. I'll be back shortly."

She fingered the passport and looked up at him, her cheeks slightly red. "Why don't you come with us, Charlie?"

He turned slowly back around and stared at her. "What?"

LuAnn looked down at her hands and spoke hurriedly. "I was thinking I got all this money now. And you been real nice to me and Lisa. And I never been anywhere before and all.

And, well, I'd like you to come with us — that is, if you want to. I'll understand if you don't."

"That's a very generous offer, LuAnn," he said softly. "But you don't really know me. And that's a big commitment to make to someone you don't really know."

"I know all I need to," she said stubbornly. "I know you're a good person. I know you been taking care of us. And Lisa took to you like nobody's business. That counts for a durn lot in my book."

Charlie smiled in the little girl's direction and then looked back at LuAnn. "Why don't we both think on it, LuAnn. Then we'll talk, okay?"

She shrugged and slid several strands of hair out of her face. "I ain't proposing marriage to you, Charlie, if that's what you think."

"Good thing, since I'm almost old enough to be your grandfather." He smiled at her.

"But I really like having you with me. I ain't had that many friends, least that I can count on. I know I can count on you. You're my friend, ain't you?"

There was a catch in his throat when Charlie answered. "Yes." He coughed and assumed a more businesslike tone. "I hear what you're saying, LuAnn. We'll talk about it when I get back. Promise."

When the door closed behind him, LuAnn got Lisa ready for her nap. While the little girl drifted off to sleep, LuAnn restlessly walked the parameters of the hotel suite. She looked out the window in time to see Charlie exit the building and head down the street. She followed him with her eyes until he was out of sight. She had not seen anyone who appeared to be tracking him, but there were so many people around, she couldn't be sure. She sighed and then frowned. She was out of her element here. She just wanted to see him back safe and sound. She began to think about the press conference, but as she envisioned a bunch of strangers asking her all sorts of questions, her nerves began to jangle too much and she quit thinking about it.

The knock at the door startled her. She stared at the door, unsure what to do.

"Room service," the voice said. LuAnn went to the door and squinted through the peephole. The young man standing there was indeed dressed in a bellman's uniform.

"I didn't order anything," she said, trying hard to keep her voice from quaking.

"It's a note and package for you, ma'am."

LuAnn jerked back. "Who from?"

"I don't know, ma'am. A man in the lobby asked me to give it to you."

Charlie? LuAnn thought. "Did he ask for me by name?"

"No, he pointed you out when you were walking to the elevator, and just said give it to you. Do you want it, ma'am?" he said patiently. "If not, I'll just put it in your box behind the registration desk."

LuAnn opened the door slightly. "No, I'll take it. She stuck out her arm and the bellman put the package in it. She immediately closed the door. The young man stood there for a moment, upset that his errand and patience had not resulted in a tip. However, the man had already rewarded him handsomely for it, so it had worked out okay.

LuAnn tore open the envelope and unfolded the letter. The message was brief and written on hotel stationery.

Dear LuAnn, how's Duane feeling lately? And the other guy, what'd you hit him with anyway? Dead as a doornail. Sure hope the police don't find out you were there. Hope you enjoy the story, a little hometown news. Let's chat. In one hour. Take a cab to the Empire State Building. It's truly a landmark worth seeing. Leave the big guy and the kid at home. XXXOOOs

LuAnn ripped off the brown packing paper and the newspaper fell out. She picked it up and looked at it: It was the *Atlanta Journal and Constitution.* It had a page marked with a yellow piece of paper. She opened to that page and sat down on the sofa.

In her agitation at seeing the headline, she jumped up. Her eyes fed voraciously on the

167

words, occasionally darting to the accompanying photo. If possible, the trailer looked even dingier captured in grainy black and white; in fact it looked like it had actually collapsed and was merely awaiting the dump truck to cart it and its occupants away for burial. The convertible was also in the photo, its long hood and obscene ornament pointed straight at the trailer like some hunting dog telling its master: There's the kill.

Two men dead, the story said. Drugs involved. As LuAnn read the name Duane Harvey, a teardrop splattered onto the page and blurred some of the text. She sat down and did her best to compose herself. The other man had not yet been identified. LuAnn read quickly, and then she stopped searching when she found her name. The police were looking for her right now; the paper didn't say she had been charged with any crime, although her disappearance had probably only increased the police's suspicions. She flinched when she read that Shirley Watson had discovered the bodies. A canister of battery acid had been found on the floor of the trailer. LuAnn's eyes narrowed. *Battery acid.* Shirley had come back to avenge herself and had brought that acid to do the job, that was clear. She doubted, though, if the police would care about a crime that had not occurred when they had their hands full with at least two that had.

While she sat staring in shock at the paper, another knock on the door almost made LuAnn jump out of her chair.

"LuAnn?"

She took a deep breath. "Charlie?"

"Who else?"

"Just a minute." LuAnn jumped up, hastily ripped the news article out of the paper and stuffed it in her pocket. She slid the letter and the rest of the newspaper under the couch.

She unlocked the door and he entered the room and shrugged off his coat. "Stupid idea, like I'm going to be able to spot somebody out on those streets." He slid a cigarette from its pack and lit up, thoughtfully staring out the window. "Still can't shake the feeling that somebody was tailing us, though."

"It could've just been somebody looking to rob us, Charlie. You got a lot of that up here, don't you?"

He shook his head. "Crooks have gotten more daring lately, but if that was the case, they would've hit us and run. Grabbed your purse and disappeared. It's not like they were going to pull a gun and stick us up in the middle of a million people. I had the sense whoever it was was tracking us for a while." He turned to stare at her. "Nothing unusual happened to you on the way up, did it?"

LuAnn shook her head, staring back at him with wide eyes, afraid to speak.

"Nobody followed you up to New York that

you know of, did they?"

"I didn't see anybody, Charlie. I swear I didn't." LuAnn started to shake. "I'm scared."

He put a big arm around her. "Hey, it's okay. Probably just paranoid Charlie going off on nothing. But sometimes it pays to be paranoid. Look, how about we go do some more shopping? It'll make you feel better."

LuAnn nervously fingered the newspaper article in her pocket. Her heart seemed to be climbing up her throat, seeking a larger space in which to explode. However, when she looked up at him, her face was calm, bewitching. "You know what I really want to do?"

"What's that? Name it and it's done."

"I want to get my hair done. And maybe my nails. They both look kinda crappy. And with the press conference going on across the whole country and all, I'd like to look good."

"Damn, why didn't I think of that? Well, let's just look up the fanciest beauty parlor in the phone book —"

"There's one in the lobby," LuAnn said hurriedly. "I saw it coming in. They do hair and nails and feet, and facials, stuff like that. It looked real nice. Real nice."

"Even better then."

"Could you watch Lisa for me?"

"We can come down and hang out with you."

"Charlie, I swear. Don't you know nothing?"

"What? What'd I say?"

"Men don't come down to the beauty parlor and watch the goings-on. That's for us females to keep secret. If you knew how much trouble it takes to get us all pretty, it wouldn't be nearly as special. But you got a job to do."

"What's that?"

"You can 'ooh' and 'ahh' when I get back and tell me how beautiful I look."

Charlie grinned. "I think I can handle that one."

"I don't know how long I'll be. I might not be able to get in right away. There's a bottle ready in the refrigerator for Lisa for when she gets hungry. She's gonna want to play for a while and then you can put her down for a nap."

"Take your time, I've got nothing else on the agenda. A beer and cable TV" — he went over and lifted Lisa out of the baby carriage — "and the company of this little lady, and I'm a happy man."

LuAnn picked up her coat.

Charlie said, "What do you need that for?"

"I need to buy some personal things. There's a drug store across the street."

"You can just get them in the gift shop in the lobby."

"If they're anything like the prices at the last hotel, I'll go across the street and save myself some money, thank you very much."

"LuAnn, you're one of the richest women

in the world, you could buy the whole damned hotel if you wanted."

"Charlie, I've been scraping pennies all my life. I can't change overnight." She opened the door and glanced back at him, trying her best to hide the rising anxiety she was experiencing. "I'll be back as soon as I can."

Charlie moved over to the door. "I don't like it. If you go out, I'm supposed to go with you."

"Charlie, I'm a grown woman. I can take care of myself. Besides, Lisa's going to have to take a nap soon and we can't leave her here by herself, can we?"

"Well, no, but —"

LuAnn slid an arm across his shoulder. "You look after Lisa and I'll be back as soon as I can." She gave Lisa a kiss on the cheek and Charlie a gentle squeeze on the arm.

After she left, Charlie grabbed a beer from the wet bar and settled into his chair with Lisa on his lap and the TV remote in hand. He suddenly paused and looked over at the doorway, a frown appearing on his features as he did so. Then he turned back and did his best to interest Lisa in channel surfing.

Chapter Fourteen

When LuAnn stepped from the cab she looked up at the towering presence of the Empire State Building. She didn't have long to dwell upon the architecture, though, as she felt the arm slide around hers.

"This way, we can talk." The voice was smooth, comforting, and it made every hair on her neck stiffen.

She pulled her arm free and looked at him. Very tall and broad shouldered, his face was clean-shaven, the hair thick and dark, matching the eyebrows. The eyes were big and luminous.

"What do you want?" Now that she could actually see the man behind the note, LuAnn's fear quickly receded.

Romanello looked around. "You know, even in New York, we're bound to attract attention if we conduct this conversation out in the open. There's a deli across the street. I suggest we continue our chat there."

"Why should I?"

He crossed his arms and smiled at her. "You read my note and the news article, obviously, or you wouldn't be here."

"I read it," LuAnn said, keeping her voice level.

"Then I think it's clear we have some things to discuss."

"What the hell do you have to do with it? Were you involved in that drug dealing?"

The smile faded from the man's lips and he stepped back for a moment. "Look —"

"I didn't kill nobody," she said fiercely.

Romanello looked around nervously. "Do you want everybody here to know our business?"

LuAnn looked around at the passersby and then stalked toward the deli with Romanello right behind.

Inside they found an isolated booth far in the back. Romanello ordered coffee and then looked at LuAnn. "Anything interest you on the menu?" he asked pleasantly.

"Nothing." She glared back at him.

After the waitress departed, he looked at her. "Since I can understand your not wanting to prolong this discussion, let's get to the heart of it."

"What's your name?"

He looked startled. "Why?"

"Just make up one, that's what everybody else seems to be doing."

"What are you talking —" He stopped and considered for a moment. "All right, call me Rainbow."

"Rainbow, huh, that's a different one. You

don't look like no rainbow I've ever seen."

"See, that's where you're wrong." His eyes gleamed for an instant. "Rainbows have pots of gold at the end."

"So?" LuAnn's tone was calm, but her look was wary.

"So, you're my pot of gold, LuAnn. At the end of my rainbow." He spread apart his hands. She started to get up.

"Sit down!" The words shot out of his mouth. LuAnn stopped in midrise, staring at the man. "Sit down unless you want to spend the rest of your life in prison instead of paradise." The calm returned to his manner and he politely gestured for her to resume her seat. She did so, slowly, her eyes squarely on his.

"I ain't never been real good at games, Mr. Rainbow, so why don't you say whatever the hell it is you want to say and let's be done with it."

Romanello waited for a moment as the waitress returned with his coffee. "You sure you don't want some? It's quite chilly outside."

The chill in LuAnn's eyes compelled him to move on. He waited until the waitress had set the coffee and cream down and asked if they wanted anything else. After she left, he leaned across the table, his eyes bare inches from LuAnn's. "I was at your trailer, LuAnn. I saw the bodies."

She flinched for an instant. "What were you doing there?"

He sat back. "Just happened by."

"You're full of crap and you know it."

"Maybe. The point is, I saw you drive up to the trailer in that car, the same one in the newspaper photo. I saw you pull a wad of cash out of your kid's baby seat at the train station. I saw you make a number of phone calls."

"So what? I'm not allowed to make phone calls?"

"The trailer had two dead bodies and a shitload of drugs in it, LuAnn. That was *your* trailer."

LuAnn's eyes narrowed. *Was Rainbow a policeman sent to get her to confess?* She fidgeted in her seat. "I don't know what you're talking about. I never seen no bodies. You musta seen somebody else get out of that car. And who says I can't keep my money wherever the hell I want to keep it." She dug her hand into her pocket and pulled out the newspaper article. "Here, why don't you take this back and go try scaring somebody else."

Romanello picked up the piece of paper, glanced at it, and put it in his pocket. When his hand returned to view, LuAnn could barely keep from trembling as she saw the torn piece of bloody shirt.

"Recognize this, LuAnn?"

She struggled to maintain her composure. "Looks like a shirt with some stains on it. So what?"

He smiled at her. "You know, I didn't expect you to remain this calm about it. You're a dumb chick from Hooterville. I pictured you dropping to your knees pleading for mercy."

"Sorry I ain't what you imagined. And if you call me a dumb anything again, I'll knock you flat on your ass."

His face suddenly became hard and he slid down the zipper of his jacket until the butt of his 9-mm was revealed. "The last thing you want to do, LuAnn, is make me upset," he said quietly. "When I get upset, I can be very unpleasant. In fact I can be downright violent."

LuAnn barely glanced at the weapon. "What do you want from me?"

He zipped the jacket back up. "Like I said, you're my pot of gold."

"I ain't got any money," she said quickly.

He almost laughed. "Why are you in New York, LuAnn? I bet you've never been out of that godforsaken county before. Why of all places did you take off for the Big Apple?" He cocked his head at her, waiting for an answer.

LuAnn rubbed her hands nervously across the uneven surface of the table. She didn't look at him when she finally spoke. "Okay, maybe I knew what happened in that trailer. But I didn't do nothing wrong. I had to get out, though, because I knew it might look real bad for me. New York seemed as good as anyplace." She looked up to test his reaction to her explanation. The mirth was still there.

"What are you going to do with all the money, LuAnn?"

She nearly crossed her eyes. "What are you talking about? What money? In the baby seat?"

"I would hope you weren't going to try and stuff one hundred million dollars in a baby seat." He eyed her chest. "Or, despite its obvious capacity, your bra." She just stared at him, her mouth open a notch. "Let's see," he continued, "what's the going price for blackmail these days? Ten percent? Twenty percent? Fifty percent? I mean, even at half, you're still talking millions in your bank account. That'll keep you and the kid in jeans and sneakers for life, right?" He took a sip of his coffee and sat back, idly fingering the edges of his napkin while he watched her.

LuAnn clamped a fist around the fork in front of her. For a moment she thought about attacking him, but that impulse subsided.

"You're crazy, mister, you really are."

"The press conference is tomorrow, LuAnn."

"What press conference?"

"You know, that's where you're going to hold that big old check and smile and wave to the disappointed masses."

"I've gotta go."

His right hand shot across and gripped her arm. "I don't think you can spend that money from a prison cell."

"I said I gotta go." She jerked her hand free and stood up.

"Don't be a fool, LuAnn. I saw you buy the lottery ticket. I was at the lottery drawing. I saw the big smile on your face, the way you ran down the street whooping and hollering. And I was inside the lottery building when you went to get your winning ticket validated. So don't try to bullshit with me. You walk out of here and the first thing I'm going to do is place a call to that Podunk county and that Podunk sheriff and tell them everything I saw. And then I'm going to send them this piece of shirt. You can't believe the high-tech stuff they've got in the lab these days. They'll start piecing it together. And when I tell them you just won the lottery and maybe they should grab you before you disappear, then you can just kiss your new life good-bye. Although I guess you can afford to put your kid up somewhere nice while you rot in jail."

"I didn't do nothing wrong."

"No, what you did was stupid, LuAnn. You ran. And when you run, the cops always figure you're guilty. It's how cops think. They'll believe you were in it up to your pretty little ass. Right now, they haven't gotten around to you. But they will. It's up to you to decide whether they start focusing on you ten minutes from now, or ten days from now. If it's ten minutes, you're dead. If it's ten days, I figure your plan is to disappear forever. Because that's what I intend to do. You only pay me once, that I'll guarantee. I couldn't spend all that money even if I tried and neither could you. We all win that way. The other way, you lose, slam-dunk. So what's it gonna be?"

She stood frozen for a moment halfway out of her chair. Slowly, inch by inch, she sat back down.

"Very smart of you, LuAnn."

"I can't pay you half."

His face darkened. "Don't be greedy, lady."

"It's got nothing to do with that. I can pay you, I just don't know how much, but it'll be a lot. Enough for you to do whatever the hell you want to."

"I don't understand —" he began.

LuAnn interrupted, borrowing phraseology from Jackson. "You don't have to understand nothing. But if I do this I want you to answer one question for me and I want the truth or you can just go and call the cops, I don't care."

He eyed her cautiously. "What's the question?"

LuAnn leaned across the table, her voice low but intense. "What were you doing in that trailer? You just didn't happen on by, I know that sure as I'm sitting here."

"Look, what does it matter why I was there?" He threw his arm up in a casual motion.

LuAnn reached out as quickly as a striking rattler and grabbed his wrist. He winced as she squeezed it with a strength he had not anticipated. Big and strong as he was, it would've taken all his might to break that grip. "I said I wanted an answer, and it better be the right one."

"I earn my living" — he smiled and corrected himself — "I *used* to earn my living by taking care of little problems for people."

LuAnn continued to grip the wrist. "What problems? Did this have to do with the drugs Duane was dealing?"

Romanello was already shaking his head. "I didn't know anything about the drugs. Duane was already dead. Maybe he was holding out on his supplier or maybe skimming off the top and the other guy cut him up. Who knows? Who cares?"

"What happened to the other guy?"

"You were the one who hit him, weren't you? Like I said in the note, dead as a door-nail." LuAnn didn't answer. He paused and took a breath. "You can let go of my wrist any time now."

"You haven't answered my question. And unless you answer it, you can just go call the sheriff, because you ain't getting one red cent from me."

Romanello hesitated, but then his greed won out over his better judgment. "I went there to kill you," he said simply.

She slowly let go of his wrist after giving it one more intense ratchet. He took a minute to rub the circulation back in.

"Why?" LuAnn demanded fiercely.

"I don't ask questions. I just do what I'm paid to do."

"Who told you to kill me?"

He shrugged. "I don't know." She reached for his wrist again, but this time he was ready for her and jerked it out of danger. "I'm telling you I don't know. My clients don't just drop by and have coffee and chat about who they want me to take out. I got a call, I got half the money up front. Half when the job was done. All through the mail."

"I'm still alive."

"That's right. But only because I got called off."

"By who?"

"By whoever hired me."

"When did you get the call?"

"I was in your trailer. I saw you get out of the car and take off. I went to my car and got the call then. Around ten-fifteen."

LuAnn sat back as the truth dawned on her: Jackson. So that's how he took care of those who refused to go along.

When she didn't say anything, Romanello leaned forward. "So now that I've answered all your questions, why don't we discuss the arrangements for our little deal?"

LuAnn stared at him for a full minute before

speaking. "If I find out you're lying to me, you won't like it one bit."

"You know, somebody who kills for a living usually strikes a little more fear into people than what you're showing," he said, his dark eyes flickering at her. He partially unzipped his jacket again so that the butt of the 9-mm was once more visible. "Don't push it!" His tone was menacing.

LuAnn glanced at the pistol with contempt before settling her eyes back on his. "I growed up surrounded by crazy people, *Mr. Rainbow.* Rednecks getting drunk and pointing twelve-gauge shotguns in people's faces and then pulling the trigger just for fun, or cutting somebody up so bad their momma wouldn't have knowed them and then betting on how long they'd take to bleed to death. Then there was the black boy who ended up in a lake with his throat slashed and his private parts gone, 'cause somebody thought he was too uppity hanging around a white girl. I'm pretty sure my daddy had something to do with that, not that the police down there gave a damn. So your little gun and your big man bullshit don't mean crap to me. Let's just get this over with and then you can get the hell out of my life."

The danger in the depths of Romanello's eyes rapidly dissipated. "All right," he said quietly, zipping his jacket back up.

Chapter Fifteen

A half hour later Romanello and LuAnn exited the deli. LuAnn climbed into a cab and headed back to her hotel where, to follow through on her cover story to Charlie, she would spend the next several hours at the beauty salon. Romanello walked down the street in the opposite direction, silently whistling to himself. Today had been a very good day. The arrangements he had made with LuAnn weren't a hundred percent foolproof, but his gut told him she would honor the deal she had made. If the first installment of the money wasn't in his account by close of business two days from now, then he would be on the phone to the police in Rikersville. She would pay, Romanello was sure of that. Why bring all that grief on yourself?

Since he was in a festive mood, he decided to stop and buy a bottle of Chianti on the way to his apartment. His thoughts were already focused on the mansion he would buy in some faraway land to replace it. He had earned good money over the years exterminating human beings, but he had to be careful in how he spent it or where he kept it. The last thing he wanted was the IRS knocking on his door asking to see his W-2s. Now that problem was behind him. Instant, massive wealth allowed one to soar beyond the reach of the Revenue boys, and everyone else. Yes, it had been a great day, Romanello concluded.

Not finding a cab handy, he opted for the subway. It was very crowded and he could barely find standing room in one of the train cars. He rode the subway for a number of stops before pushing through the masses and once again hitting the street. He turned the key in his door, closed and locked it, and walked into the kitchen to drop off the bottle. He was about to take off his jacket and pour himself a glass of Chianti when someone knocked at the door. He squinted through the peephole. The brown uniform of the UPS man filled his line of vision.

"What's up?" he asked through the door.

"Got a delivery for an Anthony Romanello, this address." The UPS man was busily scanning the package, an eight-by-eleven-inch container that bulged out at the center.

Romanello opened the door.

"You Anthony Romanello?"

He nodded.

"Just sign right here, please." He handed Romanello a pen attached to what looked to be an electronic clipboard.

"You're not trying to serve me with legal papers, are you?" Romanello grinned as he signed for the package.

"They couldn't pay me enough to do that," the UPS man replied. "My brother-in-law used to be a process server up in Detroit. After he was shot the second time, he went to work driving a bakery truck. Here you go. Have a good one."

Romanello closed the door and felt the contents of the package through the thin cardboard. A smile broke across his lips. The second installment on his LuAnn Tyler hit. He had been told of the possibility of being called off. But his employer had assured him that the rest of the money would be forthcoming regardless. The smile froze on his face as it suddenly struck him that the payment should have been mailed to his post office box. Nobody was supposed to know where he lived. Or his real name.

He whirled around at the sound behind him.

Jackson emerged from the shadows of the living room. Dressed as immaculately as when he had interviewed LuAnn, Jackson leaned against the doorway to the kitchen and looked Romanello up and down behind a pair of dark glasses. Jackson's hair was streaked with gray and a neatly trimmed beard covered his chin. His cheeks were large and puffy, the ears red and flattened-looking, both the result of carefully designed latex molds.

"Who the hell are you and how did you get in here?"

In response, Jackson pointed one gloved

hand at the package. "Open it."

"What?" Romanello growled back.

"Count the money and make certain it's all there. Don't worry, you won't hurt my feelings by doing so."

"Look —"

Jackson slipped off the glasses and his eyes bored into Romanello. "Open it." The voice was barely above a whisper and spoken in an entirely nonthreatening manner that made Romanello wonder why he was shivering inside. After all, he had murdered six people in premeditated fashion over the span of the last three years. Nobody intimidated him.

He quickly ripped open the package and the contents spilled out. Romanello watched as the cut-up newspaper drifted to the floor.

"Is this supposed to be funny? If it is, I'm not laughing." He glowered at Jackson.

Jackson shook his head sadly. "As soon as I hung up with you I knew my little slip over the phone would prove to be serious. I made mention of LuAnn Tyler and money, and money, as you well know, makes people do strange things."

"What exactly are you talking about?"

"Mr. Romanello, you were hired to perform a job for me. Once that task was called off, your participation in my affairs was at an end. Or let me rephrase that: Your participation in my affairs was *supposed* to be at an end."

"They were at an end. I didn't kill the lady

and all I get from you is cut-up newspaper. I'm the one who should be pissed."

Jackson ticked the points off with his fingers. "You followed the woman back to New York. You, in fact, have been following her all over the city. You sent her a note. You met with her, and while I wasn't privy to the conversation itself, from the looks of things the subject matter wasn't pleasant."

"How the hell do you know all that?"

"There isn't much I don't know, Mr. Romanello. There really isn't." Jackson put the glasses back on.

"Well, you can't prove anything."

Jackson laughed, a laugh that sent every hair on Romanello's neck skyward and made him reach for his gun, a gun that was no longer there.

Jackson looked at the man's amazed face and shook his head sadly. "Subways are so crowded this time of night. Pickpockets, I understand, can stalk honest people with impunity. There's no telling what else you might find missing."

"Well, like I said, you can't prove it. And it's not like you can just go to the cops. You hired me to kill someone. That doesn't do a whole lot for your credibility."

"I have no interest in going to the authorities. You disobeyed my instructions and in doing so jeopardized my plans. I came here to inform you that I was aware of this, to plainly show you that the rest of your money has been forfeited because of your improper actions, and that I have decided upon the appropriate punishment. A punishment that I fully intend to mete out now."

Romanello drew himself up to his full six feet three inch height, towering over Jackson, and laughed heartily. "Well, if you came here to punish me, I hope you brought somebody else with you to do the punishing."

"I prefer to handle these matters myself."

"Well, then this is going to be your last job." In a flash, Romanello's hand went down to his ankle and he was erect again in a second, the jagged-edge blade in his right hand. He started forward and then stopped as he eyed the device in Jackson's hand.

"The touted advantages of strength and superior size are so often overrated, wouldn't you agree?" said Jackson. The twin darts shot out from the taser gun and hit Romanello dead center in the chest. Jackson continued to squeeze the trigger, sending 120,000 volts of electricity along the thin metal cords that were attached to the darts. Romanello went down as though poleaxed, and he lay there staring up as Jackson stood over him.

"I've held the trigger down for a full minute now, which will incapacitate you for at least fifteen minutes, more than ample for my purposes."

Romanello watched helplessly as Jackson

knelt down beside him and gingerly pulled the two darts free and packed the apparatus back in his pocket. He carefully opened Romanello's shirt. "Quite hairy, Mr. Romanello. A medical examiner will never pick up on the extremely small holes in your chest." The next item Jackson withdrew from his coat would have left Romanello numb if he hadn't already been. With his tongue feeling as big as a knobby tree root, Romanello thought he had suffered a stroke. His limbs were useless to him; there was no physical sensation at all. He could still see clearly, however, and suddenly wished he had been blinded as well. He watched in horror as Jackson methodically checked the hypodermic needle he held in his hand.

"It's mostly an innocuous saline solution, you know," Jackson said as though he were addressing a science class. "I say mostly, because what's lurking in here can be quite deadly under certain conditions." He smiled down at Romanello and paused for a moment as he considered the import of his own words and then continued. "This solution contains prostaglandin, a substance produced naturally in the body. Normal levels are measured in micrograms. I'm about to give you a dose several thousand times that, measured in milligrams in fact. When this dose hits your heart it will cause the coronary arteries to severely constrict, triggering what doctors would technically term a myocardial infarction or coronary occlusion, also known as a heart attack of the most devastating kind. To tell you the truth, I've never combined the effects of electrification caused by the stun gun with this method of inflicting death. It might be interesting to observe the process." Jackson was betraying no more emotion than if he were about to dissect a frog in biology class. "Since prostaglandin occurs naturally in the body, as I mentioned, it's also naturally metabolized by the body, meaning there will be no suspiciously high traces left for a medical examiner to detect. I'm currently working on a poison to which I will attach an enzyme, encapsulated by a special coating. The protective cover is quickly broken down by the components in the bloodstream; however, the poison will have ample time to do its work before that occurs. Once the protective coating is gone the enzymes will instantly react with the poison compound and break it down, in effect destroying it. They use a similar process to clean up oil slicks. It's absolutely untraceable. I was planning to use it on you tonight; however, the process is not yet perfected and I hate to rush things of that nature. Chemistry, after all, requires patience and precision. Hence, the fallback to the old reliable: prostaglandin."

Jackson held the needle very close to Romanello's neck, seeking the perfect entry site. "They will find you here, a young, strapping man felled in his prime by natural causes. Another statistic in the ongoing health debate."

Romanello's eyes almost exploded out of his head as he struggled with every ounce of will to break the grip of inertia the stun gun had caused. The veins stood out on his neck with the effort he was exerting and Jackson quietly thanked him for providing such a convenient place, right before the needle plunged into the jugular vein and its contents poured into his body. Jackson smiled and gently patted Romanello on the head as his pupils shot back and forth like a metronome.

From his bag, Jackson extracted a razor blade. "Now, a sharp-eyed medical examiner might pick up on the hypodermic's entry site, so we will have to address that." Using the razor, Jackson nicked Romanello's skin at the precise place the needle had gone in. A drop of blood floated to the surface of the skin. Jackson replaced the razor in the bag and pulled out a Band-Aid. He pressed it across the fresh cut and sat back to study his handiwork, smiling as he did so.

"I'm sorry that it's come to this, as your services might have been useful to me in the future." Jackson picked up one of Romanello's limp hands and made the sign of the cross over the stricken man's chest. "I know that you were raised Roman Catholic, Mr. Romanello," he said earnestly, "although you obviously have strayed from the teachings of the Church, but I'm afraid a priest to administer last rites is out of the question. I hardly think it matters where you're going anyway, do you? Purgatory is such a silly notion after all." He picked up Romanello's knife and placed it back in the sheath strapped to his ankle.

Jackson was about to stand up when he noted the edge of the newspaper sticking out from the inside of Romanello's jacket pocket. He nimbly plucked it out. As he read the article detailing the story of the two murders, drugs, LuAnn's disappearance, and the police's search for her, his features became grim. That explained a lot. Romanello was blackmailing her. Or attempting to. Had he discovered this piece of information a day earlier, Jackson's solution would have been simple. He would've executed LuAnn Tyler on the spot. Now he could not do that and he hated that he had lost partial control of the situation. She had already been confirmed as the winning ticket holder. She was scheduled to appear to the world in less than twenty-four hours as the lottery's newest winner. Yes, now her requests made more sense. He folded up the piece of paper and put it in his pocket. Like it or not, he was wedded to LuAnn Tyler, warts and all. It was a challenge, and, if nothing else, he loved a challenge. However, he would take control back. He would tell her exactly what she had to do, and if she didn't follow his instructions precisely, then he would kill her after she won the lottery.

Jackson gathered up the shredded newspaper and remnants of the UPS package. The dark suit he was wearing came off with a tug on certain discreet parts of the garment, and together with the now revealed body moldings that had given Jackson his girth, all of these items were packed in a pizza carrier bag that Jackson pulled from a corner of the living room. Underneath, a much slimmer Jackson was wearing the blue and white shirt proclaiming him to be a Domino's Pizza delivery person. From one of his pockets, he pulled out a piece of thread and, edging it carefully under the putty on his nose, lifted the piece cleanly off and stuck it in the pizza box. The mole, beard, and ear pieces he similarly discarded. He swabbed his face down with alcohol from a bottle pulled from his pocket, removing the shadows and highlights that had aged his face. His hands worked quickly and methodically from years of long practice. Last, he combed a gel through his hair that effectively removed the sprayed-on streaks of gray. He checked his altered appearance in a small mirror hanging on the wall. Then this chameleon landscape was swiftly altered by a small bristly mustache applied with spirit gum, and a hair extender hung in a long ponytail out from under the Yankee baseball cap he was now putting on. Dark glasses covered his eyes; dress shoes were replaced with tennis shoes. He once again checked his appearance: completely different. He had to smile. It was quite a talent. When Jackson quietly left the building a few seconds later, Romanello's features were relaxed, peaceful. They would forever remain so.

Chapter Sixteen

"Everything will be all right, LuAnn." Roger Davis, the young, handsome man who had announced the lottery drawing, said these words as he patted her on the hand. "I know you have to be nervous but I'll be right there with you. We'll make it as painless as possible for you, I give you my word," he said gallantly.

They were in a plush room inside the lottery building, just down the corridor from the large auditorium where a mass of press and regular folk awaited the latest lottery winner's arrival. LuAnn wore a pale blue knee-length dress with matching shoes, her hair and makeup impeccable thanks to the in-house staff at the Lottery Commission. The cut on her jaw had healed enough that she had opted for makeup instead of the bandage.

"You look beautiful, LuAnn," said Davis. "I can't remember a winner looking so ravishing, I mean that." He sat down right next to her, his leg touching hers.

LuAnn flashed him a quick smile, slid a couple of inches away, and turned her attention to Lisa. "I don't want Lisa to have to go out there. All them lights and people would just scare her to death."

"That's fine. She can stay in here. We'll have someone watching her of course, every minute. Security is very tight here as you can imagine." He paused while he once again took in LuAnn's shapely form. "We'll announce that you have a daughter, though. That's why your story is so great. Young mother and daughter, all this wealth. You must be so happy." He patted her on the knee and then let his hand linger for a moment before pulling it away. She wondered again whether he was in on all of it. Whether he knew she had won an enormous fortune by cheating. He looked the type, she concluded. The kind who would do anything for money. She imagined he would be very well paid for helping to pull off something this big.

"How long until we go out there?" she asked.

"About ten minutes." He smiled at her again and then said as casually as possible, "Uh, you weren't exactly clear on your marital status. Will your husband —"

"I'm not married," LuAnn said quickly.

"Oh, well, will the father of the child be attending?" He added quickly, "We just have to know for scheduling purposes."

LuAnn looked dead at him. "No, he won't."

Davis smiled confidently and inched closer. "I see. Hmmm." He made a steeple with his hands and rested them against his lips for a moment and then he laid one arm casually across the back of her seat. "Well, I don't know what your plans are, but if you need anyone to show you around town I am absolutely here for you, LuAnn, twenty-four hours a day. I know after living all your life in a small town, that the big city" — Davis lifted his other arm dramatically toward the ceiling — "must be very overwhelming. But I know it like the back of my hand. The best restaurants, theaters, shopping. We could have a great time." He edged still closer, his eyes hugging the contours of her body as his fingers drifted toward her shoulder.

"Oh, I'm sorry, Mr. Davis, I think maybe you got the wrong idea. Lisa's father ain't coming for the press conference, but he's coming up after. He had to get leave first."

"Leave?"

"He's in the Navy. He's with the SEALs." She shook her head and stared off as if digging up some shocking memories. "Let me tell you, it downright scares me some of the stuff he's told me about. But if there's anybody that can take care of himself it's Frank. Why, he beat six guys unconscious in a bar one time 'cause they were coming on to me. He probably would've killed them if the police hadn't pulled him off, and it took five of them to do it, big, strong cops, too."

Davis's mouth dropped open and he

scooted away from LuAnn. "Good Lord!"

"Oh, but don't say nothing about that at the press conference, Mr. Davis. What Frank does is all top-secret-like and he'd get real pissed at you if you said anything. Real pissed!" She stared intently at him, watching the waves of fear pour over his pretty-boy features.

Davis stood up abruptly. "No, of course not, not one word. I swear." Davis licked his lips and put a shaky hand through his heavily moussed hair. "I'd better go check on things, LuAnn." He managed a weak smile and gave her a shaky thumbs-up.

She returned the gesture. "Thanks so much for understanding, Mr. Davis." After he had gone, LuAnn turned back to Lisa. "You ain't never gonna have to do that, baby doll. And pretty soon, your momma ain't gonna have to do it no more either." She cradled Lisa against her chest and stared across at the clock on the wall, watching the time tick down.

Charlie glanced around the crowded auditorium while he methodically pushed his way toward the front of the stage. He stopped at a spot where he could see clearly and waited. He would've liked to be up on the stage with LuAnn, giving her what he knew would be much needed moral support. However, that was out of the question. He had to remain in the background; raising suspicion was not part of his job description. He would see LuAnn after the press conference was completed. He also would have to tell her his decision about whether he would accompany her or not. The problem was he hadn't made up his mind yet. He stuffed his hand in his pocket for a cigarette and then remembered smoking wasn't permitted in the building. He really was craving the soothing influences of the tobacco and for a brief instant he contemplated sneaking outside for a quick one, but there wasn't enough time.

He sighed and his broad shoulders collapsed. He had spent the better part of his life roaming from point to point with nothing in the way of a comprehensive plan, nothing resembling long-term goals. He loved kids and would never have any of his own. He was paid well, but while money went a long way toward improving his physical surroundings it didn't really contribute to his genuine overall happiness. At his age, he figured this was as good as it was going to get. The avenues he had taken as a young man had pretty much dictated what the remaining years of his life would be like. Until now. LuAnn Tyler had offered him a way out of that. He held no delusions that she was interested in him sexually, and in the cold face of reality, away from her unpretentious and yet incredibly seductive presence, Charlie had concluded that he did not want that either. What he wanted was her sincere friendship, her goodness — two elements that had been appallingly lacking in his life. And that brought him back to the choice. Should he go or not? If he went, he had little doubt that he would enjoy the hell out of LuAnn and Lisa, with an added plus of being a father figure for the little girl. For a few years anyway. But he had sat up most of the night thinking about what would happen after those first few years.

It was inevitable that beautiful LuAnn, with her new wealth, and the refinement that would come from those riches, would be the target of dozens of the world's most eligible men. She was very young, had one child, and would want more. She would marry one of these men. That man would assume the responsibilities of fathering Lisa, and properly so. He would be the man in LuAnn's life. And where would that leave Charlie? He edged forward, squeezing between two CNN cameramen as he thought about this again. At some point, Charlie figured, he would be compelled to leave them. It would be too awkward. It wasn't like he was family or anything. And when that time came it would be painful, more painful than allowing his body to be used for a punching bag during his youth. After spending only a few days with them, he felt a bond with LuAnn and Lisa that he had not managed to form in over ten years of marriage with his ex-wife. What would it be like after three or four years together? Could he calmly walk away from Lisa and her mother without suffering an irreparably broken heart, a screwed-up psyche? He shook his head. What a tough guy he had turned out to be. He barely knew these simple people from the South and he was now engulfed in a life-churning decision the consequences of which he was extrapolating out years into the future.

A part of him said simply go for the ride and enjoy the hell out of yourself. You could be dead from a heart attack next year, what the hell did it matter? The other part of him, though, he was afraid, was winning the day. He knew that he could be LuAnn's friend for the rest of his life, but he didn't know if he could do it close-up, every day, with the knowledge that it might end abruptly. "Shit," he muttered. It came down to pure envy, he decided. If he were only twenty — he shrugged — okay, thirty years younger. Envy of the guy who would eventually win her. Win her love, a love that he was sure would last forever, at least on her side. And heaven help the poor man who betrayed her. She was a hellcat, that was easy to see. A firecracker with a heart of gold, but that was a big part of the attraction: Polar opposites like that in the same fragile shell of skin and bones and raw nerve endings was a rare find.

Charlie abruptly stopped his musings and looked up at the stage. The entire crowd seemed to tense all at once, like a biceps flexing and forming a ridge of muscle. Then the cameras started clicking away as LuAnn, tall, queenly, and calm, walked gracefully into their field of vision and stood before them all. Charlie shook his head in silent wonderment. "Damn," he said under his breath. She had just made his decision that much harder.

Sheriff Roy Waymer nearly spit his mouthful of beer clear across the room as he watched LuAnn Tyler waving back at him from the TV. "Jesus, Joseph, Mary!" He looked over at his wife, Doris, whose eyes were boring into the twenty-seven-inch screen.

"You been looking for her all over the county and there she is right there in New York City," Doris exclaimed. "The gall of that girl. And she just won all that money." Doris said this bitterly as she wrung her hands together; twenty-four torn-up lottery tickets resided in the trash can in her back yard.

Waymer wrestled his considerable girth out of his La-Z-Boy and headed toward the telephone. "I phoned up to the train stations around here and at the airport in Atlanta, but I hadn't heard nothing back yet. I didn't take her to be heading up to no New York, though. I didn't put no APB out on LuAnn because I didn't think she'd be able to get out of the county, much less the state. I mean, the girl ain't even got a car. And she had the baby and all. I thought for sure she'd just hightail it over to some friend's house."

"Well, it sure looks like she slipped right out on you." Doris pointed at LuAnn on the TV. "Right or wrong there ain't many people that look like that, that's for sure."

"Well, Mother," he said to his wife, "we don't exactly have the manpower of the FBI down here. With Freddie out with his back I only got two uniformed officers on duty. And the state police are up to their eyeballs in work; they couldn't spare nobody." He picked up the phone.

Doris looked at him anxiously. "You think LuAnn killed Duane and that other boy?"

Waymer held the phone up to his ear and shrugged. "LuAnn could kick the crap out of most men I know. She sure as hell could Duane. But that other guy was a hoss, almost three hundred pounds." He started punching in numbers on the phone. "But she coulda snuck up behind him and smashed that phone over his head. She'd been in a fight. More than one person saw her with a bandage on her chin that day."

"Drugs was behind it, that's for sure," Doris said. "That poor little baby in that trailer with all them drugs."

Waymer was nodding his head. "I know that."

"I bet'cha LuAnn was the brains behind it all. She's sharp, all right, we all know that. And she was always too good for us. She tried to hide it, but we could all see through that. She didn't belong here, she wanted to get out, but she didn't have no way. Drug money, that was her way, you mark my words, Roy."

"I hear you, Mother. Except she don't need drug money no more." He nodded toward the TV.

"You best hurry up then, before she gets away."

"I'll contact the police up in New York to go pick her up."

"Think they'll do that?"

"Mother, she's a possible suspect in a double murder investigation," he said importantly. "Even if she ain't done nothing wrong, she's probably gonna be what they call a material witness."

"Yeah, but you think those Yankee police up in New York gonna care about that? Huh!"

"Police is police, Doris, North or South. The law's the law."

Unconvinced of the virtues of her Northern compatriots, Doris snorted and then suddenly looked hopeful. "Well, if she's convicted wouldn't she have to give back the money she won?" Doris looked back at the TV, at LuAnn's smiling face, wondering whether to go out to the trash and try to reconstruct all those lottery tickets. "She sure as heck wouldn't need all that money in prison, would she?"

Sheriff Waymer didn't answer. He was now

trying to get through to the NYPD.

LuAnn held the big check, waved, and smiled at the crowds and answered a barrage of questions thrown at her from all sides of the vast room. Her picture was transported across the United States and then across the world.

Had she definitive plans for the money? If so, what were they?

"You'll know," LuAnn answered. "You'll see, but you'll just have to wait."

There were a series of predictably stupid questions such as "Do you feel lucky?"

"Incredibly," she responded. "More than you'll ever know."

"Will you spend it all in one place?"

"Not likely unless it's a really, really big place."

"Will you help your family?"

"I'll help all the people I care about."

Three times her hand was sought in matrimony. She answered each suitor differently and with polite humor but the bottom line was always "No." Charlie silently fumed at these exchanges; and then, checking his watch, he made his way out of the room.

After more questions, more photos, and more laughter and smiles, the press conference was finally over and LuAnn was escorted off the stage. She returned to the holding room, quickly changed into slacks and a blouse, erased all the makeup from her face, piled her long hair under a cowboy hat, and picked up Lisa. She checked her watch. Barely twenty minutes had passed since she had been introduced to the world as the new lottery winner. She expected that the local sheriff would be contacting the New York police by now. Everyone from LuAnn's hometown watched the lottery drawing religiously including Sheriff Roy Waymer. The timing would be very tight.

Davis leaned his head in the door. "Uh, Ms. Tyler, there's a car waiting for you at the rear entrance to the building. I'll have someone escort you down if you're ready."

"Ready as I'll ever be." When he turned to leave, LuAnn called after him. "If anybody shows up asking for me, I'll be at my hotel."

Davis looked at her coldly. "Are you expecting anyone?"

"Lisa's father, Frank."

Davis's face tightened. "And you're staying at?"

"The Plaza."

"Of course."

"But please don't tell anybody else where I am. I haven't seen Frank in a while. He's been on maneuvers for almost three months. So we don't want to be disturbed." She arched her eyebrows wickedly and smiled. "You know what I mean?"

Davis managed a very insincere smile and

made a mock bow. "You can trust me implicitly, Ms. Tyler. Your chariot awaits."

Inwardly, LuAnn smiled. Now she was certain that when the police came for her, they would be directed as fast as possible to the Plaza Hotel. That would gain her the precious moments she would need to escape this town, and this country. Her new life was about to begin.

Chapter Seventeen

The rear exit was very private and thus very quiet. A black stretch limo confronted LuAnn as she left the building. The chauffeur tipped his cap to her and held open the door. She got in and settled Lisa in the seat next to her.

"Good work, LuAnn. Your performance was flawless," Jackson said.

LuAnn nearly screamed out as she jerked around and stared into the dark recesses of the limo's far corner. All the interior lights in the rear of the limo were off except for a solitary one directly over her head that suddenly came on, illuminating her. She felt as though she were back on the stage at the lottery building. She could barely make out his shape as he hunkered back into his seat.

His voice drifted out to her. "Really very poised and dignified, a touch of humor when it was called for, the reporters eat that up, you know. And of course the looks to top it all off. *Tres* marriage proposals during one press conference is certainly a record as far as I'm aware."

LuAnn composed herself and settled back into her seat as the limo proceeded down the street. "Thank you."

"Quite frankly I was concerned that you would make a complete fool of yourself. Nothing against you of course. As I said before, you are an intelligent young woman; however, anyone, no matter their sophistication, thrust into a strange situation, is more apt to fail than not, wouldn't you agree?"

"I've had a lot of practice."

"Excuse me?" Jackson leaned forward slightly but still remained hidden from her view. "Practice with what?"

LuAnn stared toward the darkened corner, her vision blocked by the shining light. "Strange situations."

"You know, LuAnn, you really do amaze me sometimes, you really do. In some limited instances your perspicacity rivals my own and I don't say that lightly." He stared at her for several more seconds and then opened a briefcase lying on the seat next to him and pulled out several pieces of paper. As he sat back against the soft leather, a smile played across his features and a sigh of contentment escaped his lips.

"And now, LuAnn, it's time to discuss the conditions."

LuAnn fumbled with her blouse before crossing her legs. "We need to talk about something first."

Jackson cocked his head. "Really? And what might that be?"

LuAnn let out a deep breath. She had stayed

awake all night deciding how best to tell him about the man calling himself Rainbow. She had first wondered whether Jackson needed to know at all. Then she decided that since it was about the money, that he would probably find out at some point. Better it be from her.

"A man came and talked to me yesterday."

"A man, you say. What about?"

"He wanted money from me."

Jackson laughed. "LuAnn, my dear, everybody will want money from you."

"No, it's not like that. He wanted half of my winnings."

"Excuse me? That's absurd."

"No it ain't. He . . . he had some information about me, things that had happened to me, that he said he would tell, if I didn't pay him."

"My goodness, what sorts of things?"

LuAnn paused and looked out the window. "Can I have something to drink?"

"Help yourself." A gloved finger came out of the darkness and pointed to the door built into one side of the limo. LuAnn did not look in his direction as she opened the refrigerator door and pulled out a Coke.

She took a long drink, wiped her lips, and continued. "Something happened to me right before I called to tell you I was going to take your offer."

"Would that possibly be the two dead bodies in your trailer? The drugs there? The fact that the police are looking for you? Or perhaps something else you tried to hide from me?" She didn't answer at first, nervously cradling the soda in her lap, the astonishment clear on her face.

"I didn't have nothing to do with those drugs. And that man was trying to kill me. I was just protecting myself."

"I should have realized when you wanted to leave town so quickly, change your name, all that, that there was something up." He shook his head sadly. "My poor, poor LuAnn. I guess I would've left town quickly too, confronted with those circumstances. And who would have thought it of our little Duane. Drugs! How terrible. But I tell you what, out of the goodness of my heart, I won't hold it against you. What's past is past. However" — here Jackson's tone became starkly forceful — "don't ever try to hide anything from me again, LuAnn. Please don't do that to yourself."

"But this man —"

Jackson spoke impatiently. "That's taken care of. You certainly won't be giving any money to him."

She stared into the darkness, amazement again spreading across her face. "But how could you have done that?"

"People are always saying that about me: How could I have done that?" Jackson looked amused and said in a slightly hushed voice, "I can do anything, LuAnn, don't you know that by now? Anything. Does that frighten you? If it doesn't, it should. It even frightens me sometimes."

"The man said he was sent to kill me."

"Indeed."

"But then he got called off."

"How terribly peculiar."

"Timewise, I figure he got called off right after I called you and said I'd do it."

"Life is chock full of coincidence, isn't it?" Jackson's tone had become mocking.

Now LuAnn's features took on their own glint of ferocity. "I get bit, I bite back, real hard. Just so we understand each other, Mr. Jackson."

"I think we understand each other perfectly, LuAnn." In the darkness, she heard papers rustling. "However, this certainly complicates matters. When you wanted your name changed, I thought we could still do everything aboveboard."

"What do you mean?"

"Taxes, LuAnn. We do have the issue of taxes."

"But I thought all that money was mine to keep. The government couldn't touch it. That's what all the ads say."

"That's not exactly true. In fact the advertising is very misleading. Funny how the government can do that. The principal is not

213

tax-free, it's *tax-deferred*. But only for the first year."

"What the hell does that mean?"

"It means that for the first year the winner pays no federal or state taxes, but the amount of that tax is simply deferred until the next year. The underlying tax is still owed, it's just the timing that's affected. No penalties or interest will accrue of course, so long as payment is made on a timely basis during the next tax year. The law states that the tax must be paid over ten years in equal installments. On one hundred million dollars, for example, you will owe roughly fifty million dollars in state and federal income tax, or one half the total amount. You're obviously in the highest tax bracket now. Divided by ten years the tax payment comes to five million dollars per year. In addition to that, generally speaking, any money you earn from the principal amount is taxable without any type of tax-deferred status.

"And I must tell you, LuAnn. I have plans for that principal, rather grand plans. You will make a great deal more money in the coming years; however, it will almost all be taxable income, dividends, capital gains, interest from taxable bonds, that sort of thing. That ordinarily would not present a problem, since law-abiding citizens who are not on the run from the police under an assumed name can file their tax returns, pay their fair share of tax, and live quite nicely. You can no longer do that. If my people filed your tax return under the name LuAnn Tyler with your current address and other personal information, don't you think the police might come knocking on your door?"

"Well, can't I pay tax under my new name?"

"Ah, potentially a brilliant solution; however, the IRS tends to get quite curious when the very first tax return filed by someone barely out of her teens has so many zeros on it. They might wonder what you were doing before and why all of a sudden you're richer than a Rockefeller. Again, the result would probably be the police, or even more likely the FBI, knocking on your door. No, that won't really do."

"So what do we do?"

When Jackson next spoke, the tone that reached LuAnn's ears made her tighten her grip on Lisa.

"You will do exactly as I tell you, LuAnn. You are ticketed on a flight that will take you out of the country. You will never return to the United States. This little mess in Georgia has bestowed upon you a life on the move. Forever, I'm afraid."

"But —"

"There's no *but* to it, LuAnn, that is the way it will be. Do you understand?"

LuAnn sat back against the leather seat and said stubbornly, "I got enough money now to where I can handle myself okay. And I don't like people telling me what to do."

"Is that right?" Jackson's hand closed around the pistol he had lifted from his briefcase. In the darkness he could have swung it up in an instant: mother and child obliterated. "Well, then why don't you take your chances on getting out of the country by yourself. Would you like to do that?"

"I can take care of myself."

"That's not the point. You made a deal with me, LuAnn. A deal I expect you to honor. Unless you're a fool you will work with me and not against me. You will see that in the long run your and my interests are the same. Otherwise, I can stop the limo right here, toss you and the child out, and I'll phone the police to come and pick you up. It's your choice. Decide. Now!"

Confronted with that option, LuAnn looked desperately around the interior of the limo. Her eyes finally settled on Lisa. Her daughter looked up at her with big, soft eyes; there was complete faith there. LuAnn let out a deep breath. What choice did she really have?

"All right."

Jackson again rustled the papers he held. "Now, we have just enough time to go over these documents. There are a number of them for you to sign, but let me discuss the principal terms first. I will try to be as simple in my explanation as possible.

"You have just won one hundred million

216

dollars and change. As we speak, that money has been placed into a special escrow account set up by the Lottery Commission under your name. By the way, I have obtained a Social Security number for you, under your *new* name. It makes life so much easier when you have one of those. Once you execute these papers my people will be able to transfer the funds out of that account and into one over which I will have complete and total control."

"But how do *I* get to the money?" LuAnn protested.

"Patience, LuAnn, all will be explained. The money will be invested as I see fit and for my own account. However, from those investment funds you will be guaranteed a minimum return of twenty-five percent per annum, which comes to approximately twenty-five million dollars per year. Those funds will be available to you all during the course of the year. I have accountants and financial advisors who will handle all of that for you, don't worry." He held up a cautionary finger. "Understand that that is income from principal. The one hundred million is never touched. I will control that principal amount for a period of ten years and invest it however I choose. It will take several months or more to fully implement my plans for the money, so the ten-year period will commence approximately in the late fall of this year. I will provide you with the exact date later. Ten years from that date, you will receive the full one hundred million dollars back. Any of the yearly income you've earned over the ten years is of course yours to keep. We will invest that for you as well, free of charge. I'm sure you're ignorant of this, but at that rate, your money, compounded, less even an exorbitant personal allowance, will double approximately every three years, particularly when you don't pay any taxes. Under practically any reasonable projection, you will be worth hundreds of millions of dollars at the end of the ten-year period, risk-free." Jackson's eyes sparkled as he rattled off the figures. "It's positively intoxicating, isn't it, LuAnn? It just beats the hell out of a hundred dollars a day, doesn't it? You've come a long way in less than a week, you truly have." He laughed heartily. "To start you off, I will advance you the sum of five million dollars, interest-free. That should be sufficient to keep you until the investment earnings come rolling in."

LuAnn swallowed hard at the mention of the gigantic sums. "I don't know nothing about investing, but how can you guarantee me so much money each year?"

Jackson looked disappointed. "The same way I could *guarantee* that you would win the lottery. If I can perform that magic, I think I can handle Wall Street."

"What if something should happen to me?"

"The contract you will be signing binds your heirs and assigns." He nodded at Lisa. "Your daughter. However, that income would go to her and at the end of the ten-year period so would the principal amount. There's also a power of attorney form. I took the liberty of already having filled in the notary panel. I'm a man of many talents." He chuckled lightly. From out of the darkness, Jackson extended the packet of documents and a pen to her. "They're clearly marked where your signature is required. I trust that you are satisfied with the terms. I told you from the start that they would be generous, didn't I?"

LuAnn hesitated for an instant.

"Is there a problem, LuAnn?" Jackson asked sharply.

She shook her head, quickly signed the documents, and handed them back. Jackson took the documents and slid open a compartment in the console of the limo.

LuAnn heard Jackson make some tapping sounds and a loud screech ensued and then stopped.

Jackson said, "Faxes are wonderful things especially when time is of the essence. Within ten minutes the funds will be wired into my account." He picked the papers up as they slid out of the machine and placed them back into his briefcase.

"Your bags are in the trunk. I have your plane tickets and hotel reservations with me. I have planned your itinerary out for the first twelve months. It will be a great deal of travel;

however, I think the scenery will be pleasant enough. I have honored your request to travel to Sweden, the land of your maternal ancestors. Think of it all as an extremely long vacation. I may have you end up in Monaco. They have no personal income tax. However, out of an abundance of caution I'm putting together and thoroughly documenting an intricate cover story for you. In sum, you left the States as a very young girl. You met and married a wealthy foreign national. The money will all be his, as far as the IRS is concerned. You see? The funds will be kept only in foreign banks and offshore accounts. U.S. banks have stringent reporting requirements to the IRS. None of your money will ever, ever be kept in the United States. However, keep in mind that you will be traveling under a United States passport as a United States citizen. Some accounts of your wealth may well trickle back here. We have to be prepared for that. However, if the money is all your husband's, who is not an American citizen, who does not reside at any time in this country, who earns no income directly in America, or from investments or business endeavors connected to this country, then, generally speaking, the IRS cannot touch you. I won't bore you with the complex tax rules having to do with U.S. source income such as interest on bonds issued by U.S. concerns, dividends paid by U.S. corporations, other transactions and sales of property having some tangible connection to the United States that could trip up the unwary. My people will take care of all that. Believe me when I say it won't be a problem."

LuAnn reached out for the tickets.

"Not quite yet, LuAnn, we have some steps to take. The police," he said pointedly.

"I took care of that."

"Oh, did you now?" His tone was one of amusement. "Well, I would be very surprised if New York's Finest weren't stationing themselves at every airport, bus, and train station right this very minute. Since you're a felon fleeing across state lines, they've probably called the FBI in as well. They're sharp. It's not like they'll be waiting patiently at your hotel for you to show up." He looked out the window of the limo. "We have some preparations to take care of. It'll give the police additional time to set up their net; however, it's a trade-off we have to make."

As Jackson was talking, LuAnn felt the limo slow down and then stop. Then she heard a long, slow clanking sound, as though a door were being raised. When it stopped, the limo pulled through and then stopped again.

The limo phone rang and Jackson quickly answered it. He listened for a few moments and then hung up. "Confirmation that the hundred million dollars has been received; though it's after regular banking hours, I'd had special arrangements in place. Omniscience is such a rewarding gift."

He patted the seat. "Now I need you to sit next to me. First, close your eyes and then give me your hand so I can guide you," Jackson said, reaching for it out of the darkness.

"Why do I have to close my eyes?"

"Indulge me, LuAnn. I can't resist a little drama in life, particularly since it's so rare. I can assure you that what I'm about to do will be absolutely essential to your safely evading the police and starting your new life."

LuAnn started to question him again but then thought better of it. She took his hand and closed her eyes.

He settled her down beside him. She could feel a light shine down on her features. She jerked as she felt the scissors cut into her hair. Jackson's breath was right next to her ear. "I would advise you not to do that again. It's hard enough to do this in such a small space with limited time and equipment. I wouldn't want to do you serious damage." Jackson continued cutting until her hair stopped just above her ears. He periodically stuffed the cut hair into a large trash bag. A wet substance was continually run through the remaining strands and then it quickly hardened almost like concrete. Jackson used a styling brush to manipulate the remaining strands into place.

Jackson next clamped a portable mirror surrounded by nonheating light bulbs to the edge of the limo's console. Ordinarily, with the nose job he was going to perform, he would employ two mirrors to test profile constantly; however, he didn't have that luxury sitting in a limo in a Manhattan underground parking garage. He opened up his kit, a ten-tray case filled with makeup supplies and a myriad of tools with which to apply them and then set to work. She felt his nimble fingers flying over her face. He blocked out her eyebrows with Kryolan's eyebrow plastic, covered them with a sealer, dressed the area with a creme stick, and then powdered it. Then he created totally new ones using a small brush. He thoroughly cleansed the lower part of her face with rubbing alcohol. He applied spirit gum to her nose, and let it dry. While it did so, he applied K-Y lubricating jelly to his fingers so the putty he was going to use wouldn't stick to them. He let the putty heat up in his hand, and then commenced applying the malleable substance to her nose, methodically kneading and pressing until a satisfactory shape was created. "Your nose is long and straight, LuAnn, classic, really. However, a little putty, a little shadowing and highlighting and, *voilà,* we have a thick, crooked piece of cartilage that isn't nearly as becoming. However, it's only temporary. Everyone, after all, is only temporary." He chuckled lightly at this philosophical statement as he went through the process of stippling the putty with a black stipple sponge, powdering the surface, stippling in a foundation color, and adding rouge to the nares to give a natural appearance. Using subtle shadowing and highlights, he made LuAnn's eyes seem closer together, and made her chin and jawline seem less prominent with the aid of powders and creams. Rouge was placed skillfully on the cheekbones to lessen their impact on her overall appearance.

She felt him gently examining the wound on her jaw. "Nasty cut. Souvenir from your trailer experience?" When LuAnn didn't answer, he said, "You know this will require some stitching. Even with that, it's deep enough that it probably will scar. Don't worry, after I'm done, it will be invisible. But eventually, you may want to consider plastic surgery." He chuckled again and added, "In my professional opinion."

Next, Jackson carefully painted her lips. "A little thinner, I'm afraid, than the classical model, LuAnn. You may want to consider collagen at some point."

It was all LuAnn could do not to jump up and run screaming from him. She had no idea what she was going to look like; it was as though he were some mad scientist bringing her back from the dead.

"I'm stippling in freckles now, along the forehead, around the nose and cheeks. If I had time, I'd do your hands as well, but I don't. No one would notice anyway, most people are so unobservant." He spread open the collar of her shirt and applied foundation and stippling around her neck. Then he buttoned her shirt up, repacked his equipment, and guided her back to her seat.

"There's a small mirror in the compartment next to you," Jackson informed her.

LuAnn slowly pulled out the mirror and held it up in front of her face. She gasped. Looking back at her was a redheaded woman with short, spiky hair, a very light, almost albino complexion, and an abundance of freckles. Her eyes were smaller and closer together, her chin and jawline less prominent, the cheeks flat and oval. Her lips were a deep red and made her mouth look huge. Her nose was much broader and bore a distinctive curve to the right. Her dark eyebrows were now tinted a much lighter color. She was completely unrecognizable to herself.

Jackson tossed something on her lap. She looked down. It was a passport. She opened it. The photo staring back at her was the same woman whom she had looked at in the mirror.

"Wonderful work, wouldn't you say?" Jackson said.

As LuAnn looked up, Jackson hit a switch and a light illuminated him. Or her, rather, as LuAnn received a second jolt. Sitting across from her was her double, or the double of the woman she had just become. The same short red hair, facial complexion, crooked nose, everything — it was as though she had suddenly discovered a twin. The only difference was she was wearing jeans and her twin was wearing a dress.

LuAnn was too amazed to speak.

Jackson quietly clapped his hands together. "I've impersonated women before, but I believe this is the first time I've impersonated an impersonation. That photo is of me, by the way. Taken this morning. I think I hit it rather well, although I don't think I did your bust justice. Well, even 'twins' needn't be identical in every respect." He smiled at her shocked look. "No need to applaud, however I do think that considering the working conditions, it does deserve some degree of acclaim."

The limo started moving again. They exited the garage and a little more than half an hour later, they arrived at JFK.

Before the driver opened the door, Jackson looked sharply at LuAnn. "Don't put on your hat or your glasses, as that suggests attempting to hide one's features and you could conceivably mess up the makeup. Remember, rule number one: When trying to hide, make yourself as obvious as possible, put yourself right out in the open. Seeing adult twins together is fairly rare, however, but while people — the police included — will notice us, perhaps even gawk, there will be no levels of suspicion. In addition, the police will be looking for one woman. When they see two together, and twins at that, even with a child, they'll discount us entirely, even as they stare at us. It's just human nature. They have a lot of ground to cover and not much time."

Jackson reached across for Lisa. LuAnn automatically blocked his hand, looking at him suspiciously.

"LuAnn, I am trying my best to get you and this little girl safely out of the country. We will shortly be walking through a squadron of police and FBI agents who will be doing their best to apprehend you. Believe me, I have no interest in keeping your daughter, but I do need her for a very specific reason."

Finally, LuAnn let go. They climbed out of the limo. In high heels Jackson was a little taller than LuAnn. She noted that he had a long, lean build that, she had to admit, looked good in the stylish clothing. He put a black coat on over his dark dress.

"Come on," he said to LuAnn. She stiffened at the new tone of his voice. Now he also *sounded* exactly like her.

"Where's Charlie?" LuAnn asked as they entered the terminal a few minutes later, a chubby skycap with the bags in tow.

"Why?" Jackson said quickly. He expertly maneuvered in the high heels.

LuAnn shrugged. "Just wondering. He'd

been taking me around before. I thought I'd see him today."

"I'm afraid Charlie's duties with you are at an end."

"Oh."

"Don't worry, LuAnn, you're in much better hands." They entered the terminal and Jackson glanced up ahead. "Please act natural; we're twin sisters, if anyone asks, which they won't. However, I have identification to support that cover just in case they do. Let me do the talking."

LuAnn looked up ahead and swallowed quickly as she eyed the quartet of police officers carefully scrutinizing each of the patrons at the crowded airport.

They passed by the officers, who did indeed stare at them. One even took a moment to check out Jackson's long legs as the coat he was wearing flapped open. Jackson seemed pleased at the attention. Then, just as Jackson had predicted, the police quickly lost interest in them and focused on other persons coming into the terminal.

Jackson and LuAnn stopped near the international flight check-in for British Airways. "I'll check in at the ticket counter for you while you wait over near that snack bar." Jackson pointed across the broad aisle of the terminal.

"Why can't I check in myself?"

"How many times have you flown overseas?"

"I ain't never flown."

"Precisely. I can get through the process a lot faster than you. If you messed up something, said something you weren't supposed to, then we might attract some attention that we don't really need right now. Airline personnel aren't the most security conscious people I've ever run across but they're not idiots either and you'd be surprised what they pick up on."

"All right. I don't want to mess nothing up."

"Good, now give me your passport, the one I just gave you." LuAnn did so and watched as Jackson, the skycap behind him, swung Lisa's baby carrier in one hand as he sauntered over to the ticket counter. Jackson had even picked up that mannerism of hers. LuAnn shook her head in awe and moved over to the spot designated by Jackson.

Jackson was in the very short first-class line and it moved very quickly. He rejoined LuAnn in a few minutes. "So far, so good. Now, I wouldn't recommend changing your appearance for several months. You can wash the red dye out of course, although, frankly, I think the color works well on you." His eyes twinkled. "Once things die down, and your hair grows out, you can use the passport I originally made up for you." He handed a second U.S. passport to her, which she quickly put in her bag.

From the corner of his eye, Jackson watched

as two men and a woman all dressed in suits moved down the aisle, their eyes sweeping the area. Jackson cleared his throat and LuAnn glanced in their direction and then away again. LuAnn had spied, in one of their hands, a piece of paper. On it was a picture of her, no doubt taken at the press conference. She froze until she felt Jackson's hand inside hers. He gave it a reassuring squeeze. "Those are FBI agents. But just remember that you don't look anything like that photo now. It's as if you're invisible." His confident tones assuaged her fears. Jackson moved forward. "Your flight leaves in twenty minutes. Follow me." They went through security and down to the departure gate and sat down in the waiting area.

"Here." Jackson handed her the passport, along with a small packet. "There's cash, credit cards, and an international driver's license in there, all in your new name. And your new appearance with respect to the driver's license." He took a moment to toy with her hair in a completely clinical fashion. He scrutinized her altered features and came away duly impressed with himself again. Jackson took a moment to grip her by the hand and even patted her shoulder. "Good luck. If you find yourself in difficulty at any time, here is a phone number that will reach me anywhere in the world day or night. I will tell you, though, that unless there is a problem you and I will never meet or speak to each other again."

He handed her the card with the number on it.

"Isn't there something you want to say to me, LuAnn?" Jackson was smiling pleasantly.

She looked at him curiously and shook her head. "Like what?"

"Perhaps, thank you?" he said, no longer smiling.

"Thank you," she said very slowly. It was difficult pulling her gaze away from him.

"You're welcome," he said very slowly back, his eyes riveted to hers.

Finally, LuAnn nervously looked down at the card. She hoped she would never have to use it. If she never looked upon Jackson's face again, it would be all right with her. The way she felt around the man was too close to the feeling she had experienced at the cemetery when her father's grave had threatened to swallow her up. When she looked up again, Jackson had disappeared into the crowd.

She sighed. She was already tired of running and now she was about to start a lifetime of just that.

LuAnn took out her passport and looked at its blank pages. That would soon change. Then she turned back to the first page and stared at the strange photo and the stranger name underneath it. A name that would not be so unusual after a while: Catherine Savage from Charlottesville, Virginia. Her mother had been born in Charlottesville before moving as a young girl into the deep South. Her mother had spoken to LuAnn often of the good times she had as a child in the beautiful, rolling countryside of Virginia. Moving to Georgia and marrying Benny Tyler had abruptly ended those good times. LuAnn thought it appropriate that her new identity should call that city her hometown as well. Her new name had been well thought out too. A savage she was and a savage she would remain despite an enormous fortune at her command. She looked at the photo again and her skin tingled as she remembered that it was Jackson staring back at her. She quickly closed the passport and put it away.

She touched her new face gingerly and then looked away after she eyed another policeman making his way toward her. She couldn't tell if he was one of the ones who might have seen Jackson check in for her. If so, what if he watched her get on the plane instead of Jackson? Her mouth went dry and she silently wished that Jackson hadn't left. Her flight was called. As the policeman approached, LuAnn willed herself to stand. As she picked up Lisa her packet of documents tumbled to the floor. Her heart trembling, she bent down to retrieve them with one hand, at the same time awkwardly balancing Lisa in her car seat with her other. She suddenly found herself staring at a pair of black shoes. The cop bent down and looked her over. In one hand he held a photo of her. LuAnn froze for an instant as his dark eyes bored into hers.

A kindly smile emerged on his face. "Let me help you, ma'am. I've got kids of my own. Traveling with them is never easy."

He scooped up the papers, replaced them in the packet, and handed it to her. LuAnn thanked him and he tipped his cap to her before moving off.

LuAnn was sure that if someone had cut her at that instant no blood would have come out. It was all frozen inside her.

Since first-class passengers could board at their leisure, LuAnn took some time to look around; however, her hopes were fading. It was clear that Charlie wasn't coming. She walked down the jetwalk and the flight attendant greeted her warmly while LuAnn marveled at the interior size of the Boeing 747.

"Right this way, Ms. Savage. Beautiful little girl." LuAnn was led up a spiral staircase and escorted to her seat. With Lisa in the seat next to her, LuAnn accepted a glass of wine from the cabin attendant. She again looked around the lavish space in awe and noted the built-in TV and phone at each seat. She had never been on a plane before. This was quite a princely way to experience it for the first time.

The darkness was rapidly gathering as she looked out the window. For now Lisa was content to look around the cabin and LuAnn used the time to think while she sipped on her wine. She took a series of deep breaths and then studied the other passengers as they entered the first-class compartment. Some were elderly and expensively dressed. Others were in business suits. One young man wore jeans and a sweatshirt. LuAnn thought she recognized him as a member of a big-time rock band. She settled back in her seat and then jumped a bit as the plane pushed back from its moorings. The flight attendants went through their preflight safety drill and within ten minutes the giant plane was lumbering down the runway. LuAnn held onto the sides of her seat and gritted her teeth as the plane rocked and swayed while it gathered speed. She didn't dare look outside the window. Oh Lord, what had she done? One of her arms flew protectively over Lisa, who appeared far calmer than her mother. Then with a graceful motion, the plane lifted into the air and the lurching and swaying stopped. LuAnn felt as though she were floating into the sky on an enormous bubble. A princess on a magic carpet; the image swept into her mind and stayed there. Her grip relaxed, her lips parted. She looked out the window and down at the twinkling lights of the city, the country she was leaving behind. Forever, according to Jackson. She gave a symbolic wave out the window and then leaned back against the seat.

Twenty minutes later she had put on her headphones and was gently swaying her head to some classical music. She jerked upright when the hand fell upon her shoulder and Charlie's voice filtered down to her. He wore the hat she had bought him. His smile was big and genuine, but there was nervousness evident in his body language, the twitching of his eyes. LuAnn took off the headphones.

"Good gosh," he whispered. "If I hadn't recognized Lisa I would've passed right by you. What the hell happened?"

"A long story." She gripped his wrist tightly and let out a barely audible sigh. "Does this mean you're finally gonna tell me your real name, Charlie?"

A light rain had started to fall on the city shortly after the 747 had lifted off. Walking slowly down the street in midtown Manhattan with the aid of a cane, the man in the black trench coat and waterproof hat seemed not to notice the inclement weather. Jackson's appearance had changed drastically since his last encounter with LuAnn. He had aged at least forty years. Heavy pouches hung under his eyes, a fringe of brittle white hair circled the back of his bald head, which was mottled all over with age spots. The nose was long and saggy, the chin and neck equally so. His gait, slow and measured, matched the feebleness of his character. He often aged himself at night, as though when darkness came he felt compelled to shrink down, to draw nearer to old age, to death. He looked up into the cloudy sky. The plane would be over Nova Scotia about now as it traveled along its convex path to Europe.

And she had not gone alone; Charlie had gone off with her. Jackson had stayed behind after dropping off LuAnn and watched Charlie board the aircraft, not knowing his employer was only a few feet away. That arrangement might work out all right after all, Jackson thought. He had doubts about LuAnn, serious doubts. She had withheld information from him, usually an unpardonable sin. He had managed to avoid a serious problem by eliminating Romanello, and he had to concede that the difficulty had been partially his in the making. He had, after all, hired Romanello to kill his chosen one if she had failed to accept his offer. However, he had never before had a winner on the run from the police. He would do what he always did when confronted with a possible disaster: He would sit back and observe. If things continued to run smoothly he would do nothing. At the slightest sign of trouble, however, he would take immediate and forceful action. So having capable Charlie along with her might prove to be a good thing. LuAnn was different from the others, that was certain.

Jackson pulled his collar up and slowly ambled down a side street. New York City in the darkness and rain held no terror for him. He was heavily armed and expertly skilled in innumerable ways of killing anything that breathed. Anyone targeting the "old man" as easy pickings would painfully realize the mistake. Jackson had no desire to kill. It was sometimes necessary, but he took no pleasure in it. Only the attainment of money, power, or ideally both, would suffice as justification in his mind. He had far better things to do with his time.

Jackson turned his face once again to the sky. The light rain fell on the latex folds of his "face." He licked at them; they were cool to the touch, felt good against his real skin. Godspeed to you both, he said under his breath and then smiled.

And God help you if you ever betray me.

He continued down the street, thinking intently and whistling while he did so. It was now time to plan for next month's winner.

PART TWO

Ten Years Later

Chapter Eighteen

The small private jet landed at the airstrip at Charlottesville-Albemarle Airport and taxied to a halt. It was nearly ten o'clock at night and the airport had pretty much shut down for the day. The Gulfstream V was the day's last incoming flight in fact. The limousine was waiting on the tarmac. Three people quickly exited the plane and climbed into the limo, which immediately drove off and a few minutes later was heading south on Route 29.

Inside the limo, the woman took off her glasses and laid her arm across the young girl's shoulder. Then LuAnn Tyler slumped back against the seat and took a deep breath. Home. Finally, they were back in the United States. All the years of planning had finally been executed. She had thought about little else for some time now. She glanced over at the man who sat in the rear-facing seat. His eyes stared straight ahead, his thick fingers drummed a somber rhythm across the car's window. Charlie looked concerned, and he was concerned, but he still managed a smile, a reassuring grin. If nothing else he had always been reassuring for her over the last ten years.

He put his hands in his lap and cocked his head at her. "You scared?" he asked.

LuAnn nodded and then looked down at ten-year-old Lisa, who had immediately slumped over her mother's lap and fallen into an exhausted sleep. The trip had been a long and tedious one.

"How about you?" she asked back.

He shrugged his thick shoulders. "We prepared as well as we could, we understand the risks. Now we just live with it." He smiled again, this time more broadly. "We'll be okay."

She smiled back at him, her eyes deep and heavy. They had been through a lot over the last decade. If she never climbed aboard another airplane, never passed through another Customs post, never again wondered what country she was in, what language she should be trying to muddle through, it would be perfectly fine with her. The longest trip she wanted to take for the rest of her life was strolling down to the mailbox to pick up her mail, or driving down to the mall to go shopping. God, if it could only be that easy. She winced slightly and rubbed in a distracted fashion at her temples.

Charlie quickly picked up on this. Over the years he had acquired a heightened sensitivity to the subtle tracks of her emotions. He scrutinized Lisa for a long moment to make sure she was indeed sleeping. Satisfied, he undid his seat belt, sat down next to LuAnn, and spoke in soft tones.

"He doesn't know we've come back. Jackson doesn't know."

She whispered back to him. "We don't know that, Charlie. We can't be sure. My God, I don't know what's scaring me the most: the police or him. No, that's a lie. I know, it's him. I'd take the police over him any day. He told me never to come back here. Never. Now I am back. We all are."

Charlie laid his hand on top of hers and spoke as calmly as he could. "If he knew, do you think he'd have let us get this far? We took about as circuitous a route as anybody could take. Five plane changes, a train trip, four countries, we zigzagged halfway across the world to get here. He doesn't know. And you know what, even if he does he's not going to care. It's been ten years. The deal's expired. Why should he care now?"

"Why should he do any of the things he's done? You tell me. He does them because he wants to."

Charlie sighed, undid his jacket button, and lay back against the seat.

LuAnn turned to him and gently rubbed his shoulder. "We're back. You're right, we made the decision and now we're going to live with it. It's not like I'm going to announce to the whole world that I'm around again. We're going to live a nice, quiet life."

"In considerable luxury. You saw the photos of the house."

LuAnn nodded. "It looks beautiful."

"An old estate. About ten thousand square feet. Been on the market for a long time, but with an asking price of six million bucks, can't say I'm surprised. Let me tell you, we got a deal at three point five mil. But then I drive a hard bargain. Although, of course, we dumped another million into renovation. About fourteen months' worth, but we had the time, right?"

"And secluded?"

"Very. Almost three hundred acres, plus or minus as they say. About a hundred of those acres are open, 'gently rolling land.' That description was in the brochure. Growing up in New York, I never saw so much green grass. Beautiful Piedmont, Virginia, or so the realtor kept telling me on all those trips I took over here to scout for homes. And it was the prettiest home I saw. True it took a lot of work to get it in shape, but I got some good people, architects and what-not representing our interests. It's got a truckload of outbuildings, caretaker's house, three-stall horse barn, a couple of cottages, all vacant by the way; I don't see us taking in renters. Anyway, all those big estates have that stuff. It's got a pool. Lisa will love that. Plenty of room for a tennis court. The works. But then there's dense forest all around. Look at it as a hardwood moat.

And I've already started shopping around for a firm to construct a security fence and gate around the property line fronting the road. Probably should have already gotten that done."

"Like you didn't have enough to do. You do too much as it is."

"I don't mind. I kind of like it."

"And my name's not on the ownership papers?"

"Catherine Savage appears nowhere. We used a straw man for the contract and closing. Deed was transferred into the name of the corporation I had set up. That's untraceable back to you."

"I wish I could have changed my name again, just in case he's on the lookout for it."

"That would've been nice except the cover story he built for you, the same one we used to appease the IRS, has you as Catherine Savage. It's complicated enough without adding another layer to it. Geez, the death certificate we had made up for your 'late' husband was hell to get."

"I know." She sighed heavily.

He glanced over at her. "Charlottesville, Virginia, home to lots of rich and famous, I hear. Is that why you picked it? Private, you can live like a hermit, and nobody'll care?"

"That was one of two reasons."

"And the other?"

"My mother was born here," LuAnn said,

her voice dropping a notch as she delicately traced the hem of her skirt. "She was happy here, at least she told me she was. And she wasn't rich either." She fell silent, her eyes staring off. She jolted back and looked at Charlie, her face reddening slightly. "Maybe some of that happiness will rub off on us, what do you think?"

"I think so long as I'm with you and this little one," he said, gently stroking Lisa's cheek, "I'm a happy man."

"She's all enrolled in the private school?"

Charlie nodded. "St. Anne's-Belfield. Pretty exclusive, low student-to-teacher ratio. But, hell, Lisa's educational qualifications are outstanding. She speaks multiple languages, been all over the world. Already done things most adults will never do their whole life."

"I don't know, maybe I should have hired a private tutor."

"Come on, LuAnn, she's been doing that ever since she could walk. She needs to be around other kids. It'll be good for her. It'll be good for you too. You know what they say about time away."

She suddenly smiled at him slyly. "Are you feeling claustrophobic with us, Charlie?"

"You bet I am. I'm gonna start staying out late. Might even take up some hobbies like golf or something." He grinned at LuAnn to show her he was only joking.

"It's been a good ten years, hasn't it?" Her

voice was touched with anxiety.

"Wouldn't trade 'em for anything," he said.

Let's hope the next ten are just as good, LuAnn said to herself. She laid her head against his shoulder. When she had stared out at the New York skyline all those years ago, she had been brimming with excitement, with the potential of all the good she could do with the money. She had promised herself that she would and she had fulfilled that promise. Personally, however, those wonderful dreams had not been met. The last ten years had only been good to her if you defined good as constantly on the move, fearful of discovery, having pangs of guilt every time she bought something because of how she had come by the money. She had always heard that the incredibly rich were never really happy, for a variety of reasons. Growing up in poverty LuAnn had never believed that, she simply took it to be a ruse of the wealthy. Now, she knew it to be true, at least in her own case.

As the limo drove on, she closed her eyes and tried to rest. She would need it. Her "second" new life was about to commence.

Chapter Nineteen

Thomas Donovan sat staring at his computer screen in the frenetic news room of the *Washington Tribune*. Journalistic awards from a number of distinguished organizations dotted the walls and shelves of his cluttered cubicle, including a Pulitzer he had won before he was thirty. Donovan was now in his early fifties but still possessed the drive and fervor of his youth. Like most investigative journalists, he could dish out a strong dose of cynicism about the workings of the real world, if only because he had seen the worst of it. What he was working on now was a story the substance of which disgusted him.

He was glancing at some of his notes when a shadow fell across his desk.

"Mr. Donovan?"

Donovan looked up into the face of a young kid from the mail room.

"Yeah?"

"This just came in for you. I think it's some research you had requested."

Donovan thanked him and took the packet. He dug into it with obvious zeal.

The lottery story he was working on had so much potential. He had already done a great deal of research. The national lottery took in billions of dollars each year in profits and the amount was growing at more than twenty percent a year. The government paid out about half its revenue in prize money, about ten percent to vendors and other operating costs, and kept forty percent as profit, a margin most companies would kill for. Surveys and scholars had argued for years about whether the lottery amounted to a regressive tax with the poor the chief loser. The government maintained that, demographically, the poor didn't spend a disproportionate share of their income on the game. Such arguments didn't sit well with Donovan. He knew for a fact that millions of the people who played the game were borderline poverty-level, squandering Social Security money, food stamps, and anything else they could get their hands on to purchase the chance at the easy life, even though the odds were so astronomically high as to be farcical. And the government advertisements were highly misleading when it came to detailing precisely what those odds were. But that wasn't all. Donovan had turned up an astonishing seventy-five percent bankruptcy rate per year for the winners. Nine out of every twelve winners each year subsequently had declared bankruptcy. His angle had to do with financial management companies and other scheming, sophisticated types getting hold of these poor people and basically ripping them off. Charities calling up and hounding them relentlessly. Purveyors of every type of sybaritic gratification selling them just about anything they didn't need, calling their wares "must-have" status items for the nouveaux riches and charging a thousand percent markup for their troubles. It didn't stop there. The sudden wealth had destroyed families and lifetime friendships as greed supplanted all rational emotions.

And the government was just as much to blame, Donovan felt, for these financial crashes. About twelve years ago they had bestowed the initial prize in one lump sum and given it tax-deferred status for one year to attract more and more players. The advertisements had played up this fact dramatically, touting the winnings as "tax-free" in the large print and counting on the "fine print" to inform the public that the amounts were actually tax-deferred and only for one year. Previously, the winnings had been paid out over time and taxes taken out automatically. Now the winners were on their own as far as structuring the payment of taxes went. Some, Donovan had learned, thought they owed no tax at all and went out and spent the money freely. All the earnings on that principal were subject to numerous taxes as well, and hefty ones. The Feds just hung the winners out there with a pat on the back and a big check. And when the winners weren't astute enough to set up sophisticated accounting and financial systems, the tax boys would come after them and take every last dime they had, under the guise of penalties and interest and what-not, and leave them poorer than when they started out.

It was a game designed for the ultimate destruction of the winner and it was done under the veil of the government's doing good for its people. It was the devil's game and our own government was doing it to us, Donovan was firmly convinced. And the government did it for one reason and one reason only: money. Just like everybody else. He had watched other papers give the problem lip service. And whenever a real attack or exposé was formed in the news media, government lottery officials quickly squelched it with oceans of statistics showing how much good the lottery monies were doing. The public thought the money was earmarked for education, highway maintenance, and the like, but a large part of it went into the general purpose funds and ended up in some very interesting places, far away from buying school books and filling potholes. Lottery officials received fat paychecks and fatter bonuses. Politicians who supported the lottery saw large funds flow to their states. All of it stunk and Donovan felt it was high time the truth came out. His pen would defend the less fortunate, just as it had over his entire career. If he did nothing else, Donovan would at least shame the government into reconsidering the morals of this gargantuan revenue source. It might not change anything, but he was going to give it his best.

He refocused on the packet of documents. He had tested his theory on the bankruptcy rate going back five years. The documents he was holding took those results back another seven years. As he paged through year after year of lottery winners, the results were almost identical, the ratio staying at virtually nine out of twelve a year declaring personal bankruptcy. Absolutely astonishing. He happily thumbed through the pages. His instincts had been dead-on. It was no fluke.

Then he abruptly stopped and stared at one page, his smile disappearing. The page represented the list of twelve consecutive lottery winners from exactly ten years ago. It couldn't be possible. There must be some mistake. Donovan picked up the phone and made a call to the research service he had engaged to do the study. No, there was no mistake, he was told. Bankruptcy filings were matters of public record.

Donovan slowly hung up the phone and stared again at the page. Herman Rudy, Bobbie Jo Reynolds, LuAnn Tyler, the list went on and on, twelve winners in a row. Not one of them had declared personal bankruptcy. Not one. Every twelve-month period for the lottery except this one had resulted in nine bankruptcies.

Most reporters of Thomas Donovan's caliber lived or died by two intangibles: perseverance and instincts. Donovan's instinct was that the story he might be onto right now would make his other angle seem about as exciting as an article on pruning.

He had some sources to check and he wanted to do them in more privacy than the crowded newsroom allowed. He threw the file in his battered briefcase and quickly left the office. In non–rush hour traffic he reached his small apartment in Virginia in twenty minutes. Twice divorced with no children, Donovan led a life focused solely on his work. He had a relationship slowly percolating with Alicia Crane, a well-known Washington socialite from a wealthy family, which had once been politically well connected. He had never been fully comfortable moving in these circles; however, Alicia was supportive and devoted to him, and truth be known, flitting around the edges of her luxurious existence wasn't so bad.

He settled into his home office and picked up the phone. There was a definite way to obtain information on people, particularly rich people, no matter how guarded their lives. He dialed the number of a longtime source at the Internal Revenue Service. Donovan gave that person the names of the twelve consecutive lottery winners who had not declared bankruptcy. Two hours later he got a call back. As he listened, Donovan checked off the names on his lists. He asked a few more questions, thanked his friend, hung up, and looked down at his list. All of the names were crossed off except for one. Eleven of the lottery winners had duly filed their tax returns each year, his source had reported. That was as far as his source would go, however. He would tell Donovan no specifics except to add that the income reported on all of the eleven tax returns was enormous. While the question still intrigued Donovan as to how all of them had avoided bankruptcy and apparently done very well over the last ten years, another more puzzling question had emerged.

He stared down at the name of the sole lottery winner that wasn't crossed off. According to his source, this person had not filed any tax returns, at least under her own name. In fact this person had outright disappeared. Donovan had a vague recollection of the reason why. Two murders, her boyfriend in rural Georgia and another man. Drugs had been involved. The story had not interested him all that much ten years ago. He would not have recalled it at all except that the woman had disappeared just after winning a hundred million dollars and the money had disappeared with her. Now his curiosity was much greater as he eyed that particular name on his list: "LuAnn Tyler." She must have switched identities on her run from the murder charge. With her lottery winnings she could easily have invented a new life for herself.

Donovan smiled for an instant as it suddenly occurred to him that he might have a way of discovering LuAnn Tyler's new identity. And maybe a lot more. At least he could try.

The next day Donovan telephoned the sheriff in Rikersville, Georgia, LuAnn's hometown. Roy Waymer had died five years ago. Ironically, the current sheriff was Billy Harvey, Duane's uncle. Harvey was very talkative with Donovan when the subject of LuAnn came up.

"She got Duane killed," he said angrily. "She got him involved in those drugs sure as I'm talking to you. The Harvey family ain't got much, but we got our pride."

"Have you heard from her in any way over the last ten years?" Donovan asked.

Billy Harvey paused for a lengthy moment. "Well, she sent down some money."

"Money?"

"To Duane's folks. They didn't ask for it, I can tell you that."

"Did they keep it?"

"Well, they're on in years and poorer'n dirt. You don't just turn your back on that kind of money."

"How much are we talking about?"

"Two hundred thousand dollars. If that doesn't show LuAnn's guilty conscience, I don't know what would."

Donovan whistled under his breath. "Did you try to trace the money?"

"I wasn't sheriff then, but Roy Waymer did. He even had some local FBI boys over to help, but they never turned up a durn thing. She's helped some other people round here too, but we could never get a handle on her whereabouts from them either. Like she was a damned ghost or something."

"Anything else?"

"Yeah, you ever talk to her, you tell her that the Harvey family ain't forgot, not even after all these years. That murder warrant is still outstanding. We get her back to Georgia, she'll be spending some nice quality time with us. I'm talking twenty to life. No statute of limitations on murder. Am I right?"

"I'll let her know, Sheriff, thanks. Oh, I'm wondering if you could send me a copy of the file on the case. The autopsy reports, investigative notes, forensics, the works?"

"You really think you can find her after all this time?"

"I've been doing this kind of stuff for thirty years and I'm pretty good at it. I'm sure going to try."

"Well, then I'll send it up to you, Mr. Donovan."

Donovan gave Harvey the *Trib*'s FedEx number and address, hung up, and wrote down some notes. Tyler had a new name, that was for certain. In order even to begin to track

256

her down, he had to find out what that name was.

He spent the next week exploring every crevice of LuAnn's life. He got copies of her parents' death notices from the *Rikersville Gazette*. Obituaries were full of interesting items: birthplaces, relatives, and other items that could conceivably lead him to some valuable information. Her mother had been born in Charlottesville, Virginia. Donovan talked to the relatives listed in the obituary, at least the few who were alive, but received few useful facts. LuAnn had never tried to contact them.

Next, Donovan dug up as many facts as he could on LuAnn's last day in the country. Donovan had conversations with personnel from the NYPD and the FBI field office in New York. Sheriff Waymer had seen her on TV and immediately notified the police in New York that LuAnn was wanted in Georgia in connection with a double murder and drug trafficking. They, in turn, had put a blanket over the bus and train stations, and the airports. In a city of seven million, that was the best they could do; they couldn't exactly put up roadblocks. However, there hadn't been one sign of the woman. That had greatly puzzled the FBI. According to the agent Donovan talked to who was somewhat familiar with the file, the Bureau wanted to know how a twenty-year-old woman with a seventh-grade education from rural Georgia, carrying a baby no less, had waltzed right through their net. An elaborate disguise and cover documents were out of the question, or so they thought. The police had thrown out their net barely a half hour after she had appeared on national television. No one was that fast. And all the money had disappeared as well. At the time, some at the FBI had wondered whether she had had help. But that lead had never been followed up as other crises of more national importance had swallowed up the Bureau's time and manpower. They had officially concluded that LuAnn Tyler had not left the country, but had simply driven out of New York or taken the subway to a suburb and then lost herself somewhere in the country or perhaps Canada. The NYPD had reported its failure to Sheriff Waymer and that had been the end of it. Until now. Now, Donovan was greatly intrigued. His gut told him that LuAnn Tyler had left the country. Somehow she had gotten past the law. If she had gotten on a plane, then he had something to work with.

He could narrow the list down in any event. He had a certain day to work with, even a block of hours on that day. Donovan would begin with the premise that LuAnn Tyler had fled the country. He would focus on international flights departing from JFK during that time frame, ten years ago. If the records at JFK turned up nothing, he would focus on LaGuardia and then Newark International

Airport. At least it was a start. There were far fewer international flights than domestic. If he had to start checking domestic flights, he concluded he would have to try another angle. There were simply too many. As he was about to start this process a package arrived from Sheriff Harvey.

Donovan munched on a sandwich at his cubicle while he looked through the files. The autopsy photos were understandably gruesome; however, they didn't faze the veteran reporter. He had seen far worse in his career. After an hour of reading he laid the file aside and made some notes. From the looks of it, he believed LuAnn Tyler to be innocent of the charges for which Harvey wanted to arrest her. He had done some independent digging of his own into Rikersville, Georgia. By virtually all accounts, Duane Harvey was a lazy good-for-nothing with no greater ambition than to spend his life drinking beer, chasing women, and adding nothing whatsoever of value to mankind. LuAnn Tyler, on the other hand, had been described to him by several persons who had known her as hardworking, honest, and a loving, caring mother to her little girl. Orphaned as a teenager, she seemed to have done as well as she could under the circumstances. Donovan had seen photos of her, had even managed to dig up a videotape of the press conference announcing her as the lottery winner ten years ago. She was a looker all right, but there was something behind that beauty. She hadn't scraped by all those years on her physical assets alone.

Donovan finished his sandwich and took a sip of his coffee. Duane Harvey had been cut up badly. The other man, Otis Burns, had also died from knife wounds to his upper torso. There had been serious but nonfatal head trauma also present, and the clear signs of a struggle. LuAnn's fingerprints had been found on the broken phone receiver and also all over the trailer. No surprise since she happened to live there. There had been one witness account of seeing her in Otis Burns's car that morning. Despite Sheriff Harvey's protests to the contrary, Donovan's research led him to believe that Duane was the drug dealer in the family and had been caught skimming. Burns was probably his supplier. The man had a lengthy rap sheet in neighboring Gwinnett County, all drug related. Burns had probably come to settle the score. Whether LuAnn Tyler knew of Duane's drug dealing was anybody's guess. She had worked at the truck stop up until the time she had bought her lottery ticket and disappeared only to resurface, however briefly, in New York City. So if she had known of Duane's sideline, she hadn't reaped any discernible benefits from it. Whether she had been in the trailer that morning and had had anything to do with either man's death was also unclear. Donovan really didn't care one way or another. He had no reason to sympathize with Duane Harvey or Otis Burns. At this point he didn't know what he felt about LuAnn Tyler. He did know that he wanted to find her. He wanted that very much.

Chapter Twenty

Jackson sat in a chair in the darkened living room of a luxurious apartment in a prewar building overlooking Central Park. His eyes were closed, his hands neatly folded in his lap. Approaching forty years of age he was still lean and wiry in build. His actual facial features were androgynous, although the years had etched fine lines around his eyes and mouth. His short hair was cut stylishly, his clothing was quietly expensive. His eyes, however, were clearly his most distinctive feature, which he had to disguise very carefully when he was working. He rose and moved slowly through the amply proportioned apartment. The furnishings were eclectic: English, French, and Spanish antiques mixed liberally with Oriental art and sculpture.

He entered an area of his apartment reminiscent of a Broadway star's dressing room. It was his makeup room and workshop. Special recessed lighting covered the ceiling. Multiple mirrors with their own special nonheating bulbs ringed the room. Two padded reclining leather chairs sat in front of two of the largest mirrors. The chairs had casters which allowed them to be rolled about the room. Innumerable photos were neatly pinned to cork bulletin boards on the walls. Jackson was an avid photographer, and many of his subjects were the basis for most of the identities he had created over the years. Both full wigs and hairpieces, neatly separated into toupees and falls, lined one wall, each hanging on special cotton-covered wire. Customized wall cabinets housed dozens of latex caps and other body pieces along with acrylic teeth, caps, and molds, and other synthetic materials and putties. One massive storage unit contained absorbent cotton, acetone, spirit gum, powders, body makeup; large, medium, and small brushes with bristles of varying rigidity; cake makeup, modeling clay, collodion to make scars and pock marks; crepe hair to make beards, mustaches, and even eyebrows; Derma wax to alter the face, creme makeup, gelatin, makeup palettes; netting, toupee tape, sponges, ventilating needles to knot hair into net or gauze for beards and wigs; and hundreds of other devices, materials, and substances designed solely to reshape one's appearance. There were three racks of clothing of all descriptions and several full-length mirrors to test the effect of any disguise. In a specially built case with multiple drawers were over fifty complete sets of identification documents that would allow Jackson to travel the world as a man or a woman.

Jackson smiled as he noted various articles

in the room. This was where he was most comfortable. Creating his numerous roles was the one constant pleasure in his life. Acting out the part, however, ran a close second as his favorite endeavor. He sat down at the table and ran his hand along its top. He stared into a mirror. Unlike anyone else looking into a mirror, Jackson didn't see his reflection staring back at him. Instead, he saw a blank countenance, one to be manipulated, carved, painted, covered, and massaged into someone else. Although he was perfectly content with his intellect and personality, why be limited to one physical identity one's whole life, he thought, when there was so much more out there to experience? Go anywhere, do anything. He had told that to all twelve of his lottery winners. His baby ducklings all in a row. And they had all bought it, completely and absolutely, for he had been dead right.

Over the last ten years he had earned hundreds of millions of dollars for each of his winners, and billions of dollars for himself. Ironically, Jackson had grown up in very affluent circumstances. "Old money" his family had been. His parents were long dead. The old man had been, in Jackson's eyes, a typical example of those members of the upper class whose money and position had been inherited rather than earned. Jackson's father had been both arrogant and insecure. A politician and insider in Washington for many years, the old man had taken his family connections as far as he could until his decided lack of merit and marketable skills had done him in and the escalator had stopped moving upward. And then he had spent the family money in a futile attempt to regain that upward momentum. And then the money was gone. Jackson, the eldest, had often taken the brunt of the old man's wrath over the years. Upon turning eighteen, Jackson discovered that the large trust fund his grandfather had set up for him had been raided illegally so many times by his father that there wasn't anything left. The continuing rage and physical abuse the old man had wielded after Jackson had confronted him with this discovery had left a profound impression on the son.

The physical bruises eventually had healed. The psychological damage was still with Jackson and his own inner rage seemed to grow exponentially with each year, as though he were trying to outdo his elder in that regard.

It might seem trite to others, Jackson understood that. Lost your fortune? So what? Who gives a damn? But Jackson gave a damn. Year after year he had counted on that money to free him from his father's tyrannical persecution. When that long-held hope was abruptly torn away, the absolute shock had carved a definite change in him. What was rightfully his had been stolen from him, and by the one man who shouldn't have done it, by a man who should have loved his son and wanted the best for him, respected him, wanted to protect him. Instead Jackson had gotten an empty bank account and the hate-filled blows of a madman. And Jackson had taken it. Up to a point. But then he hadn't taken it anymore.

Jackson's father had died unexpectedly. Parents killed their small children every day, never with good reason. By comparison, children killed their parents only rarely, usually with excellent purpose. Jackson smiled lightly as he thought of this. An early chemical experiment, administered through his father's beloved scotch, the rupturing of a brain aneurysm the result. As with any occupation, one had to start somewhere.

When those of average or below-average intelligence committed crimes such as murder, they usually did so clumsily, with no long-range planning or preparation. The result was typically swift arrest and conviction. Among the highly intelligent, serious crimes evolved from careful planning, long-term approaches, many sessions of mental gymnastics. As a result, arrests were rare, convictions even rarer. Jackson was definitely in the latter category.

The eldest son had been compelled to go out and earn the family fortune back. A college merit scholarship to a prestigious university and graduation at the top of his class had been followed by his careful nurturing of old family contacts, for those embers could not be allowed to die out if Jackson's long-range plan was to succeed. Over those years he had devoted himself to mastering a variety of skills, both corporeal and cerebral, that would allow him to pursue his dream of wealth and the power that came with it. His body was as fit and strong as his mind, the one in precise balance with the other. However, ever mindful of not following in his father's footsteps, Jackson had set a far more ambitious goal for himself: He would do all of it while remaining completely invisible from scrutiny. Despite his love of acting, he did not crave the spotlight as his politician father had. He was perfectly content with his audience of one.

And so he had built his invisible empire albeit in a profoundly illegal manner. The results were the same regardless of where the dollars had originated. Go anywhere, do anything. It didn't only apply to his ducklings.

He smiled at this thought as he continued to move through the apartment.

Jackson had a younger brother and sister. His brother had inherited their father's bad habits and consequently expected the world to offer up its best for nothing of comparable value in return. Jackson had given him enough money to live a comfortable but hardly luxurious existence. If he ran through that money there would be no more. For him, that well was dry. His sister was another matter. Jackson cared deeply for her, although she had adored the old man with the blind faith a daughter often shows to her father. Jackson had set her up in grand style but never visited her. The demands on his time were too immense. One night might find him in Hong Kong, the next in London. Moreover, visits with his sister would necessitate conversation and he had no desire to lie to her about what he had done and continued to do for a living. She would never be a part of that world of his. She could live out her days in idle luxury and complete ignorance looking for someone to replace the father she believed had been so kind, so noble.

Still, Jackson had done right by his family. He had no shame, no guilt there. He was not his father. He had allowed himself one constant reminder of the old man, the name he used in all his dealings: Jackson. His father's name was Jack. And no matter what he did, he would always be Jack's son.

As he continued to drift around his apartment he stopped at a window and looked out at a spectacular evening in New York. The apartment he was living in was the very same one he had grown up in, although he had completely gutted it after purchasing it; the ostensible reason had been to modernize and make it suitable for his particular needs. The more subtle motivation had been to obliterate, to the extent he could, the past. That compulsion did not only apply to his physical surroundings. Every time he put on a disguise, he was, in effect, layering over his real self, hiding the person his father had never felt deserved his respect or his love. None of the pain would ever be fully wiped away, though, so long as Jackson lived, as long as he could remember. The truth was, every corner of the apartment held the capability of flinging painful memories at him at any moment. But that wasn't so bad, he had long since concluded. Pain was a wonderful motivational tool.

Jackson entered and exited his penthouse by private elevator. No one was ever allowed in his apartment under any circumstances. All mail and other deliveries were left at the front desk; but there was very little of that. Most of his business was conducted by means of phone, computer modem, and fax. He did his own cleaning, but with his traveling schedule and spartan habits, these were not overly time-consuming chores, and were certainly a small price to pay for absolute privacy.

Jackson had created a disguise for his real identity and used it whenever he left his apartment. It was a worst-case-scenario plan, in the event the police ever came calling at his door. Horace Parker, the elderly doorman who greeted Jackson each time he left his apartment, was the same one who had tipped his cap to the shy, bookish boy clutching his mother's hand all those years ago. Jackson's family had left New York when he was a teenager, because his father had fallen on bad times, so the aged Parker had accepted Jackson's altered appearance as simply maturation. Now with the "fake" image firmly in people's minds, Jackson was confident that no one could ever identify him.

For Jackson, hearing his given name from Horace Parker was comforting and troubling at the same time. Juggling so many identities was not easy, and Jackson occasionally found himself not responding when he heard his real name uttered. It was actually nice being himself at times, however, since it was an escape of sorts where he could relax, and explore the never-ending intricacies of the city. But no matter which identity he assumed, he always took care of business. Nothing came before that. Opportunities were everywhere and he had exploited them all.

With such limitless capital, he had made the world his playpen for the last decade, and the effects of his manipulations could be felt in financial markets and political paradigms all across the globe. His funds had propelled enterprises as diverse as his identities, from guerrilla activities in Third World countries to the cornering of precious metal markets in the industrialized world. When one could mold world events in that way, one could profit enormously in the financial markets. Why gamble on futures markets, when one could manipulate the underlying product itself, and thereby know precisely which way the winds would be blowing? It was predictable and logical; risk was controlled. These sorts of climates he loved.

He had exhibited a distinctly benevolent side as well, and large sums of money had been funneled to deserving causes across the globe. But even with those situations he demanded and received ultimate control however invisible it was, figuring that he could exercise far better judgment than anyone else. With so much money at stake, who would deny him? He would never appear on any power list or hold any political office; no financial magazine would ever interview him. He floated from one passion to another with the utmost ease. He could not envision a more perfect existence, although he had to admit that even his global meanderings were becoming a little tedious lately. Redundancy was beginning to usurp originality in his numerous lines of business and he had begun searching around for a new pursuit that would satisfy an ever-growing appetite for the unusual, for the extremely risky, if only to test and retest his skills of control, of domination, and ultimately, of survival.

He entered a smaller room which was filled floor to ceiling with computer equipment. This represented the nerve center of his operation. The flat screens told him in real time how his many worldwide interests were doing. Everything from stock exchanges to futures markets to late-breaking news stories was captured, catalogued, and eventually analyzed here by him.

He craved information, absorbed it like a three-year-old learning a foreign language. He only needed to hear it once and he never forgot it. His eyes scanned each of the screens, and from long habit he was able to separate the important from the mundane, the interesting from the obvious in a matter of minutes. Investments of his colored in soft blue on the screens meant he was doing very well; those mired in harsh red meant he was doing less well. He sighed in satisfaction as a sea of blue blinked back at him.

He went into another, larger room that housed his collection of mementos from past projects. He pulled out a scrapbook and opened it. Inside were photographs of and background information on his twelve precious pieces of gold — the dozen individuals upon whom he had bestowed great wealth and new lives; and who, in turn, had allowed him to recoup his family's fortune. He flipped idly through the pages, occasionally smiling as various pleasant memories flickered through his mind.

He had handpicked his winners carefully, culling them from welfare rolls and bankruptcy filings; logging hundreds of hours tramping through poor, desolate areas of the country, both urban and rural, searching for desperate people who would do anything to change their fortunes — normal law-abiding citizens who would commit what was technically a financial crime of immense proportion without blinking an eye. It was wonderful what the human mind could rationalize given the appropriate inducement.

The lottery had been remarkably easy to fix. It was often that way. People just assumed institutions like that were absolutely above corruption or reproach. They must have forgotten that government lotteries had been banned on a wholesale basis in the last century because of widespread corruption. History did tend to repeat itself, if in a more sophisticated and focused manner. If Jackson had learned one thing over the years it was that nothing, absolutely nothing, was above corruption so long as human beings were involved, because, in truth, most people were not above the lure of the dollar or other material enticements, particularly when they worked around vast sums of money all day. They tended to believe that part of it was rightfully theirs anyway.

And an army of people wasn't required to carry out his plans. Indeed, to Jackson, the notion of a "widespread conspiracy" was an oxymoron anyway.

He had a large group of associates working for him around the globe. However, none of them knew who he really was, where he lived, how he had come by his fortune. None of them were privy to the grand plans he had laid, the worldwide machinations he had orchestrated. They simply performed their small slice of the pie and were very well compensated for doing so. When he wanted something, a bit of information not readily available to him, he would contact one of them and within the hour he would have it. It was the perfect setting for contemplation, planning, and then action — swift, precise, and final.

He completely trusted no one. And with his ability to create flawlessly more than fifty separate identities, why should he? With state-of-the-art computer and communications technology at his fingertips, he could actually be in several different places at the same time. As different people. His smile broadened. Could the world be any more his personal stage?

As he perused one page of the scrapbook his smile faded and was replaced with something more understated; it was a mixture of discernible interest and an emotion that Jackson almost never experienced: uncertainty. And something else. He would never have characterized it as fear; that particular demon never bothered him. Rather he could adequately describe it as a feeling of destiny, of the unmistakable conviction that two trains were on a collision course and no matter what one or the other did, their ominous meeting would take place in a very memorable manner.

Jackson stared at the truly remarkable countenance of LuAnn Tyler. Of the twelve lottery winners, she had been by far the most memorable. There was danger in that woman, danger and a definite volatility that drew Jackson like the most powerful magnet in the world. He had spent several weeks in Rikersville, Georgia, a locale he had picked for one simple reason: its irreversible cycle of poverty, of hopelessness. There were many such places in America, so well documented by the government under such categories as "lowest per capita income levels," "below standard health and education resources," "negative economic growth." Stark fiscal terms that did little or nothing to enlighten anyone as to the people behind the statistics; to shed light on a large segment of the population's free fall into misery. Ever the capitalist, Jackson surprisingly did not mind the added element of his actually doing some good here. He never picked rich people to win, although he had no doubt most of them would have been far easier to persuade than the poor he solicited.

He had discovered LuAnn Tyler as she rode the bus to work. Jackson had sat across from her, in disguise, of course, blending into the background in his torn jeans, stained shirt, and Georgia Bulldogs cap, a scruffy beard covering the lower part of his face, his piercing eyes hidden behind thick glasses. Her appearance had struck him immediately. She seemed out of place down here; everyone else looked so unhealthy, so hopeless, as though the youngest among them were already counting the days until burial. He had watched her play with her daughter; listened to her greet the people around her, and watched their dismal spirits noticeably lifted by her thoughtful comments. He had proceeded to investigate every element of LuAnn's life, from her impoverished background to her life in a trailer home with Duane Harvey. He had visited that trailer several times while LuAnn and her "boyfriend" had not been there. He had seen the small touches LuAnn had employed to keep the place neat and clean despite Duane Harvey's slovenly lifestyle. Everything having to do with Lisa was kept separate and immaculate by LuAnn. Jackson had seen that clearly. Her daughter was her life.

Disguised as a truck driver, he had spent many a night in the roadside diner where LuAnn worked. He had watched her carefully, seen the terms of her life grow more and more desperate, observed her stare woefully into her infant daughter's eyes, dreaming of a better life. And then, after all this observation, he had chosen her as one of the fortunate few. A decade ago.

And then he had not seen or spoken to her in ten years; however, a rare week went by that he did not at least think of her. At first he had kept quite a watchful eye on her movements, but as the years went by and she continued to move from country to country in accordance with his wishes, his diligence had lessened considerably. Now, she was pretty much off his radar screen entirely. The last he had heard she was in New Zealand. Next year could find her in Monaco, Scandinavia, China, he well knew. She would float from one locale to the next until she died. She would never return to the United States, of that he was certain.

Jackson had been born to great wealth, to every material advantage, and then it had all been taken away. He had had to earn it back through his skill, his sweat, his nerve. LuAnn Tyler had been born to nothing, had worked like a dog for pennies, no way out, and look at her now. He had given LuAnn Tyler the world, allowing her to become who she had always wanted to be: someone other than LuAnn Tyler. Jackson smiled. With his complete love of deception, how could he not appreciate that irony? He had spent most of his adult life pretending to be other people. LuAnn had spent the last ten years of hers living another life, filling in the dimensions of another identity. He stared into the lively hazel eyes, studied the high cheekbones, the long hair; he traced with his index finger the slender yet strong neck and began to wonder once more about those trains, and the truly wonderful collision they might one day create. His eyes began to shine with the thought.

Chapter Twenty-One

Donovan entered his apartment and sat down at the dining room table, spreading the pages he had taken out of his briefcase in front of him. His manner was one of subdued excitement. It had taken several weeks, dozens of phone calls, and a massive amount of leg work to accumulate the information he was now sifting through.

Initially, the task seemed more than daunting; indeed it had seemed destined for failure through sheer numbers. During the year LuAnn Tyler had disappeared, there had been over seventy thousand scheduled international passenger-aircraft movements at JFK. On the day she presumably fled there had been two hundred flights, or ten per hour, because there had been no flights between one and six A.M. Donovan had whittled down the parameters of his search at JFK to include women between the ages of twenty and thirty traveling on an international flight on the date of the press conference ten years ago, between the hours of seven P.M. and one A.M. The press conference had lasted until six-thirty and Donovan doubted she could have made a seven o'clock flight, but the flight could have been delayed, and he wasn't taking any chances. That meant checking sixty flights and about fifteen thousand passengers. Donovan had learned during his investigation that most airlines kept active records of passengers going back five years. After that the information was archived. His task promised to be easier because most airline records had been computerized in the mid-seventies. However, Donovan had met a stone wall in seeking passenger records from ten years ago. The FBI could get such records, he had been told, but usually only through a subpoena.

Through a contact at the Bureau who owed him a favor, Donovan had been able to pursue his request. Without going into particulars and naming names with his FBI contact, Donovan had been able to convey the precise parameters of his search, including the fact that the person he was seeking had probably been traveling under a newly issued passport and traveling with a baby. That had narrowed things down considerably. Only three people satisfied those very narrow criteria and he was now looking at a list of them together with their last known addresses.

Next, Donovan pulled out his address book. The number he was calling was a firm called Best Data, a well-known national credit check agency. Over the years the company had amassed a large database of names, addresses, and, most important, Social Security numbers. They serviced numerous firms requiring that information, including collection agencies and banks checking up on the credit of potential borrowers. Donovan gave the three names and last known addresses of the people on his list to the person at Best Data, and then provided his credit card number to pay for Best Data's fee. Within five minutes he was given the Social Security numbers for all three people, their last known addresses, and five "nearbys," or neighbors' addresses. He checked those against the records from the airlines. Two of the women had moved, which wasn't surprising given their ages ten years ago; in the interim they had probably moved on to careers and marriages. One woman, however, had not changed her address. Catherine Savage was still listed as living in Virginia. Donovan called directory assistance in Virginia, but no number came up for that name and address. Undeterred, he next called the Virginia Department of Motor Vehicles, or DMV, and gave the woman's name, last known address, and Social Security number, which in Virginia was also the driver's license number. The person at DMV would only tell Donovan that the woman had a current, valid Virginia driver's license but would not reveal when it had been issued or the woman's current address. Unfortunate, but Donovan had chased lots of leads into brick walls in the past. At least he knew she was now living in Virginia or at least had a driver's license in the commonwealth. The question now was Where in the commonwealth might she be? He had ways of finding that out, but decided in the meantime to dig up some more information on the woman's history.

He returned to the office where he had an on-line account through the newspaper and accessed the Social Security Administration's PEBES, or Personal Earnings and Benefit Estimate Statement database on the World Wide Web. Donovan was from the old school when it came to research methods, but even he occasionally lumbered out to do some Net surfing. All one needed to find out information on a person was their Social Security number, mother's maiden name, and the birthplace of the person. Donovan had all of those facts in hand. LuAnn Tyler had been born in Georgia, that he knew for certain. However, the first three digits of the Social Security number he had been given identified Catherine Savage as having been born in Virginia. If LuAnn Tyler and Catherine Savage were one and the same, then Tyler had obtained a phony SSN. It wasn't all that difficult to do, but he doubted whether the woman would've had the connections to do it. The PEBES listed a person's earnings going back to the early fifties, their contributions to the Social Security fund, and their expected benefits upon retirement based upon those contributions. That was normally what was shown. However, Donovan was looking at a blank screen. Catherine Savage had no history of wage earnings of any kind. LuAnn Tyler had worked, Donovan knew that. Her last job had been at a truck diner. If she had received a paycheck, her employers should have withheld payroll taxes, including amounts for Social Security. Either they hadn't or LuAnn Tyler didn't have a Social Security number to begin with. Or both. He called up Best Data again and went through the same process. The answer this time, however, was different. As far as the Social Security Administration was concerned, LuAnn Tyler didn't exist. She simply did not have a Social Security number. There was no more to be learned here. It was time for Donovan to take some more serious steps.

That evening Donovan returned home, opened a file, and took out IRS form 2848. The form was entitled "Power of Attorney and Declaration of Representative." A relatively simple form as Internal Revenue documents went, but one that carried extraordinary power. With it Donovan could obtain all sorts of confidential tax documents on the person he was investigating. True, he would have to stretch the truth a little in filling out the form, and a little falsification of signature was involved, but his motives were pure, and, thus, his conscience was clear. Besides, Donovan knew that the IRS received tens of millions of requests a year from taxpayers for information about their tax returns. The fact that somebody would take the time to match signatures was beyond the realm of probability. Donovan smiled. The odds of it would be greater even than the odds of winning the lottery. He filled out the form, listing the woman's name and last known address, put in her Social Security number, listed himself as the woman's representative for tax purposes, and requested the woman's federal income tax returns for the last three years, and mailed it off.

It took two months and numerous prodding phone calls, but the wait was worth it. Donovan had devoured the contents of the package from the IRS when it finally came. Catherine Savage was an awfully wealthy woman and her tax return from the prior year, at a full forty pages in length, reflected that wealth and the financial complexities that level of income bore. He had requested her last three years' worth of returns, but the IRS had only sent one for the simple reason that she had only filed one return. The mystery behind that had been cleared up quickly, because Donovan, as Catherine Savage's tax representative, had been able to contact the IRS and ask virtually every question that he wanted about the taxpayer. Donovan had learned that Catherine Savage's tax situation had sparked a great deal of initial interest with the IRS. A U.S. citizen with such an extraordinary level of income filing a tax return for the first time at age thirty was enough to jump-start even the most drone-like of Revenue agents into action. There were over a million Americans living abroad who simply never filed returns, costing the government billions in unpaid taxes, and consequently this was an area that always received the IRS's attention. However, the initial interest had quickly dissipated as every question the agency had asked had been answered and every answer had been supported by substantial documentation, Donovan had been told.

Donovan looked at his notes from the conversation with the IRS agent. Catherine Savage had been born in the United States, in Charlottesville, Virginia, in fact, and then left the country as a young girl when her father's business had taken him overseas. As a young woman living in France, she had met and married a wealthy German businessman who was a resident of Monaco at the time. The man had died a little over two years ago and his fortune had duly passed to his young widow. Now, as a U.S. citizen with control of her own money, all of which was passive, unearned income, she had begun paying her income taxes to her homeland. The documents in the file were numerous and legitimate, the IRS agent had assured Donovan. Everything was aboveboard. As far as the IRS was concerned, Catherine Savage was a responsible citizen who was lawfully paying her taxes although residing outside the United States.

Donovan leaned back in his chair and studied the ceiling, his hands clasped behind his head. The agent had also provided Donovan with another piece of interesting news. The IRS had very recently received a change of address form for Catherine Savage. She was now in the United States. In fact, she had returned, at least according to her records, to the town of her birth: Charlottesville, Virginia. The same town where LuAnn Tyler's mother had been born. That was far too much of a coincidence for Donovan.

And with all that information in hand, Donovan was fairly certain of one thing: LuAnn Tyler had finally come home. And now that he was so intimately familiar with virtually every facet of her life, Donovan felt it was time that they actually meet. How and where was what he started to think about.

Chapter Twenty-Two

Sitting in his pickup truck parked on the side of a sharp bend in the road, Matt Riggs surveyed the area through a pair of light-weight field binoculars. The tree-filled, steeply graded land was, to his experienced eye, impenetrable. The half mile of winding asphalt private road running to his right formed a **T**-intersection with the road he was on; beyond that, he knew, sat a grand country estate with beautiful vistas of the nearby mountains. However, the estate, surrounded by thick woods, couldn't be seen from anywhere except overhead. Which made him wonder again why the owner would want to pay for an expensive perimeter security fence in the first place. The estate already had the very best of nature's own handiwork for protection.

Riggs shrugged and bent down to slip on a pair of Overland boots, then pulled on his coat. The chilly wind buffeted him as he stepped from his truck. He sucked the fresh air in and put a hand through his unkempt dark brown hair, working a couple of kinks out of his muscular frame before donning a pair of leather gloves. It would take him about an hour to walk the front location of the fence. The plans called for the fence to be seven feet high, made of solid steel painted glossy black, with each post set in two feet of concrete. The fence would have electronic sensors spaced randomly across its frame, and would be topped by dangerously sharp spike finials. The front gates, set on six-foot-high, four-foot-square concrete monuments with a brick veneer, would be of similar style and construction. The job also called for a video camera, intercom system, and a locking mechanism on the huge gates that would ensure that nothing less than the head-on impact of an Abrams tank could ever open it without the permission of the owner. From what he could tell, Riggs didn't expect such permission to be granted very often.

Bordered by Nelson County on the southwest, Greene County to the north, and Fluvanna and Louisa counties on the east, Albemarle County, Virginia, was home to many wealthy people, some famous and some not. However, they all had one thing in common: They all craved privacy and were more than willing to pay for it. Thus, Riggs was not entirely surprised at the precautions being undertaken here. All the negotiations had been handled through a duly authorized intermediary. He reasoned that someone who could afford a fence such as this, and the cost was well into the hundreds of thousands of dollars, probably had better things to do with his time than sit down and chat with a lowly general contractor.

Binoculars dangling around his neck, he dutifully trudged down the road until he found a narrow pathway into the woods. The two most difficult parts of the job were clear to him: getting the heavy equipment up here and having his men work in such cramped surroundings. Mixing concrete, punching postholes, laying out the frames, clearing land, and angling sections of a very heavy fence, all of that took space, ample space that they would not have here. He was very glad to have added a healthy premium to the job, plus a provision for a cost overrun for exactly those reasons. The owner, apparently, had not set a limit as to the price, because the representative had promptly agreed to the huge dollar amount Riggs had worked up. Not that he was complaining. This single job would guarantee his best year ever in business. And although he had only been on his own for three years, his operation had been growing steadily ever since the first day. He got to work.

The BMW pulled slowly out from the garage and headed down the drive. The road going down was lined on either side with four-board oak fencing painted a pristine white. Most of the cleared land was surrounded by the same style of fencing, the white lines making a stunning contrast to the green landscape. It was not quite seven in the morning and the stillness of the day remained unbroken. These early morning drives had become a soothing ritual for LuAnn. She glanced back at the house in her rearview mirror. Constructed of beautiful Pennsylvania stone and weathered brick with a row of new white columns bracketing a deep front porch, a slate roof, aged-looking copper gutters, and numerous French doors, the house was elegantly refined despite its imposing size.

As the car passed down the drive and out of sight of the house, LuAnn turned her eyes back to the road and suddenly took her foot off the gas and hit the brake. The man was waving at her, his arms crisscrossing themselves as he flagged her down. She inched forward and then stopped the car. He came up to the driver's side window and motioned for her to open it. Out of the corner of her eye she saw the black Honda parked on a grass strip bordering the road.

She eyed him with deep suspicion but hit the button and the window descended slightly. She kept one foot on the accelerator ready to mash it down if the situation called for it. His appearance was innocent enough: middle-aged and slight of build, with a beard laced around the edges with gray.

"Can I help you?" she asked, her eyes attempting to duck his gaze at the same time she tried her best to note any sudden movements on his part.

"I think I'm lost. Is this the old Brillstein Estate?" He pointed up the road toward where the house was.

LuAnn shook her head. "We just recently moved in, but that wasn't the name of the owners before us. It's called Wicken's Hunt."

"Huh, I could've sworn this was the right place."

"Who were you looking for?"

The man leaned forward so that his face filled her window. "Maybe you know her. The name is LuAnn Tyler, from Georgia."

LuAnn sucked in a mouthful of air so quickly she almost gagged. There was no hiding the astonishment on her face.

Thomas Donovan, his face full of satisfaction, leaned even closer, his lips right at her eye level. "LuAnn, I'd like to talk to you. It's important and —"

She hit the accelerator and Donovan had to jump back to avoid having his feet crushed by the car tires.

"Hey!" he screamed after her. The car was almost out of sight. Donovan, his face ashen, ran to his car, started it up, and roared off down the road. "Christ!" he said to himself.

Donovan had tried directory assistance in Charlottesville, but they had no listing for Catherine Savage. He would have been shocked if they had. Someone on the run all these years didn't ordinarily give out her phone number. He had decided, after much thought, that the direct approach would be, if not the best, at least the most productive. He had watched the house for the last week, noted her pattern of early morning drives, and chosen today to make contact. Despite being almost run over, he had the satisfaction of knowing that he had been right. Throwing the question at her out of the blue like that, he knew, was the only sure way to get the truth. And now he had it. Catherine Savage was LuAnn Tyler. Her looks had changed considerably from the video and photos he had seen from ten years ago. The changes were subtle, no one single alteration really dramatic, yet the cumulative effect had been marked. Except for the look on her face and her abrupt departure, Donovan wouldn't have known it was her.

He now focused on the road ahead. He had just glimpsed the gray BMW. It was still far ahead, but on the curvy mountain road his smaller and more agile Honda was gaining. He didn't like playing the daredevil role; he had disdained it in his younger days when covering dangerous events halfway around the world, and he disliked it even more now. However, he had to make her understand what he was trying to do. He had to make her listen. And he had to get his story. He hadn't worked twenty-hour days the last several months tracking her down simply to watch her disappear again.

Matt Riggs stopped for a moment and again studied the terrain. The air was so clean and pure up here, the sky so blue, the peace and quiet so ethereal, he again marveled at why he had waited so long to chuck the big city, and come to calmer, if less exciting, parts. After years of being in the very center of millions of tense, increasingly aggressive people, he now found being able to feel like you were all alone in the world, for even a few minutes, was more soothing than he could have imagined. He was about to pull the property survey out of his jacket to study in more detail the dimensions of the property line when all thoughts of work amid the peaceful countryside abruptly disappeared from his mind.

He jerked his head around and whipped the binoculars up to his eyes to focus on what had suddenly destroyed the morning's calm. He quickly located the origin of the explosion of sound. Through the trees he spied two cars hurtling down from the road where the country estate was situated, their respective engines at full throttle. The car in front was a big BMW sedan. The car behind it was a smaller vehicle. What the smaller car lacked in muscle power to the big Bimmer, it more than made up for in agility around the winding road. At the speeds the two were doing, Riggs thought it most likely they would both end up either wrapped around a tree or upside down in one of the steep ditches that bordered either side of the road.

The next two visuals he made through his binoculars made him turn and run as fast as he could back to his truck.

The look of raw fear on the woman's face in the Bimmer, the way she looked behind to check her pursuer's progress, and the grim countenance of the man apparently chasing her were all he needed to kick-start every instinct he had ever gained from his former life.

He gunned the engine, unsure exactly what his plan of action would be, not that he had much time to come up with one. He pulled onto the road, strapping his seat belt across him as he did so. He normally carried a shotgun in the truck to ward off snakes, but he had forgotten it this morning. He had some shovels and a crowbar in the truck bed, although he hoped it wasn't going to come to that.

As he flew down the road, the two cars appeared in front of him on the main road. The Bimmer took the turn almost on two wheels before stabilizing, the other car right behind it. However, now on the straightaway, the three hundred plus horses of the BMW could be fully used, and the woman quickly opened a two-hundred-yard gap between herself and her pursuer, a gap that grew with every second. That wouldn't last, Riggs knew, because a curve that would qualify for deadman's status was fast approaching. He hoped to God the woman knew it; if she didn't he would be watching the BMW turn into a fireball as it sailed off the road and crashed into an army of unyielding hardwoods. With that prospect nearly upon them, his plan finally came together. He punched the gas, the truck flew forward, and he gained on what he now saw was a black Honda. The man apparently had all of his attention focused on the BMW, because when Riggs passed him on the left, the man didn't even look over. However, he took abrupt and angry notice when Riggs cut in front of him and immediately slowed down to twenty miles an hour. Up ahead, Riggs saw the woman glance back in her rearview mirror, her eyes riveted on Riggs and his fortuitous appearance on the scene as the truck and Honda fought a pitched battle for supremacy of the road. Riggs tried to motion to her to slow down, to make her understand what he was trying to do. Whether she got the message or not, he couldn't tell. Like the coils of a sidewinder, the truck and the Honda swayed back and forth across the narrow roadway, coming dangerously close to the sheer drop on the right side. Once, the truck's wheel partially skidded in the gravel shoulder and Riggs braced himself for the plunge over, before he barely managed to regain control. The driver of the Honda tried mightily to pass, leaning on the horn the whole time. But in his past career Riggs had done his share of dangerous, high-speed driving and he expertly matched the other man maneuver for maneuver. A minute later they rounded the almost V-shaped curve, a wall of sheer jutting rock on his left and an almost vertical drop to the right. Riggs anxiously looked down that steep slope for any sight of the Bimmer's wreckage. He breathed a sigh of relief as he saw none. He looked up the once again straight road. He saw the glint of a bumper far up ahead and then the big sedan was completely out of sight. Admiration was his first thought. The woman hadn't slowed down much, if any, coming around that curve. Even at twenty miles an hour Riggs hadn't felt all that safe. Damn.

Riggs reached across to his glove box and pulled out his portable phone. He was just about to punch in 911 when the Honda now took the very aggressive tack of ramming his truck from behind. The phone flew out of his hand and smashed into several pieces against the dashboard. Riggs cursed, shook off the impact, clenched the wheel hard, shifted into low gear, and slowed down even more as the Honda repeatedly smashed into him. What he was hoping would happen eventually did, as the Honda's front bumper and the truck's heavy-duty rear one locked together. He could hear the gears grinding in the Honda as the driver tried to extricate his vehicle without success. Riggs peered into the rearview mirror and he saw the man's hand slide over to his glove compartment. Riggs wasn't going to wait around to see whether a weapon emerged from it or not. He jerked the truck to a stop, slammed the gear in reverse, and the two vehicles roared backward down the road. He watched with satisfaction as the man in the Honda jerked back upright and gripped the steering wheel in a panic. Riggs slowed as he came to the curve, cleared it and then shot forward again. As he came to a straightaway, he cut the wheel sharply to the left and slammed the Honda into the rocky side of the road. The force of that collision uncoupled the two vehicles. The driver appeared unhurt. Riggs slammed the truck into drive and quickly disappeared down the road in pursuit of the BMW. He continually looked back for several minutes but there was no sign of the Honda. Either it had been disabled upon impact, or the driver had decided not to pursue his reckless actions further.

The adrenaline continued to course through Riggs's body for several minutes until it finally dissipated. Five years removed from the dangers of his former profession, Riggs was aware that this morning's five-minute episode had reminded him vividly of how many close calls he had survived. He had neither expected nor ever wanted to rekindle that anxious feeling in the sleepy morning mists of central Virginia.

His damaged bumper clanking loudly, Riggs finally slowed down, as further pursuit of the BMW was hopeless. There were innumerable roads off the main track and the woman could have taken any one of them and be long gone by now. Riggs pulled off the road and stopped, plucked a pen from his shirt pocket and wrote the license plate numbers of the Honda and BMW down on the pad of paper he kept affixed to his dashboard. He ripped the paper off the pad and tucked it in his pocket. He had a pretty good idea who was in the Bimmer. Someone who lived in the big house. The same big house he had been hired to surround with a state-of-the-art security fence. Now the owner's request started to make a whole lot more sense to Riggs. And the question he was most interested in now was why? He drove off, deep in thought, the morning's peacefulness irretrievably shattered by the look of sheer terror on a woman's face.

Chapter Twenty-Three

The BMW had indeed pulled off on a side road several miles away from where Riggs and the Honda had tangled. The driver's side door was open, the motor running. Arms clutched tightly around her sides, LuAnn walked in tight, frenetic circles in the middle of the road, shooting frosty breaths skyward in her agitation. Anger, confusion, and frustration raced across her features. All traces of fear were gone, however. The present emotions were actually far more damaging to her. Fear almost always passed; these other mental battering rams did not retreat so easily. She had learned this over the years, and had even managed to cope with it as best as she could.

Now thirty years old, LuAnn Tyler still carried the impulsive energy and sleek animal movements of her youth. The years had grafted onto her a more complete, mature beauty. However, the basic elements of that beauty had been discernibly altered. Her body was leaner, the waist even tighter. The effect was to make her appear even taller than she already was. Her hair had grown out and now was far more blond than auburn, and cut in a sophisticated manner that highlighted her more defined facial features, including the minor nose job done for disguise rather than aesthetics. Her teeth were now perfect, having benefitted from years of expensive dentistry. There was, however, one imperfection.

She had not followed Jackson's advice regarding the knife wound to her jaw. She had had it stitched, but let the scar remain. It wasn't all that noticeable, but every time she looked in the mirror, it was a stark reminder of where she had come from, how she had gotten here. It was her most visible tie to the past, and not a pleasant one. That was the reason she would not cover it over with surgery. She wanted to be reminded of the unpleasantness, of the pain.

People she had grown up with would probably have recognized her; however, she never planned to see anyone like that here. She had resigned herself to wearing a big hat and sunglasses whenever she ventured out into public, which wasn't very often. A lifetime of hiding from the world: that had come with her deal.

She went and sat back down on the front seat of the BMW, rubbing her hands back and forth across the padded steering wheel. She continually looked back down the road for any sign of her pursuer; however, the only sounds were her car's engine and her own uneven breathing. Huddled in her leather jacket, she hitched up her jeans, swung her long legs inside the car, and closed the door and locked it.

She took off and for a few moments as she drove her thoughts centered on the man in the truck. He had obviously helped her. Was he just a good Samaritan who had happened along at the right time? Or was he something else, something more complex than that? She had lived with this paranoia for so long now that it was like an exterior coating of paint. All observations had to pass through its screening first, all conclusions were based in some way upon how she perceived the motivation of anyone colliding unexpectedly with her universe. It all came down to one grim fact: fear of discovery. She took one long, deep breath and wondered for the hundredth time if she had made a grievous mistake by returning to the United States.

Riggs drove his battered truck up the private road. He had kept a close eye out for the Honda on his return down the road, but the car and driver had not reappeared. Going up to the house, he figured, was the quickest way to find a telephone, and perhaps also seek an explanation of sorts for this morning's events. Not that he deserved one, but his intervention had helped the woman and he felt that was worth something. In any event, he couldn't exactly let it rest now. He was surprised that no one stopped him on the drive up. There was no private security, apparently. He had met with the owner's representative in town; this was his first visit to the estate, which had been christened Wicken's Hunt long ago. The home was one of the most beautiful in the area. It had been constructed in the early 1920s with craftsmanship that was simply nonexistent today. The Wall Street magnate who had had it built as a summer retreat had jumped off a New York skyscraper during the stock market crash of '29. The home had passed through several hands, and had been on the market six years before being sold to the current owner. The place had required substantial renovation. Riggs had talked to some of the subcontractors employed to do that work. They had spoken with awe of the craftsmanship and beauty of the place.

Whatever moving trucks had hauled the owner's possessions up the mountain road had apparently done so in the middle of the night, because Riggs could find no one who had seen them. No one had seen the owner, either. He had checked at the courthouse land records. The home was owned by a corporation that Riggs had never heard of. The usual channels of gossip had not yielded an answer to the mystery, although St. Anne's-Belfield School had admitted a ten-year-old girl named Lisa Savage who had given Wicken's Hunt as her home address. Riggs had heard that a tall young woman would occasionally drop off and pick up the child; although she had always worn sunglasses and a large hat. Most often picking up the little girl would be an elderly man who had been described to Riggs as built like a linebacker. A strange household. Riggs had several friends who worked at the school but none of them would talk about the young woman. If they knew her name, they wouldn't say what it was.

When Riggs rounded a curve, the mansion suddenly appeared directly in front of him. His truck resembled a plain, squat tug bearing down on the *QEII*. The mansion stood three stories tall, with a double doorway spanning at least twenty feet.

He parked his truck in the wraparound drive that encircled a magnificent stone fountain that, on this cold morning, was not operating. The landscaping was as lush and as carefully planned as the house; and where annuals and even late-blooming perennials had died out, evergreens and other hardy foliage of all descriptions filled in the spaces.

He slid out of his seat, making sure he had the piece of paper with the license plate numbers still in his pocket. As he walked up to the front door, he wondered if a place like this would condescend to have a doorbell; or would a butler automatically open the door at his approach? Actually, neither happened, but as he cleared the top step, a voice did speak to him from a brand new–looking intercom built into the side of the wall next to the door.

"Can I help you?" It was a man's voice, big, solid, and, Riggs thought, slightly threatening.

"Matthew Riggs. My company was hired to build the privacy fence on the property's perimeter."

"Okay."

The door didn't budge, and the tone of the voice made clear that unless Riggs had more information to impart, this status was not going to change. He looked around, suddenly conscious that he was being observed. Sure enough, above his head, recessed within the back of one of the columns, was a video camera. That looked new as well. He waved.

"Can I help you?" the voice said again.

"I'd like to use a telephone."

"I'm sorry, that's not possible."

"Well, I'd say it should be possible since I just crashed my truck into a car that was chasing a big charcoal gray BMW that I'm pretty sure came from this house. I just wanted to make sure that the woman driving the car was okay. She looked pretty scared the last time I saw her."

The next sound Riggs heard was the front door being unbolted and thrown open. The elderly man facing him matched the six-foot-one Riggs in height, but was far broader across the shoulders and chest. However, Riggs noted that the man moved with a slight limp as though the legs and, perhaps, the knees in particular were beginning to go. The possessor of a very strong, athletic body himself, Riggs decided he would not want to have to take this guy on. Despite his advancing age and obvious infirmities, the man looked strong enough to break Riggs's back with ease. This was obviously the guy seen at the school picking up Lisa Savage. The doting linebacker.

"What the hell are you talking about?"

Riggs pointed toward the road. "About ten minutes ago, I was out doing a preliminary survey of the property line in advance of ordering up men and equipment when this BMW comes bolting down the road, a woman driving, blond from what I could see, and scared to death. Another car, a black Honda Accord, probably a 1992 or '93 model, right on her butt. A guy was driving that one and he looked determined as hell."

"The woman, is she all right?" The elderly man edged forward perceptibly. Riggs backed up a notch, unwilling to let the guy get too close until he had a better understanding of the situation. For all he knew, this guy could be in cahoots with the man in the Honda. Riggs's internal radar was all over the place on this one.

"As far as I know. I got in between them and took the Honda out, banged the crap out of my truck in the process." Riggs briefly rubbed his neck as the recollection of his collision brought several distinct painful twinges to that location. He would have to soak in the tub tonight.

"We'll take care of the truck. Where's the woman?"

"I didn't come up here to complain about the truck, mister —"

"Charlie, call me Charlie." The man extended his hand, which Riggs shook. He had not underestimated the strength the old guy possessed. As he took his hand back Riggs observed the indentations in his fingers caused by the other man's vise-like grip. Whether he was merely anxious about the safety of the woman, or he mangled visitors' fingers on a routine basis, Riggs didn't know.

"I go by Matt. Like I said, she got away, and as far as I know, she's fine. But I still wanted to call it in."

"Call it in?"

"The police. The guy in the Honda was breaking at least several laws that I know of, including a couple of felonies. Too bad I didn't get to read him his rights."

"You sound like a cop."

Had Charlie's face darkened, or was that his imagination, Riggs wondered.

"Something like that. A long while back. I got the license plate number of both cars." He looked at Charlie, studying the battered and grizzled face, trying to get beyond the stolid stare he was getting in return. "I'm assuming the BMW belongs to this house, and the woman."

Charlie hesitated for a moment and then nodded. "She's the owner."

"And the Honda?"

"Never seen it before."

Riggs turned and looked back down the road. "The guy could've been waiting partially down the entry road. There's nothing stopping him from doing that." Riggs turned and looked back at Charlie.

"That's why we contracted with you to build the fence and gate." A glint of anger rose in Charlie's eyes.

"Now I can see why that might be a good idea, but I only got the signed contract yesterday. I work fast, but not that fast."

Charlie relaxed at the obvious logic of Riggs's words and looked down for a moment.

"What about using that phone, Charlie?" Riggs took a step forward. "Look, I know a kidnap attempt when I see one." He looked up at the facade of the house. "It's not hard to see why either, is it?"

Charlie took a deep breath, his loyalties sharply divided. He was sick with worry about LuAnn — *Catherine,* he corrected himself mentally; despite the passage of ten years, he had never been comfortable with her new name. He was finding it close to impossible to allow the police to be called in.

"I take it you're her friend or family —"

"Both actually," Charlie said with renewed vigor as he stared over Riggs's shoulder, a smile breaking across his face.

The reason for that change in attitude reached Riggs's ears a second later. He turned and watched the BMW pull up behind his truck.

LuAnn got out of the car, glanced at the truck for a moment, until her eyes riveted on the damaged bumper; then she strode up the steps, passing over Riggs to focus on Charlie.

"This guy said you ran into some trouble," said Charlie, pointing at Riggs.

"Matt Riggs." Riggs extended his hand. In her boots, the woman wasn't much shorter than he. The impression of exceptional beauty he had gotten through his binoculars was considerably magnified up close. The hair was long and full, with golden highlights that seemed to catch every streak of the sun's rays as it slowly rose over them. The face and complexion were flawless to the point of seeming impossible to achieve naturally, yet the woman was young so the cut of the plastic surgeon's knife could not have beckoned to her yet. Riggs reasoned the beauty must be all her own. Then he spotted the scar that ran along her jawline. That surprised him, it seemed so out of place with the rest of her. The scar also intrigued Riggs because, to his experienced eye, the wound seemed to have been made by a knife with a serrated edge. Most women, he figured, especially those who had the kind of money she obviously did, would have paid any amount to cover up that blemish.

The pair of calm, hazel eyes that stared into Riggs made him conclude that this woman was different. The person he was looking at was one of those rare creations: a very lovely woman who cared little about her looks. As his eyes continued to sweep over her, he noted the lean, elegant, body; but from the smallish hips and waist there grew a breadth of shoulders that suggested exceptional physical strength. When her hand closed around his, he almost gasped. The grip was almost indistinguishable from Charlie's.

"I hope you're okay," said Riggs. "I got the plate number of the Honda. I was going to call it in to the cops, but my cell phone got broken when the guy hit me. The car's probably stolen anyway. I got a good look at the guy. This is a pretty isolated place. We should be able to nail him, if we act fast enough."

LuAnn looked at him, confusion on her face. "What are you talking about?"

Riggs blinked and stepped back. "The car that was chasing you."

LuAnn looked over at Charlie. Riggs watched closely but he saw no discernible signals passing between them. Then LuAnn pointed over at Riggs's truck. "I saw that truck and another car driving erratically, but I didn't stop to ask any questions. It was none of my business."

Riggs gaped for a moment before he responded. "The reason I was doing the two-step with the Honda was because he was trying his best to run you off the road. In fact, I almost took your place as the wreck of the week."

"Again, I'm sorry, but I don't know what you're talking about. Don't you think I would know if someone were trying to run me off the road?"

"So you're saying that you always drive eighty miles an hour around curvy, mountainous roads just for the fun of it?" Riggs asked heatedly.

"I don't think my driving methods are any of your concern," she snapped back. "However, since you happen to be on my property, I think it is my concern to know why you're here."

Charlie piped in. "He's the guy who's building the security fence."

LuAnn eyed Riggs steadily. "Then I would strongly suggest you concentrate on that task rather than come up here with some outrageous account of my being chased."

Riggs's face flushed and he started to say something, but then decided against it. "Have a good day, ma'am." He turned and headed back to his truck.

LuAnn didn't look back. She passed by

Charlie without a glance and walked quickly into the house. Charlie stared after Riggs for a moment before shutting the door.

As Riggs climbed back in his truck another car pulled up the drive. An older woman was driving. The back seat of the car was stacked with groceries. The woman was Sally Beecham, LuAnn's live-in housekeeper, just back from early-morning grocery shopping. She glanced over at Riggs in a cursory fashion. Though his features were laced with anger, he curtly nodded at her and she returned the gesture. As was her custom, she pulled around to the side-load garage and hit the garage door opener clipped to the car's visor. The door in from the garage led directly to the kitchen, and Beecham was an efficient person who detested wasted effort.

As Riggs pulled off he glanced back up at the massive house. With so many windows staring back at him he didn't catch the one framing LuAnn Tyler, arms folded across her chest, looking resolutely at him, a mixture of worry and guilt on her face.

Chapter Twenty-Four

The Honda slowed down, turned off the back road, then made its way over a rustic wooden bridge spanning a small creek, and then disappeared into the thickness of the surrounding forest. The antenna clipped some of the overhanging branches, sending a shower of dewdrops onto the windshield. Up ahead, under an umbrella of oak trees, a small, ramshackle cottage was visible. The Honda pulled into the tiny backyard and then into a small shed located behind the cottage. The man closed the doors of the shed and walked up to the house.

Donovan rubbed his lower back and then worked his neck around some in an attempt to overcome the aftereffects of his early morning escapade. He was still visibly shaking. Donovan stamped into the house, threw off his coat, and proceeded to make coffee in the small kitchen. Nervously smoking a cigarette while the coffee percolated, he looked outside the window with a slight feeling of apprehension, although he was fairly certain no one had followed him. He rubbed his brow. The cottage was isolated and the landlord didn't know his real name or the reason he had decided to take up temporary residence here.

The guy in the truck, who the hell had he been? Friend of the woman or some guy who had happened by? Since he had been seen, Donovan would have to shave off his beard and do something with his hair. He would also have to rent another car. The Honda was damaged and the guy in the truck could've gotten the license plate number. But the Honda was a rental, and Donovan had not used his real name in leasing it. He wasn't worried about the woman doing anything about it, but the guy might put a crimp in his plans. He wouldn't risk driving the Honda back into town to exchange it for another rental. He didn't want to be spotted driving it, and he didn't want to have to explain the damage to the bumper right now. Tonight, he'd walk to the main road and catch a bus into town, where he would pick up another rental car.

He poured a cup of coffee and walked into the dining room that had been set up as an office. A computer terminal, printer, and fax and phone were set up on one table. File boxes were stacked neatly in one corner. On two walls hung several large bulletin boards. They were filled with newspaper clippings.

The car chase had been stupid, Donovan muttered to himself. It was a miracle both of them weren't dead in some ravine right now. Tyler's reaction had absolutely astonished him. Although, thinking about it now, it probably shouldn't have. She was scared, and she had ample reason to be. Donovan's next problem was apparent. What if she disappeared again? Finding her the first time had been part hard work and part luck. There was no guarantee he would be as fortunate the next time. However, there was nothing he could do about that now. He could only wait and watch.

He had established a contact at the regional airport who would advise Donovan if any person matching LuAnn Tyler's description or traveling under the name Catherine Savage was headed out of the area via plane. Unless she had another identity already set up, it would be difficult for Tyler to travel any time soon except under the name Catherine Savage, and that would leave him a trail. If she left the area by means other than airplane, well, he could watch the house, but he couldn't do it twenty-four hours a day. He briefly contemplated calling in reinforcements from the *Trib*, but there were many factors that cautioned him against doing that. He had worked alone for almost thirty years, and bringing in a partner now was not very appealing, even if the newspaper would consent to do it. No, he would do what he could to dog her movements, and he would work very hard to set up another face-to-face. He was convinced that he could make the woman trust him, work with him. He didn't believe that she had killed anybody. But he was fairly certain that she and perhaps some of the other winners were hiding something about the lottery. He wanted that story, wherever it led him.

A fire blazed in the hearth of the spacious two-story library, which had floor-to-ceiling maple bookcases on three walls and inviting, overstuffed furniture arranged in intimate conversation patterns. LuAnn sat on a leather sofa, her legs drawn up under her, bare feet protruding, an embroidered cotton shawl covering her shoulders. A cup of tea and a plate of uneaten breakfast sat on the table next to her. Sally Beecham, dressed in a gray uniform with a sparkling white apron, was just leaving, carrying the serving tray. Charlie closed the arched double doors behind her and sat down next to LuAnn.

"Listen, are you gonna tell me what really happened or not?" When LuAnn didn't answer, Charlie gripped one of her hands. "Your hands are like ice. Drink the tea." He rose and stoked the fire until the flames made his face redden. He looked at her expectantly. "I can't help you if you don't tell me what's wrong, LuAnn."

Over the last ten years a lasting bond had been built between the two that had seen them through many crises, both minor and major, in their travels. From the time Charlie had touched her shoulder as the 747 climbed into the skies, until they had arrived back in America, they had been inseparable. Even though his given name was Robert, he had taken "Charlie" as his accepted name. It wasn't too far from the truth, as his middle name was Charles. What was in a name anyway? However, he referred to her as LuAnn only in private, as now. He was her closest friend and confidant, really her only one, since there were things she could not even tell her daughter.

As he sat back down, Charlie winced in pain. He was acutely aware that he was slowing down, a process that was exacerbated by the rough treatment of his body in his youth. The difference in years between the two was now more pronounced than ever, as nature took its toll on him. Even with all that, he would do anything for her, would face any danger, confront any enemy she had with every ounce of strength and ingenuity he had left.

It was the look in Charlie's eyes as LuAnn read these very thoughts that made her finally start talking.

"I had just left the house. He was standing in the middle of the driveway waving for me to stop."

"And you did?" Charlie's tone was incredulous.

"I didn't get out of the car. I couldn't exactly run over the man. If he tried anything, or pulled a gun, you can bet I would've done just that."

Charlie hitched one leg up over the other,

an action that was accompanied by another painful wince. "Go on. Eat while you're talking, and drink your tea! Your face is white as a sheet."

LuAnn did as he said, managing to get some bites of egg and toast down and a few sips of the hot tea. Putting the cup back down, she wiped her mouth with a napkin. "He motioned for me to roll the window down. I cracked it a bit and asked him what he wanted."

"Wait a minute, what'd he look like?"

"Medium height, full beard, a little gray at the edges. Wire-rimmed glasses. Olive complexion, maybe a hundred sixty pounds. Probably late forties or early fifties." Over the last ten years, memorizing minute details of people's appearances had become second nature to LuAnn.

Charlie mentally filed away her description of the man. "Go on."

"He said he was looking for the Brillstein Estate." She hesitated and took another sip of the tea. "I told him that this wasn't the place."

Charlie suddenly leaned forward. "What'd he say then?"

Now LuAnn was perceptibly shaking. "He said he was looking for somebody."

"Who? Who?" Charlie asked again as LuAnn's blank stare dropped to the floor.

She finally looked up at him. "LuAnn Tyler from Georgia."

Charlie sat back. After a decade, they had pretty much put the fear of exposure on the back burner, though it was still there and always would be. Now that flame had just been rekindled.

"Did he say anything else?"

LuAnn rubbed the napkin across her dry lips and then sat back up. "He said something about wanting to talk to me. Then . . . I . . . I just went blank, slammed the accelerator, and almost ran over him." She let all the air drain out of her after speaking. She looked over at Charlie.

"And he chased you?"

She nodded. "I've got strong nerves, Charlie, you know that, but they have their limits. When you're going out for a relaxing early morning drive and you get hit with something like that instead?" She cocked her head at him. "God, I was just starting to feel comfortable here. Jackson hasn't shown up, Lisa loves school, this place is so beautiful." She fell silent.

"What about the other guy, Riggs? Is his story true?"

Suddenly agitated, LuAnn stood up and paced the room. She stopped and ran her hand fondly along a row of finely bound novels resting on the shelves. Over the years, she had read just about every book in the room. Ten years of intensive education with some of the finest private tutors had produced an articulate, polished, cosmopolitan woman far re-moved from the one who had run from that trailer, from those bodies. Now those bloody images would not budge from her mind.

"Yes. He just jumped right into the middle of it. I probably would've lost the guy, any-way." She added quietly, "But he did help me. And I would've liked to have thanked him. But I couldn't exactly do that, could I?" She threw up her hands in frustration and sat back down.

Charlie rubbed his chin as he pondered the situation.

"You know, legally, the lottery scam amounts to a bunch of felonies, but the statute of limitations has expired on all of them. The guy can't really hurt you there."

"What about the murder charge? There's no statute of limitations on that. I did kill the man, Charlie. I did it in self-defense, but who the hell would believe me now?"

"True, but the police haven't pursued that case in years."

"Okay, do you want me to go turn myself in?"

"I'm not saying that. I just think you might be blowing this out of proportion."

LuAnn trembled. Going to jail over the money or the killing was not her biggest con-cern. She put her hands together and looked over at Charlie.

"My daddy probably never said one word

to me that was true. He did his best to make me feel like the most worthless piece of trash in the world and any time I built up some confidence he'd come along and tear it down. The only thing I was good for according to him was making babies and looking pretty for my man."

"I know you had it rough, LuAnn —"

"I swore to myself that I would never, ever do that to any child of mine. I swore that to God on a stack of Bibles, said it on my mother's grave, and whispered it to Lisa while I was carrying her and every night for six months after she was born." LuAnn swallowed hard and stood up. "And you know what? Everything I've told her, everything she knows about herself, you, me, every damned molecule of her existence is a lie. It's all made up, Charlie. Okay, maybe the statute of limitations is expired, maybe I won't go to jail because the police don't care that I killed a drug dealer. But if this man has found out my past and he brings it all out into the open, then Lisa will know. She'll know that her mother told her more lies than my daddy probably ever thought of in his entire life. I'll be a hundred times worse than Benny Tyler, and I'll lose my little girl as certain as the sun comes up. I'll lose Lisa." After this outburst, LuAnn shuddered and closed her eyes.

"I'm sorry, LuAnn, I hadn't thought about it like that." Charlie looked down at his hands.

LuAnn's eyes opened and they held a distinctly fatalistic look. "And if that happens, if she finds out, then it's over for me. Jail will seem like a day in the park, because if I lose my little girl, then I won't have any reason to be anymore. Despite all this." She swept her arms around the room. "No reason at all."

LuAnn sat back down and rubbed at her forehead.

Charlie finally broke the silence. "Riggs got the license plate number. On both cars." He fiddled with his shirt and added, "Riggs is an ex-cop, LuAnn."

Her head in her hands, LuAnn looked at him. "Oh God! And I didn't think it could get any worse."

"Don't worry, he runs your plate, he gets nothing except Catherine Savage with this address, legit Social Security number, the works. Your identity has no holes in it. Not after all this time."

"I think we have a very big hole, Charlie. The guy in the Honda?"

Charlie conceded the point with a quick nod of his head. "Right, right, but I'm talking about Riggs. Your end with him is okay."

"But if he tracks the other guy down, maybe talks to him?"

"Then maybe we got a big problem." Charlie finished the thought for her.

"You think Riggs might do that?"

"I don't know. I do know that he didn't buy

your story about not knowing you were being chased. Under the circumstances, I don't blame you for not acknowledging it, but an ex-cop? Hell, he's got to be suspicious. I don't think we can count on him letting it lie."

LuAnn rubbed the hair out of her eyes. "So what do we do?"

Charlie gently took one of her hands. "*You* do nothing. You let old Charlie see what he can find out. We've been in tight places before. Right?"

She slowly nodded and then licked her lips nervously. "But this might be the tightest one of them all."

Matt Riggs walked quickly up the steps of the old Victorian with a wraparound porch that he had meticulously restored over the last year. He had had a few years of carpentry and woodworking experience before coming to Charlottesville. They had been pursuits he had taken up to alleviate the stress that had come with what he used to do for a living. He wasn't thinking about the graceful lines of his home right now, however.

He went inside and down the hall to his office, for his home also housed his business. He shut the door, grabbed the phone, and placed a call to an old friend in Washington, D.C. The Honda had D.C. tags. Riggs was pretty sure what running the license plate would reveal: either a rental or stolen. The

BMW would be another matter. At least he would find out the woman's name, since it had suddenly occurred to him on the drive home that neither the man calling himself Charlie nor the woman had ever mentioned it. He was assuming the last name would be Savage and that the woman in the BMW was either Lisa Savage's mother or perhaps, from her youthful looks, an older sister.

A half hour later he had his answers. The Honda was indeed a rental out of the nation's capital. Tom Jones was the name of the lessee and he had rented the vehicle two weeks ago. Tom Jones! That was real clever, Riggs thought. The address he had for the man would be as phony as the name, he was certain. A total dead-end; he had expected nothing less.

Then he stared down at the woman's name he had written on a piece of paper. Catherine Savage. Born in Charlottesville, Virginia. Age: thirty. Social Security number had checked out, current address was correct: Wicken's Hunt. Unmarried. Excellent credit, no priors. No red flags at all in her background. He had a good slice of her past right there in his hand in less than half an hour. Computers were wonderful. And yet . . .

He looked at her age again. Thirty years old. He thought back to the house and substantial grounds, three hundred acres of prime Virginia real estate. He knew the asking price for

Wicken's Hunt had been six million dollars. If she had struck a wonderful deal, Ms. Savage could conceivably have gotten it for between four and five million, but from what he heard the renovation work had easily run to seven figures. Where the hell does a woman that young get that kind of money? She wasn't a movie star or rock star; the name Catherine Savage meant nothing to him, and he wasn't that far out of the loop on popular culture.

Or was it Charlie who had the bucks? They weren't husband and wife, that was clear. He had said he was family, but something was off there too. He leaned back in his chair, slid open a drawer of his desk, and popped a couple of aspirin, as his neck threatened to stiffen up again. It could be she had inherited serious family money or been the extraordinarily rich widow of some old duffer. Recalling her face, he could easily see that. A lot of men would shower her with everything they had.

So what now? He looked out the window of his office at the beauty of the surrounding trees with their vibrant fall colors. Things were going well for him: An unhappy past behind him; a thriving business in a place he loved. A low-key lifestyle that he figured would add lots of quality years to his life. And now this. He held the piece of paper with her name on it up to eye level. Despite having no material incentive to care at all about her, Riggs's curiosity was at a high pitch.

"Who the hell are you, Catherine Savage?"

Chapter Twenty-Five

"You about ready, honey?" LuAnn peeked in the door and cast her gaze fondly on the back of the young girl who was finishing dressing.

Lisa looked around at her mother. "Almost."

With a face and athletic build that mirrored LuAnn's, Lisa Savage was the one immovable landmark in her mother's life.

LuAnn stepped into the room, closed the door, and settled on the bed. "Miss Sally says you didn't eat much breakfast, are you feeling all right?"

"I have a test today. I guess I'm just a little nervous." One result of having lived all over the world was that her speech carried myriad traces of the different cultures, dialects, and accents. The mesh was a pleasing one, although several months in Virginia had already started to graft upon Lisa the beginnings of a mild Southern inflection.

LuAnn smiled. "I would've thought that by now, after so many straight A's, you wouldn't get so nervous." She touched her daughter's shoulder. During the time spent traveling, LuAnn had thrown every ounce of energy and a great deal of money into reshaping herself to be who she had always wanted to be, which was as far from Southern white trash named LuAnn Tyler as she could get. Well-educated, able to speak two foreign languages, she noted with pride that Lisa could speak four, as much at home in China as in London. She had covered several lifetimes in the last ten years. With this morning's developments, maybe that was a good thing. Had she run out of time?

Lisa finished dressing and sat down with her back to her mother. LuAnn picked up a brush and started doing her daughter's hair, a daily ritual between the two that allowed them to talk and catch up with each other.

"I can't help it, I still do get nervous. It's not always easy."

"Most things worthwhile in life aren't easy. But, you work hard and that's the important thing. You do your best, that's all I'll ever ask, regardless of what your grades are." She combed Lisa's hair into a thick ponytail and then clipped on a bow. "Just don't bring home any B's." They both laughed.

As they walked downstairs together, Lisa looked over at her mother. "I saw you talking to a man outside this morning. You and Uncle Charlie."

LuAnn tried to hide her apprehensiveness. "You were up? It was pretty early."

"Like I said, I was nervous about the test."

"Right."

"Who was he?"

"He's putting up the security fence and gate around the property. He had some questions about the plans."

"Why do we need a security fence?"

LuAnn took her hand. "We've talked about this before, Lisa. We're, well, we're very well-off financially. You know that. There are some bad people in the world. They might try to do things, to get money from us."

"Like robbing us?"

"Yes, or maybe something else."

"Like what?"

LuAnn stopped and sat down on the steps, beckoning Lisa to join her. "Remember how I'm always telling you to be careful, watch out for people?" Lisa nodded. "Well, that's because some bad people might try to take you away from me."

Lisa looked frightened. "I'm not telling you that to scare you, baby, but in a way I guess I do want you to be concerned, to be aware of what's going on. If you use your head and keep your eyes open, everything will be fine. Me and Uncle Charlie won't let anything happen to you. Mommy promises. Okay?"

Lisa nodded and they went down the stairs hand in hand.

Charlie met them in the hallway. "My, don't we look extra pretty this morning."

"I've got a test."

"You think I don't know that? I was up last night until ten-thirty with you going over the stuff. You're gonna ace it, sure as anything. Go get your coat, I'll be out front in the car."

"Isn't Mommy taking me today?"

Charlie glanced over at LuAnn. "I'm gonna give your mom a break this morning. Besides, it'll give us one more time to go over the test stuff, right?"

Lisa beamed. "Right."

After Lisa had gone, Charlie turned a very serious face to LuAnn. "I'm gonna check some things out in town after I drop Lisa off."

"You think you can find this guy?"

Charlie shrugged as he buttoned up his overcoat. "Maybe, maybe not. It's not a big town, but it's got lots of hiding places. One reason *we* picked it, right?"

LuAnn nodded. "What about Riggs?"

"I'll save him for later. I go knock on his door now, he might get more suspicious than he already is. I'll call from the car if I find out anything."

LuAnn watched the two climb into Charlie's Range Rover and drive off. Deep in thought, she pulled on a heavy coat, walked through the house and out the back. She passed the Olympic-size pool with surrounding flagstone patio and three-foot-high brick wall. At this time of year, the pool was drained and protected by a metal cover. The tennis court would probably go in next year. LuAnn cared little for either activity. Her underprivileged childhood had yielded no opportunities to idly hit a yellow ball around or lounge in chlorinated water. But Lisa was an avid swimmer and tennis player, and upon arriving at Wicken's Hunt, she had pressed eagerly for a tennis court. Actually, it was nice to know she was going to be around in one spot long enough actually to plan something like the construction of a tennis court down the road.

The one activity LuAnn had picked up in her travels was what she was heading to do right now. The horse barn was about five hundred yards behind the main house and surrounded on three sides by a thick grove of trees. Her long strides took her there quickly. She employed several people full-time to care for the grounds and horse barn, but they were not yet at work. She pulled the gear from the tack room and expertly saddled her horse, Joy, named for her mother. She snagged a wide-brimmed Stetson hat and leather gloves off the wall, and swung herself up onto her ride. She had had Joy for several years now; the horse had traveled with them to several countries, not an easy task, but one that was quite manageable when your pocketbook was bottomless. LuAnn and company had arrived in the United States via plane. Joy had made the crossing by boat.

One reason she and Charlie had decided upon the property was its myriad of riding trails, some probably dating from Thomas Jefferson's days.

She started off at a good pace and soon left the house behind. Twin clouds of breath escorted the pair as they made their way down a gradual decline and then around a curve, the trees hugging either side of the trail. The morning's briskness helped to clear LuAnn's head, let her think about things.

She had not recognized the man, not that she had expected to. Counterintuitively, she had always expected discovery to come from unknown quarters. He had known her real name. Whether that was a recent discovery on his part or he had found out long ago, she had no way of knowing.

Many times she had thought about going back to Georgia and telling the truth, just making a clean breast of it and attempting to put all of it behind her. But these thoughts had never managed to work themselves into cohesive actions and the reasons were clear. Although she had killed the man in self-defense, the words of the person calling himself Mr. Rainbow had continually come back to her. She had run. Thus, the police would assume the worst. On top of that, she was vastly rich, and who would have any sympathy or compassion for her now? Especially people from her hometown. The Shirley Watsons of the world were not so rare. Added to that was the fact that she had done something that was absolutely wrong. The horse she was riding, the clothes she was wearing, the home she was living in, the education and worldliness she had obtained over the years for herself and Lisa, all had been bought and paid for with what amounted to stolen dollars. In stark fiscal terms, she was one of the biggest crooks in history. If need be, she could endure prosecution for all that, but then Lisa's face sprung up in her thoughts. Almost simultaneously, the imagined words of Benny Tyler that day at the graveyard came filtering back to her.

Do it for Big Daddy. When did I ever lie to you, baby doll? Daddy loves you.

She pulled Joy to a halt and sunk her head in her hands as a painful vision entered her head.

Lisa, sweetheart, your whole life is a lie. You were born in a trailer in the woods because I couldn't afford to have you anywhere else. Your father was a no-account loser who got murdered over drugs. I used to stick you under the counter at the Number One Truck Stop in Rikersville, Georgia, while I waited tables. I've killed a man and run from the police over it. Mommy stole all this money, more money than you could dream of. Everything you and I have came from that stolen money.

When did Mommy ever lie to you, baby doll? Mommy loves you.

LuAnn slowly dismounted and collapsed on a large stone that jutted at an angle from the ground. Only after several minutes did she slowly come around, her head swaying in long, slow movements, as though she were drunk.

She finally rose and took a handful of pebbles from the ground. She idly skipped the stones across the smooth surface of a small pond, sending each one farther and farther with quick, graceful flicks of her wrist. She could never go back now. There was nothing to go back to. She had given herself a new life, but it had come with a terrifyingly high cost. Her past was total fabrication, thus her future was uncertain. Her day-to-day existence vacillated between fear of total collapse of the flimsy veneer shrouding her true identity and immense guilt for what she had done. But if she lived for anything, it was to ensure that Lisa's life would not be harmed in any way by her mother's past — or future — actions. Whatever else happened, her little girl would not suffer because of her.

LuAnn remounted Joy, cantering along until she slowed the mare down to a walk as they passed through some overhanging tree branches. She guided Joy to the edge of the trail and watched the swift, powerful thrust of the swollen creek that cut a jagged path across her property. There had been recent heavy rains, and early snow in the mountains had turned the usually docile water into a dangerous torrent. She backed Joy away from the edge and continued on.

Ten years ago, just after she, Charlie, and Lisa had landed in London, they had immediately boarded a plane for Sweden. Jackson had given them detailed marching orders for the first twelve months and they had not dared to deviate from them. The next six months had been a whirlwind zigzag through western Europe and then several years in Holland and then back to Scandinavia where a tall, light-haired woman would not seem so out of place. They had also spent time in Monaco and surrounding countries. The last two years had them in New Zealand, where they had all enjoyed the quiet, civilized, and even somewhat old-fashioned lifestyle. While Lisa knew multiple languages, English had been her primary one; LuAnn had been firm on that. LuAnn was an American despite spending so much time away.

It had indeed been fortunate that Charlie was a seasoned traveler. It had been largely through his efforts that potential disaster had been avoided at several different times. They had not heard from Jackson, but both assumed that he knew Charlie was with her. Thank God he was. If he hadn't gotten on that plane, LuAnn didn't know what she would've done. As it stood now, she couldn't function without him. And he wasn't getting any younger. She shook at the thought of life without the man. To be robbed of the one person in her life who shared her secret, who loved her and Lisa. There was nothing Charlie wouldn't do for them, and when his life ended and that void erupted . . . She drew in a deep breath.

Their new identities had been cemented over the years as LuAnn had taken great pains to establish the history Jackson had concocted for her and her daughter. The toughest part by far had been Lisa. Lisa believed her father to have been an extremely wealthy European financier who had died when Lisa was very young and who had left behind no family other than them. Charlie's role, while never fully explained, was clearly one of family and the "uncle" label had seemed a natural one. There were no photographs of Mr. Savage. LuAnn had explained to Lisa that her father was very reclusive and a touch eccentric and had allowed none to be taken. LuAnn and Charlie had long debated whether actually to create a man, photos and all, but had decided that it would be too dangerous. A wall with holes punched through it would eventually fall. Thus, Lisa believed her mother to be the very young widow of an extremely wealthy man, whose wealth, in turn, had made her mother one of the wealthiest women in the world. And one of the most generous.

LuAnn had sent Beth, her former coworker, enough money to start her own chain of restaurants. Johnny Jarvis from the mall had received enough to pay for several advanced degrees at the country's most prestigious universities. Duane's parents had received enough money to keep them secure in their retirement. LuAnn had even sent money to Shirley Watson, a guilty reaction to having lashed the woman with a negative reputation in the only place where Shirley would ever have the ambition or courage to live. Finally, LuAnn's mother's gravesite was now marked with a far more elaborate monument. The police, she was sure, had done all they could to track her down through this largesse, but without success. Jackson had hidden the money well and there had been absolutely no trace for the authorities to follow.

In addition, half her yearly income had been donated anonymously to a number of charities and other good works that she and Charlie had identified over the years. They were ever on the lookout for more deserving homes for the lottery money. LuAnn was determined to do as much good as she could with the money to atone, at least in part, for the manner in which she had acquired it. Even with all that, the money came in far faster than they could dispose of it. Jackson's investments had paid off more handsomely than even he had envisioned and the anticipated twenty-five million dollars in earnings each year had actually exceeded forty million per annum. All money unspent by LuAnn had also been reinvested by Jackson and the surplus had kept compounding until the assets LuAnn now held in her own name were almost half a billion dollars. She shook her head at the thought of the staggering sum. And the original lottery prize money, one hundred million dollars, was to be returned to her very shortly, the ten-year period having expired, as her contract with Jackson had stated. That mattered little to LuAnn. Jackson could keep it; it wasn't as though she needed it. But he would return it. The man, she had to admit, had been utterly faithful to his promise.

Over all these years, every quarter the detailed financial statements had arrived, no matter where they happened to be in the world. But since only the papers and never the man showed up, LuAnn's anxiety finally had passed. The letter accompanying all the financial packets was from an investment company with a Swiss address. She had no idea of Jackson's ties to this firm, nor did she care to explore that area further. She had seen enough of him to be respectful of his volatility; and more disturbingly, of the extreme consequences which he was capable of causing. She also remembered how he had been prepared to kill her if she had rejected his offer. There was something not quite natural about him. The powers he seemed to possess could hardly be of this world.

She stopped at a large oak. From one of its branches a long knotted rope dangled. LuAnn gripped the rope and lifted herself off the saddle, while Joy, already quite familiar with this ritual, waited patiently. Her arms moving like wonderfully calibrated pistons, LuAnn swiftly climbed to the other end of the rope, which was tied around a thick branch almost thirty feet off the ground, and then made her way back down. She repeated the process twice more. She had a fully equipped gymnasium in her home where she worked out diligently. It wasn't vanity; she had little interest in how it made her look. She was naturally strong, and that physical strength had carried her through many a crisis. It was one of the few constant things in her life and she was loath to let it disappear.

Growing up in Georgia, she had climbed many trees, run through miles of countryside, and jumped many ravines. She had just been having fun; the concept of exercise hadn't come into the equation. And so, in addition to pumping the iron, she had built a more natural exercise course across her extensive grounds. She pulled herself up the rope one more time, the muscle cords in her arms and back tight as rebar.

Breathing hard, she settled lightly back into the saddle and made her way back to the horse barn, her heart lightened and her spirits raised by the invigorating ride through the country-side and the strenuous rope climb.

In the large storage building next to the horse barn, one of the groundspeople, a beefy man in his early thirties, had just started splitting logs with a sledgehammer and wedge.

LuAnn glanced at him through the open doorway as she rode by. She quickly unsaddled Joy and returned the horse to its stall. She walked over to the doorway of the outbuilding. The man briefly nodded to her and then continued his work. He knew she lived in the mansion. Other than that, he knew nothing about her. She watched the man for a minute and then took off her coat, lifted a second sledgehammer off the wall, squeezed a spare wedge between her fingers, testing its weight, set a log up on the block, tapped the wedge into its rough surface, stepped back, and swung cleanly. The wedge bit deep, but didn't cleave the log in two. She hit it again, dead center, and then again. The log broke clean. The man glanced at her in surprise, then shrugged and kept splitting. They both pounded away, barely ten feet from each other. The man could split a log with one swing of the hammer, while it continued to take LuAnn two and sometimes three blows. He smiled over at her, the sweat showing on his brow. She kept pounding away, though, her arms and shoulders working in precise unity, and within five minutes she was cracking a log with one blow, and before he knew it she was doing it faster than he.

The man picked up his pace, the sweat falling faster across his brow, his grin gone as his breaths became more painful. After twenty minutes, he was taking two and three strikes to crack a log as his big arms and shoulders started to tire rapidly, his chest heaving and his legs rubbery. He watched in growing amazement as LuAnn continued, her pace steady, the strength of her blows against the wood totally undiminished. In fact, she seemed to be hitting the wedge harder and harder. The sound of metal on metal rang out louder and louder. Finally, the man dropped the sledgehammer and leaned back against the wall, his gut heaving, his arms dead, his shirt drenched in perspiration despite the chilly weather. LuAnn finished her pile of logs and, barely missing a stroke, finished off his stack as well. Her work complete, she wiped her forehead and replaced the sledgehammer on the wall hook before glancing over at the puffing man as she shook out her arms.

"You're very strong," she said, looking at the substantial pile of wood he had split as she put her coat back on.

He looked at her in surprise and then started laughing. "I was thinking that too before you came along. Now I've half a mind to go work in the kitchen."

She smiled and patted him on the shoulder. She had chopped wood virtually every day of her life from the time she had started school until she was sixteen. She hadn't done it for exercise, like now; back then she had done it to keep warm. "Don't feel bad, I've had a lot of practice."

As she walked back up to the house she took a moment to admire the rear facade of the mansion. The purchase and renovation of this house had been, by far, her greatest extravagance. And she had done it for two reasons. First, because she was tired of traveling and wanted to settle down, although she would've been happy in something far less magnificent than what she was staring at. Second, and more important, she had done it for the same reason she had done most things over the years: for Lisa. To give her a real home with a sense of permanence where she could grow up, marry, and have children of her own. Home the last ten years had been hotels, rented villas, and chalets, not that LuAnn was complaining about existing in such luxury, but none of them were home. The tiny trailer in the middle of the woods all those years ago had had far deeper roots for her than the most extravagant residence in Europe. Now they had this. LuAnn smiled at the sight: big, beautiful, and safe. At the thought of the last word, LuAnn suddenly huddled in her coat as a wind broke through the stand of trees.

Safe? When they had gone to bed last night they had been safe and secure, or as much as one could be living the kind of existence they all did. The face of the man in the Honda sprang up before her and she closed her eyes tightly until it finally went away. In its place came another image. The man's face stared at her with many emotions passing across it. Matthew Riggs had risked his life for her and the best she could do was accuse him of lying. And with that response she had only served to make him more suspicious. She pondered a moment, and then sprinted toward the house.

Charlie's office was straight out of a men's club in London, with a magnificent wet bar of polished walnut occupying one corner. The custom-built mahogany desk had neatly sorted piles of correspondence, bills, and other household matters. LuAnn quickly flipped through his card file until she found the one she wanted and plucked it out. She then took out a key Charlie kept high up on a shelf and used it to open a drawer in his desk. She took out the .38 revolver, loaded it, and carried it upstairs with her. The weight of the compact weapon restored some of her confidence. She showered, changed into a black skirt and sweater, threw on a full-length coat, and went down to the garage. As she drove down the private road, one hand tight around the pistol in her coat pocket, LuAnn anxiously looked around, for the Honda could be lurking. She breathed a sigh of relief when she hit the main road and was still all alone. She glanced at the address and phone number on the business card and wondered whether she should call first. Her hand hesitated over the car phone and then she decided just to chance it. If he wasn't there, then maybe it was best. She didn't know whether what she was planning would help or hurt matters. Ever one to choose action over passivity, she couldn't change her ways now. Besides, it was her problem, not anyone else's. She would have to deal with it eventually.

Eventually, she would have to deal with it all.

Chapter Twenty-Six

Jackson had just arrived back from a cross-country trip and was in his makeup room divesting himself of his most recent disguise when the phone rang. It was not his residential phone. It was his business line, an untraceable communications linkage, and it almost never rang. Jackson called out on the line often during the business day to convey precise instructions to his associates across the globe. Almost no one ever called him, however; and that was the way he wanted it. He had a myriad of other ways to ascertain whether his instructions were being carried out. He snatched up the phone.

"Yes?"

"I think we might have a problem here, or it may be nothing," the voice said.

"I'm listening." Jackson sat down and used a long piece of string to lift the putty off his nose. Then he removed the latex pieces adhering to his face by tugging gently on their edges.

"As you know, two days ago we wired income from the last quarter to Catherine Savage's account in the Caymans. To Banque Internacional. Just like always."

"So? Is she complaining about the rate of

return?" Jackson said sarcastically. He tugged firmly on the back edges of his snow white wig and then pulled up and then forward. He next removed the latex skullcap and his own hair sprang free.

"No, but I got a call from the wire department at Banque and they wanted to confirm something."

"What was that?" Jackson cleansed his face while he was listening, his eyes scanning the mirror as layer after layer of concealment was removed.

"That they had wired all the monies from Savage's accounts to Citibank in New York."

New York! As he absorbed this stunning news, Jackson opened his mouth wide and removed the acrylic caps. Instantly, dark, misshapen teeth became white and straight. His dark eyes glittered menacingly and he stopped removing his disguise. "First, why would they call you if it was her account?"

"They shouldn't have. I mean they never have before. I think the guy at the wire desk down there is new. He must have seen my name and phone number on some of the paperwork and figured I was a principal on the receiving account instead of being on the other end of the transaction, the sending account."

"What did you tell him? I hope you didn't excite any suspicion."

"No, not at all," the voice said nervously. "I simply thanked him and said that was correct. I hope I did the right thing, but of course I wanted to report it to you right away. It seemed unusual."

"Thank you."

"Anything you want me to do on follow-up?"

"I'll handle it." Jackson hung up the phone. He sat back and fiddled absently with the wig. None of LuAnn's money was ever, ever supposed to end up in the United States. Money in the United States was traceable. Banks filed 1099s with the IRS, and other documents detailing income and account balances. Social Security numbers were communicated and kept as part of the official record; filings with the IRS on behalf of the taxpayer were required. None of that was ever supposed to happen in LuAnn's case. LuAnn Tyler was a fugitive. Fugitives did not return to their homeland and start paying their taxes, even under assumed names.

He picked up his phone and dialed a number.

"Yes, sir?" the voice asked.

Jackson said, "The taxpayer's name is Catherine Savage." Jackson provided her Social Security number and other pertinent information. "You will find out immediately whether she has filed a U.S. tax return or any other type of documents with the IRS. Use all the sources at your disposal, but I need this information within the hour."

He hung up again. For the next forty-five minutes, he walked around his apartment, wearing the portable phone and headset, a requirement when you liked to pace and your apartment was as large as Jackson's was.

Then the phone rang again.

The voice was crisp. "Catherine Savage filed an income tax return last year. I couldn't get full particulars in such a short time frame; however, according to my source, the income reported was substantial. She also recently filed a change of address form with the IRS."

"Give it to me." Jackson wrote the Charlottesville, Virginia, address down on a piece of paper and put it in his pocket.

"One more thing," the voice said. "My source pulled up a very recent filing in connection with Savage's tax account."

"By her?"

"No. It was a Form 2848. It gives a third party a power of attorney to represent the taxpayer with respect to just about anything having to do with their tax matters."

"Who was the requesting party?"

"A fellow named Thomas Jones. According to the file, he's already received information on her account, including her change of address and last year's income tax return. I was able to get a facsimile of the 2848 form he filed. I can send it to you right now."

"Do so."

Jackson hung up and a minute later had the

fax in his hands. He looked at Catherine Savage's signature on the form. He pulled out the originals of the documents LuAnn had signed ten years earlier in connection with their agreement for the lottery winnings. The signatures weren't even close, not that the IRS, cumbersome institution that it was, would ever have taken the time to compare signatures. A forgery. Whoever the man was, he had filed this document without the woman's knowledge. Jackson studied the address and phone number that Tom Jones had given for himself. Jackson called the number. It was no longer in service. The address was a P.O. box. Jackson was certain that would also be another dead end. The man was privy to Catherine Savage's tax situation and her new address and his background was a complete sham.

That startling fact was not what annoyed Jackson the most, troubling as it was. He sat down in a chair and studied the wall as his mind moved in ever expanding circles of thought. LuAnn had come back to the United States, despite his explicit instructions to the contrary. She had disobeyed him. That was bad enough. The problem was compounded by the fact that someone else was now interested in her. For what reason? Where was this person now? Probably the same place Jackson was just about to head to: Charlottesville, Virginia.

The lights of the two trains were becoming

clearer. The possibility of that collision with LuAnn Tyler crept closer and closer to reality. Jackson went back to his makeup room. It was time for another creation.

Chapter Twenty-Seven

After dropping Lisa off at St. Anne's, taking care to walk her directly into the classroom, as was his and LuAnn's practice, Charlie had wheeled the Range Rover out of the parking lot and headed into town. Over the last few months while LuAnn had remained reclusive inside their mountainside fortress, Charlie had been the point man, meeting with prominent townsfolk, making the rounds of businesses and charities and university officials. He and LuAnn had decided that they could not keep secret her wealth and presence in this small, albeit cosmopolitan town and any attempt to do so would invite more suspicion rather than less. Thus, Charlie's task was to lay the groundwork with the town's leaders for the eventual emergence of LuAnn into their society. However, it would only be a very limited emergence. Everyone could understand the need for privacy of the extremely wealthy. And there were many organizations very eager to receive donations from LuAnn, so that maximum cooperation and understanding would likely be forthcoming. That pipeline had already been opened, as LuAnn had donated over a hundred thousand dollars to several local causes. As he headed down the road Charlie shook his head wearily. All these plans, strategies, and what-not. Being phenomenally wealthy was a big pain in the ass. Sometimes he yearned for the old days. A few bucks in his pocket, a beer nearby, and a pack of smokes when he wanted it; a fight on the tube. He smiled wryly. LuAnn had finally gotten him to stop smoking about eight years ago and he knew that had prolonged his life considerably. But he was allowed an occasional cigar. She wasn't about to mother him to death.

Charlie's earlier forays into Charlottesville society had produced one contact in an extremely useful position, a contact that he now intended to pump for information that would allow him and LuAnn to check out her pursuer and, if possible, forestall any real problem. If the man wanted money, that was one thing. Money was not an issue. LuAnn's pocketbook was more than sufficient to satisfy even the most outrageous blackmailer. But what if the issue wasn't simply money? The problem was, Charlie was unsure exactly what the man knew or didn't know. He had mentioned LuAnn's real name. Did he also know about Duane Harvey's murder and LuAnn's relationship to the dead man? The warrant that had been issued for LuAnn's arrest ten years ago? And how had he tracked LuAnn down after all these years?

The next issue was even more critical: Did the man know about the lottery fix? LuAnn had told Charlie all about the man calling himself Rainbow. Rainbow might have figured it out. He had followed her, watched her buy a lottery ticket, leave immediately for New York, and win a fortune. Had the man known it was rigged? And had he told anyone? LuAnn had not been sure.

And what had happened to Rainbow? Charlie licked his lips nervously. He had never really known Jackson, never even seen him. But while he had worked for him, he had talked to the man often. The tones of Jackson's voice had been unremarkable: even, calm, direct, supremely confident. Charlie had known people just like that. These men weren't the blusterers, the ones who always said a hell of a lot more than they ever had the courage or ability to back up in reality. They were the ones who looked you dead in the eye, said precisely what they intended to do with little fanfare or hyperbole, and then simply did it. These types would efficiently disembowel you and not lose any sleep over it. Jackson, Charlie had long ago decided, was one of those. Despite his own toughness and strength, Charlie shivered slightly. Wherever Rainbow was, it wasn't among the living, that was for damn sure. Charlie drove on, lost in thought.

Chapter Twenty-Eight

LuAnn pulled her car into the driveway and stopped in front of the house. She didn't see the pickup truck anywhere. He probably was off at another job. She was about to leave, but the simple beauty of Matt Riggs's home made her stop, get out of the BMW, and go up the plank steps. The graceful lines of the old structure, the obvious care and skill which had gone into rehabbing it, made her eager to explore the place, even if its owner was absent.

She moved around the broad porch, running her hand along its intricate wooden scrollwork. She opened the screen door and knocked at the front door, but there was no answer. She hesitated and then tried the doorknob. It turned easily in her hand. People had not locked their doors where she had grown up either. As security conscious as she was now, it was good to know there were still places like that left in the world. She hesitated again. Entering the man's home without his knowledge might only compound matters. However, if he never found out? She might be able to obtain some useful information about him, something she could use to help extricate herself from this potential disaster.

She pushed open the front door and then closed it softly behind her. The living room had random-width oak flooring splotched and mottled with age. The furnishings were simple but carefully arranged and each was of excellent quality. LuAnn wondered whether Matt Riggs bought the pieces in broken condition and then worked on them. She moved through the rooms, stopping to admire the man's handiwork here and there. The slight smell of varnish hovered over various pieces of furniture. The place was neat and clean. There were no pictures of family: no wife, no kids. She didn't know why but this struck her as odd. She reached his office and peered inside. Quietly moving over to his desk, she stopped for a moment as she thought she heard a sound come from somewhere within the house. Her heart started to race and she briefly contemplated fleeing. The sound wasn't repeated, however, and she calmed down and seated herself behind the desk. The first thing that caught her eye was the paper on which Riggs had jotted down the notes. Her name and other information about her. Then she glanced at the information on the Honda. She looked at her watch. Riggs was clearly not a man who believed in idleness. And he was able to get information from sources that were obviously more than a little sophisticated. That was troubling. LuAnn jerked her head up as she looked out the broad window into the backyard. There was a barn-like structure there. The door was open slightly. LuAnn had thought she had noted movement there. As she got up to go outside, her hand dipped into her jacket pocket and closed around the .38.

When she exited the house she started to head back to her car. Then her curiosity got the better of her and she crept over to the barn door and peered inside. An overhead light illuminated the area well. It was set up as a workshop and storage facility. In front of two entire walls were sturdy work benches and tables and more tools than LuAnn had ever before seen in one place. The two other walls had shelving where wood supplies and other materials were stacked in precise configurations. As LuAnn moved inside she eyed the staircase at the rear of the structure. In former times she was certain it would have led to a hayloft. Riggs, however, had no animals in need of hay, at least that she could see. She wondered what it housed now.

She took the steps slowly. When she reached the top, she stared in amazement. The place was set up as a small study and observation area. Two bookcases, a beat-up leather chair and ottoman, and an ancient potbellied stove stared back at her. In one corner, an old-fashioned telescope was set up to look out a huge window in the rear of the barn. As LuAnn climbed up and looked through the window, her heart started to pound. Riggs's truck was parked behind the barn.

As she turned to run down the stairs, she found herself staring down the barrel of a twelve-gauge shotgun.

When Riggs saw who it was he slowly lowered the weapon. "What the hell are you doing here?" She tried to move past him, but Riggs grabbed her arm. She just as quickly pulled it free.

"You scared me to death," she said.

"Sorry. Now what the hell are you doing here?"

"Is this how you usually welcome company into your home?"

"Company usually comes in through the front door, and only after I've opened it." He looked around. "This sure as hell isn't my front door, and I don't remember inviting you in."

LuAnn moved away from him as she looked around the space and then returned her gaze to his angry features.

"This is a nice place to come and think. How would you like to build me something like this at my house?"

Riggs leaned up against the wall. He still held the shotgun in the down position but he could swing it up into a firing position in the matter of a second. "I would think you'd want to see my work on the fence before you hired me for something else, Ms. Savage."

She feigned surprise at the sound of her

name but apparently not enough to satisfy Riggs.

"So, did you find anything else of interest in my office besides my homework on you?"

She looked at him with even more respect. "I'm a little paranoid about my privacy."

"So I noticed. Is that why you carry a pistol?"

LuAnn looked down at her pocket. A sliver of the .38 was visible.

"You have good eyes."

"A thirty-eight doesn't have such great stopping power. If you're serious about your privacy, and your security, you might want to step up to a nine millimeter. A semiautomatic over a revolver is a no-brainer." The hand holding the shotgun twitched for an instant. "I tell you what, you take the revolver out, muzzle first, and I'll stop fussing with my shotgun here."

"I'm not going to shoot you."

"That's absolutely right, you're not," he said evenly. "Please do as I say, Ms. Savage. And do it very slowly."

LuAnn took the pistol out, holding it by the barrel.

"Now unload it and put the bullets in one pocket and the pistol in the other. And I can count to six so don't try to be cute."

LuAnn did as she was told, looking at him angrily. "I'm not used to being treated like a criminal."

"You break into my house carrying a weapon, that's exactly how I'm going to treat you. Count yourself lucky that I didn't shoot first and ask questions later. Buckshot can be very irritating to the skin."

"I didn't break in. The door was open."

"Don't try that one in a court of law," he fired back.

When Riggs had confirmed that she had emptied the revolver, he broke open the shotgun and laid it down on the bookcase. He crossed his arms and studied her.

Slightly unnerved, LuAnn went back to her original train of thought. "My circle of friends is very small. When somebody intrudes on that circle I tend to get curious."

"That's funny. You call it intrusion, but what I did this morning ordinarily would be called coming to the rescue."

LuAnn brushed a strand of hair out of her face and looked away for a moment. "Look, Mr. Riggs —"

"My friends call me Matt. We're not friends, but I'll allow you the privilege," he said coolly.

"I'd rather call you Matthew. I don't want to break any of your rules."

Riggs looked startled for a moment before settling back down. "Whatever."

"Charlie said you were a cop."

"I never said so."

She looked at him, surprise now clear on

her features. "Well, were you?"

"What I was really isn't any of your business. And you still haven't told me what you're doing here."

She rubbed her hand across the old leather chair. She didn't answer right away and Riggs was content to let the silence endure until she broke it. "What happened this morning is a little more complicated than it appeared. It's something that I'm taking care of." She paused and looked up at him, her eyes searching his. "I appreciate what you did. You helped me and you didn't have to. I came here to thank you."

Riggs relaxed a little bit. "Okay, although I didn't expect any thanks. You needed some help and I was around to give it. One human being to another. The world would be a hell of a lot better place if we all lived by that rule."

"I also came to ask a favor."

Riggs inclined his head toward her, waiting.

"The situation this morning, I would appreciate it if you'd just forget about it. Like I said, Charlie and I are taking care of it. If you got involved, it might make things more difficult for me."

Riggs took this in for a few moments.

"Do you know the guy?"

"I really don't want to get into it."

Riggs rubbed his chin. "You know, the guy banged me up. So I already feel like I'm involved."

LuAnn moved closer to him. "I know you don't know me, but it would mean a lot if you would just drop it. It really would." Her eyes seemed to widen with each word spoken.

Riggs felt himself drawing closer to her although he hadn't physically budged an inch. Her gaze seemed to be pasted onto his face, all the sunlight streaming through the window seemed to be blocked out as though an eclipse were occurring.

"I'll tell you what: Unless the guy gives me any more trouble, I'll forget it ever happened."

LuAnn's tensed shoulders slumped in relief. "Thank you."

She moved past him toward the stairs. The scent of her perfume drifted through his nostrils. His skin started to tingle. It had been a long time since that had happened.

"Your home is beautiful," she said.

"It certainly doesn't compare to yours."

"Did you do it all yourself?"

"Most of it. I'm pretty handy."

"Why don't you come by tomorrow and we can talk about you doing some more work for me."

"Ms. Savage —"

"Call me Catherine."

"Catherine, you don't have to buy my silence."

"Around noon? I can have some lunch ready."

Riggs gave her a searching look and then

shrugged. "I can make that."

As she started down the stairs, he called after her. "That guy in the Honda. Don't assume he's going to give up."

She glanced back at the shotgun for one significant moment before settling her gaze on him.

"I never assume anything anymore, Matthew."

"Well, it's a good cause, John, and she likes to help good causes." Charlie leaned back in his chair and sipped the hot coffee. He was sitting at a window table in the dining room of the Boar's Head Inn, off Ivy Road a little west of the University of Virginia. Two plates held the remnants of breakfast. The man across from him beamed.

"Well, I can't tell you how much it means to the community. Having her here — both of you — is just wonderful." Wearing a costly double-breasted suit, with a colorful handkerchief dangling from the outer pocket and matching his polka-dot tie, the wavy-haired John Pemberton was one of the area's most successful and well-connected real estate agents. He also sat on the boards of numerous charities and local committees. The man knew virtually everything that happened in the area, which was precisely the reason Charlie had asked him to breakfast. Further, the commission on the sale of

LuAnn's home had landed six figures in Pemberton's pocket and he was, thus, an eternal friend.

Now he looked down at his lap and a sheepish grin appeared on his handsome features when he looked back up at Charlie. "We are hoping to actually *meet* Ms. Savage at some point."

"Absolutely, John, absolutely. She's looking forward to meeting you too. It'll just take some time. She's a very private person, you understand."

"Of course, of course, this place is full of people like that. Movie stars, writers, people with more money than they know what to do with."

An involuntary smile played across Pemberton's lips. Charlie assumed the man was daydreaming about future dollars of commission when these wealthy folk moved in or out of the area.

"You'll just have to live with my company for a little while longer." A grin creased Charlie's features.

"And very enjoyable company it is too," Pemberton replied automatically.

Charlie put down his coffee cup and pushed his breakfast plate away. If he still smoked cigarettes he would've stopped to light one up. "We have Matt Riggs doing some work for us."

"Putting in the security fence. Yes, I know.

Undoubtedly his biggest job to date."

Upon noting Charlie's surprised look, Pemberton smiled in an embarrassed fashion. "Despite its cosmopolitan appearance, Charlottesville really is a small town. There is very little that happens that isn't known by most people soon thereafter."

At those words, Charlie's spirits plummeted. *Had Riggs already told someone? Had they made a mistake coming here? Should they have planted themselves amid the seven million residents of New York City instead?*

With an effort, he shook off these numbing thoughts and plunged ahead. "Right. Well, the guy had some terrific references."

"He does very good work, dependable and professional. He hasn't been here all that long by the standards of most locals, about five years, but I've never heard a bad word said about him."

"Where'd he come from?"

"Washington. D.C., not the state of." Pemberton fingered his teacup.

"So he was a builder up there then?"

Pemberton shook his head. "No, he got his general contractor's license after he got here."

"Still, he could've apprenticed up there."

"I think he had some natural talent for the trade. He's a first-rate carpenter, but he apprenticed with Ralph Steed, one of our best

362

local builders for two years. Ralph passed away about that time and that's when Riggs went out on his own. He's done very well. He's a hard worker. And landing that fence job doesn't hurt any."

"True. Still, the guy just shows up in town one day and plunges into something new. That takes some balls. I mean I've met him, and it wasn't like he would've been fresh out of college when he came here."

"No, he wasn't." Pemberton looked around the small dining area. When he spoke next it was with a lowered voice. "You're not the first person who has been curious about Riggs's origins."

Charlie leaned forward, adding to the conspiratorial image of the pair. "Is that right? What do we have here, a little local intrigue?" Charlie tried to make his tone appear light and unconcerned.

"Of course rumors come and go, and you know the questionable veracity of most of them. Still, I have heard from various sources that Riggs held some important position in Washington." Pemberton paused for effect. "In the intelligence community."

Behind the stone mask Charlie fought the urge to abruptly give back his breakfast. Although LuAnn had had the good luck to be one of the recipients of Jackson's control of the lottery, she might have just matched that luck with a dose of incredibly bad fortune. "In intelligence, you say? Like a spy?"

Pemberton threw up his hands. "Who knows. Secrets are a way of life with people like that. Torture them and they won't say a thing. Probably bite on their cyanide pill or whatever and go peacefully into the night." Pemberton obviously enjoyed a touch of the dramatic mixed in with elements of danger and intrigue, particularly at a safe distance.

Charlie rubbed at his left knee. "I had heard he was a cop."

"Who told you that?"

"I don't recall. Just heard it in passing."

"Well, if he was a policeman that's something that can be checked. If he was a spy, there'd be no record of it, would there?"

"So he never talked to anyone here about his past?"

"Only in vague terms. That's probably why you heard he was a policeman. People hear bits and pieces, they start to fill in the holes themselves."

"Well, son of a gun." Charlie sat back, trying hard to appear calm.

"Still, he's an exceptional builder. He'll do good work for you." Pemberton laughed. "Just so long as he doesn't start snooping around. You know if he was a spy, those habits probably die hard. I've led a pretty squeaky clean life, but everybody has skeletons in their closet, don't you think?"

Charlie cleared his throat before answering. "Some more than others."

Charlie leaned forward again, his hands clasped in front of him on the table; he was quite eager to change the subject and had the vehicle to do so. "John," Charlie's voice dipped low, "John, I've got a small favor to ask of you."

Pemberton's smile broadened. "Just ask it, Charlie. And consider it done."

"A man came by the house the other day asking for a donation to a charitable foundation he said he headed."

Pemberton looked startled. "What was his name?"

"He wasn't local," Charlie said quickly. "He gave me a name but I'm not sure it was his real one. It all seemed suspicious, you understand what I'm saying."

"Absolutely."

"Someone in Ms. Savage's position has to be careful. There are a lot of scams out there."

"Don't I know it. How upsetting."

"Right. Well, anyway, the guy said he was staying in the area for a while. Asked for a follow-up meeting with Ms. Savage."

"I hope you're not going to agree to that."

"I haven't yet. The guy left a phone number, but it's not a local one. I called it. It was an answering service."

"What was the name of the foundation?"

"I don't remember exactly, but it had something to do with medical research of some kind."

"That's so easy to concoct," Pemberton said knowingly. "Of course I have no personal experience with frauds like that," he added huffily, "but I understand that there is a proliferation of them."

"That was exactly my read. Well, to make a long story short, since the guy said he was going to be around awhile, I thought it probable that he was renting someplace hereabouts, instead of sacking out at a hotel. That gets to be expensive after a while, especially if you're living scam to scam."

"And you want to know if I can find out where he might be staying?"

"Exactly. I wouldn't ask it if it weren't real important. With things like this I'm never too careful. I want to know who I'm dealing with in case he shows up again."

"Of course, of course." Pemberton let out a shallow breath and sipped at his tea. "I'll certainly look into it for you. My sympathies lie with you and Ms. Savage."

"And we will be very grateful for any assistance you can give us. I've mentioned several of the other charities you head up to Ms. Savage and she spoke very positively about all of them and your work with them."

Pemberton was glowing now. "Why don't you give me a description of the man? I have the morning free and I can start my own little investigation. If he's within fifty miles of here, with my connections, I'm certain I can find him."

Charlie described the man, laid some cash on the table for the meal, and stood up. "We really appreciate it, John."

Chapter Twenty-Nine

Thomas Donovan scanned the city streets for a parking spot. Georgetown was not known for its abundance of places to leave one's vehicle. He was driving a new rental car, a late model Chrysler. He turned right from M Street onto Wisconsin Avenue, and finally managed to snag a spot on a side street not too far from where he was heading. A light rain began to fall as he walked down the street. The quiet area he soon found himself in harbored an elite neighborhood of towering brick and clapboard residences which were home to high-ranking businessmen and political types. He eyed some of the homes as he walked along. In the lights visible through intricately designed windows Donovan could make out well-dressed owners settling down in front of warm fires, coddling drinks and exchanging light kisses as they went through their rituals of relaxation after another day of perhaps changing the world, or merely adding to their already hefty investment portfolios.

So much wealth and power rested in this area that an energy seemed to wash up from the brick sidewalks and hurtle Donovan along at a furious clip. Money and power had never been overriding ambitions of his. Despite that, his occupation often placed him in close proximity to those who held the attainment of one or both of these prizes above all else. It was a wonderful position from which to play the altruistic cynic and Donovan often played that role to the fullest for the simple reason that he genuinely believed in what he did for a living. The irony of this was not lost on him. For without the rich and powerful and their evil ways, at whom would he throw his sharp-edged stones?

Donovan finally stopped at one formidable residence: a one-hundred-year-old three-story brick townhouse sitting behind a waist-high brick wall topped by black steel wrought-iron fencing of a style found throughout the area. He inserted a key into the gate's lock and went up the sidewalk. Another key allowed him entry through the massive wooden front door and he shook off his coat.

The housekeeper appeared immediately and took the wet coat from him. She wore a traditional maid's uniform and spoke with a practiced degree of deference.

"I'll tell the missus you're here, Mr. Donovan."

He nodded quickly and moved past her into the drawing room where he took a moment to warm himself before the blazing fire and then looked around with contentment. His upbringing had been decidedly blue collar but he did not attempt to hide his pleasure at occasionally dabbling in luxury. It was an incongruity in his nature that had bothered him greatly in his youth, but much less so now. Some things did become better as one aged, he mused, including layers of personal guilt that one ended up shedding like peeling an onion.

By the time he had mixed himself a drink from the stock housed behind a cabinet in one corner of the drawing room, the woman had appeared.

She moved quickly to him and gave him a deep kiss. He took her hand and caressed it lightly.

"I missed you," she said.

He led her over to the large sofa against one wall. Their knees touched as they sat close together.

Alicia Crane was petite, in her mid-thirties, with long hair that was looking more ash than blond with each passing day. Her dress was costly and the jewelry clinging to her wrists and ears easily matched the richness of the garment; however, the image was one of quiet wealth and sophistication. Her features were delicate, the nose so small as to be barely noticeable between the deep luster of the dark brown eyes. While she was not a traditional beauty, her obvious wealth and refinement had inspired a certain look that was pleasant enough. On her best days she would be described as very well put together.

Her cheek trembled slightly as he stroked it.

"I missed you too, Alicia. A lot."

"I don't like it when you have to be away." Her voice was cultured and dignified, its cadence slow and exact. It was a voice seemingly too formal for a relatively young woman.

"Well, it's part of the job." He smiled at her. "But you're making that job a lot more difficult to do." He *was* attracted to Alicia Crane. While not the brightest star in the universe, she was a good person, without the pretenses and airs that her level of wealth usually stamped on its possessors.

With a start, she stared. "Why in the world did you shave off your beard?"

Donovan rubbed his hand across the smooth skin. "Change of pace," he said quickly. "You know men go through their own form of menopause. I think it took about ten years off the mug. What do you think?"

"I think you're just as handsome without it as you were with it. In fact, you remind me a little of Father. When he was a younger man, of course."

"Thanks for lying to an *old* man." He smiled. "But being compared to him, well that's high praise."

"I can have Maggie put on some supper. You must be starved." She gripped his hand with both of hers.

"Thank you, Alicia. And maybe a hot bath after that."

"Of course, the rain is so chilling this time of year." She hesitated for a moment. "Will you have to leave again soon? I was thinking we could go down to the islands. It's so beautiful this time of year."

"That sounds wonderful, but I'm afraid it'll have to keep. I have to leave tomorrow."

Her disappointment shone through on her face before her gaze dropped. "Oh, I see."

He tucked one hand under her chin and stared into her eyes. "Alicia, I had a breakthrough today. A breakthrough that I wasn't sure would happen. It was a risk on my part, but sometimes you have to take risks if you want the payoff." He remembered from that morning, the haunted look in LuAnn Tyler's eyes. "All that sniffing around, never sure if anything's going to turn up. But that's all part of the game."

"That's wonderful, Thomas, I'm so happy for you. But I hope you didn't place yourself in personal danger. I don't know what I would do if anything happened to you."

He sat back as he contemplated his daredevil morning. "I can take care of myself. But I don't take unnecessary risks. I leave that for the kiddies coming up." His voice was calming.

He glanced over at her; the look on her face was that of a child listening to her favorite hero recount a past adventure. Donovan finished his drink. A hero. He liked the feeling. Who wouldn't? Who didn't need that kind of un-adulterated admiration every now and then? He smiled deeply and gripped Alicia's small hand in his.

"I promise you something. After I break this story, we're going to take a long vacation. Just you and me. Someplace warm, with plenty to drink, and I can dust off my talents as a sailor. I haven't done that in a long time and I can't think of anyone I'd rather do it with. How's that sound?"

She laid her head against his shoulder and squeezed his hand tightly. "Wonderful."

Chapter Thirty

"You invited him for lunch?" Charlie stared at LuAnn with a mixture of anger and frustration on his grizzled face. "Would you mind telling me why you did that? And would you mind telling me why the hell you went there in the first place?"

They were in Charlie's office. LuAnn stood next to the bulky desk while Charlie sat in front of it. He had unwrapped a thick cigar and was about to light it when LuAnn had delivered the news of her excursion that morning.

Defiance was all over LuAnn's features as she scowled back at him. "I couldn't just sit around and do nothing."

"I told you I was going to handle it. What, you don't trust my judgment anymore?"

"Of course I do, Charlie, it's not that." LuAnn dropped her defiant stance, perched on the edge of his chair and ran her fingers through his thinning hair. "I figured if I could get to Riggs before he had a chance to do anything, apologize and then get him to drop it, we'd be free and clear."

Charlie shook his head, wincing as a small pain worked at his left temple. He took a deep breath and put an arm around her waist. "LuAnn, I had a very informative conversation with John Pemberton this morning."

"Who?"

"Real estate agent. Guy who sold us the house. That's not important. What is relevant is the fact that Pemberton knows everybody and everything that goes on in this town. He's trying to track down the guy in the Honda for us right now."

LuAnn jerked back. "You didn't tell him —"

"I concocted a cover story and fed it to him. He slurped it up like it was the sweetest ice cream in the world. We both have gotten real good with making up stuff over the years, haven't we?"

"Sometimes too good," LuAnn said gloomily. "It's getting harder and harder to remember what's true and what's not."

"I also talked to Pemberton about Riggs. Trying to get some of the guy's history out, to try and get a feel for the guy."

"He's not a cop. I asked him and he said he wasn't. You said he was."

"I know, a screw-up on my part, but Riggs led me to believe he was."

"So what the heck was he? And why all the secrecy?"

"A funny question coming from you." LuAnn jabbed an elbow playfully into Charlie's side. Her smile disappeared with Charlie's next words. "Pemberton thinks Riggs was a government spy."

"A spy? Like the CIA?"

"Who the hell knows. It's not like the guy's gonna advertise what outfit he was with. Nobody really knows for sure. His background is kind of a blur as far as Pemberton can tell."

LuAnn shuddered, remembering the info Riggs had gathered on her so quickly. Now it perhaps made sense. But she was still unconvinced. "And now he builds fences in rural Virginia. I didn't think they ever let spies retire."

"You've been watching too many mob movies. Even spies change jobs or retire, especially with the Cold War ending. And there are a lot of specialties in intelligence gathering. Not all of them involve trench coats, pistols up the sleeve, and assassination plots against foreign dictators. He could've been just some schlep working in an office looking at aerial photos of Moscow."

LuAnn recalled her meeting with Riggs at his home. The way he had handled the shotgun, his observation skills and his knowledge of firearms. And finally his confident and cool demeanor. She shook her head firmly. "He doesn't strike me as the office type."

Charlie sighed deeply. "Me either. So how did it go?"

LuAnn stood back up and leaned against the doorjamb, her fingers hooked through the belt loops on the jeans she had changed into. "He had already dug up some info on me and the Honda. The cover stuff came up on me, so we're okay there."

"Anything on the Honda?"

LuAnn shook her head. "Rental up in D.C. Name looked phony. Probably a dead-end."

"Riggs moves fast. How'd you find that out?"

"I did a little snooping around his office. When he caught me he was holding a shot-gun."

"Good gosh, LuAnn, if the guy was a spy you're lucky he didn't blow your head off."

"It didn't seem so risky while I was doing it. It turned out all right anyway."

"You and your risk-taking. Like going to the drawing that night in New York. I should really start putting my foot down around here. What else?"

"I admitted to him that the car chase was something we were concerned about and that we were handling it."

"And he accepted that? No questions?" Charlie's tone was skeptical.

"I was telling the truth, Charlie," she said heatedly. "I get kind of tingling all over when the rare occasion happens along that I can do that."

"Okay, okay. I didn't mean to put a stick in your spokes. God, we sound like an old married couple here."

LuAnn smiled. "We *are* an old married couple. We just have a few more secrets to share than most."

Charlie flashed her a quick grin and took a moment to light his cigar. "So you really think Riggs is okay? He won't keep nosing around?"

"I think he's very curious, and he should be. But he told me he wasn't going to pursue it and I believe him. I'm not exactly sure why, but I do. There doesn't appear to be much B.S. in the man."

"And him coming over for lunch tomorrow? I take it you want to get to know him a little better."

LuAnn studied Charlie's face for a moment. Was there a touch of jealousy there? She shrugged her shoulders. "Well, it's a way to keep an eye on him, and maybe learn a little more about him. Maybe he's got some secrets, too. It certainly sounds like it, anyway."

Charlie puffed on his cigar. "So if things are cool with Riggs then we got only the guy in the Honda to worry about."

"Isn't that enough?"

"It's better than two headaches at one time. If Pemberton can trace him maybe we have clear sailing."

LuAnn looked nervously at him. "If he finds him, what are you going to do?"

"I've been thinking about that. I think I've decided to play straight with the man, call his hand and see what the hell he wants. If it's

378

money, maybe we see what we can work out."

"And if it's not just money he wants?" She had difficulty getting the next part out. "What if he knows about the lottery?"

Charlie took the cigar from his mouth and stared at her.

"I can't see how he could. But in the billion to one chance he does, there are a lot of other places in the world we can live, LuAnn. We could be gone tomorrow if need be."

"On the run again," she said, her tone bone-tired.

"Consider the alternative. It's not pleasant."

She reached out and plucked the cigar from between his fingers. Clenching it between her teeth, she drew the smoke in and then let it slowly out. She handed it back to him.

"When is Pemberton supposed to get back to you?"

"No set time. Could be tonight, could be next week."

"Let me know when you hear from him."

"You'll be the first to know, milady."

She turned to leave.

"Oh, am I invited to this lunch tomorrow?" he asked.

She glanced back. "I was kind of counting on it, Charlie." She smiled prettily and left. He stood up and watched her glide gracefully down the hallway. Then he closed the door to his study and sat down at his desk puffing thoughtfully on his stogie.

Riggs had put on a pair of chino pants, and the collar of his button-down shirt peeked out from under his patterned sweater. He had driven over in a Jeep Cherokee he had borrowed while his pickup truck was in the shop having its bumper repaired. The Jeep seemed more fitting to the affluent surroundings than his battered truck anyway. He smoothed down his freshly washed hair before climbing out of the Cherokee and walking up the steps of the mansion. These days he didn't usually dress up, except for the occasional social event he attended in town. He had finally decided a jacket and dress slacks was too pretentious. It was only lunch after all. And who knew? The lady of the house might ask him to do some on-site work.

The door was answered by the maid who escorted Riggs to the library. Riggs wondered if he had been watched as he had pulled up in the circle. Maybe there were video cameras trained on that area as well, with Catherine Savage and her sidekick Charlie sitting in some observation room crammed floor to ceiling with TV monitors.

He looked around the spacious area and noted with due respect the numerous volumes lining the walls. He wondered if they were for show only. He had been in places where that was the case. Somehow he didn't think that was true here. His attention fell upon the photos lining the fireplace mantel. There were ones there of Charlie and a little girl who strongly resembled Catherine Savage, but none of Catherine Savage. That seemed odd, but the woman was odd, so there was some semblance of consistency there.

He turned when the double doors to the library opened. His first real encounter with the woman, in his reconfigured hayloft, had not prepared him for his second.

The golden hair tumbled down the stylishly flared shoulders of a black one-piece dress that ended at her bare calves and didn't miss any contour of her long, curvy body along the way. It struck him that on her the garment would have seemed equally appropriate at a state fair or a White House dinner. She wore matching black low heel shoes. The image of a sleek, muscular panther gliding toward him held fast in his mind. After giving it some thought, Riggs had decided that the woman's beauty was undeniable, but wasn't perfect. After all, whose was? And another remarkable detail now emerged: While there were fine lines beginning to carve themselves around her eyes, Riggs noticed the almost complete absence of lines around her mouth, as though she had never smiled.

Curiously, the small scar on her jaw considerably heightened her attraction, he felt. Perhaps by silently forging a layer of danger, of adventure into her past?

"I'm glad you could make it," she said, moving briskly forward and extending a hand, which Riggs shook. He was again amazed at the strength he felt in that grip; her long fingers seemed to swallow his big, callused hand. "I know contractors have numerous emergencies during the day. Your time is never your own."

Riggs eyed the walls and ceilings of the library. "I heard about some of the renovations you had done here. I don't care how good the G.C. is, something this complex, things get out of whack every now and then."

"Charlie handled all of that. But I think things went fairly smoothly. I'm certainly pleased with the end product."

"I could see that."

"Lunch will be ready in a few minutes. Sally is setting it up in the rear verandah. The dining room seats about fifty and I thought it might be a little overwhelming for three. Would you like something to drink beforehand?"

"I'm okay." He pointed at the photos. "Is that your daughter? Or younger sister?"

She blushed and then followed his gesture, but settled herself on the couch before answering. "My daughter, Lisa. She's ten years old. I can't believe that, the years go by so quickly."

Riggs looked her over in an unassuming manner. "You must have had her very young then."

"Younger than I probably should have, but I wouldn't give her back for anything in the world. Do you have children?"

Riggs shook his head quickly and looked down at his hands. "Never been that lucky."

LuAnn had noted the absence of a wedding ring, although some men never wore them. She assumed a man who worked with his hands all day might not wear it simply for safety reasons.

"Your wife —"

"I'm divorced," he interjected. "Almost four years now." He put his hands in his pockets and again ran his eye around the room. He could sense her following the path of his observations. "You?" he asked, settling his eyes back upon her.

"Widowed."

"I'm sorry."

She shrugged. "It was a long time ago," she said simply. There was a ring in her voice that told Riggs the years had not managed to diminish the impact of the loss.

"Ms. Savage —"

"Please, call me Catherine." She smiled impishly. "All my close friends do."

He smiled back and sat down next to her. "So where's Charlie?"

"He's out running some errands. He'll be joining us for lunch though."

"So he's your uncle?"

LuAnn nodded. "His wife passed on years ago. Both my parents are dead. We're really all the family left."

"I take it your late husband did very well for himself. Or maybe you did. I don't want to sound politically incorrect." Riggs grinned suddenly. "Either that, or one of you won the lottery."

LuAnn's hand tightened perceptibly on the edge of the couch. "My husband was a brilliant businessman who obviously left me very well-off." She managed to say this with a casual air.

"He sure did," Riggs agreed.

"And you? Have you lived here all your life?"

"Gee, after my visit here yesterday I thought you would have checked out my background thoroughly."

"I'm afraid I don't have quite the level of sources you obviously do. I didn't think builders had such an information network." Her eyes remained fixed on his.

"I moved here about five years ago. Apprenticed with a local builder who taught me the trade. He died about three years ago and that's when I set up my own shop."

"Five years. So your wife lived here with you for a year."

Riggs shook his head. "The divorce was *final* four years ago, but we had been separated for about fourteen months. She's still up in D.C. Probably always will be."

"Is she in politics?"

"Attorney. Big partner, at a big firm. She

has some politically connected clients. She's very successful."

"She must be good then. That's still very much a man's world. Like a lot of other ones."

Riggs shrugged. "She's smart, a great business-getter. I think that's why we broke up. The marriage thing got in the way."

"I see."

"Not what you'd call an original story, but it's the only one I have. I moved down here and never looked back."

"I take it you like what you do."

"It can be a hassle sometimes, just like any job. But I like putting things together. It's therapeutic. And peaceful. I've been lucky, got some good word of mouth and the business has been steady. As you probably know, there's a lot of money in this area. Even before you came."

"So I understand. I'm glad your career change has worked out."

He sat back while he digested her words, his lips pursed, his hands balled up into fists, but not in a threatening way.

He chuckled. "Let me guess, you heard that I was either a CIA operative or an international assassin who abruptly decided to chuck all that and take up hammering and sawing in more placid surroundings."

"Actually, I hadn't heard the assassin angle."

They exchanged brief smiles.

"You know if you just told people the truth, they'd stop speculating." She couldn't believe she had just made that statement, but there it was. She looked at him with what she hoped was an air of complete innocence.

"You're assuming that I care if people speculate about me. I don't."

"That's beneath you, I take it."

"If I've learned anything in life, it's that you don't worry about what other people think or say. You worry about yourself and that's good enough. Otherwise you're setting yourself up to be a basket case. People can be cruel. Especially people who supposedly cared about you. Believe me, I speak from experience."

"I take it the divorce wasn't exactly amicable?"

He didn't look at her when he spoke. "I'm not taking anything away from you, but sometimes losing a spouse isn't as traumatic or painful as going through a divorce. They each have their own degrees of hurt, I guess."

He looked down at his hands. There was a definite ring of sincerity in his words and LuAnn felt instant guilt that she in fact had not been widowed, at least not by the falsehood of losing a wealthy husband. It was as though he were baring his wounds in return for LuAnn baring hers. As usual, it was all lies on her part. Could she even speak the truth anymore? In fact how could she? Speaking the truth would destroy her, all the lies would immediately fall to earth like those old buildings demolished by explosives that caused them to implode.

"I can understand that," she said.

Riggs didn't appear inclined to continue.

LuAnn finally looked at her watch. "Lunch should be just about ready. I thought after we eat you could look at a site at the rear grounds where I'm thinking of having you build a small studio." She stood up and Riggs did too. He appeared immeasurably relieved that this particular conversation was over.

"That sounds good, Catherine. In my business, work is always welcome."

As they walked to the rear of the house, Charlie joined them. The two men shook hands. "Glad to see you again, Matt. I hope you're hungry. Sally usually puts out a good spread."

Lunch was devoted to enjoying the food and drink and discussing innocuous subjects of local interest. However, there was an energy between Charlie and Catherine Savage that was unmistakable to Riggs. A strong bond, he concluded. Unbreakable, in fact. They were family, after all.

"So what're we looking at timewise on the fence, Matt?" Charlie asked. He and Riggs were on the rear terrace overlooking the grounds. Lunch was over and LuAnn had gone to pick up Lisa. School had ended early because of a scheduled teacher workshop. She had asked Riggs to remain until she returned so they could talk about the studio construction. Riggs wondered if her going to get Lisa had been a deliberate maneuver to leave Charlie behind to pump him for information. Whatever the reason, he remained on guard.

Before Riggs had a chance to answer him about the fence, Charlie extended a cigar. "You smoke these things?"

Riggs took it. "After a meal like that, and a gorgeous day like this, even if I didn't, I'd be tempted." He snipped off the end with a cutter Charlie handed him and they took a moment to get their respective smokes going.

"I figure a week to dig all the postholes. Two weeks clearing land, and assembling and installing the fencing. That includes pouring the cement for the posts. Another week to install the gate and security systems. One month total. That's about what I estimated in the contract."

Charlie looked him over. "I know, but sometimes what you put on paper doesn't work exactly that way in reality."

"That pretty much sums up the construction business," Riggs agreed. He puffed on his cigar. "But we'll get in before the frost, and the lay of the land isn't as bad as I originally thought." He paused and eyed Charlie. "After yesterday, I wish I could have that sucker in today. I'm sure you do too."

It was an open invitation for discussion and Charlie didn't disappoint Riggs. "Have a seat, Matt." Charlie indicated a pair of white wrought-iron chairs next to the balustrade. Charlie sat down gingerly. "God these suckers are uncomfortable as hell, and for what they cost you'd think they were made out of gold. I'm thinking the interior designer we used must've gotten some kind of kickback on them." He smoked his cigar while he looked over the landscape. "Damn, it's beautiful here."

Riggs followed his gaze. "It's one reason I came here. A big reason."

"What were the other reasons?" Charlie grinned at him. "I'm just kidding. That's *your* business." The emphasis on the word was not lost on Riggs. Charlie wriggled in the seat until he managed to find a semicomfortable position. "Catherine told me about your little discussion yesterday."

"I assumed she would. She shouldn't go sneaking around people's houses, though. That's not always a healthy thing to do."

"That's exactly what I told her. I know it might be hard to see, but she's rather headstrong."

The two men exchanged knowing chuckles.

"I do appreciate your agreeing not to pursue it," Charlie said.

"I told her so long as the guy didn't bother me, I wouldn't bother him."

"Fair enough. I'm sure you can see that with all of Catherine's wealth, she's a target for a variety of scams, hustles, or downright threats. We have Lisa to worry about too. We keep a real close eye on her."

"You sound like you speak from experience."

"I do. This isn't the first time. And it won't be the last. But you can't let it get to you. I mean Catherine could buy a deserted island somewhere and make it impossible for anyone to reach her, but what kind of life would that be? For her or Lisa?"

"And you. It's not like you're tapping on the grave, Charlie. You look like you could suit up for the Redskins on Sunday."

Charlie beamed at the compliment. "I actually played some semipro ball way back when. And I take care of myself. And Catherine nags me about my diet. I think she lets me smoke these things out of pity." He held up the cigar. "Although lately I'm feeling old beyond my years. But yeah, I don't want to live on a deserted island."

"So any luck finding the guy in the Honda?" Riggs asked.

"I'm working on it. Got some inquiries going."

"Don't take offense at this, but if you find him, what do you plan on doing about it?"

Charlie looked over at him. "What would you do?"

390

"Depends on his intentions."

"Exactly. So until I find him and determine what his intentions are, I don't know what I'm going to do." There was a slight trace of hostility in Charlie's tone that Riggs chose to ignore. He looked back over the countryside.

"Catherine says she wants to put up an outdoor studio. Do you know where?"

Charlie shook his head. "I really haven't discussed it with her. I think it was a recent impulse on her part."

Riggs again looked over at him. Had that been a conscious slip on his part? It was as though Charlie were telling him point-blank that the potential new piece of business was the payoff for Riggs keeping his mouth shut. Or was there another reason?

"What would she be using it for, the studio?"

Charlie glanced at him. "Does it matter?"

"Actually it does. If it's an art studio, I'd make sure there was sufficient lighting, maybe put in some skylights, and a ventilation system to carry the paint fumes out. If she just wants to use it to get away, read or sleep, I'd configure it differently."

Charlie nodded thoughtfully. "I see. Well, I don't know what she plans to use it for. But she doesn't paint, that I know."

The men fell silent until that silence was interrupted by the sounds of LuAnn and Lisa approaching. The door to the terrace opened and the pair came out.

In person, Lisa Savage resembled her mother even more than in the photo. They both walked the same way, easy glides, no wasted energy.

"This is Mr. Riggs, Lisa."

Riggs had not been around many children in his life, but he did what came naturally. He put out his hand. "Call me Matt, Lisa. Pleased to meet you."

She smiled and squeezed his hand in return. "Pleased to meet you, Matt."

"That's quite a grip." He glanced up at LuAnn and then Charlie. "That particular attribute must run in the family. If I keep coming over here I might have to start wearing a steel glove."

Lisa smiled.

"Matthew is going to build a studio for me, Lisa. Out there somewhere." She pointed toward the rear grounds.

Lisa looked up at the house in undisguised wonderment. "Isn't our house big enough?"

All the adults burst into laughter at that one and finally Lisa joined in too.

"What's the studio for?" Lisa asked.

"Well, maybe it'll be kind of a surprise. In fact, I might let you use it too, sometimes."

Lisa grinned broadly at the news.

"But only if you keep your grades up," said Charlie. "By the way, how'd your test go?" Charlie's tone was gruff, but it clearly was all a facade. It was obvious to Riggs that the old guy loved Lisa as much as he did her mother, if not more.

Lisa's mouth dropped into a pout. "I didn't get an A."

"That's okay, sweetie," Charlie said kindly. "Probably my fault. I'm not all that good with math."

Lisa suddenly broke into a big smile. "I got an A plus."

Charlie playfully cuffed her head. "You got your mother's sense of humor, that's for sure."

LuAnn said, "Miss Sally has some lunch ready for you. I know you didn't get a chance to eat at school. Run along and I'll see you after I finish up with Matthew."

LuAnn and Riggs walked through the rear grounds. Charlie had begged off. He had some things to do, he had said.

After Riggs had walked the property he pointed to a clearing that was level, had an unobstructed view of the distant mountains, but still had shade trees on two sides. "That looks like a nice spot. Actually, with this much land, you probably have a number of potential locations. By the way, if I knew what you were going to use the place for I could make a more informed choice for the site." He looked around. "And you have a number of outbuildings already. Another option would be to convert one of those into a studio."

"I'm sorry, I thought I was clear on that. I

want it done from scratch. None of the other buildings would really do. I want it set up like yours. Two stories. The first floor could be set up as a workshop for some of my hobbies, that is, when I get around to having some hobbies. Lisa is into drawing and she's getting pretty good. Maybe I could take up sculpting. That seems like a very relaxing pastime. On the second level I want a wood-stove, a telescope, comfortable furniture, built-in bookcases, maybe a small kitchen, bay windows."

Riggs nodded and looked around. "I saw the pool area. Are you planning on a pool-house and maybe tennis courts?"

"Next spring. Why?"

"I was just thinking that we might want to tie those and the studio into an overall plan. You know, use the same materials or some combo thereof with the poolhouse and the studio."

LuAnn shook her head. "No, I want it sepa-rate. We'll put in a large gazebo for outdoor entertaining and all that. It'll be mostly Lisa using the pool and tennis courts. I want those facilities closer to the main house. The pool is already close. The studio I want farther away. Sort of hidden."

"That's fine. You certainly have the land." He checked out the slope of the property. "So do you swim or play tennis?"

"I can swim like a fish, but I've never played

tennis and I really don't have any desire to start."

"I thought all rich people played tennis. That and golf."

"Maybe if you're born with money. I haven't always been wealthy."

"Georgia."

LuAnn looked sharply at him. "What?"

"I've been trying to place your accent. Lisa's is all over the place. Yours is very faint, but it's still there. I'd guess you spent a lot of years in Europe, but you know what they say, you can take the girl out of Georgia but you can't take Georgia out of the girl."

LuAnn hesitated for a moment before replying. "I've never been to Georgia."

"I'm surprised. I'm usually pretty good at gauging that."

"Nobody's perfect." She flicked her hair out of her eyes. "So what do you think?" She looked at the clearing.

Riggs stared at her curiously for a moment before answering. "We'll have to draw up plans. They'll help you get it exactly the way you want, although it sounds like you have a pretty good idea already. Depending on the size and complexity, it could take anywhere from two to six months."

"When could you start?"

"Not any time this year, Catherine."

"You're that busy?"

"It's got nothing to do with that. No sane

builder would start on a project like that now. We need architectural plans and we also need to get building permits. The ground will be freezing soon and I don't like to pour footers after that. And we wouldn't be able to get it framed and under roof before winter set in. Weather can get real nasty up here. This is definitely a next spring project."

"Oh." LuAnn sounded deeply disappointed. She stared off at the site as though she were seeing her hideaway fully completed.

Trying to make her feel better Riggs said, "Spring will be here before you know it, Catherine. And the winter will allow us to work up a really good set of plans. I know a first-rate architect. I can set up a meeting."

LuAnn was hardly listening. Would they even be here next spring? Riggs's news about the construction schedule had dissipated much of her enthusiasm for the project.

"I'll see. Thanks."

As they walked back to the house Riggs touched her shoulder. "I take it you're not into delayed gratification. If I could put it up for you right now, I would. Some sleazy builders might take on the job and charge you a healthy premium and then proceed to turn out a piece of crap that'll fall down in a year or two. But I take pride in my work and I want to deliver a quality job for you."

She smiled at him. "Charlie said you had

excellent references. I guess I can see why."

They were passing by the horse barn. LuAnn pointed at it and said, "I guess that counts as a hobby. You ride?"

"I'm no expert, but I won't fall off either."

"We should go for a ride sometime. There are some beautiful trails around here."

"I know," was Riggs's surprising reply. "I used to walk them before this property was sold. You made an excellent choice in real estate, by the way."

"Charlie found it."

"He's a good person to have around."

"He makes my life a lot easier. I don't know what I'd do without him."

"Nice to have somebody like that in your life."

She cast a furtive glance at him as they continued back to the house.

Chapter Thirty-One

Charlie met them at the rear entrance. There was a suppressed excitement in his manner, and the darting glances he gave LuAnn told her the reason: Pemberton had found where the man in the Honda was staying.

While not showing it, Riggs picked up on the subtle undercurrents.

"Thanks for the lunch," he said. "I'm sure you've got things to do and I've got some appointments to take care of this afternoon." He looked over at LuAnn. "Catherine, let me know about the studio."

"I will. Call me about going for a ride."

"I'll do that."

After he left, Charlie and LuAnn went into Charlie's study and closed the door.

"Where is the guy?" she asked.

"He's our neighbor."

"What?"

"A little rental cottage. Pretty isolated. It's not more than four miles from here up Highway Twenty-two. I looked at some land up near there when we were thinking of building. Used to be a big estate up there but now there's just the caretaker's cottage. Remember, we took a drive up there a while back?"

"I remember exactly. You could walk or ride it through the back trails. I've done it. The guy could have been spying on us for a while."

"I know. That's what worries me. Pemberton gave me exact directions to the place." Charlie laid the paper with the directions down on his desk while he pulled on his coat.

LuAnn took the opportunity to scan surreptitiously the directions and commit them to memory.

Charlie unlocked a drawer of his desk. LuAnn's eyes widened as she watched him pull out the .38. He proceeded to load it.

"What are you going to do?" she said fiercely.

He didn't look at her as he checked the safety and put the gun in his pocket. "Like we planned, I'm going to go check it out."

"I'm going with you."

He looked at her angrily. "The hell you are."

"Charlie, I am."

"What if there's trouble?"

"You're saying that to me?"

"You know what I mean. Let me check it out first, see what the guy's up to. I'm not going to do anything dangerous."

"So why the gun?"

"I said *I'm* not going to do anything dangerous. I don't know about him."

"I don't like it, Charlie."

"You think I do? I'm telling you, it's the only way. Something happens, the last thing

I want is you in the middle of it."

"I've never expected you to fight my battles for me."

He touched her cheek gently. "You're not exactly twisting my arm here. I want you and Lisa to be safe and sound. In case you hadn't noticed, I've kind of made that my life's work. By choice." He smiled.

She watched him open the door and start to head out. "Charlie, please be careful."

He looked back, noting the worry in her features.

"LuAnn, you know I'm always careful."

As soon as he left, LuAnn went to her room, changed into jeans and a warm shirt, and pulled on sturdy boots.

In case you hadn't noticed, Charlie, my *life's work is to make sure* you and Lisa *are safe and sound.*

She grabbed a leather jacket from her closet and raced out of the house in the direction of the horse barn. She saddled Joy and then galloped off toward the maze of trails behind the mansion.

As soon as Charlie hit the main road, Riggs started to follow from a safe distance in the Cherokee. Riggs had thought it a fifty-fifty possibility that something was going to happen as soon as he left. A friend of Riggs had mentioned seeing Pemberton and Charlie having breakfast the day before. That was smart on

Charlie's part, and indeed, was probably the path Riggs would have taken to track down the man in the Honda. That and Charlie's excited manner had been enough to convince Riggs that something was up. If he had been wrong, he wouldn't have wasted much time. He kept the Range Rover just in sight as it turned north onto Highway 22. It wasn't easy being invisible on the rural road, but Riggs was confident he could manage it. On the seat next to him was his shotgun. This time he would be prepared.

Charlie glanced to the right and left as he pulled the Range Rover underneath the cover of trees and then stopped. He could see the cottage up ahead. He might have wondered who would have built the place in the middle of nowhere, but Pemberton had informed him that the house had been a caretaker's cottage for a vast estate that was no longer in existence. Ironic that the tiny structure had outlived the main house. He gripped the pistol in his pocket and got out. Threading his way through the thick trees behind the cottage, he made his first stop the shed. Rubbing away the dirt and grime on the window he was able barely to make out the black Honda inside. For this, he and LuAnn owed Pemberton a nice little donation to a charity of his choice.

Charlie waited about another ten minutes, his gaze glued to the small cottage, looking for any movement, any shadows falling across the windows. The place appeared unoccupied but the car in the shed belied that appearance. Charlie moved forward cautiously.

He glanced around but did not notice Riggs crouched behind a stand of thick holly bushes to the left of the house.

Riggs lowered his binoculars and surveyed the area. Like Charlie, he had detected no movement or sound coming from the cottage but that didn't mean anything. The guy could be in there just waiting for Charlie to put in an appearance. Shoot first and ask questions later. Riggs gripped his shotgun and waited.

The front door was locked. Charlie could have smashed a glass pane next to the door and unlocked the door from the inside, or simply kicked the door until it tore loose from the doorjamb — it didn't look all that sturdy. However, if the house was indeed occupied, knocking down the door might prompt a deadly response. And, if it wasn't occupied, he didn't want to leave any evidence that he had been to the cottage. Charlie knocked on the door, his pistol half out of his pocket. He waited and knocked again. There was no answer. He slid the gun back in his pocket and looked at the lock, a common pin tumbler, to his expert eye. He pulled out two items from his inner coat pocket: a straight pick and a tension tool. Fortunately, arthritis had not yet

402

set into his fingers or he would not have had the dexterity needed to pick the lock. He first slid the pick into the keyhole and then eased the tension tool underneath the pick. Using the pick, Charlie raised the tumbler pins to their open position, and the constant pressure from the tension tool kept the tumbler pins open. Charlie manipulated the pick, sensing the subtle vibrations of the pins until he was rewarded with a click. He turned the doorknob and the door swung open. He replaced his tools in his coat. His State Pen degree had once again worked its magic. All the while he listened intently. He was well aware that a trap could be awaiting him. His hand closed around the .38. If the guy gave Charlie the opportunity to use it he would. The ramifications of such an act were too numerous to analyze; however, at least a few of them would be better than outright exposure.

The cottage's interior was of a simple configuration. The hallway ran from front to back, splitting the space into roughly equivalent halves. The kitchen was in the back on the left; the small dining room fronted that. On his right was an equally modest living room. Tacked on to the rear of that was a combination mud room/laundry room. Plain wooden stairs on the right made their way to the bedrooms on the second floor. Charlie observed little of this, because his attention was riveted on the dining room. He stared in amazement at the computer, printer, fax, and stacks of file boxes. He moved closer as his eyes swept to the bulletin board with all the news clippings and photos affixed to it.

He mouthed the headlines. LuAnn's face was prominent among the various photos. The whole story was there: the murders, LuAnn winning the lottery, her disappearance. Well, that had confirmed his suspicions. Now it remained to discover who the man was and, more important, what he wanted from them.

He made his way around the room, carefully lifting papers here and there, studying the clippings, examining the file boxes. His eyes diligently searched for anything that would identify the man; however, there was nothing. Whoever was pursuing them knew what he was doing.

Charlie moved to the desk and carefully slid open a drawer. The papers in there yielded nothing new. He tried the other drawers with similar results. For a moment he thought about turning on the computer but his skills with that technology were about nil. He was about to begin a search of the rest of the house when a solitary box in the far corner caught his eye. He might as well hit that too, he figured.

Lifting off the top, Charlie's eyes immediately started to twitch uncontrollably. The word "shit" passed almost silently from between his lips and his legs made a serious threat of giving out on him.

A single piece of paper stared back at him. The names were listed neatly on it. LuAnn's name was there. Most of the remaining names represented people Charlie was also familiar with: Herman Rudy, Wanda Tripp, Randy Stith, Bobbie Jo Reynolds among others. All past lottery winners. Most of them Charlie had personally escorted, like LuAnn. All of them, he knew, had won their fortunes with Jackson's help.

Charlie steadied himself by placing a shaking hand on top of the windowsill. He had been prepared to find evidence of the man knowing all about the murders and LuAnn's involvement. He had not been at all prepared to learn that the lottery scam had been uncovered. The hairs on his forearms felt like they had suddenly been electrified.

How? How could the guy have found out? Who the hell was he? He quickly put the boxtop back, turned, and headed out the door. He made sure it was locked before shutting it. He swiftly retraced his steps to the Range Rover, climbed in, and drove off.

Donovan headed down Route 29. He had been on the road the better part of two hours on his return trip from Washington and he was anxious to get back on the hunt. He sped up as he neared his final destination. On the drive down, he had thought of the next steps he would employ against LuAnn Tyler. Steps designed to make her cave in and do so quickly. If one approach failed, he would find another. The saving grace in all of this — a look of deep satisfaction came to his features as he thought of it — was that he had LuAnn Tyler over a barrel. The oft-quoted phrase was quite true: A chain was only as strong as its weakest link. And LuAnn, you are that rusty link, he said to himself. And you're not going to get away. He checked his watch. He would be at the cottage shortly. On the seat next to him was a small-caliber pistol. He didn't like guns, but he wasn't stupid either.

Chapter Thirty-Two

As Riggs watched Charlie drive off he caught only a glimpse of the man's face. However, it was enough to tell him that something was up. And that what was up was all bad. After the Range Rover disappeared from his line of sight, Riggs turned around and stared at the cottage. Should he make an attempt as well to search the place? It might answer a lot of questions. He had almost decided to flip a coin when another development caused him to crouch down behind the holly tree again and return to his role of observer.

LuAnn had tethered Joy to a tree in the woods about a hundred yards from the clearing in which the cottage stood. She emerged from outside the tree line with the same graceful movements Riggs had observed in her before. She squatted down on her haunches and waited, surveying the area with quick, darting movements of her head. Despite the impenetrable bulk of the holly tree, Riggs almost felt naked before her intense gaze.

LuAnn studied the road at the same time Riggs studied her. Was she aware that Charlie had already come and gone? Probably not. However, her features gave away nothing.

LuAnn silently watched the cottage for a time before moving over to the shed. Glancing through the same window Charlie had, she looked over the Honda. Then she lifted some dirt and grime from the windowsill and covered over the small opening Charlie had made in the filth. Riggs watched this procedure with growing respect. Even he might not have thought to do that. Charlie certainly hadn't.

LuAnn turned her attention to the house. Both hands were in the pockets of her coat. She knew Charlie had been here but had already left. The smeared window had told her that. She also deduced he hadn't stayed very long because she had ridden Joy hard on the way over, and her route had been far more direct than the one Charlie had had to drive, although he had had a head start. His short stay meant he had found either nothing, or something highly incriminating. Her instincts told her that it was almost undoubtedly the latter. Should she leave and return home and let him fill her in? While that would have been the most prudent thing to do, LuAnn quickly made her way to the front porch and her hand closed around the doorknob. It didn't budge despite the immense pressure she was exerting. She had no special tools to jimmy it as Charlie had; thus she moved on, looking for another way in and finding it at the rear of the cottage. The window finally opened under her persistent tuggings and she quickly climbed inside.

She silently descended from the windowsill to the floor and immediately crouched down. From her line of sight she could make out the kitchen. She had very acute hearing, and if someone had been in the small house she was certain she would have heard his breathing no matter how shallow. She edged forward until she reached what should have been the dining room but had been set up as an office. LuAnn's eyes widened as she saw the news clippings on the bulletin board. As LuAnn's gaze swept around the room, she sensed there was something more at work here than a blackmail scheme.

"Oh, hell." Riggs ducked down after saying the words and watched in dismay as the Chrysler passed by him on the way to the cottage. The man was hunched over the steering wheel, but Riggs had no trouble recognizing him despite the beard's having been shaved off. Thinking quickly, Riggs gripped his shotgun and hurried to his Cherokee.

LuAnn flew to the back of the cottage as soon as she heard the car drive up. She raised her head a few inches above the windowsill; her heart sank. "Dammit!" She watched Donovan pull around to the rear of the cottage and climb out of the Chrysler. Her eyes were riveted on the pistol he held in his right hand. He headed straight for the rear door. LuAnn backed away, her eyes darting every which way, looking desperately for an exit. The problem was there wasn't any, at least none that would be unobserved. The front door was locked and if she attempted to open it, he would hear her. There was no time to wriggle through a window. The cottage was so small that he couldn't possibly fail to see her if she remained on the first floor.

Donovan inserted the key in the door lock. If he had glanced through the paned door window, he would have spotted LuAnn immediately. The door began to open.

LuAnn edged back into the dining room and was about to head upstairs and try for an escape from the second floor when she heard it.

The car horn was loud and shrill and the sound pattern kept repeating itself, like a car alarm that had been activated. She crept back to the window and watched as Donovan jerked to a halt, slammed the door closed, and then ran around to the front of the cottage.

LuAnn lost no time. She launched herself through the same window she had used to enter, did a roll, and came up running. She made it to the shed and crouched down. The horn was still beeping. She ran to the far side of the shed, peered around the edge, and watched as Donovan advanced down the road, away from her, toward the sound, his pistol making wide sweeps as he did so.

The hand that suddenly gripped LuAnn's shoulder almost made her scream.

"Where's your horse?" Riggs's voice was even and calm.

She looked at him, the whiplash of fear receding as quickly as it had appeared. "About a hundred yards that way." She jerked her head in the direction of the thick woods. "Is that your car alarm?"

Riggs nodded and gripped his car keys tightly. One eye on Donovan and the other on their avenue of escape, Riggs rose to his feet and pulled LuAnn up with him. "Ready, go." Bursting out from their cover they raced across the open ground. Keeping his eyes on Donovan's back, Riggs unfortunately caught his foot on a root and he went down, his finger gripping the key ring, accidentally pressing the alarm's shut-off button. Donovan whipped around and stared at them. LuAnn had Riggs up again in a moment and they raced off into the woods. Donovan lurched toward them, his pistol making broad sweeps. "Hey," he screamed. "Dammit, hold it right there." Donovan waved the gun around, but he wasn't going to shoot; he wasn't a killer.

LuAnn ran like the wind and Riggs found it impossible to keep up with her. He had slightly twisted his ankle, he told himself, but truth be known, even at full speed he probably could not have caught her. They reached Joy, who stood patiently awaiting her owner's arrival. LuAnn quickly released the tether and jumped into the saddle without even bothering to use the stirrup. She flicked out a hand and hauled Riggs up behind her. The next moment they were racing up the trail astride the fleet mare. Riggs looked back for an instant, but Donovan was nowhere in sight. They had moved so fast he wasn't surprised. Riggs gripped LuAnn's waist with both hands and hung on for dear life as she whipped Joy at a breakneck pace through the swerving trails.

They had returned Joy to the horse barn and were walking back to the main house before Riggs broke the silence. "I take it that's how you handle those kind of situations. Break into the place. See what you can find. I don't know why I should be surprised. That's what you did with me." He looked at LuAnn with angry eyes.

She matched the look. "I didn't break into your place. And I don't remember asking you to follow me."

"I followed Charlie, not you," he corrected her. "But it's a damn good thing I was there, wasn't it? Two times in two days. At this rate you'll wear out your nine lives in a week." She kept walking, her arms crossed in front of her, her eyes staring resolutely ahead. Riggs stopped.

She stopped too and looked down for an instant. When she looked up there was a far softer countenance confronting him. "Thank you. Again. But the more distance you put between the three of us and yourself, the better off you'll be, I guarantee it. Forget the fence. I don't think we'll be staying on here. Don't worry, I'll pay you for it anyway." She stared at him for a moment longer, trying to push away feelings that had been strangers to her for so long that they now simply frightened her. "Have a good life, Matthew." She turned and headed for the house.

"Catherine?" She kept walking. "Catherine," he said again.

She finally stopped.

"Would you please tell me what's going on? I might be able to help you."

"I don't think so."

"You never know."

"Believe me, I know."

She started toward the house again.

Riggs stood there staring after her. "Hey, in case you forgot, I don't have a car to get home in."

When she turned around, the key ring was already sailing through the air. Riggs caught it in the palm of his hand.

"Take my car. It's parked out front. Keep it as long as you like. I've got another one."

On that she spun back around and disappeared into the house.

Riggs slowly pocketed the keys, shaking his head in absolute frustration.

Chapter Thirty-Three

"Where the hell have you been?" Charlie came out of his study and leaned up against the doorjamb. His face was still pale, a detail LuAnn picked up on immediately.

"Same place you were," she said.

"What? LuAnn, I told you —"

"You weren't alone. Riggs followed you. In fact he managed to save me again. If he happens to do it once more, I might have to consider marrying the man."

Charlie went a shade paler. "Did he go inside the house?"

"No, but I did."

"How much did you see?" Charlie asked nervously.

LuAnn swept past him and into the office. "I don't want Lisa to hear."

Charlie closed the door behind them. He went straight over to the liquor stand and poured himself a drink. LuAnn watched his movements in silence for a moment before speaking.

"Apparently, you saw more than I did."

He turned to her and downed the drink in one motion. "The news clippings on the lottery? The murders?"

LuAnn nodded. "I saw them. After my first encounter with the man, I wasn't very surprised to see that."

"I wasn't either."

"Apparently there was more, though." She looked at him pointedly at the same time she sat down on the sofa, folding her hands in her lap and collecting her nerves as best she could.

There was a haunted look in Charlie's features, as though he had awoken from a nightmare and attempted to laugh it off, only to find out he wasn't dreaming. "I saw some names. A list of them in fact. Yours was on there." He paused and put the glass down. His hands were shaking. LuAnn braced herself. "Herman Rudy. Wanda Tripp. Randy Stith. They were on there too. I escorted them all in New York."

LuAnn slowly rested her head in her hands.

Charlie sat down beside her, put one beefy hand on her back, and slowly rubbed it.

She sat back and slumped against him; a painful weariness laced her words. "We have to go, Charlie. We have to pack up and go. Tonight."

He considered the request before running a hand across his forehead. "I've been thinking about that. We can run, like we've done before. But there's a difference now."

LuAnn's response was immediate. "He knows about the lottery fix *and* he knows LuAnn Tyler and Catherine Savage are one

416

and the same. Our cover isn't going to work anymore."

Charlie nodded glumly. "We've never been confronted with both of those before. It makes disappearing a little trickier."

She suddenly stood up and started her ritualistic pacing, moving in fluid circles around the room. "What does he want, Charlie?"

"I've been thinking about that too." He went over to the liquor stand with his empty glass, hesitated, and decided against a second round. "You saw the guy's setup. What did it look like to you?" he asked.

LuAnn stopped pacing and leaned up against the fireplace mantel. In her mind, she went through every detail of the place.

"His car was a rental, under an assumed name. So he doesn't want us to be able to trace his real identity. I didn't recognize the man, but there must be another reason he's going incognito."

"Right." Charlie studied her. Over the years, he had learned that LuAnn missed almost nothing and her instincts were first-rate.

"He tried to spook me, which he did. I take that as a warning, a message that he's a player and he wants us to be aware of that for the next time he calls."

"Go on," he encouraged.

"The place, the little I saw of it, was set up like an office. Very neat, very orderly. Computer, fax, printer, files. It was like he had made all of this some special research project."

"Well, he would've had to do a ton of research to figure out the lottery scam. Jackson is no dummy."

"How do you think he did it, Charlie?"

He rubbed his chin and sat down in front of his desk. "Well, we don't know for absolute certain that he has figured it all out. I just saw the list. That's all."

"With the names of all those lottery winners? Come on. How long did Jackson run the scam anyway?"

Charlie shook his head. "I don't know. I mean, I was there for nine of them, including you. Started in August. You were Miss April, my last gig."

LuAnn shook her head stubbornly. "He knows, Charlie; we have to assume that to be true. However he did it, he did it."

"Okay. So it seems pretty clear the guy wants money."

She shook her head. "We don't know that. I mean, why would he set up shop here and bring all that stuff with him? He didn't need to do that. He could just send me a letter from parts unknown with the same info, and a demand for money to be wire-transferred to his bank account."

Charlie sat back, his face carrying extreme confusion. He had not looked at the matter in that light. "That's true."

"And I don't think the guy's hurting for money. He was wearing really nice clothes. Two leased cars, the rent on that cottage isn't cheap, I'm thinking, and all that equipment he had. He's not digging his dinner out of garbage cans."

"Right, but unless he's already a millionaire, going after you would significantly enrich his bank account," said Charlie.

"But he hasn't done that. He hasn't asked for anything. I wish I knew why." She was lost deep in thought for a moment and then looked up. "How long did Pemberton say the cottage had been rented?"

"About a month."

"That makes it even more unlikely he was going to blackmail us. Why wait? Why come right out and warn me that he knows everything? How does he know I won't just disappear in the middle of the night? If I do that, he's not going to be filling up his bank account with my funds."

Charlie sighed deeply. "So what do we do now?"

"Wait," was finally the answer from LuAnn's lips. "But make arrangements for us to leave the country on a moment's notice. By private jet. And since he knows about Catherine Savage, we're going to need another set of identification papers. Can you get them?"

"I'll have to look up some old contacts, but I can do it. It'll take a few days."

LuAnn stood up.

"What about Riggs?" Charlie asked. "The man's not going to let it go now."

"There's nothing we can do about that. He doesn't trust us and I don't blame him."

"Well, I doubt if he'll do anything that'll end up hurting you."

She looked sharply at him. "How do you know that?"

"Look, LuAnn, it doesn't take a rocket scientist to see Riggs has a thing for you." A hint of resentment tinged his response. His tone softened, however, with his next words. "Seems like a nice guy. Under different circumstances, who knows. You shouldn't spend your life alone, LuAnn."

A flush swept over her face. "I'm not alone. I've got Lisa and I've got you. I don't need anybody else. I can't handle anybody else." She looked away. How could she invite anyone into her life? It was impossible. Half truths competing with complete falsehoods. She was no longer a real person. She was a thirty-year-old shell, period. Everything else had been bartered away. Jackson had taken the rest of it. He and his offer. If she hadn't made that call way back when. If she hadn't panicked? She wouldn't have spent ten years turning herself into the woman she always wanted to be. She wouldn't be living in a million-dollar mansion. But as ironic as it sounded, she would probably have far more of a life than she had now. Whether it was to be spent in another wrecked mobile trailer or slinging fried foods at the truck stop, LuAnn Tyler, the pauper, would probably have been happier than Catherine Savage, the princess, ever dreamt of being. But if she hadn't accepted the offer, Jackson would have had her killed. There was no way out. She turned back to Charlie and spread her arms wide.

"That's the trade-off, Charlie. For this. For all this. You, me, and Lisa."

"The Three Musketeers." Charlie attempted a smile.

"Let's pray for a happy ending." LuAnn opened the door and disappeared down the hallway in search of her daughter.

Chapter Thirty-Four

"Thank you for meeting with me on such short notice, Mr. Pemberton."

"John, please call me John, Mr. Conklin." Pemberton shook the other man's hand and they sat down at the small conference table in Pemberton's real estate office.

"I go by Harry," the other man said.

"Now you mentioned over the phone that you were interested in a house, but you really didn't say what area or price range."

Without seeming to do so, Pemberton looked Harry Conklin over. Probably in his sixties, expensive clothing, air of assurance, undoubtedly liked the good things in life. Pemberton swiftly calculated his potential commission.

"I got your name on good reference. I understand that you specialize in the upper-end market around here," Conklin said.

"That's correct. Born and raised here. Know everybody and every property worth knowing about. So would that be the price range you're interested in? The upper end?"

Conklin assumed a comfortable look. "Let me tell you a little about myself. I make my living on Wall Street and it's a damn good living if I do say so myself. But it's also a young man's game and I'm not a young man anymore. I've made my fortune and it's substantial. I've got a penthouse in Manhattan, a place in Rio, a home on Fisher Island in Florida, and a country estate outside London. But I'm looking to get out of New York and radically simplify my life. And this place is about as beautiful as they come."

"Absolutely right," Pemberton chimed in.

"Now, I do a lot of entertaining, so it would have to be a substantial place. But I want privacy as well. Something old, and elegant, but restored. I like old things, but not old plumbing, you understand me?"

"Perfectly."

"Now, I'm assuming that there are probably a number of properties around here that fit that bill."

"There are. Most assuredly," Pemberton said excitedly.

"But see, I've got one in mind. One I heard about from my father, in fact. He was in the stock market too. Back in the twenties. Made a bundle and was fortunate to get out before the crash. He used to come here and stay with a good friend of his who was in the market too. My father, God rest his soul, loved it there, and I thought it would be appropriate for his son to buy it and live in it."

"What a truly inspiring idea. Certainly makes my job easier. Do you know the name of the place?" Pemberton's smile was broadening.

"Wicken's Hunt."

Pemberton's smile quickly faded.

"Oh." He licked his lips, made a clicking sound with his tongue against his teeth. "Wicken's Hunt," he repeated, looking depressed.

"What's the matter? Did it burn down or something?"

"No, no. It's a beautiful place, wonderfully restored." Pemberton sighed deeply. "Unfortunately it's no longer on the market."

"You sure?" Conklin sounded skeptical.

"I'm certain. I was the selling agent."

"Damn, how long ago?"

"About two years, although the people have only been in it for several months. There was a lot of renovation work to do."

Conklin looked at him slyly, eyebrows cocked. "Think they might want to sell?"

Pemberton's mind raced through the possibilities. Flipping a property like that within the relatively short span of two years? What a wonderful impact on his wallet.

"Anything's possible. I've actually gotten to know them — well, one of them anyway — fairly well. Just had breakfast with him, in fact."

"So it's a couple then, old like me, I guess. Wicken's Hunt isn't exactly a starter home from what my father told me."

"Actually, they're not a couple. And he's older, but the property doesn't belong to him. It belongs to her."

Conklin leaned forward. "To her?"

Pemberton looked around for a moment, got up and fully shut the door to his conference room, and then sat back down.

"You understand that I'm telling you this in confidence."

"Absolutely. I didn't survive all those years on Wall Street without understanding confidences."

"While the land records show a corporation as the title holder, the real owner of Wicken's Hunt is a young woman. Catherine Savage. Obviously incredibly wealthy. Quite frankly, I'm not certain what the source of that wealth is, nor is it my business to ask. She lived abroad for years. Has a little girl about ten. Charlie Thomas — the older man — he and I have had some nice little discussions. They've been very generous with several local charities. She doesn't come out in public very much, but that's understandable."

"Sure is. If I moved here, you might not see me for weeks on end."

"Exactly. They seem to be real good people, though. They seem very happy here. Very happy."

Conklin sat back and it was his turn to sigh. "Well, I guess they won't be looking to move any time soon. Damn shame too." He eyed

Pemberton intently. "Real damn shame, since I make it my practice to pay a finder's fee on top of any real estate commission you might collect from the seller."

Pemberton perked up noticeably. "Is that right?"

"Now, there aren't any ethical considerations that would prevent you from accepting such an inducement, are there?"

"None that I can think of," Pemberton said quickly. "So, how much would that inducement come to?"

"Twenty percent of the purchase price." Harry Conklin drummed his fingers on the tabletop and watched Pemberton's face turn different colors.

If Pemberton hadn't been sitting down, he would've toppled to the floor. "That's very generous," he finally managed to say.

"If I want something done, I find the best way to accomplish my goal is to provide decent incentives to those in a position to help me achieve that goal. But from the looks of things here, I don't think it's likely. Maybe I'll try North Carolina, I hear good things about it." Conklin started to get up.

"Wait a minute. Please wait just a minute."

Conklin hesitated and then slowly resumed his seat.

"Actually, your timing may be perfect."

"Why's that?"

Pemberton leaned even closer to him.

"There have been recent developments, very recent developments, that might give us an opening to approach them about selling."

"If they just moved in, seem happy here, what kind of developments are we talking about? The place isn't haunted, is it?"

"No, nothing like that. As I said, I had a breakfast meeting with Charlie. He was concerned about a person who had come to visit them. Asking for money."

"So? That happens to me all the time. You think that'll make them pack up and leave?"

"Well, I wouldn't have thought so at first either, but the more I thought about it, the more unusual it sounded. I mean, you're right, the rich get approached all the time, so why should this man upset them so? But he obviously did."

"How do you know that?"

Pemberton smiled. "In many ways, in fact, in more ways than people around here care to admit, Charlottesville is a small town. Now I know for a fact that very recently Matt Riggs was up surveying Ms. Savage's property line when he became engaged in a reckless chase with another car that almost got him killed."

Conklin shook his head in confusion. "Who's Matt Riggs?"

"A local contractor hired by Ms. Savage to install a security fence around her property."

"So he was chasing another car? How does that tie in with Catherine Savage?"

"A friend of mine was heading to work that morning. He lives up in that same area and works in town. He was about to turn on to the main road heading into town when a charcoal gray BMW flew by. He said it must've been doing eighty. If he had pulled out a second sooner that BMW would've torn his car in half. He was so shaken, he couldn't budge for a full minute. Good thing too, because while he's sitting there trying to keep his breakfast down, Matt Riggs's pickup comes barreling by and another car is locked on his bumper. They were obviously going at it."

"Do you know who was in the BMW?"

"Now, I've never met her but I know people who have seen her. Catherine Savage is a tall, blond woman. Real good-looking. My friend only got a glimpse of the driver, but he said she was blond and pretty. And I saw a charcoal gray BMW parked up at Wicken's Hunt when I went up to do a preclosing walk-through with Charlie."

"So you think somebody was chasing her?"

"And I think Matt Riggs must've run smack into it. I know that his truck's in the shop with a busted bumper. I also know that Sally Beecham — she's the maid up at Wicken's — saw Riggs walking off in a huff from the house later that same morning."

Conklin stroked his chin. "Very interesting. Guess there's no way to find out who was chasing her?"

"Yes there is. I mean I did. At least his location. You see, it gets even more interesting. As I said, Charlie invited me to breakfast. That's when he told me about this man who had come by the house wanting money. Charlie wanted my help in finding out if the man was staying in the area. Of course, I agreed to do what I could. At that point I didn't know about the car chase. I found that out later."

"You said you were able to find the man? But how could you? Lots of places to hide around here, I would think." Conklin asked this in a nonchalant manner.

Pemberton smiled triumphantly. "Not much escapes my notice, Harry. Like I said, I was born and raised here. Charlie gave me a description of the man and the car. I used my contacts and in less than twenty-four hours I had located him."

"Probably holed up pretty far away, I'll bet."

Pemberton shook his head. "Not at all. He was right under their noses. A small cottage. It's barely ten minutes from Wicken's Hunt by car. But very isolated."

"Help me out here. I don't have my bearings here yet. Is it near Monticello?"

"Well, in the general vicinity, but the area I'm talking about is north of that, north of Interstate Sixty-four, in fact. The cottage isn't too far from the Airslie Estate, off Highway Twenty-two, the Keswick Hunt area it's called. The man had leased the cottage about a month ago."

"Good gosh, did you get a name?"

"Tom Jones." Pemberton smiled knowingly. "Obviously false."

"Well, I guess they appreciated your help. So what happened?"

"I don't know. My business keeps me hopping. I really haven't talked to them about it any more."

"Well, this Riggs fellow, I bet he's sure sorry he got involved."

"Well, he can take care of himself."

"Maybe so, but getting banged around in a car in a high-speed chase? Most general contractors don't do that."

"Well, Riggs wasn't always a G.C."

"Really?" Conklin said, his features inscrutable. "You really do have the Peyton Place here. So what's his story?"

Pemberton shrugged his shoulders. "Your guess is as good as mine. He never talks about his past. He just appeared one day about five years ago, started learning the building trade and he's been here ever since. Pretty mysterious. Charlie thought he was a policeman. Frankly, I think he was with the government in some secret capacity and they put him out to pasture. Call it my gut."

"That's real interesting. Old guy then."

"No. Mid- to late thirties. Tall, strong, and very capable. Excellent reputation."

"Good for him."

"Now about our arrangement. If this man really is dogging them, I can talk to Charlie, see what he has to say. Maybe they will agree to move. It's certainly worth asking."

"I tell you what, you let me think about it for a few days."

"I can get the process started anyway."

Conklin put up one hand. "No, I don't want you doing that. When I'm ready to move, we'll move fast, don't you worry about that."

"I just thought —"

Conklin abruptly got up. "You'll hear from me very soon, John. I appreciate the insight, I really do."

"And if they won't move, there are at least a dozen other estates I can show you. They would serve your purposes equally well, I'm sure."

"This fellow in the cottage intrigues me. You wouldn't happen to have an exact address and directions, would you?"

Pemberton was startled at the question. "You certainly don't want to talk to him, do you? He might be dangerous."

"I can take care of myself. And I've learned in my business that you never know where you might find an ally." Conklin looked at him keenly until understanding spread across Pemberton's face. He wrote the information down on a piece of paper and handed it to the other man.

Conklin took an envelope out of his pocket and handed it to Pemberton, motioning for him to open it.

"Oh my God." Pemberton sat there gaping at the wad of cash that spilled out. "What's this for? I haven't done anything yet."

Conklin eyed Pemberton steadily. "You've given me information, John. Information is always worth a great deal to me. I'll be in touch." The men shook hands and Conklin took his leave.

Back at the country inn where he was staying, Harry Conklin walked into the bathroom, closed the door, and turned on the water. Fifteen minutes later the door opened and Jackson emerged, the remnants of Harry Conklin bundled in a plastic bag which Jackson deposited in a side pouch of his luggage. His conversation with Pemberton had been very enlightening. His encounter with the man had not been by chance. Upon arriving in Charlottesville, Jackson had made discreet inquiries around town that had quickly identified Pemberton as the selling agent for Wicken's Hunt. He sat on the bed and opened a large, detailed map of the Charlottesville area, noting and committing to memory the places he and Pemberton had discussed and the written directions to the cottage. Before talking to Pemberton he had educated himself on some of the history of

Wicken's Hunt, which had been nicely detailed in a book on local area estates and their original owners at the county library. It had given him enough background information to form his cover story and draw out Pemberton on the subject.

Jackson closed his eyes, deep in thought. Right now he was planning how best to begin his campaign against LuAnn Tyler and the man who was pursuing her.

Chapter Thirty-Five

Riggs had given it a day before he had attempted to retrieve his Jeep. Just in case the guy was still around, he went armed and he went at night. The Cherokee looked undamaged. Riggs made a quick check of it before heading toward the cottage. The Chrysler was nowhere to be seen. He shone his flashlight in the window of the shed. The Honda was still there. Riggs went up to the front door and wondered for the hundredth time if he should just leave this business alone. Dangerous things seemed to happen around Catherine Savage. He had had his fill of such events and he had come to Charlottesville in search of other things. Still, he could not stop his hand from carefully turning the doorknob. The door swung open.

The flashlight in one hand, his pistol in the other, Riggs moved forward slowly. He was reasonably certain that the place was empty, but assumptions like that could earn you an unwanted trip to the morgue with a tag around your big toe. He could see most of the first floor from where he was standing. He shone his flashlight slowly around the room. There was a light switch on the wall, but he wasn't about to use it. In what had been the dining room, he discerned dust patterns on the floor that showed certain objects had been removed. He ran his fingers over these areas and then moved on. He moved into the kitchen where he lifted the phone. There was no dial tone. He moved back into the dining room.

As Riggs's eyes swept the room, they passed right over the figure dressed all in black standing just inside the half-opened closet door next to the stairs.

Jackson closed his eyes the second before the light moved across his hiding place so that his pupils would not reflect off it. When the arc of illumination had passed, Jackson reopened his eyes and gripped the handle of the knife tightly. He had heard Riggs before he had ever set foot on the porch. It was not the man who had leased the cottage. He was long gone; Jackson had already searched the place thoroughly. This man had come to reconnoiter the place as well. Riggs, it must be, Jackson concluded. In fact, Jackson found Riggs almost as interesting as the man he had come to kill tonight. Ten years ago Jackson had predicted that LuAnn would be a problem, and now that prediction was coming true. He had done some preliminary checking on Riggs's background after his discussion with Pemberton. The fact that there was little to find out had intrigued him greatly.

When Riggs passed within a few feet of him,

Jackson contemplated killing him. It would take just a flick of the razor-sharp blade against his throat. But as quickly as the homicidal impulse flared through his system, it passed. Killing Riggs would further no purpose, at least not at present. Jackson's hand gripping the knife relaxed. Riggs would live another day. If there was a next time, Jackson decided, the outcome might be far different. He didn't like people meddling in his business. If nothing else, he would now check into Riggs's background with far greater intensity.

Riggs left the cottage and headed toward his Cherokee. He glanced back at the cottage. A sensation had just come over him, as though he had just survived a close call. He shrugged it off. He had once lived by his instincts; however, he assumed they had rusted somewhat since his occupation had changed. It was an empty house and nothing more.

Watching from the window, Jackson picked up on Riggs's slight hesitation, and with it his curiosity grew even more. Riggs would possibly make an interesting project, but he would have to wait. Jackson had something more pressing to take care of. From the floor of the closet Jackson picked up what looked like a doctor's bag. He moved to the dining room, crouched down, and unpacked the contents of a first-rate fingerprint kit. Jackson then moved over to the light switch and hit it from various angles with a handheld laser carried in his jacket pocket. Several latent prints sprang to life under the beam. Jackson dusted the area with a fiberglass brush dipped in black powder and gently brushed around the area of the light switch, outlining the latent prints. The kitchen counter, telephone, and doorknobs were subjected to the same process. The telephone, especially, evidenced very clear fingerprints. Jackson smiled. Riggs's real identity would not be a mystery much longer. Using pressure-wound tape, he then lifted the prints from each of the areas and transferred them to separate index cards. Humming quietly to himself, Jackson marked the cards with special identification hieroglyphics and placed them in separate plastic-lined containers. He then carefully removed all evidence of the fingerprint powder from each of the surfaces. He loved the methodology of it all. Precise steps that reached a precise conclusion. It took him only a few minutes to repack his kit and then he left the cottage. He took a side trail to his waiting car and drove off. It was not often that one captured two birds with one stone. Tonight's work was beginning to look like precisely that.

Chapter Thirty-Six

"I like Mr. Riggs, Mom."

"Well, you don't really know him, do you?"

LuAnn sat on the edge of her daughter's bed and fingered the bed covers absentmindedly.

"I have good instincts about these things."

Mother and daughter exchanged smiles. "Really? Well, maybe you can share some of your insights with me."

"Seriously, is he going to come back soon?"

LuAnn took a deep breath. "Lisa, we may have to go away soon."

Lisa's hopeful smile faded away at this abrupt change of subjects. "Go away? Where?"

"I'm not sure just yet. And it's not for certain. Uncle Charlie and I haven't finished talking about it yet."

"Were you going to include me in those discussions?"

The unfamiliar tone in her daughter's voice startled LuAnn. "What are you talking about?"

"How many times have we moved in the last six years? Eight? And that's just as far back as I can remember. God knows how many times we did when I was really little. It's not fair." Lisa's face colored and her voice shook.

LuAnn swept an arm around her shoulders. "Sweetie, I didn't say it was for certain. I just said maybe."

"That's not the point. Okay, so it's maybe now. Or maybe next month. But then one day it'll be 'we're moving' and there's nothing I can do about it."

LuAnn put her face in Lisa's long hair. "I know it's hard on you, baby."

"I'm not a baby, Mom, not anymore. And I'd really like to know what we're running from."

LuAnn stiffened and raised her head back up, her eyes searching out Lisa's.

"We're not running from anything. What would we possibly be running from?"

"I was hoping you would tell me. I like it here, I don't want to leave, and unless you can give me a really good explanation why we have to, I'm not going."

"Lisa, you're ten years old and even though you're a very intelligent and mature ten-year-old, you're still only a child. So where I go, you go."

Lisa turned her face away. "Do I have a big trust fund?"

"Yes, why?"

"Because when I turn eighteen I'm going to have my own home and I'm going to stay there until I die. And I don't want you to ever visit me."

LuAnn's cheeks reddened. "Lisa!"

"I mean it. And then maybe I'll have friends and can do the things I want to do."

"Lisa Marie Savage, you've been all over the world. You've done things most people will never get a chance to do their entire lives."

"Well, you know what?"

"What?" LuAnn shot back.

"Right now, I'd trade with them in a heartbeat."

Lisa lay down in the bed and put the covers up almost over her head. "And right now, I'd like to be alone."

LuAnn started to say something and then thought better of it. Biting her lip hard, she raced down the hallway to her room, where she collapsed on the bed.

It was unraveling. She could feel it, like a big ball of twine someone had tossed down a long set of stairs. She rose, went into the bathroom, and started the shower. She pulled off her clothes and stepped under the steaming water. Leaning up against the wall she closed her eyes and tried to tell herself that it would be okay, that in the morning Lisa would be all right, that her love for her mother remained undiminished. This was not the first serious argument mother and daughter had had over the years. Lisa did not just share her mother's physical attributes; LuAnn's independence

440

and stubborn streak had been replicated in her daughter. After a few minutes LuAnn finally calmed down and let the soothing water envelop her.

When she opened her eyes another image invaded her thoughts. Matthew Riggs must believe her to be insane by now. Insane and dishonest as hell. Quite a combination if you were trying to make an impression. But she wasn't. If anything, she felt sorry for him, for having risked his life twice and gotten kicked in the gut both times for his trouble. He was a very attractive man, but she wasn't looking for a relationship. How could she? How could she even contemplate partnering with someone? She'd be afraid to speak for fear of letting a secret scurry free. With all that, the image of Matt Riggs remained fixed in her head. A very handsome man. Strong, honest, courageous. And there was secrecy in his background too. And hurt. She suddenly cursed out loud that her life wasn't normal. That she couldn't attempt even a friendship with him.

She moved her hands fiercely along her limbs as she soaped up and released her frustrations at the same time. The harsh movements against her skin rekindled a disturbing revelation. The last man she had slept with was Duane Harvey over ten years ago. As her fingers moved over her breasts, Riggs's face appeared again in her thoughts. She shook her head angrily, closed her eyes again, and laid her face against the wall of the shower. The costly imported tile was wet and warm. She remained in that position despite danger signs flashing in her mind. So wet. So warm. So safe. Almost unconsciously her hands dipped to her waist and then over her buttocks and all the while Matthew Riggs resided in her thoughts. She kept her eyes scrunched tight. The fingers of her right hand slithered around to her navel. Her breaths became heavier. Under the sounds of the water, a low moan passed over her lips. A large tear made its way down her face before it was washed away. Ten years. Ten damned years. The fingers of her two hands were touching now, intermeshed in a way, like the gears of a clock. Slow, methodical, reliable. Back and forth . . . She jerked straight up so quickly she almost smashed her skull against the showerhead.

"Good Lord, LuAnn!" She exclaimed this to herself. She cut off the water and stepped out of the shower. She sat down on the lid of the toilet and hung her head between her knees; the light-headedness was already passing. Her wet hair sprawled across her long, bare legs. The floor became sopping wet as the water poured off her body. She glanced over at the shower, a guilty look on her face. The muscles in her back bunched together, the veins in her arms swelled large. It wasn't easy. It just wasn't easy at all.

She rose on unsteady legs, toweled off, and

went into the bedroom.

Among the costly furnishings of her bedroom was a very familiar object. The clock her mother had given her ticked away, and as LuAnn listened, her nerves began to reassemble themselves. Thank God she had stuffed it in her bag right before almost being killed in that trailer so many years ago. Even now she would lie awake at night listening to its clunkiness. It skipped every third beat and at around five o'clock in the afternoon it would make a noise like someone had lightly smacked a cymbal. The gears and wires, the guts of the contraption, were tired; but it was like listening to an old friend strum on a weathered guitar, the notes not what they should be, ideally, but holding comfort for her, some peace.

She pulled on a pair of panties and then went back into the bathroom to dry her hair. Looking in the mirror she saw a woman on the brink of something: disaster probably. Should she start seeing a shrink? Didn't you have to be truthful in therapy in order to make any progress? She mouthed this question to her reflection in the mirror. No, psychotherapy wasn't going to be an option. As usual, she would just go it alone.

She traced the scar on her face, letting her finger feel each contour of the ridged, damaged skin, in essence reliving the painful events of her past. *Never forget,* she told herself. *It's all a sham. All a lie.*

She finished drying her hair, and was about to go back into the bedroom and collapse onto the bed when Lisa's words came back to her. She just couldn't let that resentment and anger fester all night. She had to talk to her daughter again. Or at least try to.

She went back into the bedroom to put on her robe before heading for Lisa's room.

"Hello, LuAnn."

So stunned was LuAnn that she had to reach out and grip the doorjamb or she would've sagged to the floor. As LuAnn stared at him, she found that the muscles in her face had ceased to function. She couldn't even form a response, as though she had just suffered a stroke.

"It's been a long time." Jackson stepped away from the window and sat down on the edge of the bed.

His casual movements finally broke LuAnn free from her inertia. "How the hell did you get in here?"

"Not relevant." The words and tone were instantly familiar to her. All those years ago came rushing back with such speed that the effect was nearly incapacitating.

"What do you want?" She forced the words to come out.

"Ah, very relevant. However, we have much to discuss, and I would suggest you do so in the comfort of some clothing." He stared pointedly at her body.

LuAnn found it extremely difficult to take her eyes off him. Being half naked in front of the man was far less disturbing than having to turn her back on him. Finally, she threw open her closet door, pulled out a knee-length robe, and quickly put it on. She cinched the robe tightly around her waist and turned back around. Jackson wasn't even looking at her. His eyes roamed the spectacular parameters of her boudoir; his gaze rested on the clock on the wall briefly and then moved on. Apparently, the brief view of her body — a sight many men would have paid hard cash for — had inspired in him nothing more than extreme diffidence.

"You've done well for yourself. If I remember correctly, your previous decorating tastes were limited to dirty linoleum and Goodwill castoffs."

"I don't appreciate this intrusion."

He swiveled his head around and his eyes flashed into hers. "And I don't appreciate having to take time away from a very busy schedule to rescue you yet again, LuAnn. By the way, do you prefer LuAnn or Catherine?"

"I'll let you choose," she said sharply. "And I don't need to be rescued by anyone, certainly not by you."

He rose from the bed and scrutinized her altered appearance closely. "Very good. Not quite as good as I could have done, but I won't nitpick," he finally said. "Still, the look is very chic, very sophisticated. Congratulations."

LuAnn responded by remarking, "The last time I saw you, you were wearing a dress. Other than that, you haven't changed much."

Jackson still had on the dark clothing he had worn at the cottage. His features were the same as for their first meeting, although he had not covered his lean frame with padding. He thrust his head forward; the smile seemed to engulf his entire face. "Didn't you know?" he said. "Aside from my other remarkable abilities, I also never age." His smile receded as quickly as it had appeared. "Now, let's talk." He once again perched on the edge of the bed and motioned for LuAnn to sit at a small antique writing desk situated against one wall. She did so.

"What about?"

"I understand you had a visitor. A man who chased you in a car?"

"How the hell do you know that?" LuAnn said angrily.

"You just won't accept the fact that you can't conceal information from me. Like the fact that you have reentered the United States against my most explicit instructions."

"The ten years are up."

"Funny, I don't remember setting an expiration date on those instructions."

"You can't expect me to run for the rest of my life."

"On the contrary, that is exactly what I expect. That is exactly what I *demand*."

"You cannot run my life."

Jackson looked around the room again and then stood up. "First things first. Tell me about the man."

"I can handle this situation by myself."

"Is that right? From what I can tell, you've committed one blunder after another."

"I want you to leave right now. I want you to get the hell out of my house."

Jackson calmly shook his head. "The years have done nothing to ameliorate your temper. An unlimited supply of money can't purchase good breeding or tact, can it?"

"Go to hell."

In response Jackson reached one hand inside his jacket.

In an instant LuAnn had snatched up a letter opener from her writing desk. She cocked her arm back in preparation to hurl it. "I can kill you with this from twenty feet. Money *can* buy a lot of things."

Jackson shook his head sadly. "Ten years ago I found you, a young girl with a good head on her shoulders in very difficult circumstances. But you were still white trash, LuAnn. And, I'm afraid to say, some things just don't change." His hand slowly came out of his jacket. In it he held a slip of paper. "You can put your little toy away. You won't need it." He looked at her with a calmness that managed, under the circumstances, to paralyze her. "At least not tonight." He unfolded the paper. "Now, I understand that two men have recently entered your life: Matthew Riggs is one; the other is as yet unidentified."

LuAnn slowly dropped her arm, but she still clutched the letter opener in her hand.

Jackson looked up from the paper. "I have a vested interest in ensuring that your secret never be found out. I have a number of ongoing business activities, and above all I value anonymity. You're one in a line of dominoes. And when they start to fall, they tend to keep falling until they reach the end. I am that end. Do you understand?"

LuAnn sat back down in the chair and crossed her legs. "Yes," she answered curtly.

"You have unnecessarily complicated my life by coming back to the United States. The man who is following you discovered your identity, in part, through your tax records. That is why I never wanted you to come back here."

"I probably shouldn't have," LuAnn conceded. "But you try moving just about every six months, a new country, a new language. And try doing it with a little girl."

"I appreciate your difficulties; however, I assumed that being one of the richest women on earth would more than make up the difference."

"Like you said, money can't buy everything."

"You never met the man before? In your extensive travels? You're absolutely certain?"

"I would've remembered. I've remembered everything the last ten years." She said this softly.

Jackson studied her closely. "I believe you. Do you have any reason to think that he knows about the lottery?"

LuAnn hesitated a second. "No."

"You're lying. Tell me the truth immediately or I'll kill everyone in this house starting with you." This abrupt threat, delivered calmly and precisely, made her suck in her breath.

She swallowed with difficulty. "He had a list. A list with twelve names on it. Mine, Herman Rudy, Bobbie Jo Reynolds, and some others."

Jackson assimilated this information rapidly and then looked down at the paper. "And the man Riggs?"

"What about him?"

"There's some confusion as to his background."

"Everyone has secrets."

Jackson smiled. "Touché. Under other circumstances that would not bother me. However, in this instance it does."

"I'm not following you."

"Riggs has a mysterious past and he just

happens to be around when you need assistance. I take it he did help you."

LuAnn looked at him quizzically. "Yes, but he's been here for five years, long before I got here."

"That's not the point. I'm not suggesting the man is a plant. I am suggesting that he could well be something entirely different than what he claims. Now he coincidentally collides with your world. That's what worries me."

"I don't think it was anything other than a coincidence. He was hired to do a job for me. It was perfectly natural that he would be nearby when the other man started chasing me."

Jackson shook his head. "I don't like it. I saw him tonight." LuAnn stiffened perceptibly. "At the cottage. I was this close to him." He spread his hands about two feet apart. "I contemplated killing him on the spot. It would have been extremely easy."

LuAnn's face turned white and she licked dry lips. "There's no reason to do that."

"You have no way of knowing that. I'm going to check him out and if I find anything in his background to suggest trouble for me, then I will eliminate him. It's that simple."

"Let me get that information for you."

"What?" Jackson looked startled.

"Riggs likes me. He's already helped me, probably saved my life. It would be natural for me to show my gratitude. Get to know him better."

"No, I don't like it."

"Riggs is a nobody. A local builder. Why trouble yourself with him? Like you said, you're busy."

Jackson studied her intensely for a moment. "All right, LuAnn, you do that. However, any information you obtain better be reported to me in a timely fashion or, with respect to Mr. Riggs, I will take matters into my own very capable hands. Clear?"

LuAnn let out a deep breath. "Clear."

"The other man, of course, I must find. It shouldn't be too terribly difficult."

"Don't do that."

"Excuse me?"

"You don't have to do that. Find him."

"I am very much certain that I do."

The memory of Mr. Rainbow came flooding back to her. She did not want another death on her conscience. She wasn't worth it. "If he shows up again, we're just going to leave the country."

Jackson refolded the paper and replaced it in his pocket. He made a precise steeple with his hands. "You obviously do not fully understand the situation. Were you the only one he was onto, then perhaps your simplistic solution might resolve the matter, at least temporarily. However, the man has a list with the names of eleven other people with whom I worked. I would submit that a resolution involving all of them fleeing the country almost simultaneously would be essentially unworkable."

LuAnn drew in a sharp breath. "I could pay the man. How much money can he want? That would take care of it."

Jackson smiled tightly. "Blackmailers are a bad lot. They never seem to go away." He added sharply, "Unless they receive extreme persuasion to do so."

"Mr. Jackson, please don't do it," she said again.

"Don't do what, LuAnn? Ensure your survival?" He glanced around. "And with it all of this?" He rested his gaze back upon her. "How is Lisa, by the way? As beautiful as her mother?"

LuAnn felt her throat constrict. "She's fine."

"Excellent. Let's keep it that way, shall we?"

"Can't you just let it go? Let me handle it."

"LuAnn, many years ago we were confronted with a situation regarding another would-be blackmailer. I took care of that incident and I will take care of this one. In matters like this I almost never opt for delegation. Count your blessings that I'm allowing Riggs to live. For now."

"But that man can't prove anything. How can he? And even if he could, they'll never be able to trace anything to you. Maybe I'll go to jail, but you won't. Hell, I don't even know who you really are."

Jackson stood up, his lips pursed. He took a moment to rub his left hand delicately along the edge of the bedspread.

"Beautiful needlework here," Jackson commented. "Indian isn't it?"

Distracted for an instant by his query, LuAnn was suddenly staring down the barrel of a 9-mm, a suppressor attached to its muzzle.

"One potential solution could involve my killing all twelve of you. That would certainly qualify as a startling dead-end for our inquisitive friend. Remember that the ten-year period is up. The lottery's principal amount has already been returned to a Swiss account that I have set up in your name. I would strongly advise against transferring that money into the United States." He pulled another slip of paper from his pocket and put it down on her bed. "Here are the authorization codes and other account information that will enable you to access it. The funds are untraceable. There you have it. As agreed." Jackson's finger curled around the trigger of his weapon. "However, now I really don't have any incentive to keep you around, do I?" He advanced toward her. LuAnn's fingers tightened around the letter opener.

"Put it down, LuAnn. Granted, you're remarkably athletic, but you're not faster than a bullet. Put it down. *Now!*"

She dropped the letter opener and backed up against the wall.

Jackson stopped a few inches from her. While he lined up the pistol with her left cheekbone, he ran a gloved hand along her right cheek. There was no sexual content to the motion. Even through the glove, LuAnn could sense the purely clinical chill of his touch.

"You should have thrown it the first time, LuAnn. You really should have." His eyes were mocking.

"I'm not going to kill someone in cold blood," said LuAnn.

"I know. You see, that is your greatest short-coming, because that's precisely when you should strike."

He removed his hand and looked at her.

"Ten years ago I felt you were the weak link in the chain. During the intervening years, I thought perhaps I was wrong. Everything was going so smoothly. But now I find my initial intuition was correct. Even if I were in no personal danger of discovery, were I to let this man blackmail you or perhaps even expose the manipulations of the lottery, then that would be a failure on my part. I do not fail. Ever. And I do not let other people have any control whatsoever over plans of mine, for that, in itself, would be a form of failure. Besides, I couldn't bear to let such a grand performance be ruined.

"Just think about the wonderful life I've given you, LuAnn. Remember what I told you all those years ago: 'Go anywhere, do anything.' I gave that to you. The impossible. All yours. Look at you now. Flawless beauty." His hand went to the front of her robe. With slow movements he undid the strap and the robe fell open, fully exposing her quivering breasts and flat belly. He slid the robe over her shoulders and it fell to the floor.

"The most prudent action on my part, of course, would be to kill you. Right here and right now. In fact, what the hell." He pointed the gun directly at her head and pulled on the trigger. LuAnn jerked back, her eyes slamming shut.

When she reopened them, Jackson was studying her reaction. She was shaking terribly; her heart was thumping around inside her, she couldn't catch her breath.

Jackson shook his head. "Your nerves don't seem to be as strong, LuAnn, as when we were last together. And nerves, or a lack thereof, really are the whole ball of wax." He looked at the pistol for a moment, slipped off the safety, and continued speaking calmly. "As I was saying, the most prudent thing, when one is confronted with a weak link, is to snip it out." He paused and then continued, "I'm not going to do that with you, at least not yet. Not even after you've disobeyed me, jeopardized

455

everything. Would you like to know why?"

LuAnn remained planted against the wall, afraid to move, her eyes fixed on his.

He took her silence for assent. "Because I feel you have a greater destiny to fulfill. A dramatic statement, but I'm a dramatic person; I think I'll allow myself that. It's really as simple as that. And in very large measure, you are a creation of mine. Would you be living in this house, speaking and thinking as an educated person, traveling the world on a whim, without me? Of course not. In killing you, I would, in effect, be killing part of myself. That, as I'm sure you can appreciate, I am loath to do. Nevertheless, please keep in mind that a wild animal, when trapped, will ultimately sacrifice a limb in order to escape and survive. Don't think for one moment that I am not capable of that sacrifice. If you do, you're a fool. I sincerely hope that we are able to extricate you from this little problem." He shook his head sympathetically, much as he had ten years earlier during their very first meeting. "I really do, LuAnn. However, if we can't, we can't. Problems come up in business all the time, and I'm counting on you to do your part, to do all you can to ensure that we successfully navigate this one." Jackson's tone once again became businesslike as he ticked off items with his fingers. "You will not leave the country. You obviously went to a great deal of trouble to get back in, so stay and enjoy it for a while.

You will immediately report to me any further contact with our mysterious stranger. The number I gave you ten years ago will still reach me. I will be in touch on a regular basis. Whatever additional instructions I give you, you will follow precisely. Understood?"

She quickly nodded.

"I'm quite serious, LuAnn. If you disobey me again, I will kill you. And it will be slow and unbelievably painful." He studied her reaction to these words for a moment. "Now go into the bathroom and compose yourself."

She started to turn away.

"Oh, LuAnn?"

She looked back.

"Keep in mind that if we do fail to contain this problem and I have to eliminate that weak link, there will be no reason that I can see to stop there." He glanced ominously in the direction of the doorway leading to the hallway, where barely twenty feet away Lisa lay sleeping. He turned back to her. "I like to give my business associates as much incentive as possible to achieve success. I find that they're much more likely not to disappoint."

LuAnn ran into the bathroom, locking the door after her. She gripped the cold marble of the vanity, every limb shaking uncontrollably, as though she had left her skeleton back there with him. Wrapping a thick, full-length towel around her, she sank down to the floor. Her natural courage was tempered with a strong dose of common sense and she understood quite clearly the serious personal jeopardy she was in. But that was far from her greatest fear. The fact that Jackson might set his murderous sights on Lisa made her nearly delirious with terror.

Curiously enough it was with this thought that LuAnn's features grew deadly still in their own right. Her eyes stared across at the doorway, on the other side of which stood a person to whom she was probably more similar than dissimilar. They both had secrets; they both were incredibly rich from ill-gotten gains. They both had mental and physical abilities above and beyond the norm. And perhaps most telling, they both had killed someone. Her act had been spontaneous, survival the only motive. Jackson's had been premeditated, but survival of sorts had also been his motivation. Perhaps not as wide a chasm as it looked on the surface. The results, after all, had been the deaths of two human beings.

She slowly rose from the floor. If Jackson ever came after Lisa, then either he would die or LuAnn would; there would be no other possibilities. She let the towel fall to the floor. She unlocked the door. There seemed to exist an ethereal connection between Jackson and LuAnn Tyler that defied a logical explanation. It was as though, even after all this time apart, that their synapses had become fused together at a certain, almost psychic level. For she was absolutely certain what she would find when she returned to the bedroom. She threw open the door.

Nothing. Jackson was gone.

LuAnn pulled on some clothes and hurried down the hallway to check on Lisa. The little girl's steady breathing told her mother that she was asleep. For a while, LuAnn simply hovered over Lisa, afraid to leave her. She didn't want to wake her. She wouldn't be able to hide the terror she was feeling from her daughter. Finally, LuAnn made certain the windows were locked and left the room.

Next she made her way to Charlie's bedroom and gently roused him from sleep.

"I just had a visitor."

"What? Who?"

"We should've known he'd find out," she said wearily.

When the meaning behind her words worked through his grogginess, Charlie sat straight up in bed, almost knocking over the lamp on the nightstand. "Good God, he was here? Jackson was here?"

"When I finished my shower I found him waiting for me in my bedroom. I don't think I've ever been that scared in my life."

"Oh, God, LuAnn, baby." Charlie hugged her tightly for several moments. "How the hell — how the hell did he find us?"

"I don't know, but he knows everything.

The man who chased me. About Riggs. I, I told him about the list of lottery winners. I tried to lie, but he knew I was. He threatened everyone in the house if I didn't tell him the truth."

"What's he going to do?"

"He's going to find the guy and then he's going to kill him."

Charlie leaned up against the headboard and LuAnn sat down next to him. Charlie put a big hand across his face and shook his head. He looked over at her. "What else did he say?"

"That we weren't to do anything. Be careful around Riggs and to let him know if the other guy showed up again."

"Riggs? Why'd he mention him?"

She looked over at him. "Jackson seemed very suspicious of him. Like maybe he has an ulterior motive for being involved."

"Son of a bitch," Charlie moaned and abruptly rolled out of bed. He stood up and started getting dressed.

"What are you doing?"

"I don't know, but I feel like I've got to do something. Warn Riggs. If Jackson's after him —"

She reached up and gripped his arm. "If you tell Riggs about Jackson, then all you're doing is guaranteeing his death. Somehow, some way, Jackson will find out. He always does. I've got Riggs safe, at least for now."

"How'd you do that?"

"Jackson and I worked out a little arrangement. At least I think he bought it. Who can tell with him?"

Charlie stopped pulling on his pants and looked over at her.

LuAnn continued, "For now anyway, Jackson's going to focus on the other man. He'll find him, and it's not like we can warn him, because we don't even know who he is."

Charlie sat back down on the bed. "So what do we do?"

LuAnn took his hand in hers. "I want you to take Lisa away. I want both of you to go away."

"There's no way I'm leaving you alone with that guy in the neighborhood. No way in hell."

"Yes you will, Charlie, because you know I'm right. By myself, I'm okay. But if he were to get hold of Lisa . . ." She didn't need to finish the thought.

"Why don't you go with her and let me stay here and handle it?"

LuAnn shook her head. "That won't work. If I leave Jackson will come looking. Looking hard. So long as I'm around, he's not going to stray too far. In the meantime, you two can get away."

"I don't like it. I don't want to abandon you, LuAnn. Not now."

She put her arms around his burly shoulders. "My God, you're not abandoning me. You're going to be taking care of the most

461

precious thing I have —" She broke off here, as Jackson's face planted itself squarely in her thoughts.

Finally Charlie took her hand. "Okay. When do you want us to leave?"

"Right now. I'll go get Lisa ready while you pack. Jackson just left, so I doubt if he's going to be watching the place. He probably figures I'm too frozen with fear to do anything. Actually, he wouldn't be too far from the truth."

"Where do we go?"

"You pick the place. I don't want to know. That way nobody can get the information out of me. Call when you get there and then we'll make arrangements to safely communicate after that."

Charlie shrugged. "I never thought it would come to this."

She kissed him lightly on the forehead. "We'll be okay. We just need to be really careful."

"And what about you? What are you going to do?"

LuAnn took a deep breath. "Whatever it takes to make sure we all survive this."

"And Riggs?"

She looked squarely at him. "Especially Riggs."

"I hate this, Mom. I hate it." Lisa stomped around the room in her pajamas as LuAnn hurriedly packed her daughter's bags.

"I'm sorry, Lisa, but you're just going to have to trust me on this."

"Trust, ha, that's a funny one coming from you." Lisa glared at her from across the room.

"I don't need that kind of talk right now, young lady."

"And I don't need this." Lisa sat down on the bed and stubbornly crossed her arms.

"Uncle Charlie is ready, you need to get a move on."

"But we're having a party at school tomorrow. Can't it at least wait until after that?"

LuAnn slammed the suitcase shut. "No, Lisa, I'm afraid it really can't."

"When is this going to stop? When are you going to stop dragging me all over the place?"

LuAnn ran a shaky hand through her hair and sat down next to her daughter, putting an arm around Lisa's quaking form. She sensed the pain coursing through the small body. Could the truth hurt her daughter any worse than this? LuAnn clenched her fist and pushed it against her right eye as she tried to stop her nerves from pouring right out of her body.

She turned to her daughter. "Lisa?" The little girl refused to look at her mother.

"Lisa, please look at me."

Finally, Lisa looked at her mother, her small face a blend of anger and disappointment, a combination that was crushing to LuAnn.

LuAnn spoke slowly. The words she was

uttering would have been unthinkable an hour ago. But then Jackson had shown up and his appearance had changed a lot of things. "I promise that one day, very soon, I will tell you everything you want to know. In fact, more than you will ever want to know about me, about you, about everything. All right?"

"But why —"

LuAnn put her hand gently across her daughter's mouth, silencing her. "But I'm telling you right now that when I do it will shock you, it will hurt you and you might never understand or appreciate why I did what I did. You may hate me for it, you may be sorry I'm your mother" — she paused, biting hard into her lip — "but however you feel, I want you to know that I did what I thought was best at the time. I did what I thought was best for you. I was very young and I really didn't have anyone to help me make my decision."

She cupped Lisa's chin with her hand and tilted her daughter's face up to hers. Lisa's eyes were now filled with tears. "I know I'm hurting you now. I don't want you to go away, but I will die before I'd let anything happen to you. So would Uncle Charlie."

"Mom, you're scaring me."

LuAnn gripped Lisa with both hands. "I love you, Lisa. More than I've ever loved anything in my whole life."

"I don't want anything to happen to you."

Lisa touched her mother's face. "Mom, will you be okay?"

LuAnn managed a reassuring smile. "A cat always lands on its feet, sweetie. Mommy'll be just fine."

Chapter Thirty-Seven

The next morning LuAnn rose early after a mostly sleepless night. Saying good-bye to her daughter had been the most wrenching thing she had ever done; however, she knew that task would seem easy compared to the day she would tell Lisa the truth about her life, about her mother's life. LuAnn hoped she would have the opportunity to do that. And yet a huge wave of relief had swept over her when she had watched the lights of the Range Rover disappear down the road the night before.

Now her biggest concern was devising a way to reapproach Riggs without making him even more suspicious. But she didn't have much time. If she didn't report back to Jackson with some information soon, then he would turn his attention fully on Riggs. She was not going to let that happen.

She was thinking this through as she drew back her bedroom curtains and peered out onto the rear lawn. Her bedroom was on the third floor and provided an inspiring view of the surrounding countryside. A balcony opened off the bedroom through a pair of French doors. LuAnn wondered if that was how Jackson had gained access to the room last night. Normally she activated the burglar alarm right before she went to bed. She might start doing it earlier, although she had little hope that any security system would pose much of a challenge for the man. He seemed to be able to walk right up and then through walls.

She brewed a pot of coffee in the small kitchenette next to her dressing room. Then she put on a silk robe and, holding a cup of steaming coffee in one hand, she stepped out onto the balcony. A table and two chairs were set up there; however, she chose to perch on the marble railing and look out over her property. The sun was on its way up and the rays of pink and gold formed a backdrop to a sea of equally colorful foliage. The view was almost enough to raise her sagging spirits. What she saw next almost caused her to fall off the balcony.

Matthew Riggs was kneeling in the grass near the spot where she had wanted her studio to be built. From her vantage point LuAnn watched in growing amazement as Riggs unrolled a thick set of blueprints and eyed the lay of the land. LuAnn clambered up on top of the railing and, one hand clinging to the brick wall of the house for support, she stood on tip-toe for a better look. Now she could make out stakes planted in the ground at various points. While she watched, Riggs unraveled some twine and, tying one end to a stake, he started laying out what looked to be the footprint of a building.

She tried calling to him, but her voice couldn't carry far enough.

LuAnn jumped down from the railing, raced through her bedroom, not even pausing to put on shoes. She took the stairs two at a time and unlocked the back door. Sprinting across the dewy grass in her bare feet, the silk robe clung to her form, showing a good deal of her long legs in the process.

Breathing hard, she reached the spot where Riggs had been and looked around. Her breaths were visible in the early morning chill and she pulled the sheer robe tight around her.

Where the hell had he gone? She hadn't imagined it. The stakes were there, the string affixed to them. She stared at them as if they would eventually reveal the secret of the man's whereabouts.

"Morning."

LuAnn whirled around and stared at him as he emerged from the stand of trees, a large rock in his hand. He set it down ceremoniously in the middle of the staked-out area.

"Your stone chimney," he proclaimed, grinning.

"What are you doing?" LuAnn asked in an amazed tone.

"You always run around outside in that? You're going to catch pneumonia." He stared at her and then discreetly looked away as the emerging sun's rays cleared the tops of the trees and made the thin robe virtually transparent; she wasn't wearing anything underneath. "Not to mention what it's doing to me," he muttered to himself.

"I don't usually see someone on my property at the crack of dawn putting stakes into the ground."

"Just following orders."

"What?"

"You wanted a studio, I'm building you a studio."

"You said there wasn't enough time before winter set in. And you needed plans and permits."

"Well, you admired mine so much, I had the brilliant idea of using those diagrams for this one. That'll save a lot of time. And I've got contacts at the inspector's office so we can expedite the approval process." He paused and looked at her as she stood there shivering. "Now don't rush to thank me," he said.

She crossed her arms. "It's not that, I —" She shuddered again as a brisk wind sailed down the tree line. Riggs took off his heavy coat and draped it around her shoulders.

"You know you really shouldn't be outside in your bare feet."

"You don't have to do this, Matthew. I think I've intruded on your time and patience enough."

He shrugged and looked down at the ground, tapping one of the stakes lightly with his foot. "I don't really mind, Catherine." He coughed in an embarrassed fashion and looked up at the tree line. "There are a lot worse things than hanging out with a woman like you." He shot her a quick glance and then looked away.

LuAnn blushed, biting nervously at her bottom lip while Riggs shoved his hands in his pockets and stared off at nothing. The pair unconsciously emulated two teens nervously feeling each other out for that vital first date.

She looked over at the staked-out area. "So, it'll be just like yours?"

Riggs nodded. "I had the time since you fired me on the fence job."

"I told you I'd pay you and I meant it."

"I'm sure you meant it, but I have a policy of not accepting payment for a job I didn't do. I'm kind of funny that way. Don't worry, I'll charge you plenty for this one."

Riggs once again looked at the surrounding country. "It doesn't get much prettier than this, I can tell you that. Once I build this thing, you probably won't want to leave it."

"That sounds very nice, but hardly realistic."

He glanced over at her. "I guess you travel a lot. A person in your position."

"It's not that. But I do travel a lot." She added wearily, "Too much."

Riggs looked around again. "It's good to see the world. But it's nice to come home too."

"You sound like you speak from experience." She looked at him curiously.

He grinned sheepishly. "Me? I haven't really been anywhere."

"But you still like to come home. For some peace?" she said quietly, her big eyes locked on his.

His grin disappeared and he looked at her with renewed respect. "Yes," he finally said.

"How about some breakfast?"

"I already ate, but thanks."

"Coffee?" She was balancing on one bare foot and then the other as the cold ate at her skin.

Riggs watched her movements and then said, "I'll take you up on that one." Riggs tugged off his work gloves and stuffed them in his pants pocket. He turned around and bent down. "Climb on."

"Excuse me?"

"Climb on." He patted his back. "I know I'm not as bulky as your horse but just pretend."

LuAnn didn't budge. "I don't think so."

Riggs turned and looked at her. "Will you come on? I'm not kidding about the pneumonia. Besides, I do this with billionaires all the time, I'm telling you."

LuAnn laughed, pulled his coat on all the way, and hoisted herself up piggyback style, wrapping her arms around his neck. He locked his arms around her bare thighs. "Are you sure you're up to it? It's a pretty long way and I'm not exactly petite."

"I think I can manage, just don't shoot me if I collapse." They started off.

Halfway there she jabbed him playfully in the sides with her knees.

"What the hell was that for?"

"I'm pretending, just like you said. So giddy-up."

"Don't push it," he groused back and then smiled.

In the woods near the horse barn, Jackson repacked his sound wand and made his way through the woods to his car parked on a side road. He had watched in some amusement as Riggs carried LuAnn back to the house. He had also noted the rough footprint for the structure Riggs was apparently building for her. Considering how she was dressed, Jackson thought it likely that LuAnn and the handsome Riggs would probably be enjoying an intimate moment very shortly. That was good, since it would give her an opportunity to pump him for information. Using the sound wand, he had also recorded Riggs's voice, an asset that might prove valuable later. He reached his car and drove off.

Riggs sipped on a cup of coffee in the

kitchen while LuAnn munched on a piece of buttered toast. She rose and fixed herself another cup of coffee and freshened his.

Riggs couldn't help but stare when her back was turned. She hadn't changed her clothes and the clingy robe was making him think about things he probably shouldn't be. He finally looked away, his face hot.

"If I get another horse, I think I'll name it after you," LuAnn said.

"Thanks bunches." He looked around. "Everybody else still sleeping?"

She put the coffeepot back down and took a moment to sponge up a bit of spillage on the counter. "Sally has the day off. Charlie and Lisa went on a little vacation."

"Without you?"

She sat back down, her eyes roaming the room before she looked back at him and spoke casually. "I had some things to take care of. I might have to leave for Europe soon. If I do, I'll meet up with them and then we'll all go together. Italy is beautiful this time of year. Have you ever been?"

"The only Rome I've been to is in New York."

"In your past life?" She looked at him over the top of her coffee cup.

"There we go with that past life thing again. It's really not all that exciting."

"So why not tell me about it then?"

"So what's the quid pro quo?"

"Ah, I assume you learned that phrase from your attorney ex-wife."

"Assumptions are dangerous things. I like facts a lot better."

"So do I. So shower me with them."

"Why are you so interested in what I did before I came to Charlottesville?"

Because I'm doing my best to keep you alive, and it sickens me every time I think how close you came to being dead because of me. LuAnn struggled to keep her tone at an even level despite that painful reality. "I'm just a naturally curious person."

"Well, so am I. And I have a hunch your secrets are a lot more interesting than mine."

She tried her best to look surprised. "I don't have any secrets."

He put down his coffee cup. "I can't believe you can actually say that with a straight face."

"I have a lot of money. Some people would like to take it away from me any way they can. That doesn't exactly qualify for shocker status."

"So, you've concluded the guy in the Honda was a potential kidnapper."

"Maybe."

"Funny kidnapper."

"What do you mean?"

"I've been thinking a lot about it. The guy looked like a college professor. He rented a place in the area and furnished it. When he attempted to 'kidnap' you he wasn't even wearing a mask. And when I showed up on the scene, instead of hightailing it off, he tried to drive right through me even though he had no chance of catching you. And in my experience most kidnappers don't work solo. Logistically, it's difficult to go it alone."

"In your experience?"

"See, I'm showering you with secrets."

"Maybe he was trying to frighten me before he actually made the kidnap attempt."

"Don't think so. Why put you on your guard? Kidnappers kind of like the element of surprise."

"If he's not a kidnapper, what then?"

"I was hoping you could tell me. Charlie went into the cottage and so did you. What did you find?"

"Nothing."

"That's bullshit and you know it."

LuAnn stood up and glared at him. "I don't appreciate being called a liar."

"Then stop lying."

Her lips trembled and she abruptly turned away from him.

"Catherine, I'm trying to help you here. Okay, in my past life I did deal with the criminal class quite a bit. I've got some insights and some skills that might prove useful if you'd just tell me the truth."

He rose and put a hand on her shoulder. He turned her around to face him. "I know you're scared. And I also know you've got stronger nerves and more spirit than just about anybody I've ever run across, so I'm assuming whatever you're facing is pretty bad. And I want to help you. I *will* help you, if you'll just let me." He cupped her chin with his hand. "I'm playing straight with you, Catherine. I really am."

She winced slightly as he said her name again. Her *fake* name. She finally reached up and lightly caressed his fingers with her own. "I know you are, Matthew. I know." She looked up at him and her lips parted slightly. Their eyes did not budge from each other as their fingers exchanged touches that were suddenly electrifying both their bodies. The spontaneity of the sensation absolutely immobilized them. But not for long.

Riggs swallowed hard, dropped his hands to her bottom, and abruptly pulled LuAnn against him. The warmth and softness of her breasts burned invisible holes through his thick flannel shirt. Their mouths erupted against each other as he yanked the robe free and it fell to the floor. LuAnn moaned and closed her eyes, her head swaying drunkenly from side to side as Riggs attacked her neck. She pulled at his hair and then wrapped her arms around his head as he hoisted her up in the air, his face buried in her chest. She wrapped her legs around his torso.

Following her frantic, whispered directions, Riggs lunged blindly along the hallway to the small first-floor guest bedroom. Riggs pushed open the door. LuAnn jerked away from him and sprawled flat on her back on the bed, the muscles in her long legs tensing in anticipation. She reached up and pulled at him.

"Dammit, Matthew, hurry!" At his subconscious level Riggs noticed the abrupt return of the Georgia drawl but he was far too intoxicated with the passion of the moment to do anything about it.

Riggs's heavy work boots hit the hardwood floor with a loud thump and his pants followed immediately. She jerked his shirt off, popping several buttons in the process, then slid his boxers down. They didn't bother with the bed covers although Riggs did manage to back-kick the door closed before he plunged on top of her.

Chapter Thirty-Eight

Jackson sat at the table and studied the laptop's small screen. His suite was large and airy and furnished with eighteenth-century reproductions. The aged hardwood floors were partially covered with area rugs stitched with early American colonial themes. A large wooden carving of a duck in flight hung on one wall. A set of framed prints, each depicting a Virginia native who had gone on to become president of his country long ago, was on another wall. The inn was located in close proximity to his areas of focus, was quiet, and allowed Jackson the greatest freedom of unobserved movement. The night before, he had checked out as Harry Conklin and checked back in under another name. He liked to do that. He became uncomfortable staying in one character too long. Besides, he had met with Pemberton in the Conklin role and he didn't want to run into the man again. Now a baseball cap covered his head. Heavy latex eye pouches bracketed the fake nose. The hair was blondish-gray and tied in a ponytail that sprouted out the back of the cap. His neck was long and wrinkled and his build was stocky. He looked like an aging hippie. His luggage was stacked neatly in one corner. He had a practice of not unpacking when he traveled; his line of work sometimes necessitated rapid exits.

Two hours earlier he had scanned one set of the fingerprints lifted from the cottage into his hard drive and transmitted them via modem to one of his information contacts. He had already called this person and told him what was coming. This particular contact had access to a database that housed oceans of the most interesting facts, the sole reason that Jackson had enlisted his services many years ago. It wasn't certain that the man who was pursuing LuAnn would have his fingerprints on file anywhere, but Jackson had nothing to lose by checking. If the man did, Jackson's task of tracking him down would become far easier.

Jackson smiled as his computer screen started filling up with data. A digitized photo of the man had even accompanied the personal details.

Thomas J. Donovan. The photo was three years old, but Jackson reckoned that at this time of life, Donovan wouldn't have changed all that much. He studied the nondescript features of the man carefully and then checked the contents of his portable makeup kit and various hairpieces he had brought with him. Yes, if it came down to it, he could impersonate the man. Donovan's name was actually familiar to Jackson. Donovan was an award-winning journalist at the *Washington Tribune.* In fact, about a year ago he had done an in-depth piece on Jackson's father's career as a United States senator.

Jackson had read the story and quickly condemned it as a fluff piece that came nowhere near to addressing the personal side of his father and his monstrous behavior. The history books would smile upon the man; his son knew better.

Jackson's hunch had proven correct. He had figured the man trailing LuAnn wasn't your typical blackmailer. It had taken a lot to track her down and an investigative journalist or perhaps ex–law enforcement person would have the skills, knowledge, and more important, the informational resources to have successfully done so.

Jackson sat back and mused for a moment. Actually, a true blackmailer would have posed less of a difficulty for him. Donovan was undoubtedly onto a story, an enormous story, and he would not stop until he achieved his goal. Or until someone stopped him. It was an interesting challenge. Simply killing the man wouldn't do any good, however. That might make people suspicious. Also, Donovan might have told others of his investigations, although most journalists of Donovan's capabilities, Jackson was aware, kept their cards close to the vest until they broke the story, for a variety of reasons not the least of which was the fear of being scooped.

He had to determine how much Donovan knew and whether he had told anyone else. He picked up the phone, got the number for the *Trib*, and dialed it. He asked for Thomas Donovan. He was told that Donovan had taken a leave of absence. He slowly hung up the phone. He wouldn't have talked to the man if he had come on the phone. He did want to hear his voice, though, in case that knowledge should become useful later. Jackson was also an accomplished mimic and impersonating someone's voice was a wonderful way to manipulate others.

According to Pemberton, Donovan had been in the Charlottesville area for at least a month. Jackson focused briefly on one obvious question: Of all the lottery winners why had the man targeted LuAnn? Jackson almost immediately answered his own query. Because she was the only one running from a murder charge. The only one who had disappeared for ten years and then resurfaced. But how could Donovan possibly have picked up her trail? The cover had been deep and it had been buried even deeper with the passage of ten years, even though LuAnn had committed a tremendous blunder by coming back to the States.

He had a sudden thought. Donovan apparently knew the names of all or some of the lottery winners for the year Jackson had fixed the game. What if he attempted to contact some of the others? If he didn't get what he wanted from LuAnn, and Jackson felt reasonably sure he wouldn't, the next logical step would be to seek out the others. Jackson took out his electronic Rolodex and started making phone calls. After half an hour he had finished contacting the other eleven. Compared to LuAnn, they were sheep to be led around. What he told them to do, they did. He was their savior, the man who had led them to the Promised Land of wealth and leisure. Now, if Donovan bit, the trap would spring.

Jackson began to pace the room. He paused and opened his briefcase. He pulled out the photos. They had been taken on his first day in Charlottesville, even before meeting with Pemberton. The quality of the photos was good considering he had been using a long-range lens and the early morning light had not been the best. The faces stared back at him. Sally Beecham looked tired and bothered. In her forties, tall and slender, she was LuAnn's live-in housekeeper. Her suite was on the first floor on the north side of the mansion. He studied the next two photos. The two young Hispanic women constituted the cleaning staff. They came at nine and left at six. Finally came the photos of the groundspeople. Jackson studied each of their faces. When taking the photos, he had watched the people intently; how they moved, how they gestured.

His handheld sound wand had picked up their voices perfectly. He had listened to their voices over and over as he had just listened to Riggs's. Yes, it was coming together nicely. Like pieces in a strategic battle plan, he was positioning his soldiers to optimal advantage. Possibly, none of the information he had painstakingly gathered about Catherine Savage's daily world would ever come into play. But, on the chance that it might, he would be more than ready. He put the photos away and closed the briefcase.

From a hidden compartment in his suitcase he drew out a short-handled throwing knife. Hand-crafted in China, the blade was so sharp it couldn't even be touched by a bare hand without drawing blood; it was thrown by means of the perfectly balanced teak handle. Jackson strolled around the room, as his mind was sidetracked for a moment. LuAnn was uncommonly fast, lithe, agile, words that could equally be applied to himself. Yes, she had certainly upgraded herself. What else had she learned? What other skills had she acquired? He wondered whether she had experienced the same premonition he had: that their paths would cross again one day like two trains colliding. And had she done her utmost to prepare for that eventuality? Twenty feet. Using the letter opener, she could have killed him from that distance. Fast as he was, the blade would have been imbedded in his heart before he had a chance to react.

On this last thought Jackson wheeled around and let the knife fly. It sailed across the room, splitting the duck's head completely in half upon impact and burrowing several inches into the wall. Jackson eyed the distance between himself and his target: At least *thirty* feet, he estimated. He smiled. LuAnn would have been far wiser to have killed him. She had, no doubt, been constrained by her conscience. That was her greatest weakness and Jackson's greatest advantage, for he had no such parallel compunction.

Ultimately, if it came down to it, he knew that would be the difference.

Chapter Thirty-Nine

LuAnn watched Riggs, who lay dozing next to her. She let out a small breath and stretched her neck. She had felt like a virgin while they made love. An incredibly energetic display of sex, she was surprised the bed hadn't caved in; they'd probably be sore tomorrow. A grin spread over her face. She stroked his shoulder and huddled next to him, putting one of her bare legs across both of his. With this movement he finally stirred and looked over at her.

A boyish smile cracked his face.

"What?" she asked, her eyes impish.

"I'm just trying to remember how many times I said 'oh, baby.' "

She rubbed her hand across his chest, letting the nails bite in just enough to make him playfully grab her hand. LuAnn said, "I think it was more often than I screamed 'yes, yes,' but that was only because I couldn't catch my breath."

He sat up and put a hand through her hair. "You make me feel young and old all at the same time."

They kissed again and Riggs lay back while LuAnn nestled on his chest. She noticed a scar on his side.

"Let me guess, old war wound?"

He looked up surprised and then followed her gaze to the scar. "Oh, yeah, real exciting, appendicitis."

"Really? I didn't think people came with two appendixes."

"What?"

She pointed to another scar on his other side.

"Hey, can we just enjoy the moment here and stop with the observations and questions?" His tone was playful, but she noted the serious intent just below the surface.

"Well, you know, if you come over every day to work on the studio, we might make this a regular thing, sort of like breakfast." LuAnn smiled and then almost immediately caught herself. *What was the chance of that happening?* The impact of this thought was crushing.

She quickly moved away from him and started to get up.

Riggs could hardly miss this dramatic transformation.

"Was it something I didn't say?"

She turned to find him looking at her. As if suddenly self-conscious about her nakedness, she pulled the bedspread off the bed and draped it around her. "I've got a lot to do today."

Riggs sat up and grabbed at the bedspread. "Well, excuse the hell out of me. I didn't mean to get in the way of your schedule. I guess I had the six A.M. to seven A.M. slot. Who's up next? The Kiwanis Club?"

She jerked the bedspread free. "Hey, I don't deserve that."

Riggs rubbed his neck and started to pull on his clothes. "Okay. It's just that I'm having trouble switching gears as fast as you. Going nonstop from the most intensive passion I can ever remember to discussing the day's workload sort of rubbed me the wrong way. I'm sorry as hell if I offended you."

LuAnn looked down and then moved over and sat next to him. "That's how it was for me too, Matthew," she said quietly. "I'm embarrassed to tell you how long it's been." She paused and then said almost to herself, "Years."

He looked at her incredulously. "You've gotta be kidding." She didn't answer and he was reluctant to break the silence. The ringing phone did.

Hesitating for a moment, LuAnn picked it up. She hoped to God it was Charlie and not Jackson. "Hello?"

It turned out to be neither. "We're going to talk, Ms. Tyler, and we're going to do it today," Thomas Donovan said.

"Who is this?" LuAnn demanded.

Riggs quickly looked over at her.

"We had a brief meeting the other day when you were out driving. The next time I saw you was when you were sneaking out of my place with your boyfriend."

"How did you get this number? It's unlisted."

Donovan silently laughed. "Ms. Tyler, no information is safe, if you know where to look. I'm assuming by now that you realize I know where to look."

"What do you want?"

"Like I said, I want to talk."

"I don't have anything to say to you."

Riggs went over to the phone and held the receiver with her. At first LuAnn tried to push him off but Riggs held firm.

"Sure you do. And I have a lot to say to you. I can understand your reaction the other day. Maybe I should have approached you differently, but that's past. I know beyond a doubt that you're sitting on a story of immense importance, and I want to know what it is."

"I have nothing to say to you."

Donovan considered this for a moment. He ordinarily didn't like to take this tack, but right now he couldn't think of an alternative strategy. He made up his mind. "I'll give you this as an inducement. If you talk to me, I'll give you forty-eight hours to leave the country before I go public. If you don't talk to me then I go public with everything I have as soon as I get off the phone." He struggled internally for a moment and then added quietly, "Murder doesn't have a statute of limitations, LuAnn."

Riggs stared over at LuAnn, wide-eyed. She looked away from him.

"Where?" she asked.

Riggs was shaking his head fiercely but LuAnn ignored him.

"Let's make it a very public place," Donovan said. "Michie's Tavern. I'm sure you know where that is. One o'clock. And don't bring anyone with you. I'm way too old for guns and speeding cars. I catch a whiff of your boyfriend or anyone else, the deal is off and I call the sheriff in Georgia. Do you understand?"

LuAnn ripped the phone free from Riggs and slammed it down.

Riggs faced her. "Would you like to fill me in on what's going on? Who are you supposed to have murdered? Somebody in Georgia?"

LuAnn stood up and pushed past him, her face crimson from the abrupt revealing of this secret. Riggs grabbed her arm and pulled her back roughly. "Dammit, you're going to tell me what's going on."

She snapped around and, quick as a ferret, connected her right fist flush with his chin, causing his head to snap back and hit hard against the wall.

When he came to Riggs was lying on the bed. LuAnn sat next to him holding a cold compress to his bruised chin and then pressed it against the growing knot on his head.

"Damn!" he said as the cold went through his system.

"I'm sorry, Matthew. I didn't mean to do that. I just —"

He rubbed his head in disbelief. "I can't believe you knocked me out. I'm not a chauvinist, but I can't believe a woman just flattened my butt with one punch."

She managed a feeble smile. "I had a lot of practice growing up, and I'm pretty strong." She added kindly, "But I think your head hitting the wall had a lot to do with it."

Riggs rubbed his jaw and sat up. "Next time we're having an argument and you're thinking about popping me, just let me know and I'll surrender on the spot. Deal?"

She touched his face gently and kissed him on the forehead. "I'm not going to hit you anymore."

Riggs looked over at the phone. "Are you going to meet him?"

"I don't have a choice — that I can see."

"I'm going with you."

LuAnn shook her head. "You heard him."

Riggs sighed. "I don't believe you murdered anyone."

LuAnn took a deep breath and decided to tell him. "I didn't murder him. It was self-defense. The man I was living with ten years ago was involved in drugs. I guess he was skimming off the top and I walked right into the middle of it."

"So you killed your boyfriend?"

"No, the man who killed my boyfriend."

"And the police —"

"I didn't stay around long enough to find out what they were going to do."

Riggs looked around the room. "The drugs. Is that where all this came from?"

LuAnn almost laughed. "No, he was a small-timer. Drug money didn't have anything to do with this."

Riggs wanted desperately to ask what did, but refrained from doing so. He sensed that she had divulged enough of her past life for now. Instead he watched in silent frustration as LuAnn slowly got up and started to leave the room, the bedspread dragging behind her, the well-defined muscles in her bare back tensing with each stride.

"LuAnn? That's your real name?"

She turned to look at him and nodded faintly. "LuAnn Tyler. You were right about Georgia. Ten years ago I was a lot different. A lot."

"I believe it, although I bet you've always had that right cross." He attempted a smile, but neither of them was buying it.

She watched Riggs as he dug into his pants pocket. He tossed something to her. She caught the keys in the palm of her hand. "Thanks for letting me use your BMW; you might need the horsepower in case he starts chasing you again."

She frowned, looked down, and then walked out of the room.

Chapter Forty

Wearing a long black leather coat and a matching hat, her eyes hidden behind a pair of Ray-Bans, LuAnn stood outside the "Ordinary," an aged wooden building that was part of Michie's Tavern, a historic structure originally built in the late 1700s and later moved to its current location down the road from Monticello in the late 1920s. It was lunchtime and the place was starting to fill up with tourists either lining their stomachs with the fried chicken buffet offered there after touring Jefferson's home and its neighbor Ash Lawn, or fueling up before setting out on the tour. Inside, a fire blazed in the hearth and LuAnn, who had arrived early to check things out, had soaked in the warmth from the flames before deciding to wait for him outside. She looked up when the man walked toward her. Even without his beard she recognized him.

"Let's go," Donovan said.

LuAnn looked at him. "Go where?"

"You follow me in your car. I'll be checking my rearview mirror. If I see anyone who remotely looks like they're following us, then I pick up my cell phone and you go to prison."

"I'm not following you anywhere."

He leaned into her face and said quietly, "I think you might want to reconsider."

"I don't know who you are or what you want. You said you wanted to meet. Well, I'm here."

Donovan looked around at the line of people making their way into the tavern. "I had in mind a little more privacy than this."

"You picked the place."

"That I did." Donovan jammed his hands in his pocket and stared at her in obvious discomfort.

LuAnn broke the silence. "I'll tell you what, we'll go for a drive in my car." She stared at him ominously and spoke in low tones. "But don't try anything because if you do, I *will* hurt you."

Donovan snorted for a moment and then just as quickly stopped as he stared into her eyes. An involuntary shiver swept over him. He followed her long strides to her car.

LuAnn got on Interstate 64 and put the big sedan on cruise control.

Donovan turned to her. "You know, you threatened me back there with bodily injury. Maybe you did kill that guy in the trailer."

"I didn't *murder* anyone. I didn't do anything wrong in that trailer."

Donovan studied her features and then looked away. When he spoke next, his tone was softer, calmer. "I didn't spend the last several months tracking you down, LuAnn, in order to destroy your life."

She glanced over at him. "Then what did you track me down for?"

"Tell me what did happen in that trailer."

LuAnn shook her head in frustration and remained silent.

"I've dug through a lot of dirt over the years, and I can read between the lines with the best of them. I don't believe you murdered anyone," Donovan said. "Come on, I'm not a cop. You can check me for a wire if you want. I've read all the newspaper accounts. I'd like to hear your version."

LuAnn let out a deep sigh and looked over at him. "Duane was dealing drugs. I didn't know anything about it. I just wanted to get out of that life. I went to the trailer to tell him so. Duane was cut up very badly. A man grabbed me, tried to cut my throat. We fought. I hit him with the telephone and he died."

Donovan looked puzzled. "You just hit him with the telephone?"

"Really hard. I guess I cracked his skull."

Donovan rubbed his chin thoughtfully. "The man didn't die from that. He was stabbed to death."

The BMW almost ran off the road before LuAnn regained control. LuAnn stared over at him, her eyes wide. "What?" she gasped.

"I've seen the autopsy reports. He did have a wound to the head, but it wasn't fatal. He died from multiple stab wounds to his chest. No doubt about it."

It didn't take LuAnn long to realize the truth. *Rainbow.* Rainbow had killed him. And then lied to her. She shook her head. Why should that be such a big surprise, she thought. "All these years, I believed that I had killed him."

"That's a horrible thing to carry around inside. I'm glad I could clear your conscience on it."

"The police can't still be interested in all this. It's been ten years," LuAnn said.

"That's where you've run into some incredibly bad luck. Duane Harvey's uncle is the sheriff in Rikersville now."

"Billy Harvey is sheriff?" LuAnn said in astonishment. "He's one of the biggest crooks down there. He had an auto chop shop. He ran gambling in the back rooms of the bars; he was into everything you could earn a buck from illegally. Duane kept trying to get in on it, but Billy knew Duane was too stupid and unreliable. That's probably why he ended up selling drugs over in Gwinnett."

"I don't doubt it. But the fact is he's sheriff. Probably figured the best way to avoid trouble with the police was to become the police."

"So you talked to him?"

Donovan nodded. "According to him, the whole family has never gotten over poor Duane and his hasty exit from the living. He said the drug dealing sort of besmirched the whole family. And the money you sent? Instead of salving over those wounds, they took it as pouring salt on them, like you were trying to buy them off somehow. I mean they spent it and all, but they still didn't like it, at least according to the illustrious Billy Harvey. Bottom line is, he told me that the investigation is still active and he's not going to rest until LuAnn Tyler is brought in for trial. From what I can tell his theory is that you're the one who was involved in the drug dealing because you wanted to escape Duane and the boring life. Duane died trying to protect you and then you murdered the other guy, who allegedly was your partner."

"That's a bunch of lies."

Donovan shrugged. "You know it is, I know it is. But the people deciding that will be a jury of your peers down in Rikersville, Georgia." He took a moment to appraise her expensive clothing. "Or a jury of whom your peers *used* to be. I wouldn't recommend that you wear that outfit to the trial. It might rub people the wrong way. Duane being flower food and all these last ten years while you were living the high life and doing a pretty good impersonation of Jackie O, it just wouldn't sit well with the good folks down there."

"Tell me something I don't know." She paused for a moment. "So is that your deal?

If I don't talk, you're going to throw me to Billy Harvey?"

Donovan patted the dashboard. "It may surprise you to know that I don't give a damn about all that stuff. If you hit that man, you did it in self-defense. That I believe."

LuAnn lifted her sunglasses and stared across at him. "Then what do you care about?"

He leaned toward her. "The lottery." His eyebrows arched.

LuAnn spoke evenly. "What about it?"

"You won it ten years ago. One hundred million dollars."

"So?"

"So, how'd you do it?"

"I bought a ticket that turned out to be the winning number, how else do you do it?"

"I don't mean that. Let me fill you in on something. Without getting too technical, I went back through years' worth of lottery winners. There's a constant rate of bankruptcy declared by all those winners. Nine out of twelve every year. Bang, bang, you can set your clock by it. Then I run across twelve consecutive winners who somehow managed to avoid the big B and you were smack in the middle of that unique group. Now how is that possible?"

She glanced over at him. "How should I know? I've got good money managers. Maybe they do too."

"You haven't paid taxes on your income nine out of the last ten years; I guess that helps."

"How do you know that?"

"Again, all sorts of information is available. You just have to know where to look. I know where to look."

"You'd have to talk to my financial people about that. I was in other parts of the world during that time, maybe the income wasn't taxable in the U.S."

"I doubt that. I've written enough financial stories to know that there's almost nothing Uncle Sam won't tax, if he can find it, that is."

"So call up the IRS and report me."

"That's not the story I'm looking for."

"Story?"

"That's right. I forgot to fill you in on the reason I came to visit you. My name's Thomas Donovan. You probably haven't heard of me, but I'm a journalist for the *Washington Trib* going on thirty years now and a damned good one even if I am blowing my own horn. A while back I decided to do a story on the national lottery. Personally, I think the whole thing is a travesty. Our own government doing that to the poorest among us. Dangling carrots like that, all the catchy ads, enticing people to cash in their Social Security checks to play something with odds at millions to one. Excuse the soapbox, but I only write about things

I feel passionate about. Anyway, my original angle was the rich sucking it back out of the poor after they hit the jackpot. You know, investment shysters, people peddling one scheme after another, and the government just letting them go right ahead and do it, and then when the winners' finances are so screwed up, they haven't paid enough tax or what-not, the IRS comes in and takes every last dime, leaving them poorer than before they won. A good story, and one I feel needs to be told. Well, while I'm researching the story, I find out this interesting coincidence about all the lottery winners from your year: They didn't lose a dime of their money. In fact, using their tax returns as a gauge, they're all richer now. A lot richer. So I track you down and here I am. What I want is simple: the truth."

"And if I don't tell you, I end up in a Georgia prison, is that it? That's what you implied over the phone."

Donovan stared across at her angrily. "I won two Pulitzers before I was thirty-five. I've covered Vietnam, Korea, China, Bosnia, South Africa. Gotten my ass shot up twice. I've spent my life chasing every hot spot in the world. I'm as legit as they come. I'm not going to blackmail you, because I don't operate that way. I told you that over the phone just to get you to meet with me. If Sheriff Billy catches up to you it's not going to be with my help.

Personally, I hope he never does."

"Thank you."

"But if you don't tell me the truth, I'll find it out someplace else. And then I'm going to write that story. And if you don't tell me your side of things, I can't guarantee how flatteringly I can portray you. I report the facts, guilt will fall where it may. If you're willing to talk to me, I can guarantee only one thing: that your side of the story will be heard. But if you've broken the law somehow, there's nothing I can do about that. I'm not a cop, and I'm not a judge." He paused and looked at her. "So what's it going to be?"

She didn't speak for several minutes, her eyes staring down the road. He could see the conflict going on inside her.

Finally she looked over at him. "I want to tell you the truth. God, I want to tell somebody the truth." She took a deep breath that almost turned into a shudder. "But I can't."

"Why not?"

"You're already in a great deal of danger. If I were to talk to you, that danger would turn to an absolute certainty that you're going to die."

"Come on, LuAnn, I've been in dangerous spots before. It comes with the territory. What is it, and who's behind it?"

"I want you to leave the country."

"Excuse me?"

"I'll pay. You pick a place, I'll make all the

arrangements. I'll set up an account for you."

"Is that your way of dealing with problems? Send them off to Europe? Sorry, but I've got a life right here."

"That's just it. If you stay you're not going to have a life."

"You're really going to have to do better than that. If you'd work with me, we could really accomplish something here. Just talk to me. Trust me. I didn't come down here to shake you down. But I also didn't come down here to be thrown a bunch of bullshit."

"I'm telling you the truth. You are in serious danger!"

Donovan wasn't listening now. He rubbed his chin as he thought out loud. "Similar backgrounds. All poor, desperate. It made for great stories, really picked up the numbers of players." He looked at her, clutched her arm. "Come on, LuAnn, you had help leaving the country ten years ago. You've gotten a whole lot richer. I can smell the story here, if you'd just give me the right angle. This could rank right up there with the Lindbergh baby and who shot JFK. I've got to know the truth. Is the government behind this, whatever this is? They're making billions off this thing every month, sucking it out of the rest of us. Taxation without representation." Donovan rubbed eager hands together. "Are we talking all the way to the White House? Please tell me we are."

"I'm not telling you anything. And I'm doing it to keep you as safe as I can."

"If you work with me, we both win."

"I don't consider being murdered winning. Do you?"

"Last chance."

"Will you please believe me?"

"Believe what? You haven't told me anything," he bellowed.

"If I tell you what I know, it's like I'm putting a pistol against your head and pulling the trigger myself."

Donovan sighed. "Then why don't you take me back to my car. I don't know, LuAnn, I guess I expected more from you. You grew up dirt-poor, raised a kid by yourself, and then got this incredible break. I thought you might give a crap."

LuAnn put the car in gear and they started off again. She glanced once or twice at him and then started speaking in a very low voice, as though she were afraid of being overheard. "Mr. Donovan, the person who is looking for you right this very minute is not someone you want to mess around with. He told me he's going to kill you because you might know too much. And he will. Unless you leave right now, he'll find you for sure and when he does it won't be pretty. This person can do anything. Anything."

Donovan snorted and then his face froze. He slowly turned and looked at her as the answer finally hit him. "Including making a poor woman from Georgia rich?"

Donovan saw LuAnn jerk slightly as he said the words. His eyes widened. "Jesus, that's it, isn't it? You said this man can do anything. He made you the lottery winner, didn't he? A woman barely out of her teens running from the police after believing she committed a murder —"

"Mr. Donovan, please."

"She stops to buy a lottery ticket and then just happens to travel to New York where the lottery drawing is being held. And what do you know, she wins a hundred million bucks." Donovan slapped the dashboard with the palm of his hand. "Good God, the national lottery was fixed."

"Mr. Donovan, you have got to let it drop."

Donovan's face flushed crimson. "No way, LuAnn. No way am I letting this drop. Like I said, you couldn't have eluded the NYPD and the FBI all by yourself. You had help, a lot of help. This elaborate cover story you had in Europe. Your 'perfect' money managers. This guy set all of it up. All of it, didn't he? Didn't he?" LuAnn didn't answer. "God, I can't believe I didn't see it all before. Sitting here talking to you, it just all fell into place. I've been drifting in circles for months and now —" He turned sideways in his seat. "You're not the only one either, are you? The other eleven nonbankrupts? Maybe more. Am I right?"

LuAnn was shaking her head hard. "Please stop."

"He didn't do it for free. He must've gotten some of your winnings. But, Christ, how did he fix it? Why? What's he doing with all that money? It can't be just one guy." Donovan fired questions left and right. "Who, what, when, why, how?" He gripped her shoulder. "Okay, I'll accept your statement that whoever is behind this is one very dangerous individual. But don't discount the power of the press, LuAnn. It's toppled crooks bigger than this guy. We can do it, if we work together." When LuAnn didn't respond, Donovan let go of her shoulder. "All I'm asking is that you think about it, LuAnn. But we don't have a lot of time."

When they returned to his car Donovan got out and then poked his head back in the door. "This number will reach me." He handed across a card. LuAnn didn't take it.

"I don't want to know how to reach you. You'll be safer that way." LuAnn suddenly reached across and grabbed his hand. Donovan winced from the pressure of her fingers.

"Will you please take this?" She reached in her purse and took out an envelope. "There's ten thousand dollars in here. Pack your bags, go to the airport, get on a plane, and get the hell out of here. Call me when you get to wherever you're going and I'll send enough money to keep you in hotels and restaurants for as long as you want."

"I don't want money, LuAnn. I want the truth."

LuAnn pushed back the urge to scream. "Dammit I'm trying my best to save your life."

He dropped the card onto her front seat. "You warned me and I appreciate that. But if you won't help me, I'll get it from somewhere else. One way or another, this story is being told." He looked at her ominously. "If this person is half as dangerous as you say he is, you might want to think about getting the hell out of here. My butt may be in the crosshairs now, but it's only my butt. You've got a kid." He paused again and right before he turned to leave he said, "I hope we both make it through this, LuAnn. I mean that."

He walked across the parking lot to his car, got in, and drove off. LuAnn watched him go. She took a deep breath, trying to calm her shaken nerves. Jackson was going to kill the man unless she did something. But what could she do? For one thing, she wasn't going to tell Jackson about her meeting with Donovan. She looked around the parking lot for any sign of him. But what was the use? He could be anyone. Her heart took another jolt. He could've tapped her phone lines. If so he would know about Donovan's phone call, that they had planned to meet. If he knew that, it was highly likely that he had followed her. Then Jackson would already be tracking Donovan. She looked down the road. Donovan's car was already out of sight. She slammed her fists into the steering wheel.

Although LuAnn didn't know it, Jackson had not tapped her phone line. However, as she drove off, she also had no inkling that directly beneath her seat a small transmitter had been affixed to the floorboard. Her entire conversation with Donovan had just been heard by someone else.

Chapter Forty-One

Riggs turned off the receiving unit and the sounds of LuAnn's BMW coming through his earphones vanished. He slowly took off the headphones, sat back in his desk chair, and let out a long breath. He had anticipated obtaining some information about LuAnn Tyler and her discussions with the man he now knew to be Thomas Donovan, a newspaper reporter. The name was familiar to Riggs; he had seen the guy's byline in past years. However, Riggs hadn't anticipated stumbling across something that had all the earmarks of a major conspiracy.

"Damn." Riggs stood up and looked out the window of his home office. The trees were stunning, the sky a pale blue that was both dazzling and soothing. To the right a squirrel scampered up a tree, a chestnut secured between its jaws. Farther back, through the thickness of the trees, Riggs could make out a slender procession of deer headed by a six-point buck as they made their way cautiously toward the small spring-fed pond situated on Riggs's property. So peaceful, so serene, all that he had hoped for. He looked back at the receiving device he had used to listen in on

LuAnn and Donovan's conversation. "LuAnn Tyler," Riggs said out loud. Not Catherine Savage, not even close, she had said. New identity, new life, far, far away. That was something Riggs could certainly relate to. He eyed the phone, hesitated, then picked it up. The number he was calling had been given to him five years ago, for emergencies, just as, unknown to Riggs, Jackson had provided one to LuAnn ten years ago. Just for emergencies. Well, Riggs decided as he punched in the numbers, he supposed this qualified as such.

An automated voice came on the line. Riggs left a series of numbers and then his name. He spoke slowly in order to let the computer verify the authenticity of his voice patterns. He put down the phone. One minute later it rang. He picked it up.

"That was fast," Riggs said, sitting back down.

"That number gets our attention. What's the situation? You in trouble?"

"Not directly. But I've come across something I need to check up on."

"Person, place, or thing?"

"Person."

"I'm ready, who is it?"

Riggs took a silent breath and hoped to God he was doing the right thing. He would at least hedge his bets until he understood matters a little better. "I need to find out about someone named LuAnn Tyler."

LuAnn's car phone buzzed as she was driving back home.

"Hello?"

The voice on the other end of the line made her breathe easier.

"Don't tell me where you are, Charlie, we can't be sure this line is safe." She checked where she was on the road. "Give me twenty minutes and then call me at the prearranged spot." She hung up. When they had come to the area, they had identified a pay phone at a McDonald's that would receive incoming calls. That was their safe phone.

Twenty minutes later she was standing at the pay phone, snatching it up on the first ring.

"How's Lisa?"

Charlie's tone was low. "Fine, we're both okay. She's still bumming, but who can blame the kid."

"I know. Did she talk to you at all?"

"A little. Although, I think we're both the enemy as far as she's concerned right now. That little girl's playing it close to the vest. Chip off the old block, right?"

"Where is she?"

"Crashed on the bed. We drove all night, and she didn't sleep much, just stared out the car window."

"Where are you?"

"Right now we're at a motel on the outskirts of Gettysburg, Pennsylvania, just across the

Maryland state line. We had to stop, I was falling asleep at the wheel."

"You didn't use a credit card, did you? Jackson can trace that."

"You think I'm a novice at being on the run? All cash."

"Any sign that you've been followed?"

"I've varied my route, gone the interstate, back roads, lots of stops in very public places. I've checked every car that even looks remotely familiar. No one's onto us. How's it on your end? You hook up with Riggs?"

LuAnn blushed at the question. "You could say that." She paused and cleared her throat. "I met up with Donovan."

"Who?"

"The guy from the cottage. His name is Donovan. He's a reporter."

"Aw, crap!"

"He knows about the twelve lottery winners."

"How?"

"It gets complicated, but basically because none of us declared bankruptcy. In fact we all became a lot richer through shrewd investment advice. I guess that's pretty unusual with lottery winners."

"Damn, I guess Jackson isn't infallible."

"That's a comforting thought. I've got to go. Give me the number there." Charlie did so.

"I brought the portable cell phone too,

511

LuAnn. You've got the number, right?"

"Memorized."

"I don't like it that you're all alone in this. I really don't."

"I'm holding my own. I've just got to think things through a little. When Jackson shows up again, I want to be ready."

"I'm not sure that's possible. The guy's not human."

LuAnn hung up the phone and walked back to her car. As unobtrusively as she could, she scanned the parking lot for anyone looking remotely suspicious. But that was the problem: Jackson never looked suspicious.

Charlie hung up the phone, checked on Lisa, and then went to the window of the ground-floor motel room. The building was constructed in the shape of a horseshoe so that Charlie was looking out not only at the parking lot but also at the motel units on the other side of the parking lot. He had a habit of checking the parking lots every thirty minutes to see who had pulled in after them. He had selected fairly isolated places that would make it easier to flush out someone who was following them. Despite his sharp scrutiny he could not have seen the pair of binoculars focused on him from the dark recesses of the motel room directly across from his. This person's car was not in the parking lot because he was not a paying guest of the motel. He had broken into the room when Charlie and Lisa had gone out to eat. The man put down the binoculars and jotted some words down in a notebook before taking up his sentry once again.

Chapter Forty-Two

The BMW pulled into the front drive. LuAnn sat in the car and stared up at the house. She had not gone home. After driving around for a while, she had decided to come here. The Jeep was there, so he must be as well. She got out of the sedan and walked up the wide steps of the Victorian.

Riggs heard her coming. He was just finishing up his phone call, the paper in front of him covered with notes, more information than he had ever wanted to know. His gut was cramping up just thinking about it all.

He opened the door to her knock and she passed through the doorway without looking at him.

"How'd it go?" he asked.

LuAnn drifted around the room before settling down on the couch and looking up at him with a shrug. "Not all that well, really." Her voice was listless. Riggs rubbed his eyes and sat down in the chair opposite her.

"Tell me about it."

"Why? Why in the hell would I want to get you involved in all this?"

He paused and briefly considered what he was about to say. He could walk away from this. She was obviously giving him the opportunity to do so. He could just say you're right and escort her to the door and out of his life. As he looked at her, so tired, so alone, he spoke quietly and intensely.

"I want to help you."

"That's nice, but I really wouldn't know where to begin."

"How about ten years ago, Georgia, and you're running from the cops for a murder you didn't commit."

She stared over at him, biting her lip. She wanted desperately to trust the man; it was an almost physiologically compelling need. And yet, as she stared down the hallway to where his study was, where she had previously seen the information he had obtained on her so easily, so quickly, the doubts came flooding back to her. Jackson was suspicious of the man. Who was he? Where had he come from? What had he done in his past life?

When she looked back over at him, he was watching her closely. He read the uncertainty, the suspicions there.

"LuAnn, I know you really don't know me. Yet. But you *can* trust me."

"I want to, Matthew. I really do. It's just —" She stood up and started her ritualistic pacing. "It's just that I've made a habit the last ten years of never trusting anyone. Anyone other than Charlie."

"Well, Charlie's not here, and from the

looks of things, you're not going to be able to handle this alone."

She stiffened at the words. "You'd be surprised at what I can handle."

"I don't doubt that. Not at all," he said in a sincere, if disarming, manner.

"And getting you involved means, ultimately, placing you in danger. That's not something I want on my conscience."

"You'd be surprised at how accustomed I am to dangerous things. And people."

She stared at him, a glimmer of a smile on her lips. Her deep hazel eyes were intoxicating to him, calling up the fresh memory of their lovemaking.

"I still don't want you to get hurt."

"Then why are you here? In spite of how terrific this morning was, I doubt if you're here for a nooner. You've got other things on your mind, I can tell."

She sat back down and clasped her hands together. After thinking the matter over a minute she started speaking earnestly. "The man's name was Thomas Donovan. He's a reporter of some kind. He started investigating me."

"Why? Why you? The murder?"

LuAnn hesitated before answering. "That was part of it."

"What was the other part?"

LuAnn didn't answer now; she looked at the floor. Imparting personal information to anyone other than Charlie went against every instinct she possessed.

Riggs decided to take a shot. "Did it have to do with the lottery?"

She slowly looked up, the astonishment starkly on her face.

"I knew your real name; something clicked. You won a hundred million dollars ten years ago, a lot of stories about you back then. Then you disappeared."

She studied him warily, alarm bells ringing. His face, though, was one of complete sincerity, and finally that look subdued her suspicions, at least temporarily.

"Yes, I won that money."

"So what did Donovan want? Your story on the killing?"

"Partly."

"What was the other part?" he asked persistently.

Now the alarm bells started ringing again, and this time Riggs's honest features did not silence them. LuAnn rose. "I've got to be going."

"Come on, LuAnn. Talk to me."

"I think I've said more than I should have."

Riggs knew far more than she had already told him, but he had wanted to hear it from her. His source for the information on LuAnn had naturally desired to know why he wanted it. He had lied, or gotten close to it. He wasn't going to give LuAnn Tyler away, at least not yet. He had no reason to trust her, and many reasons not to. But he did trust her. He did believe in her.

As her hand closed over the doorknob he called to her.

"LuAnn, if you change your mind, I'll be here."

She didn't look at him, fearful of what might happen if she did. She wanted to tell him everything. She wanted his help, she wanted to make love to him again. After all these years of fabrication, of lies, deceit, and constant fear of exposure, she just wanted to be held; to be loved for herself, not for the enormous wealth she possessed.

Riggs watched the BMW pull out of his driveway. When it had disappeared from view he turned and went back to his study. Because of his inquiries into LuAnn Tyler, Riggs knew the Feds would undoubtedly get around to dispatching some agents to Charlottesville to talk to him or at least get the local FBI office involved. But because of his special status, they would have to jump through some bureaucratic hoops before that could be accomplished. He had some time, but not much. And once the Bureau boys showed up, it was over for LuAnn Tyler. All of her diligent work over the last ten years to remain hidden Riggs could blow up in the next few days. A very strong emotion told Riggs he could not allow that to happen, despite what he knew about the woman. In the course of his past career, deception had become a way of a life. So also had reading people, telling the good ones from the bad, to the extent you could. LuAnn was a good person, Riggs had long ago concluded. Even if she didn't want his help, she was going to get it. But she was obviously involved with some very dangerous people. And now, Riggs thought to himself, so was he.

Chapter Forty-Three

When LuAnn arrived home it was late; the household staff had gone, and Sally Beecham would not return until tomorrow. She went in the house through the garage, punched in the alarm code, and threw her coat and purse down on the kitchen island. She went upstairs to shower and change. She had a lot of things to think through right now.

In the shrubs bordering the edge of the expansive lawn by the garage side of the house, Jackson knelt in the mulch and smiled to himself. He lowered the small piece of equipment he was holding in his hand. On its digital face were the six numbers constituting LuAnn's pass code for the home's alarm system. The scanner had picked up the electrical impulses thrown off when LuAnn inputted her pass code and then it had unscrambled them. With the pass code Jackson could come and go freely.

When he got back to his rental car, his cell phone buzzed. He spoke for a few minutes and then hung up. Charlie and Lisa were at a motel outside of Gettysburg. They would probably be on the move again soon. LuAnn had tried to get them away from him, or rather Lisa away from him. Charlie could take care of himself, Jackson well knew. If it came to it, Lisa was the Achilles' heel of her mother.

LuAnn had watched out the window as the figure made its way down the tree line toward the main road. The steps had been animal-like in their stealth and precision, much as hers would have been. She didn't know what had drawn her to the window at that precise instant. She felt no fear or even apprehension as she watched Jackson move down the hillside. She had expected him to be there. For what specific reason or for how long Jackson had been watching the house, she wasn't sure; but it was completely logical that he should be. She was now his main focus, she knew. And to be the main focus of the man was akin to treading on the very edge of the grave. She drew the curtains shut and sat on her bed. The enormous house felt cold and threatening, as though she were all alone in a mausoleum of immense proportion, just waiting for something unspeakably horrible to happen to her.

Was Lisa truly safe, beyond the reach of the man? The answer to that question was so obvious that it hit her like a hard slap in the face.

I can do anything, LuAnn.

The mocking words came back to her after all these years and sent a shiver through her. Riggs was right, she couldn't get through this alone. He had offered help, and this time she needed it. Whether she was making the right decision or not, she didn't care. Right now, she just needed to do something. She jumped up, grabbed her car keys, unlocked a box in her closet, and placed the loaded nickel-plated .44 Magnum in her purse. She ran down the stairs and into the garage. A minute later the BMW was flying down the road.

Riggs was in the room over his barn when he heard the car drive up and park next to the garage. He watched out the window as LuAnn came into view. She started toward the house but then, as if sensing his presence, she turned to stare at him. Their eyes stayed locked for a long moment as each silently probed the other. A minute later she was sitting across from him, warming her hands from the heat of the stove.

This time Riggs felt no compunction to mince words.

"The lottery was fixed, wasn't it? You knew you were going to win, didn't you?"

LuAnn jolted upright for an instant, but then let out an almost simultaneous breath of relief.

"Yes." With that one word she felt as though the last ten years of her life had suddenly evaporated. It was a cleansing feeling. "How'd you figure it out?"

"I had some help."

LuAnn tensed and slowly rose. Had she just made the biggest mistake of her life?

Riggs sensed her sudden change and put up a hand. As calmly as he could, he said, "Nobody else knows right now. I pulled some pieces of information from different sources and then took a wild stab." He hesitated and then added, "I also bugged your car. I heard your entire conversation with Donovan."

"Who the hell are you?" LuAnn hissed, her hand feeling for her purse catch and the gun inside even as she stared at him.

Riggs just sat there and stared back at her. "I'm someone very much like you," was his surprising reply. Those words stopped her cold. Riggs stood and put his hands in his pockets, leaned up against the bookcase, and eyed the gently swaying trees through the window. "My past is a secret, my present is all made up." He looked over at her. "A lie. But for a good reason." He raised his eyebrows. "Like you."

LuAnn trembled for an instant. Her legs felt weak and she abruptly sat down on the floor. Riggs swiftly knelt beside her, taking her hand in his. "We don't have a lot of time so I'm not going to sugarcoat things. I made some inquiries about you. I did it discreetly, but it's going to have ripple effects nonetheless." He looked at her intently. "Are you ready to hear this?"

LuAnn swallowed hard and nodded; the fear passed from her eyes and was replaced with an inexplicable calmness.

"The FBI has been interested in you ever

since you fled the country. The case has been dormant for a while, but that's not going to last. They know something is up with you, and maybe with how you won the money, but they don't know what, and they haven't been able to prove anything."

"If you bugged the car, you know how Donovan got onto it."

Riggs nodded and helped her up. They both sat on the couch. "Bankruptcy. Pretty clever. I know the Feds haven't latched on to that angle yet. Do you know how it was rigged?"

LuAnn shook her head.

"Is it a group, an organization behind it? Donovan thought it was the government. Please don't tell me it is. That gets way too complicated."

"It's not." LuAnn was speaking clearly now, although traces of fear, the effect of the sudden exposure of long-held secrets, flitted over her features. "It's one person, as far as I know."

Riggs sat back with an amazed look. "One person. That isn't possible."

"He had some people working for him, at least two that I know of, but I'm pretty sure he was the boss." That was an understatement. LuAnn could not imagine Jackson taking orders from anyone.

"Was Charlie one of those people?"

LuAnn started again. "What makes you say that?"

Riggs shrugged. "The uncle story was a little

lame. And you two seemed to be sharing a secret. There wasn't any mention in all my research about you of any uncle, so I assumed he came into the picture after the lottery scam."

"I'm not going to answer that." The last thing she was going to do was incriminate Charlie.

"Fair enough. What about this person behind it? What can you tell me about him?"

"He calls himself Jackson." LuAnn stopped suddenly, astonished that she was telling anyone this. As the name passed over her lips, she closed her eyes and imagined for an instant what Jackson would do to her, to all of them, if he had any idea what she was revealing. She instinctively looked over her shoulder.

Riggs gripped her arm. "LuAnn, you're not alone anymore. He can't hurt you now."

She almost laughed out loud. "Matthew, if we're the luckiest people in the world, he'll kill us quick instead of making us suffer."

Riggs felt her arm shaking. As strong and resourceful as he knew her to be, she was clearly afraid.

"If it makes you feel any better," he said, "I've dealt with some pretty bad people in my time, and I'm still here. Everyone has weaknesses."

"Sure, right." LuAnn's voice was hushed, her words lifeless.

Riggs's tone was harsh. "Well, if you want

to roll over for him and play dead, go ahead. I don't see how that's going to help Lisa, though. If this guy's as scary as you say, you think he's going to let her walk?"

"I haven't told her about any of this."

"Jackson's not going to assume that. He's going to assume that she knows everything, and that she's going to have to be eliminated if things turn against him."

"I know," she finally said. She rubbed her face and glanced wearily at him. "I don't understand. Why do you want to help me? You don't even know me. And I just told you I did something illegal."

"Like I said, I checked you out. I know your background. Jackson took advantage of you. Hell, if it had been me in your same position, I would've jumped at the chance to be rich too."

"That's just it, I didn't. I had decided not to go along, but then I walked into Duane's drug deal, and the next thing I know two men are dead and I'm running as fast as I can with a baby in my arms. I . . . I didn't think I had any choice left. I just wanted to get away."

"I can understand that, LuAnn. I really can."

"I've been running ever since, scared of my shadow, afraid somebody would find everything out. It's been ten years, but it's felt like a hundred." She shook her head and gripped her hands together.

"So I take it Jackson's in the area."

"He was in my garden about forty-five minutes ago."

"What?"

"I'm not sure what he was up to, but I'm assuming he's laying the groundwork for whatever plan he's about to implement."

"What sort of plan?"

"He's going to kill Donovan for starters."

"So I heard you tell Donovan."

"And then Jackson will probably come after us." LuAnn put her face in her hands.

"Well, you won't be seeing him again."

"You're wrong there, Matthew. I have to meet with him. And very soon."

He looked at her in absolute shock. "Are you crazy?"

"Jackson suddenly appeared in my bedroom last night. We had quite a lengthy discussion. I told him I was going to get to know you better. I don't think he had sex in mind, it just worked out that way."

"LuAnn, you don't —"

"He was going to kill you. In the cottage last night. I guess you went back for your truck. He said he was two feet from you. You're lucky to be alive. Very lucky."

Riggs sat back. His instincts had been right. That was a little heartening, despite the close call he had unwittingly experienced.

"He was going to check you out. He was concerned about your background, it was fuzzy. He was going to look into your background, and if he found anything worrisome, he was going to kill you."

"But?"

"But I told him I'd check you out instead."

"You took a risk there."

"Not as many as you've taken for me. I owed you. And I didn't want anything to happen to you. Not because of me."

Riggs spread his hands wide. "So why? Why the lottery fix? Did you give him some of your winnings?"

"All of it." Riggs looked blankly at her. LuAnn said, "He had control of the money for ten years; that period just ended. He invested the money and paid me some of the income from those investments."

"He had a hundred million to invest. How much did you earn each year?"

"Around forty million on the initial principal. He also invested any amounts I didn't spend. I earned tens of millions more on that each year."

Riggs gaped at her. "That's a forty percent return on your lottery money alone."

"I know. And Jackson made a lot more than that, I'm certain. He wasn't in this out of the goodness of his heart. It was a business transaction, plain and simple."

"So if you made forty percent, he probably made at least that and maybe more. That's a minimum of eighty percent return on your money. He could only have done that through illegal channels."

"I don't know about that."

"And at the end of ten years?"

"I got the hundred million back."

Riggs rubbed at his brow. "And if there were twelve of you at, say, an average of seventy million dollars each, this guy had almost one billion dollars to invest."

"He's got a lot more than that now, I'm sure." She looked at him, saw the worry lines. "What, what are you thinking?"

He looked at her steadily. "Another thing that's had the FBI's dander up." She looked puzzled. Riggs started to explain. "I know for a fact that for years now the FBI, Interpol, and a few other foreign law enforcement agencies have been aware of something: Tremendous amounts of money have been funneled into lots of activities across the globe, some legit, others not. At first the Feds thought it was drug cartel money, either from South America or Asia, partly to launder it. That didn't turn out to be the case. They picked up threads here and there, but the leads always fizzled. Someone with that much money can cover himself really well. Maybe that someone is Jackson." Riggs fell silent.

"You're sure the Feds don't know about the lottery?"

Riggs looked uneasy. "I can tell you, if they do, they didn't learn it from me. But they do

529

know of my inquiries about you. There was no getting around that."

"And if they've figured it out for themselves? Then we have Jackson *and* the federal government coming for us. Right?"

Riggs looked away for a moment and then stared her directly in the eye. "Right."

"And to tell you the truth, I'm not sure which one frightens me more."

They looked at each other, similar thoughts running through their minds. Two people against all of this.

"I need to go now," LuAnn said.

"Go where?"

"I'm pretty certain that Jackson's been following my movements closely. He'll know we've seen each other several times. He may know I've met with Donovan. If I don't report back to him right away" — here she took a painful swallow — "well, it won't be pretty."

Riggs gripped her shoulders tightly. "LuAnn, this guy is a psycho, but he must be brilliant as well. That makes him even more dangerous. You walk in there, the guy gets the least bit suspicious . . ."

She gently rubbed his arms with her hands. "Well, I just have to make sure he doesn't get suspicious."

"How in the hell are you going to do that? He already must be. I say we bring in the troops, set the guy up and take him."

"And me, what about me?"

Riggs stared at her. "I'm sure you could probably work a deal with the authorities," he said lamely.

"And the folks down in Georgia? You heard Donovan, they want to lynch me."

"The Feds could talk to them, they . . ." Riggs broke off as he realized absolutely none of what he was saying could be guaranteed.

"And maybe I work a deal with all of them. I give back the money. It might surprise you, but I really don't care about that. And then maybe I get a sympathetic judge, or judges, and they give me a break. Cumulatively what could I be looking at? Twenty years?"

"Maybe not that much."

"How much then?"

"I can't tell you that. I don't know."

"I'd make a real sympathetic defendant, wouldn't I? I can see the headlines now: Drug dealer-turned-murderess-turned-dream-stealer-turned-fugitive LuAnn Tyler living like a queen while people blow their Social Security checks on the lottery. Maybe they'd give me a prize instead of throwing away the key. What do you think?"

Riggs didn't answer and he couldn't manage to look at her either.

"And let's say we set Jackson up. What if we miss and he gets away? Or what if we nail him? Do you think with all his money, all his power, he might beat the rap? Or maybe he just might pay someone to carry out his revenge for him. Given that, what do you think my life is worth? And my daughter's life?"

Riggs did answer this time. "Nothing. Okay, I hear where you're coming from. But listen, why can't you report back to the guy over the phone? You don't need to see him in person."

LuAnn considered this for a minute. "I'll try," was all she could promise.

LuAnn stood up to her full height and gazed down at him. She looked twenty again, strong, rangy, confident. "Despite having zillions of dollars and traveling all over the world, I'm not the FBI. I'm still just a dumb girl from Georgia, but you might be a little surprised at what I can do when I set my mind to it." Lisa's face was conjured up in her thoughts. "And I've got a lot to lose. Too much." Her eyes seemed to look right through his, seeing something far, far down the road. When she spoke, her voice carried the full measure of her deep Southern roots. "So I'm not going to lose."

Chapter Forty-Four

George Masters stared down at the file intently. He was sitting in his office at the Hoover Building in Washington. Masters had been with the FBI for over twenty-five years. Ten of those years had been spent in the FBI's New York office. And now Masters was staring down at a name that he had become intimately familiar with ten years ago: LuAnn Tyler. Masters had been part of the federal investigation of Tyler's flight from the United States, and although the investigation had been officially closed years ago due to basic inertia, Masters had never lost interest mainly because none of it made sense. Things that didn't make sense bothered the veteran FBI agent greatly. Even after transferring to Washington, he had kept the case in the back of his mind. Now there were recent events that had ignited that spark of interest into a full flame. Matthew Riggs had made inquiries about LuAnn Tyler. Riggs, Masters knew, was in Charlottesville, Virginia. Masters knew Riggs, or who Riggs used to be, very well. If someone like Riggs was interested in Tyler, so was Masters.

After failing to prevent LuAnn Tyler's escape from New York, Masters and his team had spent considerable time trying to reconstruct the last several days leading up to her disappearance. He had figured that she would have either driven up from Georgia to New York or taken the train. She didn't have a driver's license or a car. The big convertible she had been spotted in had been found in front of the trailer, so she hadn't used that vehicle. Masters had then focused on the trains. At the station in Atlanta, Masters had hit the jackpot. LuAnn Tyler had taken the Amtrak Crescent to New York City on the day the authorities believed the murders were committed. But that wasn't all she had done. LuAnn had made a phone call from Otis Burns's car phone. Burns was the other dead man in the trailer. The FBI had traced the phone call. The number was an eight hundred number, but it had already been disconnected. Investigations into who had leased the phone number had run into a complete dead-end. That had gotten Masters's curiosity up even more.

Now that he was once again focused on LuAnn Tyler, Masters had instructed his men to go over NYPD records looking for any unusual events occurring around the time of LuAnn's disappearance. One item his men had just discovered had interested Masters greatly. A man named Anthony Romanello had been found dead in his New York apartment the night before the press conference announcing LuAnn as the lottery winner. The discovery of a dead body in New York City was hardly news; however, the police had been suspicious of Romanello's death because he had a long arrest record and was suspected of hiring himself out as an assassin. The police had probed into the details of what he had done on his last day among the living. Romanello and a woman had been seen at a restaurant shortly before Romanello had died; they had been observed having a serious argument. Barely two hours later, Romanello was dead. The official cause of death had been ruled cardiac arrest; however, the autopsy had revealed no sign of heart trouble in the youthful and strongly built man. None of those details had gotten Masters excited. What had gotten his adrenaline going was the description of the woman: It matched LuAnn Tyler precisely.

Masters shifted uncomfortably in his chair and lit up a cigarette. And then came the kicker: Found on Romanello's person was a receipt for a train ticket. Romanello had been in Georgia and returned to New York on the very same train with LuAnn, although they had been seated in separate compartments. Was there a connection? Drawing on information that had been long buried in his mind, the veteran FBI agent was beginning to piece things together from a clearer perspective. Maybe being away from the case all these years had been a good thing.

He had finished poring over the files he had accumulated on LuAnn Tyler, including records from the lottery. The winning ticket had been purchased at a 7-Eleven in Rikersville, Georgia, on the day of the trailer murders, presumably by LuAnn Tyler. Pretty nervy for her to stop and buy a ticket after a double homicide, Masters thought. The winning ticket had been announced on the following Wednesday at the drawing in New York. The woman fitting LuAnn's description had been seen with Romanello on Friday evening. And the press conference announcing LuAnn as the winner had been held on Saturday. But the thing was, according to Amtrak records and the ticket found on Romanello, both Tyler and Romanello had taken the Crescent train on the *previous* Sunday getting them into New York on Monday. If so, that meant LuAnn had left for New York City *before* she had known she had even won the lottery. Was she just running from a possible murder charge and coincidentally chose New York in which to hide, and then just happened to win a hundred million bucks? If so, she must be the luckiest person in the world. George Masters did not believe that anyone could be that lucky. He ticked off the points on his hand. Murders. Telephone call. Purchase of lottery ticket. Train to New York before winning ticket announced. LuAnn Tyler wins the lottery. Romanello and Tyler argue. Romanello dies. LuAnn Tyler, a twenty-year-old with a seventh-grade education and a baby, walks right through a massive police net and successfully disappears. She could not, Masters decided, have done that alone. All of this had been planned well in advance. And that meant one thing. Masters suddenly gripped the arms of his chair tightly as the conclusion hit him.

LuAnn Tyler knew that she was going to win the lottery.

The implications of that last thought sent a deep shudder through the grim-faced agent. He couldn't believe he hadn't seen that possibility ten years ago, but he had to admit it had never even occurred to him. He was looking for a potential murderer and nothing else. He drew solace from the fact that ten years ago he didn't have the Romanello angle to chew on.

Masters obviously wasn't old enough to remember all the lottery corruption from the last century, but he certainly remembered the game show scandals in the 1950s. Those would seem laughable by comparison to what the country might be now facing.

Ten years ago someone may have corrupted the United States Lottery. At least once, possibly more. The ramifications were truly terrifying to think about. The federal government depended on the revenue from that lottery to fund a myriad of programs, programs that were now so entrenched politically that it would be impossible to repeal them. But if the source of those funds was contaminated? If the American people ever discovered that fact?

Masters's mouth went dry with the thought. He swallowed some water from a carafe on his desk and downed a couple of aspirin to combat the beginnings of what would still become a torturous headache. He composed himself and picked up his phone. "Get me the director," he instructed. While he waited for the call to go through, Masters sat back in his chair. He knew this eventually would have to go up to the White House. But he'd let the director talk to the attorney general and the A.G. could talk to the president. If his conclusions were right, so much shit would hit the fan that everyone would eventually be covered in it.

Chapter Forty-Five

Jackson was again in his suite and was again staring at his laptop. LuAnn had met with Riggs several times now. Jackson would give her another few hours to call. He was disappointed in her nonetheless. He had not tapped LuAnn's phone line, an oversight that he had decided was not worth remedying at this point. She had caught him a little off-guard by sending Lisa away so quickly. The associate he had retained to track LuAnn's movements had been compelled to follow Charlie and Lisa, thereby depriving Jackson of a valuable pair of eyes. Thus, he did not know that LuAnn and Donovan had already met.

He had contemplated sending for more people so that all bases would be covered, but too many strangers lurking around town would probably raise suspicion. He wanted to avoid that if possible. Particularly because there was a wild card out there he was unsure of: Matt Riggs. He had transmitted Riggs's fingerprints to the same information source and was awaiting a reply.

Jackson's mouth sagged as the information spread over the screen. The name that appeared as the owner of the fingerprints was not Matthew Riggs. For a moment Jackson wondered if he could have lifted someone else's prints in the cottage by mistake. But that was impossible; he had seen the exact area the man calling himself Matt Riggs had touched. There could have been no mistake there. He quickly decided to check the other source of a possible mistake. He dialed the number and spoke at length to the person on the other end.

"This one was tricky," the voice said. "We went through normal channels initially to avoid any suspicions. We believe the request was kicked to senior level and we received back a 'no-fingerprint-found' reply."

"But a person was identified," Jackson said.

"Right, but only after we went back through other channels." Jackson knew that meant hacking into a database. "That's when we pulled up the information we transmitted to you."

"But it's a different name than the one he's using now and it lists him as being deceased."

"Right, but the thing is, when a criminal dies, the standard procedure is to fingerprint the corpse and transmit the prints to the FBI for verification. When that's completed, the pointer — the linkage used to retrieve the print from the database — is deleted. The result is that there are, technically, no prints of deceased criminals on the database."

"So how do you explain what you just sent

me? Why would they want to have this person listed as deceased but under another name?"

"Well, that tells me that the name listed on the database is his real one and the one he's using now is phony. The fact that he's listed as dead tells me that the Feds want people to believe he's dead, including anyone who might try to get access to their database to check. I've seen the Feds do that before."

"Why?"

The answer the man gave him caused Jackson to slowly hang up the phone. Now it all made sense. He stared at the screen.

Daniel Buckman: Deceased.

It was less than three minutes after LuAnn left that Riggs received a telephone call. The message was terse, but still managed to chill Riggs to the bone.

"Someone just made an unauthorized access of your fingerprint file through the Automated Fingerprint Identification System. And it was somebody who knew what he was doing because we didn't realize it happened until after the fact. Exercise extreme care, we're checking it out right now."

Riggs slammed down the phone and grabbed his receiving unit. He took a moment to unlock a drawer of his desk. He pulled out two pistols, two ammo clips, and an ankle holster. The larger pistol he put in his pocket and the smaller one he inserted in the holster he belted around his ankle. Then he ran for his Jeep. He hoped to God LuAnn hadn't found and removed the transmitter from her car.

Chapter Forty-Six

From the car phone LuAnn called the number Jackson had given her. He buzzed her back less than a minute later.

"I'm on the move too," he said. "We need to talk."

"I'm reporting back to you, like you said."

"I'm sure you are. I trust you have a good deal to tell me."

"I don't think we have a serious problem on our hands."

"Oh, really, I'm so very glad to hear it."

LuAnn responded testily. "Do you want to hear it or not?"

"Yes, but in person."

"Why?"

"Why not?" he fired back. "And I have some information that might be of interest to you."

"About what?"

"No, about whom. Matt Riggs. Like his real name, his real background, and why you should take every caution in dealing with him."

"You can tell me all that over the phone."

"LuAnn, perhaps you didn't hear me. I said you're going to meet me in person."

"Why should I?"

"I'll give you a wonderful reason. If you don't I'll find Riggs and kill him in the next half hour. I'll cut off his head and mail it to you. If you call to warn him, then I'll go to your home and kill everyone there from the maids to the gardeners and then I'll burn it to the ground. Then I'll go to your precious daughter's exclusive school and slaughter everyone there. You can keep calling, trying to warn the whole town, and I'll just start killing people at random. Is that a good enough reason, LuAnn, or do you want to hear more?"

LuAnn, pale and trembling at this verbal onslaught, had to force her next breath out. She knew that he meant every insane word. "Where and when?"

"Just like old times. Speaking of old times, why don't you ask Charlie to join us. This applies to him as well."

LuAnn held the phone away from her, staring at it as though she wanted to melt it down along with the man on the other end. "He's not around right now."

"My, my. And I thought he never left your side, the faithful sidekick."

Something in his tone touched a chord in LuAnn's memory. She couldn't think of what it was. "We're not exactly joined at the hip. He's got a life to live."

For now, Jackson thought. *For now, just like you. I'm having my doubts, though, I really am.*

"Let's meet at the cottage where our inquisi-

544

tive friend was nesting. Thirty minutes, can you manage it?"

"I'll be at the cottage in thirty minutes."

Jackson hung up the car phone and with an automatic motion felt for the knife hidden in his jacket.

Ten miles away LuAnn almost mirrored that movement, slipping off the safety on her .44.

Dusk was gathering as LuAnn drove down the tree-lined, leaf-strewn dirt road. The area was very dark. It had rained heavily the night before and a spray of water kicked up on her windshield as she drove through a deep puddle; she was momentarily startled. The cottage was up ahead. She slowed down and swept the terrain with her eyes. She saw no car, no person. She knew that meant nothing. Jackson seemed to appear and disappear whenever he damn well pleased with less rippling than a pebble flung across the ocean. She pulled the BMW to a stop in front of the ramshackle structure and climbed out. She knelt down for a moment and eyed the dirt. There were no other tire tracks and the mud would have shown any very clearly.

LuAnn studied the exterior of the cottage. He was already there, she was certain. It was as though the man carried a scent that was detectable only to her. It smelled like the grave, moldy and dank. She took one last deep breath and started toward the door.

Upon entering the cottage, LuAnn surveyed the small area.

"You're early." Jackson stepped from the shadows. His face was the same one from each of their face-to-face encounters. He liked to be consistent. He wore a leather jacket and jeans. A black ski cap covered the top of his head. Dark hiking boots were on his feet. "But at least you came alone," he added.

"I hope the same can be said of you." LuAnn shifted slightly so that her back was against a wall rather than the door.

Jackson interpreted her movements and smiled slightly. He folded his arms and leaned against the wall, his lips pursed. "You can start delivering your report," he ordered.

LuAnn kept her hands in her jacket, one fist closed around her pistol; she managed to point the muzzle at Jackson through the pocket.

Her movements were slight but Jackson cocked his head and smiled. "Now I distinctly remember you saying you wouldn't kill in cold blood."

"There are exceptions to everything."

"Fascinating, but we don't have time for games. The report?"

LuAnn started speaking in short bursts. "I met with Donovan. He's the man who was following me, Thomas Donovan." LuAnn assumed that Jackson had already run down Donovan's identity. She had decided on the drive over that the best approach was to tell Jackson mostly the truth and to only lie at critical junctures. Half truths were a wonderful way to inspire credibility, and right now she needed all she could muster. "He's a reporter with the *Washington Tribune*."

Jackson squatted on his haunches, his hands pressed together in front of him. His eyes remained keenly on her. "Go on."

"He was doing a story on the lottery. Twelve of the winners from ten years ago." She nodded toward Jackson. "You know the ones; they've all flourished financially."

"So?"

"So, Donovan wanted to know how, since so many of the other winners have gone belly-up. A very consistent percentage, he said. So your twelve sort of stuck out."

Jackson hid his chagrin well. He didn't like having loose ends, and this one had been glaring. LuAnn studied him closely. She read the smallest of self-doubts in his features. That was enormously comforting to her, but this was not the time to dwell on it.

"What did you tell him?"

"I told him I had been referred to an excellent investment firm by someone from the lottery. I gave him the name of the investment firm you used. I'm assuming they're legitimate."

"Very," Jackson replied. "At least on the surface. And the others?"

"I told Donovan I didn't know about them, but that they could have been referred to the same firm for all I knew."

"And he bought that?"

"Let's just say that he was disappointed. He wanted to write a story about the wealthy screwing the poor — you know, they win the lottery and then parasitic investment firms churn their accounts, earn their pieces of the pie, and leave the winner with nothing but attorney fees for filing bankruptcy. I told him that I certainly didn't support that conclusion. I had done just fine."

"And he knew about your situation in Georgia?"

"That's what drew him to me initially, I would imagine." LuAnn drew in a small breath of relief as she saw Jackson nod slightly at this remark. He apparently had arrived at the same conclusion. "He thought I would confess to some big conspiracy, I guess."

Jackson's eyes glittered darkly. "Did he mention any other theories, like the lottery being fixed?"

To hesitate now would be disastrous, LuAnn knew, so she plunged ahead. "No. Although he thought he had a big story. I told him to talk directly to the investment firm, that I had nothing to hide. That seemed to take the wind out of his sails. I told him if he wanted to contact the Georgia police he could go ahead. Maybe it was time to get things out in the open."

"You weren't being serious."

"I wanted him to believe I was. I figured if I made a big deal out of resisting or wanting to hide anything, he'd get even more suspicious. As it was, everything sort of fizzled for him."

"How did you leave it?"

"He thanked me for meeting with him, even apologized for troubling me. He said he might contact me later, but kind of doubted it." Once again LuAnn saw Jackson incline his head slightly. This was working out better than she could have expected. "He got out of my car and into his. That's the last I saw of him."

Jackson was silent for several moments and then he slowly rose, silently clapping his hands together. "I love a good performance and I think you handled the situation very well, LuAnn."

"I had a good teacher."

"What?"

"Ten years ago. The airport, where you impersonated an impersonation. You told me the best way to hide is to stick out, because it runs counterintuitive to human nature. I used the same principle. Be overly open, cooperative, and honest, and even suspicious people tend to rethink things."

"I am honored that you remembered all that."

A little ego-stroking went a long way with most men, LuAnn knew, and Jackson, exceptional though he was in many ways, was no exception in that regard. In an understatement of mammoth proportions, LuAnn said, "You're a little hard to forget. So you don't have to do anything with Donovan, he's harmless. Now tell me about Riggs."

A smile formed on the man's lips. "I witnessed your impromptu meeting with Riggs on the rear grounds this morning. It was rather picturesque. From your state of undress, I imagine he had quite a pleasant morning."

LuAnn hid her anger at this barb. Right now she needed information. She replied, "All the more reason why I should know all about him."

"Well, let's start with his real name: Daniel Buckman."

"Buckman? Why would he have a different name?"

"Funny question coming from you. Why do people change their names, LuAnn?"

Perspiration sprouted on her forehead. "Because they have something to hide."

"Precisely."

"Was he a spy?"

Jackson laughed. "Not quite. Actually, he's not anything."

"What do you mean by that?"

"I mean that dead men, technically, can't be anything other than dead, correct?"

"Dead?" LuAnn's entire body froze. *Had Jackson killed Matthew? It couldn't be.* She fought with all her might not to plunge to the floor. Luckily, Jackson continued.

"I obtained his fingerprints, had them run through a database and the computer told me that he's dead."

"The computer's wrong."

"The computer only relays what it's been told. Someone wanted it to appear that Riggs was dead in case anyone came looking."

"Came looking? Like who?"

"His enemies." When LuAnn didn't respond, Jackson said, "Have you ever heard of the Witness Protection and Relocation Program?"

"No. Should I?"

"You've lived abroad for so long, I suppose not. It's run by the federal government, more particularly by the United States Marshal's Service. It's to protect persons testifying against dangerous criminals or organizations. They get new identities, new lives. Officially, Riggs is dead. Shows up in a small town, starts a new life under a new identity. Maybe his features have been altered somewhat. I don't know for certain, but it's an educated guess on my part that Riggs is a member of that select group."

"Riggs — Buckman — was a witness? To what?"

Jackson shrugged. "Who knows? Who

cares? What I'm telling you is that Riggs is a criminal. Or was a criminal. Probably drugs or something like that. Maybe Mafia informant. Witness Protection isn't used for purse snatchers."

LuAnn settled back against the wall to keep herself from falling. *Riggs was a criminal.*

"I hope you haven't confided anything to him. There's no telling what his agenda might be."

"I haven't," LuAnn managed to say.

"So what can you tell me about the man?"

"Not as much as you just told me. He doesn't know any more than he did before. He's not pushing the issue. He thinks Donovan was a potential kidnapper. From what you just said, I'm sure he doesn't want to draw any attention to himself."

"True, that's very good for us. And I'm sure your little rendezvous this morning didn't hurt at all."

"That's really none of your business," she retorted hotly. With their exchange of information at an end, she wasn't going to let that remark pass.

"Ah, your first mistake this session. You just can't make it through without committing some blunder, can you?" He pointed a slender finger at her. "Everything about you is my business. I made you. And in a real sense I feel responsible for your well-being. I don't take that responsibility lightly."

LuAnn blurted out, "Look, the ten years is up. You've made your money. I've made mine. I say we call it a day, forever. In thirty-six hours I'll be on the other side of the world. You go your way, I'll go mine, because I'm more than real tired of all this."

"You disobeyed me."

"Right, well I spent ten damn years in twenty different countries, constantly looking over my shoulder, obeying *your* instructions. And I guess now I'll spend the rest of my life doing the same thing. So let me get to it." The two engaged in a stare-down of prolonged duration.

"You'll leave right away?"

"Just give me time to pack my bags. We'll be gone by tomorrow morning."

Jackson rubbed his chin as he considered this proposal. "Tell me something, LuAnn, tell me why I shouldn't kill you right now."

She had been prepared for that question. "Because Donovan might find it a little peculiar that right after he talks to me I end up a corpse. He's not suspicious now. I think I can guarantee you that would get his radar going. You really want that kind of trouble?"

Jackson pursed his lips for a moment and then motioned to the door. "Go pack."

LuAnn looked at him and motioned to the door. "You first."

"Let's leave together, LuAnn. That way, we'll each have a reasonable chance at reciprocating in kind in the event one of us tries something violent."

They went to the door together, their gazes glued to each other.

Right when Jackson put his hand on the doorknob, the door burst open, almost knocking him down.

Riggs stood there, his gun leveled on Jackson. Before he could fire, Jackson pulled LuAnn in front of him, his hand edging downward.

"Matthew, don't," LuAnn cried out.

Riggs shot her a glance. "LuAnn —"

LuAnn sensed rather than saw Jackson cock his arm. He was using an underhanded throwing method to hurl the knife, but it wouldn't be any less deadly that way.

Her hand shot out, partially colliding with Jackson's forearm. The next instant Riggs was grunting in pain, the knife sticking out of his arm. He dropped to the floor, clutching at the blade's handle. LuAnn pulled her gun out of her pocket and whipped around, trying to draw a bead on Jackson. At the very same time, Jackson pulled her backward against him.

Their combined momentum sent Jackson and LuAnn crashing through the glass window. LuAnn landed on top of him as they hit the porch, hard. LuAnn's pistol squirted free from her hand and slid across the porch. Each felt the subtle but undeniable strength of the other as they wrestled amid the thick, slippery shards of glass, trying to gain some footage. He clutched at her neck, she kicked at his groin, one of her elbows levered against his chin. Locked tightly together, they both rose slowly, each seeking an advantage. She noted the blood pouring from the grisly wound on Jackson's hand; he must have cut it going through the window. His grip couldn't be a hundred percent, she thought. With a sudden burst of strength that seemed to astonish even Jackson, LuAnn tore free from him, seized him by his belt and shirt front, and threw him face first against the side of the cottage where he slumped down, momentarily stunned from the impact. Without wasting an instant or any unnecessary motion, LuAnn propelled herself forward, straddled his back, gripped his chin with both hands, and pulled it backward, trying her best to crack his spine. Jackson screamed in pain as she pulled harder and harder. Another inch and he was a dead man. Her hands, however, suddenly slipped and she fell backward, landing in the glass. She exploded up and then froze as she looked down. In her hands was Jackson's face.

Jackson staggered up. For one terrible instant their eyes locked on each other. And for the first time, LuAnn was staring at Jackson's real face.

Jackson looked down at her hands. He

touched his face, felt his own skin, his own hair, his breath coming in great gasps. Now she could identify him. Now she had to die.

The same thought occurred to LuAnn. She dove for the gun at the same time Jackson pounced on her; they slid together along the porch, both straining for the gun.

"Get off her, you bastard!" Riggs screamed. LuAnn turned to see the man, deathly pale, standing at the window, his shirt entirely red, the gun in his shaky hands. With an enviable bit of speed Jackson leapt over the porch railing. Riggs fired an instant too late, the bullets striking the porch instead of flesh.

"Shit!" Riggs groaned and dropped to his knees, disappearing from LuAnn's line of sight.

"Matthew!" LuAnn sprung to the window. Meanwhile, Jackson had disappeared into the woods.

LuAnn raced through the door, pulling off her jacket as she did so. She was next to Riggs in an instant. "Wait, don't pull it out, Matthew." Using her teeth, she tore her jacket sleeve apart and into strips. Next, she ripped open his shirtsleeve and exposed the wound. At first she tried to staunch the bleeding with the cloths, but she couldn't. She searched under Riggs's armpit and applied pressure with her finger at a certain spot. The flow of blood finally stopped. As gently as she could LuAnn pulled the knife free while Riggs's fingers dug into her arm, his teeth almost biting through his lip. She tossed the blade down.

"Matthew, hold your finger right here, don't push too hard, you need to allow a little blood to flow through." She guided his finger to the pressure point under his arm that she had been pressing against.

"I've got a first-aid kit in my car. I'll dress it as best as I can. Then we need to get you to a doctor."

LuAnn retrieved her gun from the porch and they hustled out to the BMW, where LuAnn cleaned and dressed the wound using the first-aid kit from her glove compartment. As she cut the last piece of tape off with her teeth and wound it around the gauze, Riggs looked at her. "Where did you learn to do this stuff?"

LuAnn grunted. "Hell, the first time I ever saw a doctor was when Lisa was born. And even then it was only for about twenty minutes. You live in the boonies with no money, you have to learn how to do this just to survive."

When they got to an urgent care center off Route 29, LuAnn started to get out of the car to help Riggs in. He stopped her.

"Look, I think it'll be better if I go in alone. I've been to this place before, they know me. General contractors get hurt a lot. I'll tell 'em I slipped and stuck a hunting knife in my arm."

"You're sure?"

"Yeah, I think I made a big enough mess for you already."

He struggled out of the car.

"I'll be here when you get out, I promise," she said.

He smiled weakly, and holding his injured arm, he went inside.

LuAnn pulled the BMW around and backed into the parking space so she could see anyone coming in. She locked the doors and then swore under her breath. Riggs had come to her rescue, for that she could hardly fault him. But right before that she had Jackson convinced that everything was okay. Another minute and they would've been home free. God, the timing. She slumped against the seat. It was possible that she could explain Riggs's sudden and armed presence away. Riggs had been concerned for her safety, followed her, thinking maybe that the man she was meeting was Donovan. But Riggs had done something else, something that she couldn't explain away. She let out a loud groan as she watched the traffic pass by on Route 29.

In front of Jackson, Riggs had called her LuAnn. That one word had destroyed everything. There was no way he would've missed that. Now, Jackson knew she had lied to him about what Riggs knew. She had no doubt what the punishment for that would be. Her spirits had been so high barely thirty minutes ago. Now all bets were off.

She glanced down at the seat and saw the white piece of paper there. She picked up Donovan's card and looked at the phone number. She thought for a moment and then picked up the phone. She silently cursed when she only got the answering machine. She left a lengthy message telling Donovan what had happened. She implored him once again to go underground, that she would pay for everything. He was a good man looking for the truth. She didn't want him to die. She didn't want anyone else to die because of her. She hoped to God he would live to get the message.

Jackson pressed the cloth against his palm. He had indeed badly cut his hand going through the glass. Damn the woman. Riggs would've been dead if she hadn't hit Jackson's arm a millisecond before he released the knife.

He gingerly touched his real skin. A small lump had appeared thanks to one of her blows. He had finally felt her raw strength and he had to admit, it exceeded his own. Who would have thought it? The big muscle-bound types never possessed genuine God-given strength like that; that kind you couldn't manufacture in a health spa. It was a combination of both inner and outer phenomena, working in precise, albeit spontaneous, bursts when called upon. One couldn't measure it or quantify it, because it came and went upon demand by its owner and varied in its intensity depending on the situation, rising to the occasion and mustering just enough reserve so that failure was never a possibility. Either you had that type of power or you didn't. LuAnn Tyler clearly did. He would not forget that. He would not seek to conquer her that way, but, as always, he would adapt around it. And the stakes were as high as they were ever likely to climb, for one specific reason.

The irony was he had believed her. He had been prepared to let her walk away. LuAnn had confided in Riggs, that was clear. Riggs knew her real name. There were few actions that angered Jackson more than prevarication by his own people. Disloyalty could not and would not be tolerated. If she had lied about Riggs, it was more than probable that she had lied about Donovan. Jackson had to assume that the *Trib* reporter was closing in on the truth. Thus, he had to be stopped as well.

As these thoughts were going around in Jackson's mind, his portable phone rang. He picked it up. He listened, asked a few questions, conveyed some clear instructions, and when he hung up, a deep look of satisfaction graced his true features. The timing couldn't have been better: His trap had just been sprung.

Chapter Forty-Seven

The Bell Ranger helicopter landed in a grassy field where three black sedans bearing government license plates were waiting. George Masters alighted from the chopper, another agent, Lou Berman, right at his elbow. They climbed in one of the cars and started off. Riggs had seriously underestimated the quickness of the response time from Washington.

Twenty minutes later the procession made its way down the gravel road and stopped in front of Riggs's home. Car doors swung open and serious-looking men, weapons out and ready, swarmed the front and back of the house and barn.

Masters strode up to the front door. When his knocks were not answered, he motioned to one of his men. The burly agent planted one foot directly against the lock and the door flew open, crashing against the interior wall. After they searched the house thoroughly, they finally converged in Riggs's office.

Masters sat down at the desk and quickly rustled through the papers, his eyes alighting on one set of notes. Masters leaned back in the chair and intently studied Riggs's scribbles on LuAnn Tyler and someone named Catherine Savage. He looked up at Berman. "Tyler disappears and Catherine Savage reappears. That's the cover."

"We can check the airports, see if Catherine Savage flew out ten years ago," Berman said.

Masters shook his head. "We don't need to do that. They're one and the same. Tyler is here. Find out Savage's address pronto. Call up some of the high-end real estate agents around here. I don't think her highness will be living in another trailer."

Berman nodded, pulled out a portable phone, and went to confer with the local FBI agents who had accompanied them here.

Masters ran his eyes around Riggs's office. He was wondering how Riggs fit into all this. He had it nice here, new life, new career, peaceful, lot of good years left to live. But now? Masters had been at the White House meeting with the president, the attorney general, and the director of the FBI. As Masters had outlined his theory, he had watched each of their faces go sickly pale. A scandal of horrific proportions. The government lottery, fixed. The American people would believe that their own government had done it to them. How could they not? The president had publicly announced his support for the lottery, even appeared in a TV commercial touting it. So long as the billions flowed in, and a few lucky people were elevated to millionaire status, who cared?

The concept of the lottery had received attacks claiming that what it spent on furthering the public welfare was largely negated by what it cost in others: breakup of families, gambling addiction, making poor people even poorer, causing people to eschew hard work and industriousness for the unrealistic dream of winning the lottery. One critic had said it was much like inner city kids striving for the NBA instead of an MBA. However, the lottery had remained bulletproof from those attacks.

If it came out, however, that the game was fixed, then the bullets would rapidly shatter that bubble. There would be a tremendous blood-letting and everyone from the president on down was going to take a major hit. As Masters had sat in the Oval Office he saw that clearly in all their features: the FBI director, the nation's top lawman; the attorney general, the nation's top lawyer; the president, the number one of all. The responsibility would fall there and it would fall heavily. So Masters had been given explicit instructions: Bring in LuAnn Tyler, at any cost and by any means possible. And he intended to do just that.

"How's it feel?"

Riggs climbed slowly into the car. His right arm was in a sling. "Well, they gave me enough painkillers to where I'm not sure I can feel anything."

LuAnn put the car in gear and they sped out onto the highway.

"Where are we going?" he asked.

"McDonald's. I'm starving and I can't remember the last time I had a Big Mac and fries. Sound good?"

"Sounds good."

She pulled into the drive-through of a McDonald's, ordering some burgers, fries, and two coffees.

They ate as they drove. Riggs put down his coffee, wiped his mouth, and nervously fingered the dashboard with his good arm. "So tell me, how badly did I screw things up for you?"

"Matthew, I'm not blaming you."

"I know," he said sheepishly. He slapped the seat. "I thought you were walking into a trap."

She stared over at him. "And why's that?"

Riggs looked out the window for a long moment before answering. "Right after you left I got a call."

"Is that right. Who from, and what did it have to do with me?"

He sighed deeply. "Well, for starters, my name's not Matthew Riggs. I mean it's been my name for the last five years, but it's not my real name."

"Well, at least we're even on that score."

He said with a forced grin, "Daniel Buck-man." He held out his hand. "My friends call me Dan."

LuAnn didn't take it. "You're Matthew to me. Do your friends also know that technically you're dead and that you're in the Witness Protection Program?"

Riggs slowly withdrew his hand.

She flipped him an impatient look. "I told you that Jackson can do anything. I wish you'd start believing me."

"I was betting he was the one who tapped into my file. That's why I followed you. If he knew about me, I didn't know how he'd react. I thought he might kill you."

"That's always a possibility with the man."

"I got a good look at him."

LuAnn was exasperated. "That wasn't his real face. Dammit, it's never his real face." She thought of the rubbery flesh she had held. She had seen his real face. *His real face.* She knew what that meant. Jackson would now do everything in his power to kill her.

She slid her hands nervously over the steering wheel. "Jackson said you were a criminal. So what'd you do?"

"Are you telling me you believe everything that guy says to you? Just in case you didn't notice, he's a psycho. I haven't seen eyes like that since they executed Ted Bundy."

"Are you saying you're not in Witness Protection?"

"No. But the program isn't just for the bad guys."

She looked at him, puzzled. "What does that mean?"

"Do you think criminals can pick up the phone and get the sort of info I got on you?"

"I don't know, why can't they?"

"Pull over."

"What?"

"Just pull the damn car over!"

LuAnn turned into a parking lot and stopped the car.

Riggs leaned over and pulled out the listening device from under LuAnn's seat. "I told you I had bugged your car." He held up the sophisticated device. "Let me tell you, they almost never give out equipment like this to felons."

LuAnn looked at him, her eyes wide.

Riggs took a deep breath. "Up until five years ago, I was a special agent with the FBI. I'd like to think a *very* special agent. I worked undercover infiltrating gangs operating both in Mexico and along the Texas border. These guys were into everything from extortion to drugs to murder for hire; you name it, they were doing it. I lived and breathed with that scum for a year. When we busted the case open, I was the lead witness for the prosecution. We knocked out the entire operation, sent a bunch of them to prison for life. But the big bosses in Colombia didn't take all that kindly to my depriving them of about four hundred million a year in disposable income from the drug operation component. I knew how badly they'd want me. So I did the brave, honorable thing. I asked to disappear."

"And?"

"And the Bureau turned me down. They said I was too valuable in the field. Too experienced. They did have the courtesy to set me up in another town, in another gig. A desk job for a while."

"So there was no wife. That was all made up."

Riggs rubbed his injured arm again. "No, I was married. After I relocated. Her name was Julie."

LuAnn said very quietly, "Was?"

Riggs shook his head slowly and took a weary sip on his coffee. The steam from the liquid fogged the window and he traced his real initials in it, forming the D and the B for Dan Buckman with great care as though doing it for the very first time. "Ambush on the Pacific Coast Highway. Car went over the cliff with about a hundred bullet holes in it. Julie was killed by the gunfire. I took two slugs; somehow neither of them hit any vitals. I was thrown clear of the car, landed on a ledge. Those were the scars you saw."

"Oh, God. I'm so sorry, Matthew."

"Guys like me, we probably shouldn't get married. It wasn't something I was looking for.

It just happened. You know, you meet, you fall in love, you want to get married. You expect everything to sort of click after that. Things that you know might come up to ruin it, you sort of will them away. If I had resisted that impulse, Julie would still be alive and teaching first grade." He looked down at his hands as he spoke. "Anyway, that was when the brilliant higher-ups at the Bureau decided I just might want to retire and change my identity. Officially, I died in the ambush. Julie's six feet under in Pasadena and I'm a general contractor in safe, pastoral Charlottesville." He finished his coffee. "Or at least it used to be safe."

LuAnn slid her hand across the front seat and took his in a firm grip.

He squeezed back and said, "It's tough wiping out so many years of your life. Trying not to think about it, forgetting people and places, things that were so important to you for so long. Always afraid you're going to slip up." He stared at her. "It's damn tough," he said wearily.

She raised her hand up and stroked his face. "I never realized how much we had in common," she said.

"Well, here's another one." He paused for a second as their eyes locked. "I hadn't been with a woman since Julie."

They kissed tenderly and slowly.

"I want you to know," Riggs said, "that that

wasn't the reason this morning happened. I've had other opportunities over the years. I just never felt like doing anything about them." He added quietly, "Until you."

She traced his jaw line with her index finger and then her finger curled up to his lips. "I've had other chances too," she said. They kissed again and then their bodies instinctively embraced and held tightly like two pieces from a mold, joined at last. They sat and rocked together for several minutes.

When they finally pulled away, Riggs checked the parking lot, refocusing on the present situation.

"Let's get to your house, pack some clothes, and whatever else you need. Then we'll go to my house and I'll do the same. I left the notes I made from my phone calls about you on my desk. I don't want to leave a trail for anyone."

"There's a motel off twenty-nine about four miles north of here."

"That's a start."

"So, what do you think Jackson's going to do now?"

"He knows I lied about you. He has to assume I lied about Donovan. Since I have every reason not to reveal the truth and Donovan is trying his best to do that, Jackson will go after him first and me second. I called Donovan and left a message warning him."

"Boy, that's real encouraging, being number

two on Master Psycho's hit list," Riggs said, tapping his hand against the gun in his pocket.

A few minutes later they pulled up the private drive to Wicken's Hunt. The house was dark. LuAnn parked in front and she and Riggs got out. LuAnn punched in the home's security code and they went inside.

Riggs sat alertly on the bed while LuAnn stuffed some things in a small travel bag.

"You're sure Lisa and Charlie are okay?"

"As sure as I can be. They're far away from here. And him. That can only be a good thing."

Riggs went over to the window that overlooked the front drive. What he saw coming up the driveway made his knees buckle for an instant. Then he snatched LuAnn by the hand and they were racing down the stairs and out the rear entrance.

The black sedans stopped in front of the house and the men quickly scrambled out. George Masters laid a hand on the BMW's hood and immediately scanned the area. "It's warm. She's here somewhere. Find her." The men fanned out and surrounded the house.

LuAnn and Riggs were racing past the horse barn and were headed into the deep woods when LuAnn pulled up.

Riggs stopped too, clutching at his arm, sucking in air. They were both trembling.

"What are you doing?" he gasped.

She motioned toward the horse barn. "You can't run with that arm. And we can't just go floundering around in the woods."

They entered the horse barn. Joy immediately started to make some noise and LuAnn quickly darted over and soothed the animal. While LuAnn readied their mount, Riggs pulled a pair of binoculars off the wall and went outside. Setting up in some thick bushes that hid the horse barn from the house, Riggs focused the binoculars. He automatically jerked back as he saw, under the flood lights that fully illuminated the entire rear lawn, the man moving across the back of the house, rifle in hand and the letters "FBI" emblazoned across his jacket. The next sight made Riggs mutter under his breath. It was five years since he had seen the man. George Masters hadn't changed much. The next instant the men disappeared from view as they entered the house.

Riggs hustled back to the horse barn where LuAnn was checking the cinches on the saddle. She patted Joy's neck, whispering calming words to the horse as she slid on the bridle.

"You ready?" she asked Riggs.

"Better be. As soon as they find the house empty, they're going to check the grounds. They know we're around somewhere — the car's engine would've still been warm."

LuAnn planted a wooden crate next to Joy,

swung up, and reached out a hand for Riggs. "Step on the crate and hold on tight to me."

Riggs managed to struggle up in this fashion, clutching his arm as he did so. He planted his good arm around LuAnn's waist.

"I'll go as slow as I can, but it's going to jostle you a lot regardless. Horseback riding does that."

"Don't worry about me. I'll take a little pain to having to try and explain everything to the FBI."

As they started off on the trail LuAnn said, "So that's who it was? Your old friends?" Riggs nodded.

"At least one old friend in fact. Used to be a friend anyway. George Masters. He's the one at the Bureau who said I was too valuable in the field, who wouldn't let me enter Witness Protection until my wife was dead."

"Matthew, it's not worth it. There's no reason you should be running from them, you haven't done anything wrong."

"Look, LuAnn, it's not like I owe those guys anything."

"But if I'm caught and you're with me?"

"Well, we just won't get caught." He grinned.

"What's so funny?"

"I was just thinking how bored I'd been the last few years. I guess I'm not really happy unless I'm doing something where I have a reasonable shot at getting my head blown off.

I might as well own up to it."

"Well, you picked the right person to hang with then." She looked up ahead. "The motel's probably out of the question."

"Yep, they'll cover every place like that. Besides, riding up on a horse might make the motel manager suspicious."

"I've got another car back at the house, fat lot of good that'll do us."

"Wait a minute. We do have a car."

"Where?"

"We've got to get to the cottage, pronto."

When they arrived at the cottage, Riggs said, "Keep a sharp eye out in case you know who decided to come back." He opened up the doors to the rear shed and went inside. In the darkness, LuAnn couldn't see what he was doing. Then she heard a motor turn over and then die. Then it kicked over again and this time it kept running. A moment later, Donovan's black Honda, torn-up front bumper and all, appeared in the doorway. Riggs pulled it to a stop outside the shed doors and climbed out.

"What do you want to do with the horse?"

LuAnn looked around. "I could send her back up the trail. She'd probably go back to the horse barn on her own, but in the dark like this, she might miss the trail or wander off and fall in a hole or maybe the creek."

"How about we put her in the shed and then

you can call somebody to come get her?" he offered.

"Good idea." She swung down and led Joy inside the shed.

She looked around and noted the watering trough, tack wall, and two small bales of hay stored in the back of the shed.

"It's perfect. The tenant before Donovan must have kept a horse and used this as a stable."

Lifting off the saddle and slipping off the horse's bridle, LuAnn tethered Joy to a hook on the wall with a piece of rope she found. LuAnn scrounged up a bucket and, using water from the outside tap, she filled up the watering trough, and laid out the hay in front of Joy. The horse immediately dipped her head to the trough and then started to munch on the hay. LuAnn shut the doors and climbed in the driver's seat of the Honda while Riggs eased in the other side.

There was no key in the ignition. LuAnn glanced under the steering column and saw a bundle of exposed wires hanging down. "They teach hot wiring at the FBI?"

"You learn a lot of things going through life."

She put the car in gear. "Tell me about it."

They were silent and still for a moment and then Riggs stirred. "We may only have one shot at getting out of this relatively intact."

"And what's that?"

"The FBI can be accommodating to people who cooperate."

"But, Matthew —"

He broke in, "But they can be absolutely forgiving to people who give them what they really want."

"Are you suggesting what I think you are?"

"All we need to do is deliver Jackson to them."

"That's good to hear. For a minute there I thought it might be something difficult."

They drove off in the Honda.

Chapter Forty-Eight

It was ten o'clock in the morning. Donovan stared through a pair of binoculars at the large Southern colonial home set amid mature trees. He was in McLean, Virginia, one of the most affluent locales in the United States. Million-dollar properties were the norm here and that was typically only on an acre of land or less. The home he was staring at rested on five secluded acres. You had to have substantial wealth for a place like this. As he looked at the columned portico, Donovan knew without a doubt that the current owner had more than enough.

As he watched, a brand new Mercedes drove down the street from the opposite direction and approached the massive gates to the property. As the Mercedes nosed toward the entrance, the gates parted and the car entered the private drive. Through the binoculars, Donovan eyed the woman driving. In her forties now, she still matched her lottery photo from ten years ago pretty well. Lots of money could slow down the aging process, Donovan figured.

He checked his watch. He had gotten here early just to scope things out. He had checked his answering machine and had listened to LuAnn Tyler's warning. He wasn't going to run yet, but he had taken her advice quite seriously. He would've been a fool to think there weren't some serious forces behind all this. He took out the gun from his pocket and checked to make sure it was fully loaded. He scanned the area intently once more. He waited a few more minutes to give her time to get settled, then tossed his cigarette out the window, rolled it up, and drove toward the house.

He pulled up to the gates and spoke into an intercom. The voice answering him sounded nervous, agitated. The gates opened and a minute later he was standing inside the foyer that rose a full three stories above his head.

"Ms. Reynolds?"

Bobbie Jo Reynolds was trying her best not to meet his eye. She didn't speak, but simply nodded. She was dressed in a way Donovan would describe as very put together. You wouldn't have suspected that barely ten years ago she had been a starving actress wannabe hustling tables. She had been back in the country for almost five years now after a lengthy sojourn in France. During his investigation into the lottery winners, Donovan had checked her out thoroughly. She was now a very respected member of the Washington social community. He suddenly wondered if Alicia Crane and she knew each other.

After failing to get anywhere with LuAnn, Donovan had contacted the eleven other lottery winners. They had been far easier to track down than LuAnn; none of them were fugitives from the law. Yet.

Reynolds was the only one who had agreed to speak with him. Five of the winners had hung up on him. Herman Rudy had threatened bodily harm and used language Donovan hadn't heard since his Navy days. The others hadn't called back after he had left messages.

Reynolds escorted him into what Donovan figured was the living room — large, airy, and filled, presumably under an interior designer's tasteful eye, with contemporary furnishings, sprinkled here and there with costly antiques.

Reynolds sat down in a wingback chair and motioned Donovan to the settee across from her. "Would you like some tea or coffee?" She still didn't look at him, her hands nervously clasping and unclasping.

"I'm fine." He hunched forward, took out his notebook, and slipped a tape recorder from his pocket. "You mind if I record this conversation?"

"Why is that necessary?" Reynolds was suddenly showing a little backbone now, he thought. Donovan quickly decided to squelch that tendency before it gained any further strength.

"Ms. Reynolds, I assumed when you called me back that you were prepared to talk about things. I'm a reporter. I don't want to put words in your mouth, I want to get the facts exactly straight, can you understand that?"

"Yes," she said nervously, "I suppose I can. That's why I called you back. I don't want my name besmirched. I want you to know that I've been a very respectable member of this community for years. I've given generously to numerous charities, I sit on several local boards —"

"Ms. Reynolds," Donovan interrupted, "do you mind if I call you Bobbie Jo?"

There was a perceptible wince on Reynolds's face. "I go by Roberta," she said primly.

Reynolds reminded Donovan so much of Alicia he was tempted to ask if they knew each other. He decided to pass on that impulse.

"All right, Roberta, I know you've done a ton of good for the community. A real pillar. But I'm not interested in the present. I want to talk about the past, specifically ten years ago."

"You mentioned that on the phone. The lottery." She swept a shaky hand through her hair.

"That's right. The source of all this." He looked around at the opulence.

"I won the lottery ten years ago, that's hardly news now, Mr. Donovan."

"Call me Tom."

"I would prefer not."

"Fine. Roberta, do you know someone named LuAnn Tyler?"

Reynolds thought a moment and then shook her head. "It doesn't seem familiar. Should I know her?"

"Probably not. She won the lottery too, in fact two months after you did."

"Good for her."

"She was a lot like you. Poor, not a lot to look forward to. No way out, really."

She laughed nervously. "You make it sound like I was destitute. I was hardly that."

"But you weren't exactly rolling in dough, were you? I mean that's why you played the lottery, right?"

"I suppose. It's not like I expected to win."

"Didn't you, Roberta?"

She looked startled. "What are you talking about?"

"Who manages your investments?"

"That's none of your business."

"Well, my guess is it's the same person who manages the money of eleven other lottery winners, including LuAnn Tyler."

"So?"

"Come on, Roberta, talk to me. Something's up. You know all about it and I want to find out all about it. In fact, you knew you were going to win the lottery."

"You're crazy." Her voice was trembling badly.

"Am I? I don't think so. I've interviewed

lots of liars, Roberta, some very accomplished. You're not one of them."

Reynolds stood up. "I don't have to listen to this."

Donovan persisted. "The story's going to come out, Roberta. I'm close to breaking through on a variety of fronts. It's only a matter of time. The question is: Do you want to cooperate and maybe get out of this whole thing relatively unscathed or do you want to go down with everybody?"

"I . . . I . . ."

Donovan continued in a steady voice. "I'm not looking to wipe out your life, Roberta. But if you participated in a conspiracy to fix the lottery, in whatever manner, you're going to take some lumps. But I'll offer you the same deal I offered Tyler. Tell me all you know, I go and write my story and you do whatever you want to do until the story hits. Like disappear. Consider the alternative. It's not nearly as pretty."

Reynolds sat back down and looked around her home for a moment. She took a deep breath. "What do you want to know?"

Donovan turned on the recorder. "Was the lottery fixed?" She nodded. "I need an audible response, Roberta." He nodded toward the recorder.

"Yes."

"How?" Donovan was almost shaking as he waited for the answer.

"Would you mind pouring me a glass of water from that carafe over there?"

Donovan jumped up, poured the water, and set the glass down in front of her. He sat back down.

"How?" he repeated.

"It had to do with chemicals."

Donovan cocked his head. "Chemicals?"

Reynolds pulled a handkerchief from her pocket and wiped at a sudden cluster of tears in her eyes.

As Donovan watched her, he figured she was near the breaking point. Ironic that the one to call him back would be the nervous Nellie type.

"I'm no scientist, Roberta, give it to me as simply as you can."

Reynolds gripped the handkerchief tightly. "All but one ball, the one with the winning number, was sprayed with some chemical. And the passageway through which the ball traveled was sprayed with something. I can't explain it exactly, but it made certain that only the one ball that wasn't sprayed with anything went through. It was the same for all the other ball bins."

"Damn!" Donovan stared at her in amazement. "Okay, Roberta, I got a million questions. Do the other winners know about this? How was it done? And by whom?" He thought back to LuAnn Tyler. She knew, that was for damned sure.

"No. None of the winners knew how it was done. Only the people who did it knew." She pointed to his tape recorder. "Your recorder's stopped." She added bitterly, "I'm sure you don't want to miss one word of this."

Donovan picked up the recorder and studied it as he reflected on her words. "But that's not exactly right, because you knew how the lottery was fixed, Roberta, you just told me. Come on, give me the whole truth."

The crunching blow to his upper torso sent Donovan over the top of the settee. He landed hard on the oak floor, his breath painfully gone. He could feel shattered ribs floating inside him.

Reynolds hovered over him. "No, the truth is only the *person* who came up with the whole scheme knew how it was done." The feminine hair and face came off and Jackson stared down at the injured man.

Donovan tried desperately to get up. "Christ."

Jackson's foot slammed into his chest, knocking him back against the wall. Jackson stood erect. "Kick-boxing is a particularly deadly art form. You can literally kill someone without using your hands."

Donovan's hand slipped down to his pocket, fumbling for his gun. His limbs would barely respond, his broken ribs were prodding internal organs they weren't meant to touch. He couldn't seem to catch his breath.

"Really, you're obviously not feeling well. Let me help you." Jackson knelt down and, using the handkerchief, pulled the gun out of Donovan's pocket. "This actually is perfect. Thank you."

He kicked Donovan viciously in the head and the reporter's eyes finally closed. Jackson pulled plastic locking binds from his pocket and within a minute had Donovan secured.

He pulled off the rest of the disguise, packed it carefully in his bag pulled from under the couch, and went up the stairs two at a time. He raced down the hallway and opened the bedroom door at the far end.

Bobbie Jo Reynolds lay spread-eagled on the bed, her arms and legs tied to the bedposts, tape over her mouth. She looked wildly up at Jackson, her body twitching in uncontrollable fear.

Jackson sat down next to her. "I want to thank you for following my directions so precisely. You gave the staff the day off and made the appointment with Mr. Donovan just as I requested." He patted her hand. "I knew that I could count on you, the most faithful of my little flock." He looked at her with soft, comforting eyes until her trembling subsided. He unloosened her straps and gently removed the tape.

He stood up. "I have to attend to Mr. Donovan downstairs. We'll be gone very soon and won't trouble you anymore. You will stay here until we're gone, do you understand?"

She nodded in a jerky motion, rubbing her wrists.

Jackson stood up, pointed Donovan's gun at her, and squeezed the trigger until the firing pin had no bullets left to ignite.

He watched for a moment as blood spread over the sheets. Jackson shook his head sadly. He did not enjoy killing lambs. But that was how the world worked. Lambs were made for sacrifice. They never put up a fight.

He went back downstairs, pulled out his makeup kit and mirror, and spent the next thirty minutes hovering over Donovan.

When the reporter finally came to his head was splitting; he could feel the internal bleeding but at least he was still alive.

His heart almost stopped when he found himself staring up at . . . Thomas Donovan. The person even had his coat and hat on. Donovan refocused his eyes. His initial impression had been one of staring at his twin. Now he could see subtle differences, things that weren't exactly right. However, the impersonation was still remarkable.

Jackson knelt down. "You look surprised, but I assure you I'm very adept at this. Powders, creams, latex, hairpieces, spirit gum, putty. It really is amazing what one can do, even if it is all an illusion of sorts. Besides, in your case it wasn't all that difficult. I don't mean this in a negative way, but you have quite an ordinary face. I didn't have to do anything special and I've been studying your features for several days now. You did surprise me by shaving off your beard, though. However, instead of beard we have beard stubble courtesy of crepe hair and adhesive."

He grabbed Donovan under his armpits and lifted him up to the couch and sat down across from him. The groggy journalist listed to one side. Jackson gently propped him up with a pillow.

"It certainly wouldn't pass the closest of scrutiny; however, the result isn't bad for a half hour's work."

"I need to get to a doctor." Donovan managed to get the words out through blood-caked lips.

"I'm afraid that's not going to happen. But I will take a couple of minutes to explain some things to you. For what it's worth, I believe that I owe you that. You were quite ingenious in figuring out the bankruptcy angle. That, I admit, had never occurred to me. My main concern was to ensure that none of my winners would want for money. Any shortage of funds might give them motivation to tell all. Fat and happy people rarely double-cross their benefactor. You found the hole in that plan."

Donovan coughed and, with a sudden motion, managed to sit up straight. "How'd you pick up my trail?"

"I knew LuAnn would tell you basically

nothing. What would you do next? Ferret out another source. I phoned all my other winners and alerted them that you might call. Ten of them I instructed to blow you off. I told Bobbie Jo — excuse me, Roberta — to meet with you."

"Why her?"

"Simple enough. Geographically, she was the closest one to me. As it is, I had to drive through the night to get here and set everything up. That was me in the Mercedes, by the way. I had a description of you. I thought that was you in the car watching the house."

"Where's Bobbie Jo?"

"Not relevant." Jackson smiled both in his eagerness to explain and in his triumph and total control over the veteran reporter. "Now, to continue. The substance applied to nine of the ten balls was a clear light acrylic. If you care for precise details, it was a diluted solution of polydimethyl siloxane that I made a few modifications to, a turbocharged version if you will. It builds up a powerful static charge and also increases the size of the ball by approximately one thousandth of an inch without, however, a measurable change in weight or appearance or even smell. They do weigh the balls, you know, to ensure that all are of equal weight. In each bin the ball with the winning number on it had no chemicals applied to it. Each passageway through which the winning ball must travel was given a small trace of the modified polydimethyl siloxane solution as well. Under those precisely controlled conditions, the nine balls with the static charge could not enter a passageway coated with the same substance; indeed, they repelled each other, much like a force field. Thus they could not be part of the winning combination. Only the uncoated ball would be able to do so."

The awe was clear on Donovan's face, but then his features clouded. "Wait a minute: If the nine balls were coated with the same charge, why wouldn't they be repelling each other in the bin? Wouldn't that make people suspicious?"

"Wonderful question. I thrive on the details. I further modified the chemical so that it would be instantly activated by the heat given off by the air flow into the machines to make the balls gyrate. Until then, the balls would remain motionless."

Jackson paused, his eyes shining. "Inferior minds seek convoluted scenarios; it takes a brilliant one to achieve simplicity. And I'm sure your background research revealed that all of my winners were poor, desperate, searching for a little hope, a little help. And I gave it to them. To all of you. The lottery loved it. The government looked like saints helping the impoverished like that. You people in the media got to write your teary-eyed stories. Everybody won. Including me." Donovan half expected the man to take a bow.

"And you did this all by your lonesome?" Donovan sneered.

Jackson's retort was sharp. "I didn't need anyone else, other than my winners. Human beings are infinitely fallible, completely unreliable. Science is not. Science is absolute. Under strict principles, if you do A and B, then C will occur. That rarely happens if you inject the inefficiencies of humanity into the process."

"How'd you get the access?" Donovan was starting to slur his words as his injuries took their toll.

Jackson's smile broadened. "I was able to gain employment as a technician at the company that provided and maintained the ball machines. I was drastically overqualified for the position, which was one reason I got it. No one really cared about the geeky little techie, it was like I wasn't even there. But I had complete and unrestricted access to the machines. I even bought one of the ball machines so that I could experiment in private as to the right combinations of chemicals. So there I am, mister technician, spraying the balls with what everyone thought was a cleansing solution to get rid of dust and other grime that might have gotten into the bins. And all I had to do was hold the winning ball in my hand while I did so. The solution dries almost immediately. I surreptitiously drop the winning ball back into the bin and I'm all set."

Jackson laughed. "People really should respect the technicians of the world more, Mr. Donovan. They control everything because they control the machines that control the flow of information. In fact, I use many of them in my work. I didn't need to buy off the leaders. They're useless because they're incompetent showpieces. Give me the worker bees any day."

Jackson stood up and put on a pair of thick gloves. "I think that covers everything," he said. "Now, after I finish with you, I'm going to visit LuAnn."

Damn me for a fool for not listening to you, LuAnn, Donovan thought to himself.

Through the glove Jackson rubbed his injured hand where the glass had cut him. He had many paybacks planned for LuAnn.

"Piece of advice, A-hole," Donovan sputtered, "tangle with that woman and she'll cut your balls off."

"Thank you for your point of view." Jackson gripped Donovan tightly by the shoulders.

"Why're you keeping me alive, you son of a bitch?" Donovan tried to pull back from him, but was far too weak.

"Actually, I'm not." Jackson suddenly placed both hands around the sides of Donovan's head and gave it an abrupt twist. The sound of bone cracking was slight but unmistakable. Jackson lifted the dead man up and over his shoulder. Carrying him down to the garage, Jackson opened the front door of the Mercedes and pressed Donovan's fingers against the steering wheel, dash, clock, and several other surfaces that would leave good prints. Finally, Jackson clinched the dead man's hand around the gun he had used to kill Bobbie Jo Reynolds. Wrapping the body in a blanket, Jackson loaded it in the trunk of the Mercedes. He raced back into the house, retrieved his bag and Donovan's recorder, then returned to the garage and climbed behind the wheel of the Mercedes. In a few minutes the car had left the very quiet neighborhood behind. Jackson stopped by the side of the road, rolled down the window, and hurled the gun into the woods before pulling off again. Jackson would wait until nightfall and then a certain local incinerator he had found on an earlier reconnaissance would prove to be Thomas Donovan's final resting place.

As he drove on, Jackson thought briefly of how he would deal with LuAnn Tyler and her new ally, Riggs. Her disloyalty was now firmly established and there would be no more reprieves. He would focus his undivided attention on that matter shortly. But first he had something else to take care of.

Jackson entered Donovan's apartment, closed the door, and took a moment to survey the premises. He was still wearing the dead man's face. Thus, even if he had been spotted, it was of no concern to him. Donovan's body had been incinerated, but Jackson had a limited amount of time to complete his search of the late reporter's apartment. A journalist kept records, and those records were what Jackson had come for. Very soon the housekeeper would discover Bobbie Jo Reynolds's body and would call the police. Their search would very quickly, largely through Jackson's efforts, lead to Thomas Donovan.

He searched the apartment rapidly but methodically and soon found what he was looking for. He stacked the record boxes in the middle of the small foyer. They were the same ones Donovan had kept at the cottage in Charlottesville, filled with the results of his investigation into the lottery. Next he logged on to Donovan's computer and did a search of the hard drive. Thankfully, Donovan had not bothered to employ any passwords. The hard drive was clear. He probably kept everything on disk for portability. He looked at the back of the computer and then behind the desk. No phone modem. Just to be sure, Jackson again checked the icon screen. No computer services like America Online were present. Thus there was no e-mail to search. How old-fashioned of Donovan, he thought. Next he checked a stack of floppies in the desk drawer and piled them all in one of the boxes.

He would look at them later.

He was preparing to leave when he noted the phone answering machine in the living room. The red light was blinking. He went over to the phone and hit the playback button. The first three messages were innocuous. The voice on the fourth message made Jackson jerk around and bend his head low to catch every single word.

Alicia Crane sounded nervous and scared. Where were you, Thomas, she implored. You haven't called. What you were working on was too dangerous. Please, please call me, the message said.

Jackson rewound the tape and listened to Alicia's voice again. He hit another button on the machine. Finally, he picked up the boxes and left the apartment.

Chapter Forty-Nine

LuAnn looked at the Lincoln Memorial as she drove the Honda over the Memorial Bridge. The water of the Potomac River was dark and choppy. Flecks of white foam appeared but then quickly dissipated. It was the morning rush hour and the traffic over the bridge was heavy. They had spent one night in a motel near Fredericksburg while they decided what to do. Then they had driven to the outskirts of Washington, D.C., and spent the night at a motel near Arlington. Riggs had made some phone calls and visited a couple of retail establishments preparing for the events that would take place the next day. Then they had sat in the motel room eating while Riggs had gone over the plan, the details of which LuAnn quickly memorized. With that completed they had turned out the lights. One slept while the other kept watch. That was the plan at least. However, neither one got much rest. Finally, they both sat up, one curled around the other. Under any other circumstances they would have probably made love. As it was they spent the night looking out the window onto the dark street, listening for any sound that might herald another wave of danger.

"I can't believe I'm doing this," LuAnn said as they drove along.

"Hey, you said you trusted me."

"I do. I do trust you."

"LuAnn, I know what I'm doing. There are two things I know: how to build things, and how the Bureau works. This is the way to do it. The only way that makes sense. You run, they'll eventually find you."

"I got away before," she said confidently.

"You had some help and a better head start. You'd never get out of the country now. So if you can't run, you do the reverse, you go right at them, take the offensive."

LuAnn focused on the traffic at the same time she was thinking intently about what they were about to do. What she was about to do. The only man she had ever absolutely trusted was Charlie. And that complete trust had not come quickly, it had been built and then cemented over a ten-year period. She had only known Riggs for a very short time. And yet he had earned her trust, even in a matter of days. His actions reached her far more deeply than any words he could try to tempt her with.

"Aren't you nervous?" she asked. "I mean you don't really know what you're going to be walking into."

He grinned at her. "That's the really great part, isn't it?"

"You're a crazy man, Matthew Riggs, you really are. All I want in my life is a little predictability, a semblance of tranquillity, of normalcy even, and you're salivating over walking along the edge of the cliff."

"It's all in how you look at it." He looked out the window. "Here we are." He pointed to an open spot on the curb and she pulled over and parked. Riggs got out and then poked his head back in. "You remember the plan?"

LuAnn nodded. "Going over everything last night helped. I can find it with no trouble."

"Good, see you soon."

As Riggs walked down the street to the pay phone, LuAnn looked up at the large, ugly building. THE J. EDGAR HOOVER BUILDING was stenciled on its facade. Home of the Federal Bureau of Investigation. These people were looking for her everywhere and here she was parked ten feet from their damned headquarters. She shivered and put on her sunglasses. Putting the car in gear, she tried to keep her nerves in check. She hoped to hell the man really knew what he was doing.

Riggs made the phone call. The man on the other end was understandably excited. Within a few minutes Riggs was inside the Hoover Building and being escorted by an armed guard to his destination.

The conference room he was deposited in was large but sparsely furnished. He passed by the chairs gathered around the small table, and remained standing waiting for them to arrive.

He took a deep breath and almost cracked a smile. He had come home, in a manner of speaking. He scanned the room for any hidden cameras, and saw nothing obvious, which meant the room was probably under both audio and video surveillance.

He swung around when the door opened and two men dressed in white shirts and similar ties entered.

George Masters extended his hand. He was large, nearly bald, but his figure was trim. Lou Berman sported a severe crew cut and a grim demeanor.

"It's been a long time, Dan."

Riggs shook his hand. "It's Matt now. Dan's dead, remember, George?"

George Masters cleared his throat, looked nervously around, and motioned Riggs to sit down at the nicked-up table. After they were all seated, George Masters inclined his head toward the other man. "Lou Berman, he's heading up the investigation we discussed over the phone." Berman nodded curtly at Riggs.

Masters looked at Berman. "Dan" — Masters paused, correcting himself — "Matt was one of the best damned undercover agents we ever had."

"Sacrificed a lot in the name of justice, didn't I, George?" Riggs eyed him evenly.

"You want a cigarette?" Masters asked. "If I remember correctly, you were a smoker."

"Gave it up, too dangerous." He looked

over at Berman. "George here will tell you I stayed in the ball game one inning too many. Right, George? Sort of against my will, though."

"That was all a long time ago."

"Funny, it still seems like yesterday to me."

"Goes with the territory, Matt."

"That's easy to say when you haven't watched your wife get her brains blown out because of what her husband did for a living. How's your wife by the way, George? Three kids too, right? Having kids and a wife must be nice."

"All right, Matt. I get your point. I'm sorry."

Riggs swallowed hard. He was feeling far more emotion than he had expected, but it did feel like yesterday and he had waited half a decade to say this. "It would've meant a lot more if you had said it five years ago, George."

Riggs's stare was so intense that Masters finally had to look down.

"Let's get down to it," Riggs finally said, breaking out of the past.

Masters put his elbows up on the table and glanced over at him. "FYI, I was in Charlottesville two nights ago."

"Beautiful little college town."

"Visited a couple of places. Thought I might see you."

"I'm a working man. Gotta keep busy."

Masters eyed the sling. "Accident?"

"The construction business can be very hazardous. I'm here to strike a deal, George. A mutually satisfactory deal."

"Do you know where LuAnn Tyler is?" Berman leaned forward, his eyes darting all over Riggs's face.

Riggs cocked his head at the other man. "I've got her down in the car, Lou, you want to go check? Here." Riggs reached in his pocket, pulled out a set of keys, and dangled them in front of the FBI agent. They were the keys to his house, but Riggs figured Berman wouldn't take him up on the offer.

"I'm not here to play games," Berman snarled.

Riggs put the keys away and leaned forward. "Neither am I. Like I said, I'm here to make a deal. You want to hear it?"

"Why should we deal? How do we know you're not working with Tyler?"

"What do you care if I am?"

Berman's face turned red. "She's a criminal."

"I worked with criminals most of my career, Lou. And who says she's a criminal?"

"The state of Georgia."

"Have you really looked at that case? I mean really looked at it. My sources say it's bullshit."

"Your sources?" Berman almost laughed.

Masters intervened. "I've looked at it, Matt. It probably *is* bullshit." He glowered over at

Berman. "And even if it isn't, it's Georgia's problem, not ours."

"Right, and your interests should lie elsewhere."

Berman refused to give it up. "She's also a tax evader. She won a hundred million bucks and then disappeared for ten years and hasn't paid Uncle Sam a dime."

"I thought you were an FBI agent, not an accountant," Riggs shot back.

"Let's settle down, guys," Masters said.

Riggs leaned forward. "I thought you'd be a lot more interested in the person behind LuAnn Tyler, the person behind a lot of people. The invisible guy with billions of dollars running around the planet playing games, causing havoc, making your lives miserable. Now, do you want to get to him, or do you want to talk to LuAnn Tyler about her itemized deductions?"

"What are you suggesting?"

Riggs sat back. "Just like old times, George. We reel in the big fish and let the little one go."

"I don't like it," Berman grumbled.

Riggs's eyes played over the man's features. "Based upon my experience at the Bureau, catching the big fish gets you promoted and, more important, gets you pay raises; delivering the small fry doesn't."

"Don't lecture me on the FBI, Riggs, I've been around the block a few times."

"Good, Lou, then I shouldn't have to waste time on this crap. We deliver you the man and LuAnn Tyler walks. And I mean from everything — federal, taxes, and the state of Georgia."

"We can't guarantee that, Matt. The boys at the IRS go their own way."

"Well, maybe she pays some money."

"Maybe she pays a lot of money."

"But no jail. Unless we can agree on that, it's a no go. You have to make the murder charge go away."

"How about we arrest you right now and hold you until you tell us where she is?" Berman was inching forward, crowding Riggs.

"Then how about you never break the biggest case of your career. Because LuAnn Tyler will disappear again and you'll be stuck at point A again. And on what charge would you be holding me by the way?"

"Accessory," Berman fired back.

"Accessory to what?"

Berman thought for a moment. "Aiding and abetting a fugitive."

"What proof do you have of that? What actual proof do you have that I even know where she is, or have ever even met her?"

"You've been investigating her. We saw the notes in your house."

"Oh, so you came by my house on your visit to Charlottesville? You should've called ahead. I would've fixed up something nice for dinner."

"And we found lots of interesting stuff," Berman snapped.

"Good for you. Can I see the search warrant you used to enter my premises without permission?"

Berman started to say something and then clamped his mouth shut.

A thin smile broke across Riggs's face. "Great. No search warrant. All inadmissible. And since when is it a crime to make a phone call and get some *public* information on someone? Considering that I got that information from the Feds."

"Your WPP handler, not us," Berman said threateningly.

"I guess I treat all you guys as one big, happy family."

Masters started speaking slowly. "Supposing we do go along, you haven't given us the connection between Tyler and this other person."

Riggs had been expecting this question and was surprised it hadn't come up before. "He had to get the money from somewhere."

Masters considered this statement for a moment, and then his eyes flickered. "Listen, Matt, this is a little bigger than you probably know." He looked over at Berman briefly before continuing. "We know — or rather we think — the lottery was . . ."

Masters paused, searching for the right words. "We believe the lottery may have been compromised. Was it?"

Riggs sat back in his chair and tapped his fingers on the table. "Maybe."

Masters again chose his words carefully. "Let me make this real clear to you. The president, the A.G., the director of the FBI, they've all been apprised of this possibility. I can tell you that their collective reaction was one of absolute shock."

"Bully for them."

Masters ignored Riggs's sarcastic tone. "If the lottery was fixed, then this situation has to be handled very delicately."

Riggs chuckled. "Translation: If it ever gets out to the public, half the guys in Washington, including the president, the A.G., the director, and you two guys, will probably be looking through the want ads. So what you're suggesting is a major cover-up."

"Hey, this all probably happened ten years ago. It didn't occur on our watch," Berman said.

"Gee, Lou, that'll go over real big with John Q. Public. All of your butts are on the line here and you know it."

Masters banged his fist down on the table. "Do you realize what would happen if it becomes public that the lottery was fixed?" Masters said hotly. "Can you imagine the lawsuits, the investigations, the scandals, the blow it would give the old U.S. of A. right in the gut? It would almost be like the country defaulting on its debt. It cannot be allowed to happen. It *will not* be allowed to happen."

"So what's your suggestion, George?"

Masters rapidly calmed down and ticked off the points with his fingers. "You bring in Tyler. We question her, we get her cooperation. With that information in hand we bring in the people —"

"*Person*, George," Riggs interrupted. "There's just one of him, but let me tell you, he's a very special one."

"Okay, so with Tyler's help we nail him."

"And what happens to LuAnn Tyler?"

Masters spread his hands helplessly. "Come on, Matt, she's got a state murder warrant out. She hasn't paid taxes for almost a decade. I have to assume she was in on the lottery scam. That all adds up to a few lifetimes in prison, but I'll settle for just one, maybe half of one if she's real cooperative, but I can't guarantee it."

Riggs stood up. "Well, guys, it was nice talking to you."

Berman was up in an instant and he slid over to the door, blocking Riggs's exit.

"Lou, I've still got one good arm, and the fist attached to it is just itching like hell to plant one right across your face." Riggs started to advance menacingly toward the door.

"Wait a minute, just hold it. Both of you sit

down," Masters bellowed.

Riggs and Berman engaged in a suitably lengthy stare-down and then slowly returned to their seats.

Riggs stared over at Masters. "If you think the woman's going to waltz in here so she can risk her life in order to bring this guy down and then be rewarded by spending the rest of her life in prison, then you've hung around the Bureau too long, George. Your brains are gone."

Riggs pointed a finger at him. "Let me fill you in on something. It's the game of life and it's called 'who's got the leverage.' You call up the state of Georgia and tell them that LuAnn Tyler is no longer wanted for murder there, or for anything else. If she's got a friggin' parking ticket outstanding, then it's wiped out. You understand me? Squeaky clean. Then you call up the IRS and you tell them that she'll pay what she owes, but they can forget jail time. As far as being involved in any lottery scam, if the statute of limitations hasn't already expired, then that goes away too. The tiniest infraction that could possibly put her in jail for even a second gets blotted out. Gone. She's a free person."

"Are you nuts?" Berman said.

"Or?" Masters said quietly, his eyes fixed on Riggs.

"Or, we go public with everything, George. What does she have to lose? If she's going to go to prison for life, then she's going to have to have some hobbies to fill up her days. I'm thinking appearances on *Sixty Minutes*, *Dateline*, *Prime Time Live*, maybe even *Oprah*. A book deal would probably be in the cards too. She can just talk her little heart out about the lottery being fixed, how the president and the A.G. and the FBI director wanted to cover it all up to save their jobs and how they were stupid enough to let a master criminal who's been wreaking worldwide havoc for years walk away so they could put a young woman who grew up dirt-poor in prison for doing something all of us would've done in an instant!"

Riggs sat back and looked at both men. "That, gentlemen, is what I mean by leverage."

While Masters considered this, Berman snorted. "One guy? I don't believe that. We're looking at a big organization. No way could one person do all the stuff I've been seeing on my radar screen. We haven't been able to prove anything, but we know there are multiple players."

Riggs thought back to the cottage, right before the knife sliced into his arm. He had stared right into the most deadly pair of eyes he had ever seen. Over the years working undercover in some very dangerous situations, he had been scared before; he was only human after all. But he had never before felt the nervous terror those eyes had aroused in him. If he had had a crucifix handy, he would have pulled it out to ward the guy off.

He looked at Berman. "You know, Lou, you'd be surprised. This guy is a master of disguise. He can probably play enough roles to fill a Broadway musical. And by going it alone, he never has to worry about anyone turning snitch on him or trying to cut him out."

Masters started speaking in low tones as he tried a different tack. "Remember, Matt, not so long ago, you were one of us. You might want to think about that. You've obviously gained Tyler's confidence. You bring her in, well, let's just say your government would be very grateful. No more sawing and hammering to make a living."

"Let me think about that for a second, George." Riggs closed his eyes, reopened them almost instantaneously, and said, "Go to hell."

He and Masters locked eyes. "What do you say, George? Is it a deal? Or do I go and phone Oprah?"

Slowly, almost imperceptibly, Masters nodded.

"I'd really love to hear you say it, George."

Berman started to cut in, but Masters stared him into silence.

"Yes, it's a deal," Masters said, "no jail."

"Georgia too?"

"Georgia too."

"You sure you can do that? I know your authority is limited there." Riggs's tone was taunting.

"Mine is, but I don't think the president of the United States has that same problem. My instructions are to avoid public exposure at all costs. I guarantee that either he or the A.G. will make that phone call."

"Good, now get the director and the attorney general in here, because I want to hear the same things from them. By the way, is the president busy today?"

"There's no way in hell the president is meeting with you."

"Then get the director and the A.G. in here, George. Right now."

"You don't trust my word?"

"Let's just say your track record hasn't inspired my confidence all that much. And I take comfort in numbers." He nodded at the phone. "Make the call."

Masters and Riggs stared across at each other for at least a minute. Then Masters slowly picked up the phone and spoke into it at length. It took some schedule-juggling, but within thirty minutes the director of the FBI and the attorney general of the United States were sitting across from Riggs. Riggs presented the same deal to them he had presented to Masters, and he extracted the same promises.

Riggs rose. "Thank you for your cooperation."

Berman got up too. "All right, if we're working together now, bring Tyler in, we can wire
her, get a team together, and go get this 'one
man crime wave.' "

"Uh-uh, Lou. The deal was *I'd* bring him
in, not the FBI."

Berman looked ready to explode. "Listen
you —"

"Shut up, Lou!" The FBI director's eyes
bored into him and then he turned to look at
Riggs. "You really think you can pull this off?"

Riggs smiled. "Have I ever let you guys
down before?" He glanced over at Masters.

Masters didn't return the smile, but just
continued to study Riggs's face. "If you don't,
all bets are off. For Tyler." He paused and
then added ominously, "And you. Your
cover's blown. And I'm not sure how much
incentive we'd have to reestablish it. And your
enemies are still plenty active."

Riggs walked across the room to the door,
but then turned back. "Well, George, I never
really expected anything less from you guys.
Oh, and don't try to have me followed. That'll
just piss me off and waste a lot of time. Okay?"

Masters nodded quickly. "Sure, don't sweat
it."

The big-voiced attorney general asked a final question. "Was the lottery fixed, Mr.
Riggs?"

Riggs looked back at her. "You bet it was. And you want to know the kicker? It looks like the United States Lottery was used to finance the plans of one of the most dangerous psychopaths I've personally ever seen. I truly hope this never makes it onto the six o'clock news." His eyes swept the room taking in the steadily rising panic in each of their faces. "Have a good day." Riggs closed the door behind him.

The rest of the group looked around at each other. "Holy shit," was all the director could say, his head swaying from side to side.

Masters picked up the phone and spoke into it. "He's leaving the building now. He'll know he's being followed. Make it a short leash, but give him some room. He's an expert at this stuff, so he'll take you for a waltz around the city and then try to lose you. Be alert! When he hooks up with Tyler, communicate with me immediately. Keep them under surveillance, but don't approach them." He looked over at the A.G., who nodded her assent. Masters hung up the phone and took a deep breath.

"Do you believe Riggs's story that it's only one man behind all this?" the director asked, looking nervously at Masters.

"It sounds incredible, but I hope to God it's true," said Masters. "I'd rather be dealing with one guy than some worldwide crime syndicate." The A.G. and director both nodded in agreement.

Berman looked around with questioning eyes. "So what's the plan here?"

The director cleared his throat heavily and said, "We can't ever let this come out, you all know that. No matter what happens. No matter who gets hurt. Even if Riggs is successful and we are able to apprehend this person and any others involved in the scheme, then we still face a major problem."

The A.G. folded her arms across her chest and picked up this line of thought. "Even if we can build a case against him on all the other activities this person will know he has 'leverage,' to use Riggs's term. And he'll use the same threat Riggs used. Deal with him or he goes public. I can just see his defense lawyer salivating over that one." She involuntarily shuddered.

"So what you're saying is this thing can never go to trial," Berman said. "What then?"

The A.G. ignored the question and instead asked Masters, "You think Riggs is playing straight with us?"

Masters shrugged. "He was one of the best at undercover operations. To do that you have to lie on a regular basis and appear not to be. Truth takes a backseat. Sometimes reality becomes blurred. And old habits die hard."

"Meaning we can't completely trust him," the A.G. said.

Masters looked thoughtful for a moment. "No more than he can trust us."

"Well," the director said, "there's the strong possibility that we won't bring this guy in alive." He looked around the room. "Right?"

They all nodded. Masters ventured, "If he's half as dangerous as Riggs says he is, I'd shoot first and ask no questions later. Then maybe our problem goes away."

"And what about Riggs and Tyler?" the A.G. asked.

Berman answered, "Well, if we're going to go that route, you never know who might get caught in the crossfire. I mean none of us wants that to happen, of course," he quickly added, "but like Riggs's wife, you know, innocent people sometimes die."

"Tyler is hardly innocent!" the director said angrily.

"That's right," Masters said. "And if Riggs is tying his allegiances to her instead of us, well then he has to accept the consequences. Whatever they may be."

All of them looked at each other uneasily. Under normal circumstances, none of them would have been remotely contemplating any of this. They had dedicated their lives to apprehending criminals and then seeing them receive a fair trial before a court of law for their offenses. Their now silently praying that justice wouldn't happen this time, that instead several human beings would die before a judge or jury ever heard their case, was not sitting well with any of them. However, in this present case, they were all confronted with something much larger than merely hunting down a criminal. Here the truth was far more dangerous.

"Whatever the consequences may be," the director quietly repeated.

Chapter Fifty

Walking down the street, Riggs looked at his watch. The clock housing was actually a sophisticated recording device; the tiny perforations in the leather strap were the speaker component. The day before, he had spent some time in a well-known "spy shop" four blocks from the FBI building. The technology had certainly gotten better over the years. At least his deal with the government was recorded somewhere other than in his memory. With operations like this, he shouldn't put too much faith in anyone, no matter which side he was on.

Riggs knew that the government could never allow the truth to come out. In this case capturing the criminal alive was just as bad as not capturing him, maybe worse. And anyone who knew the truth was in serious jeopardy, and not just from Jackson. Riggs knew that the FBI would never intentionally gun down an innocent person. But he knew the FBI hardly regarded LuAnn as innocent. And since Riggs had thrown his support her way, he was automatically lumped with her as the enemy. If it got dicey toward the end, which Riggs knew it would, and if LuAnn were anywhere near Jackson, well, the FBI might not be real careful about who they were firing at. Riggs didn't expect Jackson to go down quietly. He would take out as many agents as he could. Riggs had seen that in his eyes at the cottage. The man had no respect for human life. To him a person was merely a factor to be manipulated and eliminated if circumstances called for it. As an undercover agent, Riggs had dealt with people like that for years. People almost as dangerous as Jackson. Given those elements, the FBI would err on the side of killing the man rather than taking him alive; they wouldn't risk the life of an agent in order to ensure that the man would stand trial. Riggs was well aware that the government had no incentive to bring Jackson to trial and every incentive not to. So Riggs's job was to flush out Jackson and then the Feds could do what they wanted. If that was pumping the man full of lead, Riggs would be glad to help them do so. But he was going to keep LuAnn as far away from the man as humanly possible. She was not going to be caught in the crossfire. He had been through that once. History was not going to repeat itself.

Riggs didn't bother to look behind him. He knew he was already under surveillance. Despite Masters's assurances to the contrary, he would have immediately ordered a tail. Riggs would've done the same thing in his position. Now he had to beat the tail before meeting up with LuAnn. He smiled. Just like old times.

While Riggs had been dealing with the FBI, LuAnn had driven to another pay phone and dialed a certain phone number. It rang several times and LuAnn thought she would probably get the standard automated message. Then a voice answered. She could barely recognize it, the connection was so bad.

"Charlie?"

"LuAnn?"

"Where are you?"

"On the road. I can barely hear you. Hold on, I'm passing some power lines."

In a moment, the connection was much clearer.

"That's better," LuAnn said.

"Hang on, there's someone who wants to talk to you."

"Mom?"

"Hello, baby."

"Are you okay?"

"I'm fine, sweetie, I told you Mommy would be fine."

"Uncle Charlie said you and Mr. Riggs saw each other."

"That's right. He's helping me. With things."

"I'm glad you're not alone. I miss you."

"I miss you too, Lisa, I can't tell you how much."

"Can we come home soon?"

Home? Where was home now? "I think so, baby. Mommy's working really hard on that right now."

"I love you."

"Oh, sweetie, I love you too."

"Here's Uncle Charlie."

"Lisa?"

"Yes?"

"I mean to keep my promise to you. I'm going to tell you everything. The truth. Okay?"

The voice was small, a little scared. "All right, Mom."

When Charlie came back on the phone, LuAnn told him to just listen. She filled him in on the latest events including Riggs's plan and his real background.

Charlie could barely contain himself. "I'm pulling over at a rest stop in two minutes. Call me back."

When LuAnn did so, Charlie's tone was heated. "Are you crazy?"

"Where's Lisa?"

"In the rest room."

"Is it safe?"

"I'm right outside the door and the place is packed with families. Now answer my question."

"No, I don't think I'm crazy."

"You let Riggs, an ex–FBI agent, walk into

the Hoover Building and cut a deal for you. How in the hell do you know he's not selling you down the river right now?"

"I trust him."

"Trust him?" Charlie's face turned crimson. "You barely know him. LuAnn, this is a big mistake, darling. A damned big one."

"I don't think so. Riggs is playing straight. I know he is. I've learned some things about him in the last few days."

"Like he's an experienced undercover agent who's an expert at lying."

LuAnn blinked for a second as these words sank in. A small seed of doubt suddenly grew, invading her confidence in Matthew Riggs.

"LuAnn, are you there?"

She gripped the phone hard. "Yes. Well, if he did sell me down the river, it won't be long before I find out."

"You've got to get out of there. You said you've got the car. Get the hell out of there."

"Charlie, he saved my life. Jackson almost killed him while he was trying to help me."

Charlie was silent for a minute. He was having an internal conflict and was highly uncomfortable with it. From everything LuAnn had just told him, Riggs probably was going to bat for her. Charlie thought he knew why: The man was in love with her. Was LuAnn in love with him? Why shouldn't she be? And where did that leave him? The fact was, Charlie wanted Riggs to be lying. He wanted the man out of their lives. That thought was skewing his whole mental process. But Charlie did love LuAnn. And he loved Lisa too. He had always put his own interests behind theirs. And with that thought his inner conflict disappeared. "LuAnn, I'll go with your instincts. Riggs is probably okay, now that I think about it. Just keep your eyes open, will you?"

"I will, Charlie. Where are you?"

"We headed through West Virginia, then into Kentucky, skirted the edge of Tennessee, and now we're floating back toward Virginia."

"I've gotta go now. I'll call later today and fill you in."

"I hope the rest of today isn't as exciting as the last two were."

"You and me both. Thanks, Charlie."

"For what? I haven't done anything."

"Now who's lying?"

"Take care of yourself."

LuAnn hung up the phone. She would be meeting Riggs soon if everything went according to plan. As she walked back to the car, Charlie's initial reaction came back to her. Could she trust Riggs? She slid into the front seat of the Honda. She had left it running because she had no keys and didn't share Riggs's skills at hot-wiring automobiles. She was about to put the car in gear when her hand stopped. This was no time for doubts, and yet she was suddenly overwhelmed with them. Her hand refused to move.

Chapter Fifty-One

Riggs walked slowly down Ninth Street, looking casually around, as if he had all the time in the world. A gust of freezing air hit him. He stopped, gingerly slipped off the sling, and put his injured arm in the sleeve of his overcoat, buttoning it all the way up. As the bitter wind continued to blow down the street, Riggs pulled up the collar of his overcoat, took a knit cap emblazoned with the Washington Redskins logo from his pocket, and pulled it tightly over his head so that only the lower part of his reddening face was visible. He entered a corner convenience store.

The two teams of agents that were following him, one on foot, the other in a gray Ford, swiftly moved into position. One team covered the front of the store, the other the rear. They knew Riggs was an experienced undercover agent and they weren't taking any chances.

Riggs appeared carrying a newspaper under his arm, walked down the street, and hailed a taxi. The agents quickly climbed into the sedan, and it followed the taxi.

Moments after the sedan disappeared, the real Matt Riggs, wearing a dark felt cap, emerged from the store and walked quickly in the opposite direction. The key had been the brightly colored knit cap. His pursuers would have focused on the burgundy and gold colors like a ship's beacon to pinpoint their man and would not notice the subtle differences in the overcoats, pants, and shoes. He had called in a favor last night from an old friend who had thought Riggs long dead. The FBI was now tailing that old friend to his job at a law firm near the White House. The man lived near the FBI building, so his being in the vicinity would not be difficult to explain. And a lot of Washingtonians wore Redskins knit caps this time of year. Finally, the FBI couldn't possibly know of the long ago connection between the two men. The agents would question him briefly, realize their mistake, report back to Masters and the director, and get their heads handed to them for their morning troubles.

Riggs climbed in a cab and gave an address. The car sped off. He ran a hand through his hair. He was glad to get that one under his belt. He and LuAnn were a long way from being home free, but it felt good to know he still had it, at least in small doses. As the cab stopped at a red light, Riggs opened the newspaper he had purchased at the store.

Staring back at him from the front page were

two photos. One person he knew, the other was a stranger to him. He quickly read the story and then looked at the pictures again. With a press badge dangling around his neck and a small notepad and pen peeking out from his shirt pocket, a sleepy-eyed Thomas Donovan looked like he had just climbed off a plane from covering some major news event on the other side of the world.

The woman in the photo next to his could not have struck a greater contrast to the reporter's disheveled image. The dress was elegant, the hair and makeup obviously professionally done and thus impeccable, the background almost surreal in its abundant luxury: a charity event where the rich and famous caucused to raise money for the less fortunate. Roberta Reynolds had been a longtime participant in such events and the story said her brutal murder had robbed the Washington area's charitable community of a great benefactor. Only one line of the story recounted the source of Reynold's wealth: a sixty-five-million-dollar lottery win ten years earlier. She was apparently worth far more than that now. Or, at least, now her estate was.

She had been murdered — allegedly, the story reported, by one Thomas Donovan. He had been seen around the woman's home. A message from Donovan requesting an interview was on the dead woman's answering machine. Donovan's prints had been found on a carafe of water and a glass in Reynolds's home, which indicated the two had indeed met. And, finally, the pistol apparently used to slaughter Roberta Reynolds had been found in a wooded area about a mile from her home, along with her Mercedes, with Donovan's prints all over both of them. The murdered woman had been discovered lying on her bed. Evidence indicated she had been bound and held for some period of time, so that the crime was obviously premeditated, the paper said. There was an APB out on Donovan and the police were confident they would soon apprehend him.

Riggs finished reading the story and slowly folded up the newspaper. He knew the police were completely wrong. Donovan hadn't killed Reynolds. And it was highly likely that Donovan was dead as well. Riggs took a deep breath and thought about how he would break the news to LuAnn.

Chapter Fifty-Two

The burly man looked around at the other pricey homes in the Georgetown neighborhood. Fiftyish with pale skin and a neatly trimmed mustache, the man hitched up his pants, tucked his shirt in, and rang the bell next to the front door.

Alicia Crane opened the door, looking anxious and tired.

"Yes?"

"Alicia Crane?"

"Yes."

The man flashed his identification. "Hank Rollins, homicide detective, Fairfax County, Virginia."

Alicia stared at the man's photo and the badge affixed to it. "I'm not sure —"

"Are you an acquaintance of Thomas Donovan?"

Alicia closed her eyes and bit her lip on the inside. When she reopened her eyes she said, "Yes."

Rollins rubbed his hands together. "Ma'am, I've got some questions to ask you. We can either do it down at the station or you can ask me in before I freeze to death, it's your call."

Alicia immediately opened the door. "Of

course, I'm sorry." She led him down the hallway to the living room. After settling him down on the sofa she asked him if he wanted coffee.

"That'd be great, yes, ma'am."

As soon as she left the room, Rollins lurched to his feet and looked around the room. One item commanded his immediate attention. The photo of Donovan, his arm around Alicia Crane. It looked to be of recent vintage. They both looked extremely happy.

Rollins was holding the photo in his hands when Alicia walked back in carrying a tray with two cups of coffee and some creamer and two blue packets of Equal.

She lowered the tray to the coffee table. "I couldn't find the sugar. The housekeeper ran an errand. She'll be back in about an hour and I don't usually —" Her eyes caught the photo.

"May I have that?" she asked. She set down the tray and held out her hand.

Rollins quickly passed the photo over and returned to his seat. "I'll get to the point, Ms. Crane. You've read the newspaper, I assume?"

"You mean that pack of lies." Her eyes flashed for an instant.

"Well, I'll agree that it's all largely speculation at this time; however, there's a lot of things pointing toward Thomas Donovan having killed Roberta Reynolds."

"His fingerprints and his gun?"

"It's an active homicide investigation, Ms.

Crane, so I can't really go into it with you, but, yes, things like that."

"Thomas wouldn't hurt anyone."

Rollins shifted his bulk around, picked up a cup of coffee, and stirred some cream into it. He tasted the result and then poured the contents of an Equal pack into the cup before he resumed speaking. "But he did go visit Roberta Reynolds."

Alicia crossed her arms and glared at him. "Did he?"

"He never mentioned it to you, that he was going to meet with her?"

"He told me nothing."

Rollins pondered this for a moment. "Ma'am, we got your name off Donovan's answering machine at his apartment. You sounded upset, said what he was working on was dangerous." Alicia didn't take the bait. "Also his place had been ransacked, all his records, files, everything gone."

Alicia started to shake, finally steadying herself by grasping the arm of the chair she was sitting in.

"Ms. Crane, you might want to have some of that coffee. You don't look too good."

"I'm all right." However, she did raise the cup and take several nervous sips.

"Well, if, as you say, someone went through Thomas's apartment, then there must be someone else involved. You should focus your efforts on apprehending that person."

"I'm not arguing with you on that point, but I have to have something to go on. I guess I don't have to tell you that Ms. Reynolds was a very prominent member of the community and we're getting a lot of heat to find her killer, pronto. Now I've already talked to someone at the *Trib*. He told me Donovan was working on a story having to do with lottery winners. And Roberta Reynolds was one of those winners. Now, I'm not a reporter, but when you're talking that kind of money, maybe somebody would have a motive for murder."

Alicia smiled for an instant.

"Something you want to tell me?"

Alicia returned to her prim manner and shook her head.

"Ms. Crane, I've been working homicide since my youngest was born and now he's got his own kids. Don't take this the wrong way, but you're holding out on me and I'd like to know why. Murder isn't something you want to screw around with." He looked at the elegant room. "Murderers and those who *assist* murderers don't end up in places nearly as nice as this one."

Alicia's eyes bulged at him. "What are you implying?"

"I'm not implying a damn thing. I came here looking for facts. I listened to your voice on Donovan's answering machine. That voice told me two things: First, you were scared for him; second, you knew exactly why you were scared for him."

Alicia kneaded and kneaded her lap with her fisted hands. She closed and opened her eyes several times. Rollins waited patiently while she went through her decision-making process.

When she started speaking it was in quick bursts. Rollins whipped out his notebook and scribbled.

"Thomas had initially started investigating the lottery because he was convinced that several top money management firms were taking the winners' money and either losing it or charging such huge commissions, churning, he called it, that the winners were left with nothing. He also hated the government for, in essence, leaving these poor people exposed to all of that. And then so many of them not understanding how to handle their taxes, and then the IRS coming in and taking everything back. And more. Leaving them with nothing."

"How did he arrive at that conclusion?"

"Bankruptcies," she said simply. "All these people were winning all this money and then they were declaring bankruptcy."

Rollins scratched his head. "Well, I've read about that from time to time. I always chalked it up to the winners' not being money savvy. You know, spend everything they get, forget to pay taxes, that kind of stuff, like you said.

Pretty soon, you can work your way right through all those winnings. Hell, I'd probably do the same thing, just go nuts."

"Well, Thomas didn't think that was all there was to it. But then he discovered something else." She took another sip of coffee, her face coloring prettily as she recalled Thomas Donovan's cleverness.

"Which was?" Rollins prodded.

"Which was the fact that twelve lottery winners in a row didn't declare bankruptcy."

"So?"

"So Thomas's research went back many years. In all that time the ratio of winners to bankrupt was completely consistent. Then, right in the middle of this consistency were twelve who didn't. Not only didn't they declare bankruptcy but they grew far wealthier."

Rollins rubbed his chin, unconvinced. "I'm still not seeing a story here."

"Thomas wasn't clear in his mind about that yet. But he was getting closer. He called me regularly from the road to let me know how things were going, what he had found out. That's why I was so worried when I hadn't heard from him."

Rollins looked at his notebook. "Right. You mentioned danger in your phone message."

"Thomas tracked down one of the twelve lottery winners." Alicia paused and struggled to remember the name. "LuAnn somebody. Tyler, that's right, LuAnn Tyler. He said she was charged with murdering somebody right before she won the lottery and then she disappeared. He tracked her down, partly through her tax records. He went to visit her."

"Now, where was this?" Rollins was again scribbling in his notebook.

"Charlottesville. Lovely country, some of the most beautiful estates. Have you ever been?"

"On my salary, I'm not really into estate shopping. What next?"

"He confronted the woman."

"And?"

"And she cracked. Or almost did. Thomas said you can always tell by the eyes."

"Uh-huh." Rollins rolled his own eyes. "So what was Donovan's angle?"

"Excuse me?"

"His angle. What story was he going to write that you thought put him in danger?"

"Oh, well, the woman was a murderer. She had killed once, she could kill again."

Rollins smiled lightly. "I see."

"I don't think you're taking this seriously."

"I take my work very seriously. I just don't see the connection. Are you suggesting that this LuAnn person killed Roberta Reynolds? Why would she do that? We don't even know if they knew each other. Are you suggesting that she may have threatened Donovan?"

"I'm not suggesting that LuAnn Tyler threatened or murdered anyone. I mean I have no proof of that."

"Then what?" Rollins was struggling to maintain his patience.

Alicia looked away. "I . . . I don't know. I mean I'm not sure."

Rollins stood up, closing his notebook. "Well, if I need any more information I'll be in touch."

Alicia just sat there, her face pale, her eyes shut. Rollins was almost at the door when she spoke. "The lottery was fixed."

Rollins slowly turned and walked back into the living room. "Fixed?"

"He called two days ago and told me that. Thomas made me promise not to breathe a word to anyone." She clutched at the hem of her skirt in her anxiety. "That LuAnn Tyler person practically admitted that the lottery was fixed. Thomas sounded, well, he sounded a little frightened. And now, I'm just so worried about him. He was supposed to call again, but never did."

Rollins parked his bulk on the sofa once more. "What else did he tell you?"

"That he had contacted the other eleven winners, but that only one had called him back." Her lips trembled. "Roberta Reynolds."

"So Donovan did meet with her." His tone was accusatory.

Alicia rubbed a tear from her eye. She didn't speak but merely shook her head. Finally she said, "He had been working on this story for a long time, but he only recently confided in me. He was scared. I could tell in his voice." She cleared her throat. "He had at least arranged to meet with Roberta Reynolds. The meeting was to take place yesterday morning. I haven't heard from him since that time, and he'd promised to call me right after it was over. Oh, God, I know something terrible has happened."

"Did he tell you who fixed the lottery?"

"No, but LuAnn Tyler told him to watch out for somebody. A man. That this person would kill him, that he was on Thomas's trail and would find him. That he was very dangerous. I'm sure this person had something to do with that woman's death."

Rollins sat back and stared sadly at her and took a big gulp of the hot coffee.

Alicia didn't look up. "I told Thomas to go to the police with what he knew."

Rollins sat forward. "Did he?"

She shook her head fiercely. "Dammit no!" A huge breath escaped her lungs. "I pleaded with him to. If someone had fixed the lottery, all that money. I mean people would kill for that. You're a policeman, aren't I right about that?"

"I know people who'd cut your heart out for a couple of singles," was Rollins's chilling reply. He looked down at his empty coffee cup. "Got any more?"

Alicia started. "What? Oh, yes, I just made a fresh pot."

Rollins took out his notepad again. "Okay, when you get back, we'll have to go over every detail and then I'm calling in some reinforcements. I'm not afraid to admit that this one is looking like it's way over my head. You up for a trip to police headquarters?"

Alicia nodded without much enthusiasm and left the room. She came back a couple of minutes later balancing the wooden tray, her eyes focused on the filled coffee cups, trying not to spill them. When she looked up her eyes widened in utter disbelief and she dropped the entire tray on the floor.

"Peter?"

The remnants of Detective Rollins — wig, mustache, facial mask, and malleable rubber padding — were neatly positioned on the wingback chair. Jackson, or Peter Crane, Alicia Crane's elder brother, was looking back at her, his features infinitely troubled as his right cheek rested on his right palm.

Donovan's observation that Bobbie Jo Reynolds had looked a lot like Alicia Crane was right on the mark. However, it had been Peter Crane's alias, Jackson, disguised as Bobbie Jo Reynolds, who looked a lot like Alicia Crane. The family resemblance was remarkable.

"Hello, Alicia."

She stared at the discarded disguise. "What

633

are you doing? What is all this?"

"I think you should sit down. Would you like me to clean up that mess?"

"Don't touch it." She put one hand against the doorjamb to steady herself.

"I didn't mean to upset you so," said Jackson with sudden sincere remorse. "I . . . I guess when faced with confrontation, I'm just more comfortable not being myself." He smiled weakly.

"I don't appreciate this at all. I almost had a heart attack."

He rose quickly, encircled her waist with one of his arms, and guided her over to the sofa. He patted her hand kindly. "I'm sorry, Alicia, I really am."

Alicia again stared over at the remains of the beefy homicide detective. "What is this all about, Peter? Why were you asking me all those questions?"

"Well, I needed to know how much you knew about everything. I needed to know what Donovan had told you."

She jerked her hand from under his. "Thomas? How do you know about Thomas? I haven't seen or spoken to you in three years."

"Has it been that long?" he said evasively. "You don't need anything, do you? You just had to ask."

"Your checks come like clockwork," she said, a bit bitterly. "I don't need any more money. It would have been nice to have seen you once in a while. I know you're very busy, but we are family."

"I know." He looked down for a moment. "I always said I would take care of you. And I always will. Family is family."

"Speaking of, I spoke with Roger the other day."

"And how is our decadent, undeserving younger brother?"

"He needed money, like always."

"I hope you didn't send him any. I gave him enough to last a lifetime, even invested it for him. All he had to do was stay within a reasonable budget."

"There's nothing reasonable about Roger, you know that." She looked at him a little nervously. "I sent him some money." Jackson started to say something, but she hurried on. "I know what you said all those years ago, but I just couldn't let him be thrown out on the street."

"Why not? It might be the best thing that ever happened to him. He shouldn't live in New York. It's too expensive."

"He wouldn't survive. He's not strong, not like Father."

Jackson held his tongue at the mention of their father. The years had not cleared up his sister's blindness in that regard. "Forget it, I'm not going to waste my time discussing Roger."

"I want you to tell me what's going on, Peter."

"When did you meet Donovan?"

"Why?"

"Please just answer the question."

"Almost a year ago. He did a lengthy piece on Father and his distinguished career in the senate. It was a wonderful, compelling testimonial."

Jackson shook his head in disbelief. She would have viewed it that way: the exact opposite of the truth.

"So I called Thomas up to thank him. We had lunch and then dinner and, well, it's been wonderful. Extraordinarily wonderful. Thomas is a noble man with a noble purpose in life."

"Like Father?" Jackson's mouth curled into a smirk.

"Very much like him," she said indignantly.

"It's truly a small world." He shook his head at the irony.

"Why do you say that?"

Jackson stood up and spread his arms to show the entire sweep of the room. "Alicia, where exactly do you think all of this came from?"

"Why, from the family money, of course."

"The family money? That was gone. All of it. Has been for years."

"What are you talking about? I know that Father ran into some financial difficulties along the way, but he recovered. He always did."

Jackson looked at her with contempt. "He recovered shit, Alicia. He didn't earn a dime of it. It was all made long before he was around. All he did was blow it. My inheritance, your inheritance. He pissed it away on himself and his lousy dreams of greatness. He was a fake and a loser."

She jumped up and slapped his face. "How dare you! Everything you have is because of him."

Jackson slowly rubbed his skin where she had hit him. His real skin was pale, smooth as though he had lived his life in a temple like a Buddhist monk, which in one sense he had.

"Ten years ago, *I* fixed the national lottery," he said quietly, his dark eyes glittery as he stared at her small, stunned face. "All that money, everything you have came from that money. From me. Not dear old Dad."

"What do you mean? How could you —"

Jackson pushed her down on the sofa as he interrupted.

"I collected almost one billion dollars from twelve lottery winners, the very same ones Donovan was investigating. I took their winnings and I invested the money. You remember Grandfather's network of Wall Street elite? He actually *earned* his money. I maintained those contacts over the years for a very specific purpose. With the fortune I amassed from the lottery winners, which Wall Street assumed came from the 'family money,' I was one of their preferred customers. I negotiated the best deals, was given first choice of all the initial public offerings, the sure-fire winners. That's a well-kept secret of the rich, Alicia. They get first dibs on everything: A stock that I get at ten dollars a share right before it hits the market goes to seventy dollars a share in the twenty-four hours after it hits the market. I sell it to the ordinary folks, collect my six hundred percent return, and move on to the next windfall. It was like printing money; it's all in who you know and what you bring to the table. When you bring a billion dollars, believe me, everybody sits up and takes notice. The rich get richer and the poor never will."

Alicia's lips had begun trembling halfway through her brother's explanation, as his speech and mannerisms grew more and more intense, more and more feverish. "Where is Thomas?" Her question was barely audible.

Jackson looked away and licked his dry lips. "He was no good for you, Alicia. No good at all. An opportunist. And I'm sure he loved all of this. All that you had. All that I had given you."

"*Was? Was* no good?" Alicia stood up, her hands clamped so tightly together the skin looked boiled.

"Where is he? What have you done to him?"

Jackson stared at her, searching her features for something. It suddenly occurred to him that he was looking for some redeeming quality. From afar he had long held idyllic visions of his only sister, putting her perhaps on a pedestal. Face-to-face with her he found that image was unsustainable. The tone of his response was casual, his words far from casual, as he finally made up his mind.

"I killed him, Alicia."

She stood there frozen for an instant and then started toppling to the floor. He grabbed her and laid her on the couch, this time not so gently. "Now don't be this way. There will be other men, I can assure you of that. You can walk the earth searching for Father. Donovan wasn't him, but I'm sure you'll keep trying." He didn't try to hide the sarcasm.

She wasn't listening to him, however. The tears stained her cheeks.

He continued despite her tears, pacing in front of her, the professor in front of his class of one. "You'll have to leave the country, Alicia. I erased your phone message to Donovan, so the police won't have that to go on. However, since your relationship has endured for a year, it must be well known to others. The police will come calling at some point. I'll make all the arrangements. As I recall, you've always loved New Zealand. Or perhaps Austria. We had several lovely times there as children."

"Stop it! Stop it, you animal."

He turned to find her on her feet.

"Alicia —"

"I'm not going anywhere."

"Let me be quite clear. You know too much. The police will ask questions. You have no experience in these matters. They will get the truth from you quite easily."

"You're right about that. I intend to call them right now and tell them everything."

She started for the phone, but he blocked her way. "Alicia, be reasonable."

She hit him with her fists as violently as she could. They did no physical damage to him; however, the blows conjured up the memory of another violent confrontation with another family member. His father, back then, had been physically stronger than he, was able to dominate him in ways that Jackson had never let himself be dominated since.

"I loved him, damn you! I loved Thomas," Alicia shrieked in his face.

Jackson focused a pair of watery eyes upon her. "I loved someone too," he said. "Someone who should have loved me back, respected me, but who didn't." Despite the years of pain, of guilt and embarrassment, Jack's son still held long-buried feelings for the old man. Feelings that he had never dwelt upon or vocalized until now. The resurgence of this emotional maelstrom had a violent impact on him.

He grabbed her by the shoulders and threw her roughly on the sofa.

"Peter —"

"Shut up, Alicia." He sat down next to her.

"You're leaving the country. You are not going to call the police. Do you understand?"

"You're crazy, you're insane. Oh, God, I don't believe this is happening."

"Actually, right now, I'm absolutely certain I'm the most rational member in the family." He stared into her eyes and repeated the words very slowly: "You're not talking to anyone, Alicia, do you understand?"

She looked at his eyes and suddenly shivered to the depths of her soul. For the first time during this confrontation, terror had suddenly replaced her anger. It had been a long time since she had seen her brother. The boy she had happily romped with, and whose maturity and intelligence she had been fascinated by, was now unrecognizable to her. The man across from her was not her brother. This manifestation was something else altogether.

She hastily changed course and spoke as calmly as she could. "Yes, Peter, I understand. I . . . I'll pack tonight."

Jackson's face took on a level of despair that it had not carried for many years. He had read her thoughts, her fears; they were so plainly written on the thin parchment of her soft features. His fingers clutched the large throw pillow on the sofa between them.

"Where would you like to go, Alicia?"

"Anywhere, Peter, anywhere you say. New Zealand, you mentioned New Zealand. That would be fine."

"It is a beautiful country. Or Austria, as I said, we had good times there, didn't we?" He tightened his grip on the pillow. "Didn't we?" he asked again.

"Yes we did." Her eyes dipped to follow his movements and she tried to swallow but her throat was too dry. "Perhaps I could travel there first and then on to New Zealand."

"And not a word to the police? You promise?" He lifted up the pillow.

Her chin trembled uncontrollably as she watched the pillow come toward her. "Peter. Please. Please don't."

His words were stated very precisely. "My name is Jackson, Alicia. Peter Crane doesn't live here anymore."

With a sudden pounce, he pushed her flat against the couch, the pillow completely covering her face. She fought hard, kicking, scratching, gyrating her body, but she was so small, so weak; he barely felt her fighting for her life. He had spent so many years making his body hard as rock; she had spent that time waiting for a precise replica of her father to stride gallantly into her life, her muscles and her mind growing soft in the process.

Soon, it was over. As he watched, the violent movements diminished quickly and then stopped altogether. Her pale right arm slid down to her side and then dangled off the couch. He removed the pillow and forced himself to look down at her. She at least deserved that. The mouth was partially open, the eyes wide and staring. He quickly closed them and sat there with her, patting her hand gently. He did not try to hold back his own tears. That would've done no good. He struggled to remember the last time he had cried but couldn't. How healthy was it when you couldn't even recall?

He placed her arms across her chest but then decided to have them clasped at her waist instead. He carefully lifted her legs up on the sofa and put the pillow he had used to kill her under her head, arranging her pretty hair so that it swept out evenly over the pillow. He thought she was very lovely in death despite the utter stillness. There was a peace there, a serenity that was at least heartening to him, as though what he had just done wasn't all that terrible.

He hesitated for a moment and then went ahead: He checked her pulse and laid her hand back down. If she'd still been alive, then he would've left the room, fled the country, and left it at that. He wouldn't have touched her like that again. She was family after all. But she was dead. He rose and looked down at her one last time.

It needn't have ended this way. Now all the family he had left was the useless Roger. He should go kill his brother right now. It should have been him lying there, not his cherished Alicia. However, Roger wasn't worth the effort. He froze for an instant as an idea occurred to him. Perhaps his brother could play a supporting role in this production. He would call Roger and make him an offer. An offer he knew his younger brother would be unable to resist as it would be all cash; the most potent drug in existence.

He gathered up the elements of his disguise, and methodically reapplied them, all the time making little darting glances at his dead sister. He had coated his hands with a lacquer-like substance, so he wasn't concerned about leaving fingerprints. He left by the back door. They would find her soon enough. Alicia had said her housekeeper had gone out to run an errand. It was a better than even chance that the police would think Thomas Donovan had continued his homicidal rampage by murdering his lady friend, Alicia Morgan Crane. Her obituary would be extensive, her family had been very important; there would be much to write about. And at some point, Jackson would have to come back, as himself once more, to bury her. Roger could hardly be trusted to do that. *I am sorry, Alicia. It shouldn't have come to this.* This unexpected turn of events had come closer than anything he could remember to completely immobilizing him. Above all else he cherished complete control and it suddenly had been stripped from him. He looked down at his hands, the instruments of his sister's death. His sister. Even now his legs felt rubbery, his body not in sync with his mind.

As he walked down the street, still reeling from what he had just done, Jackson's mental energies finally were able to focus on the one person he clearly saw as responsible for all of it.

LuAnn Tyler would experience the brunt of everything he was now feeling. The pain that slashed so viciously through him would be multiplied a hundredfold upon her until she would beg him to just finish her, make her stop breathing because every breath would be a hell, would be beyond what any person could endure. Even her.

And the grand part of it all was that he would not have to go looking for her. She would come to him. She would run to him with all the speed and strength her extraordinary physical specimen of a body could inspire. For he would have something that LuAnn would go anywhere, do anything for. He would hold something that LuAnn Tyler would die for. *And so you will LuAnn Tyler slash Catherine Savage.* As he disappeared down the street he swore this, over the mental image of a still-warm body whose dear face strongly resembled his own.

Chapter Fifty-Three

For the tenth time Riggs looked around the Mall and then checked his watch. In cutting his deal with the FBI, he had just shimmied out onto the most fragile limb in the world and LuAnn was three hours late. If she never showed up, where did that leave him? Jackson was still out there, and Riggs doubted if the knife would miss its mark a second time. If he didn't produce Jackson, fulfill his deal with his former employer, and have his cover reestablished, the cartel members who had sworn to kill him five years ago would soon learn that he was alive and they would surely try again. He couldn't return to his house. His business was probably already going to hell, and to top it off, he had five bucks in his pocket and no car. If he could have screwed up his life to any greater degree he was at a loss as to how.

He slumped on a bench and stared up at the Washington Monument while the cold wind whipped up and down the flat, open space that stretched from the Lincoln Memorial to the United States Capitol. The sky was overcast; it would be raining again soon. You could smell it in the air. Just wonderful.

And you're right between a rock and a hard place, Mr. Riggs, he said to himself. His emotional barometer had dropped to its lowest point since finding out his wife had perished in the gang attack five years ago. Had it really been less than one week ago that he had been leading a relatively normal life? Building things for wealthy people, reading books by his woodstove, attending a few night classes at the university, thinking seriously about taking a real vacation for a change?

He blew on his cold fingers and stuffed them in his pockets. His injured shoulder ached. He was just about to leave when the hand touched his neck.

"I'm sorry."

As he turned his head, his spirits soared with such swiftness that he felt dizzy. But he couldn't help smiling. He needed desperately to smile.

"Sorry for what?"

He watched as LuAnn settled in beside him, slipping her arm through his. She didn't answer right away. After staring off for a minute and then taking a heavy breath, she turned to him, stroked his hand with hers.

"I had some misgivings."

"About me?"

"I shouldn't have. After all you've done, I shouldn't have any doubts left."

He looked at her kindly. "Sure you should.

Everybody has doubts. After the last ten years, you should have more than most." He patted her hand, looked into her eyes, noted their moist edges, and then said, "But you're here now. You came. So it must be okay, right? I passed the test?"

She simply nodded her head, unable to speak.

"I vote for finding a warm place where I can fill you in on developments and we can discuss our plan of attack. Sound good?"

"I'm all yours." Her grip tightened on his hand as though she would never let go. And right now, that was just fine with him.

They ditched the Honda, which was acting up, and rented a sedan. Riggs was getting tired of hot-wiring the car anyway.

They drove to the outskirts of western Fairfax County and stopped for lunch at a nearly empty restaurant. On the drive out Riggs filled her in on the meeting at the Hoover Building. They walked past the bar area and sat at a table in the corner. LuAnn absently watched the bartender tinker with the TV to better the reception of a daytime soap he was watching. He slouched against the bar and pried between his teeth with a swizzle stick as he watched the small screen. It would be wonderful, she thought, to be that relaxed, that laid back.

They ordered their food and then Riggs pulled out the newspaper. He didn't say a word until LuAnn had read the entire story.

"Good Lord."

"Donovan should have listened to you."

"You think Jackson killed him?"

Riggs nodded grimly. "Probably set him up. Had Reynolds call him, say she was gonna spill her guts. Jackson is there and pops them both with the result that Donovan gets blamed for it all."

LuAnn let her head rest in her hands.

Riggs gently touched her head. "Hey, LuAnn, you tried to warn the guy. There was nothing else you could do."

"I could have said no to Jackson ten years ago. Then none of this would've happened."

"Yeah, but I bet if you had, he would've done you right then and there."

LuAnn wiped her eyes with her sleeve. "So now I've got this great deal with the FBI you negotiated for me, and in order to finalize it all we need to do is drop a net over Lucifer." She sipped on her coffee. "Would you care to tell me how we're going to do that?"

Riggs put away the paper. "I've been giving it a lot of thought as you might have guessed. The problem is we can't be too simplistic or too complicated. Either way, he'll smell a trap."

"I don't think he'll take another meeting with me."

"No, I wasn't going to suggest that. He wouldn't show, but he'd send somebody to kill you. That's way too dangerous."

"Didn't you know, I like danger, Matthew. If I wasn't constantly smothered in the stuff, I wouldn't know what to do with myself. Okay, no meeting, what else?"

"Like I said before, if we can find out who he really is, track him down, then we might be in business." Riggs paused as their food came. After the waitress left he picked up his sandwich and started talking in between bites. "You don't remember anything about the guy? I mean anything that could start us in the right direction to finding out who he really is?"

"He was always disguised."

"The financial documents he sent you?"

"They were from a firm in Switzerland. I've got some back at the house, which I guess I can't get to. Even with our deal?" She raised an eyebrow.

"I wouldn't advise that, LuAnn. The Feds run across you now, they might forget all about out little deal."

"I've got some other documents at my bank in New York."

"Still too risky."

"I could write the firm in Switzerland, but I don't think they're going to know anything. And if they do, I don't think they're going to talk. I mean, that's why people bank in Switzerland, right?"

"Okay, okay. Anything else? There's gotta be something you remember about the guy.

The way he dressed, smelled, talked, walked. Any particular interests? How about Charlie? Would he have any ideas?"

LuAnn hesitated. "We could ask him," she said, wiping her hands on her napkin, "but I wouldn't bet on it. Charlie told me he'd never even met Jackson face-to-face. It was always over the phone."

Riggs slumped back and touched his injured arm.

"I just don't see any way to get to him, Matthew."

"There is a way, LuAnn. In fact I had already concluded it was the only way. I was just going through the motions with all those questions."

"How?"

"You have a phone number where you can reach him?"

"Yes. So?"

"We set up a meeting."

"But you just said —"

"The meeting will be with me, not you."

LuAnn half stood up in her anger. "No way, Matthew, there is no way in hell I'm going to let you near that guy. Look what he did to you." She pointed at his arm. "The next time will be worse. A lot worse."

"It would've been a lot worse if you hadn't messed up his aim." He smiled tenderly at her. "Look, I'll call him. I tell him that you're leaving the country and all these problems behind. You know Donovan is dead, so Jackson doesn't have that issue anymore. Everybody's home free." LuAnn was vigorously shaking her head as she sat back down.

"Then I'll tell him," Riggs continued, "that I'm not such a happy camper. I've got it all figured out: I'm a little tired of construction work, and I want my payoff."

"No, Matthew, no!"

"Jackson figures I'm a criminal anyway. Trying to extort him wouldn't seem out of line at all. I'll tell him I bugged your bedroom, that I've got a recording of a conversation he had with you, that night at your house, where you both talked a lot about things."

"Are you nuts?"

"I want money. Lots of it. Then he gets the tape."

"He will kill you."

Now Riggs's face darkened. "He'll do that anyway. I don't like sitting around waiting for the other shoe to drop. I'd rather go on the offensive. Make him sweat for a change. And I may not be the killing machine he is, but I'm no slouch either. I'm a veteran FBI agent. I've killed before, in the line of duty, and if you think I'd hesitate one second before blowing his brains out, then you really don't know me."

Riggs looked down for a moment, trying to make himself calm down. His plan was risky, but what plan wouldn't be? When he looked back up at LuAnn, he was about to say something else but the look on her face froze the words in his mouth.

"LuAnn?"

"Oh, no!" Her voice was filled with panic.

"What is it? What's the matter?" Riggs grabbed her shoulder, which was quivering. She didn't answer him. She was looking at something over his shoulder. He whirled around, expecting to see Jackson coming for them, foot-long knives in either hand. He scanned the nearly empty restaurant and then his eyes settled on the TV where a special news report was being broadcast.

A woman's face spread across the screen. Two hours ago, Alicia Crane, prominent Washingtonian, had been found dead in her home by her housekeeper. The evidence collected so far suggested that she had been murdered. Riggs's eyes widened as he listened to the broadcaster mention that Thomas Donovan, prime suspect in the Roberta Reynolds murder, apparently had been dating Alicia Crane.

LuAnn could not pull her eyes away from that face. She had seen those features, those eyes staring at her from the front porch of the cottage. Jackson's eyes bored into her.

His real face.

She had shuddered when she had actually seen it, or realized what she was seeing. She had hoped to never lay eyes on those features again. Now she was staring at them. They were planted on the TV.

When Riggs looked back at her, she raised a shaky finger toward the screen. "That's Jackson," she said, her voice breaking. "Dressed up like a woman."

Riggs looked back at the screen. That couldn't be Jackson, he thought. He turned back to LuAnn. "How do you know? You said he was always in disguise."

LuAnn could barely take her eyes away from the face on the screen. "At the cottage, when he and I went through the window. We fought and his face, plastic, rubber, whatever, came off. I saw his real face. That face." She pointed to the screen.

Riggs's first thought was the correct one. *Family?* God, could it be? The connection to Donovan couldn't be a coincidence, could it? He raced to the phone.

"Sorry I lost your boys, George. Hope that didn't cost you any brownie points with the top brass."

"Where the hell are you?" Masters demanded.

"Just listen." Riggs recounted the news story he had just heard.

"You think he's related to Alicia Crane?" Masters asked, the excitement echoing in his voice, his anger at Riggs completely gone, for now.

"Could be. Ages are about right. Older or

654

younger brother maybe, I don't know."

"Thank God for strong genes."

"What's your game plan?"

"We check her family. Shouldn't be too hard to do. Her father was a U.S. senator for years. Very prominent lineage. If she has brothers, cousins, whatever, we hit 'em fast. Bring them in for questioning. Hell, it can't hurt."

"I don't think he's going to be waiting for you to knock on the front door."

"They never do, do they?"

"If he is around, be careful, George."

"Yeah. If you're right about all this —"

Riggs finished for him: "The guy just killed his own sister. I'd hate to see what he'd do to a nonfamily member."

Riggs hung up. For the very first time he actually felt hopeful. He was under no delusions that Jackson would be around for the FBI to take into custody. He would be flushed out, cut off from his home base. He'd be pissed, full of revenge. Well, let him be. He'd have to cut Riggs's heart out before he'd get to LuAnn. And they wouldn't be sitting targets. Now was the time to keep on the move.

Ten minutes later they were in the car heading for points unknown.

Chapter Fifty-Four

Jackson boarded the Delta shuttle for New York. He needed additional supplies and he was going to pick up Roger. He couldn't count on him to travel by himself and get to where he was supposed to be. Then they would head back south. During the short flight Jackson checked in with the man following Charlie and Lisa. They had made a rest stop. Charlie had talked on the phone. No doubt checking in with LuAnn. They had gone on and were now close to reentering Virginia on the southern side. It was all working out very well. An hour later, Jackson was in a cab threading its way through Manhattan toward his apartment.

Horace Parker looked around with intense curiosity. A doorman for over fifty years at a building where average apartments covered four thousand square feet and went for five million, and the penthouse that covered triple that space and went for twenty mil, he had never seen anything like this before. He watched as the small army of men in FBI windbreakers swept through the lobby and into the private elevator that went only to the penthouse. They looked deadly serious and had the weaponry to prove it.

He went back outside and looked up and down the street. A cab pulled up and out stepped Jackson. Parker immediately went over to him. The doorman had known him for most of his life. Years ago he had skipped pennies in the lobby's massive fountain with Jackson and his younger brother, Roger. To earn extra money he had baby-sat them and taken them to Central Park on the weekends; he had bought them their first beers when they were barely into puberty. Finally, he had watched them grow up and then leave the nest. The Cranes, he had heard, had fallen on hard times, and they had left New York. Peter Crane, though, had come back and bought the penthouse. Apparently, he had done awfully well for himself.

"Good evening, Horace," Jackson said cordially.

"Evening, Mr. Crane," Parker said and tipped his cap.

Jackson started past him.

"Mr. Crane, sir?"

Jackson turned to him. "What is it? I'm in a bit of a hurry, Horace."

Parker looked upward. "There's some men come to the building, Mr. Crane. They went right up to your apartment. A bunch of them. FBI. Guns and everything, never seen nothing like it. They're up there right now. I think they're waiting for you to get home, sir."

Jackson's reply was calm and immediate. "Thank you for the information, Horace. Simply a misunderstanding."

Jackson put out his hand, which Parker took. Jackson immediately turned and walked away from the apartment building. When Parker opened his hand, there was a wad of hundred-dollar bills there. He looked around discreetly before stuffing the cash in his pocket and taking up his position by the door once more.

From the shadows of an alley across the street, Jackson turned and looked up at his apartment building. His eyes kept going up and up until they came to rest upon the windows of the penthouse. His penthouse. He could see the silhouettes move slowly across the windows, and his lips started to tremble at this outrageous invasion of his home. The possibility that they could have traced him to his personal residence had not occurred to him. How in the hell? He couldn't worry about it now, though. He went down the cross street and made a phone call. Twenty minutes later a limousine picked him up. He called his brother and told him to leave his apartment immediately — not even bothering to pack a bag — and meet Jackson in front of the St. James Theater. Jackson wasn't sure how the police had found out his identity, but he couldn't be sure they wouldn't wind up at

Roger Crane's apartment at any minute. Then he made a quick stop to gather together some necessary supplies from another smaller apartment he kept under a phony name. Under the ownership of one of his myriad corporate shells he maintained a private jet and full-time crew at La Guardia. He called ahead so that the pilot on duty would be able to file his flight plan as quickly as possible. Jackson did not intend to spend time twiddling his thumbs in the waiting area. The limo would take them right to the plane. That accomplished, he collected his brother from in front of the theater.

Roger was two years younger and slimly built but wiry like his older brother. He also shared the same shock of dark hair and delicate facial features. He was certainly curious about his brother's abrupt return to his life. "I couldn't believe you called like that out of the blue. What's up, Peter?"

"Shut up, I need to think." He suddenly turned to his younger brother. "Have you seen the news?"

He shook his head. "I don't usually watch TV. Why?"

He obviously didn't know of Alicia's death. That was good. Jackson didn't answer his brother; he settled back in the seat, his mind racing through a seemingly infinite number of scenarios.

In a half hour they were at La Guardia Airport. Soon they had left the Manhattan skyline behind on their way south.

The FBI did converge on Roger Crane's small apartment building, but a little too late. Yet they were far more intrigued by what they had discovered at Peter Crane's penthouse.

Masters and Berman, walking around the massive penthouse, came across Jackson's makeup and archives rooms and his computerized control center.

"Holy shit," Berman said, his hands in his pockets as he stared at the masks, makeup bins, and racks of clothing.

Masters held the scrapbook gingerly in his gloved hands. FBI technicians roamed everywhere collecting evidence.

"Looks like Riggs was right. One guy. Maybe we *can* survive all this," Masters said.

"So what's our next move?"

Masters answered immediately. "We focus on Peter Crane. Put a blanket on the airports and train and bus stations. I want road blocks posted on all the major arteries heading out of town. You're to instruct all the men that he's extremely dangerous and a master of disguise. Send out photos of the guy everywhere, fat lot of good that'll do us. We've cut off his home base, but he's obviously got enormous financial resources. If we do manage to track him down, I want no unnecessary chances. Tell the men that if there's the slightest threat, to shoot him down."

"How about Riggs and Tyler?" Berman asked.

"So long as they don't get in the way, they'll be okay. If they get mixed up with Crane along the way, well, there's no guarantee. I'm not going to jeopardize my men to make sure they don't get hurt. As far as I'm concerned LuAnn Tyler belongs in jail. But that's why we've got some ammo with her. We can send her to jail or threaten to. I think she'll keep her mouth shut. Why don't you go oversee the rest of the evidence collection."

While Berman did so, Masters sat down and read the background information on LuAnn that accompanied her photo.

He was finishing up when Berman returned.

"You think Crane's going to go after Tyler now?" Berman asked.

Masters didn't answer. Instead he looked down at the picture of LuAnn Tyler staring back at him from the photo album. He now understood why she had been picked as a lottery winner. Why they had all been picked. He now had a much clearer idea of who LuAnn Tyler was and why she had done what she had. She had been destitute, stuck in a cycle of poverty, with an infant daughter. No hope. All of the chosen winners had shared this common denominator: no hope. They were ripe for this man's scheme. Masters's features betrayed the emotions he was feeling. Right at that very moment, and for a number of reasons, George Masters was starting to feel immense guilt.

It was nearing midnight when Riggs and LuAnn stopped at a motel. After checking in, Riggs phoned George Masters. The FBI agent had just returned from New York and he detailed to Riggs what had happened since they had last spoken. After receiving this briefing Riggs hung up the phone and looked over at a very anxious LuAnn.

"What happened? What did they say?"

Riggs shook his head. "As expected. Jackson wasn't there, but they found enough evidence to keep him in prison for the rest of his life and then some. Including a scrapbook on all the lottery winners."

"So he *was* related to Alicia Crane."

Riggs nodded grimly. "Her older brother, Peter. Peter Crane is Jackson. Or at least everything points that way."

LuAnn was wide-eyed. "Then he murdered his own sister."

"Looks that way."

"Because she knew too much? Because of Donovan?"

"Right. Jackson couldn't take a chance on that. Maybe he shows up disguised or maybe as his true self. He gets what he wants out of her, maybe he tells her he killed Donovan. Who knows. She apparently was dating the guy. She might have gone nuts, threatened to go to the police. At some point he murdered her, I feel sure of that."

LuAnn shuddered. "Where do you think he is?"

Riggs shrugged. "The Feds got to his house, but from the looks of the place the man has money to burn, a million different places he could go, a dozen faces and identities he could go there under. It's not going to be easy to catch him."

"To finish our deal?" LuAnn's tone was slightly sarcastic.

"We handed the Feds his friggin' identity. They're at his 'world' headquarters right now. When I said we'd deliver him, I didn't necessarily mean in a box with a ribbon on it, laid on the doorstep of the Hoover Building. As far as I'm concerned we've lived up to our end of the bargain."

LuAnn let out a deep breath. "So does that mean everything's square? With the FBI? And Georgia?"

"We'll have some details to work out, but yeah, I think so. Unknown to them, I recorded the entire meeting at the Hoover Building. I've got Masters, the director of the FBI, and the attorney general of the United States herself, acting upon the authority of the president of the United States no less, all on tape agreeing to the deal I proposed. They've got to play straight with us now. But I've gotta be straight with you too. The IRS is going to put a big dent in your bank account. In fact after so many years of compounded penalties and interest, I'm not sure how much money you're going to have left, if any."

"I don't care about that. I want to pay my taxes, even if it takes everything I've got. The truth is, I stole the money to begin with. I just want to know if I have to keep looking over my shoulder for the rest of my life."

"You're not going to prison, if that's what you mean." He touched her cheek with his hand. "You don't look too happy."

She blushed and smiled at him. "I am." Her smile quickly faded though.

"I know what you're thinking."

She blurted out, "Until they catch Jackson, my life's not worth spit. Or yours. Or Charlie's." Her lips trembled. "Or Lisa's." She suddenly jumped up and grabbed the phone.

"What are you doing?" Riggs asked.

"I need to see my daughter. I need to know that she's safe."

"Wait a minute, what are you going to tell them?"

"That we can meet up somewhere. I want her near me. Nothing's going to happen to her without it happening to me first."

"LuAnn, look —"

"This subject isn't open for discussion." Her tone was ferocious.

"All right, all right, I hear you. But where

are we going to meet them?"

LuAnn passed a hand over her forehead. "I don't know. Does it matter?"

Riggs said, "Where are they now?"

"The last I heard, they were heading back into southern Virginia."

He rubbed his chin. "What's Charlie driving?"

"The Range Rover."

"Terrific. It'll hold all of us. We'll meet them wherever they are right now. We'll leave the rental and head out. Go somewhere and wait for the FBI to do its thing. So call them and I'll run up to that all-night burger place we saw on the way in and get us some food."

"Good enough."

When Riggs got back with two bags of food, LuAnn was no longer on the phone.

"You reach them?"

"They're at a motel on the outskirts of Danville, Virginia. But I need to call them back and let them know when we're going to be there." She looked around. "Where the hell are we?"

"We're in Edgewood, Maryland, north of Baltimore. Danville is a little over a hundred miles south of Charlottesville, which means we're about five or six hours from Danville."

"Okay, if we start right now —"

"LuAnn, it's after midnight. They're probably in bed, right?"

"So?"

"So, we can catch some sleep, which we both really need, get up early, and meet them tomorrow around noon."

"I don't want to wait. I want Lisa safe with me."

"LuAnn, driving when you're exhausted isn't real safe. Even if we start right now, we won't make it until five or six in the morning. Nothing's going to happen between now and then. Come on, I think we've had enough excitement for one day. And if Lisa knows you're coming tonight, she won't get a wink of sleep."

"I don't care. I'd rather she'd be sleepy and safe."

Riggs shook his head slowly. "LuAnn, there's another reason we might not want to hook up with them right now, and it has to do with keeping Lisa safe."

"What are you talking about?"

Riggs put his hands in his pockets and leaned up against the wall. "Jackson is somewhere out there, that we know. Now, the last time we saw him he was running off into the woods. He could have easily come back and followed us."

"But what about Donovan and Bobbie Jo Reynolds and Alicia Crane? He killed them."

"We believe he killed them, or had someone kill them. Or he could've killed all of them personally and hired someone to follow us. That man has a deep pocketbook; there isn't much he can't buy."

LuAnn reflected briefly on Anthony Romanello. Jackson had hired him to kill her. "So Jackson could know about your meeting with the FBI? He could know where we are right now?"

"And if we go running off to see Lisa, then we lead him right to her as well."

LuAnn slumped down on the bed. "We can't do that, Matthew," she said wearily.

He rubbed her shoulders. "I know."

"But I want to see my little girl. Can't I do that?"

Riggs thought for a few minutes and then sat on the bed beside her and held her hands with his. "Okay, we'll stay here for the night. It would be a lot easier for someone to follow us at night and remain unseen. Tomorrow, we'll get an early start and head down to Danville. I'll keep an eagle eye out for anyone remotely suspicious. As an undercover agent, I got pretty good at that. We'll take secondary roads, make frequent stops, and occasionally take the interstate. It'll be impossible for anyone to tail us. We'll meet Charlie and Lisa at the motel and then we'll have Charlie take her directly to the local FBI office in Charlottesville. We'll follow in our car but we won't go in. I don't want them getting hold of you just yet. But since we struck a deal with the Feds, we might as well avail ourselves of some of their protection resources. How's that sound?"

She smiled. "So I'll see Lisa tomorrow?"

He cupped her chin in his hand. "Tomorrow."

LuAnn called Charlie back, setting the meeting time at one o'clock the following day at the motel in Danville. With Charlie, Riggs, and herself around her little girl, Jackson could just come on and try something, because she liked their odds of survival under those circumstances.

They slid into bed and Riggs wrapped his good arm around her slim waist and snuggled against her. His 9-mm was under his pillow, a chair wedged tightly under the door lock. He had unscrewed a light bulb, broken it, and sprinkled the remains in front of the door. Although he didn't expect anything to happen, he wanted as much advance warning as he could get if it did.

As he lay next to her he was both confident and uneasy. She apparently sensed this and turned to face him, her hand gently stroking his face.

"Got something on your mind?"

"Anticipation, I guess. When I was with the FBI I had to work hard to keep my patience. I seem to have a natural aversion to delayed gratification."

"That all?" Riggs slowly nodded. "You sure you're not sorry you got involved in all this?"

He pulled her closer to him. "Why in the world would I be?"

"Well, let me list some things for you. You've been stabbed, and came within an inch of dying. A madman is probably going to try his best to kill us. You stuck your neck out with the FBI for me and your cover is blown, with the result that the people who tried to kill you before may try again. You're running around the country with me trying to stay one step ahead of everybody and your business is going to hell and it doesn't look like I'll have two dimes to rub together to even begin to repay you for everything you've done. That cover it?"

Riggs stroked her hair and figured he might as well say it now. Who knew how things were going to go. He might not get another chance.

"You left out the part about me falling in love with you."

Her breath caught as her eyes drifted over him, taking in every subtle quiver, trying to give them all simultaneous meaning. All the while his words echoed in her head. She tried to say something but couldn't.

He filled in the silence. "I know it's probably the world's worst timing, but I just wanted you to know."

"Oh, Matthew," she finally managed to say. Her voice was trembling, everything about her was.

"I'm sure you've heard those words before. Lots of times, from guys probably a lot better suited —"

She covered his mouth with her hand but she didn't say anything for a long minute. He gently kissed her fingers.

Her voice was husky as though she were reaching down deep in order to utter the words. "Other men have said them. But this is the first time I've really been listening."

She stroked his hair and then her lips searched out and found his in the darkness and sunk in, slowly and deeply. They blindly undressed each other, their fingers probing and gently caressing. LuAnn began to softly cry as the unlikely twins of nervous fear and intense happiness fought for dominance. Finally, she just stopped thinking and gave herself over to what she had been looking for for so many years, across so many countries; from precious dreams that rudely dissolved into nightmares, which viciously framed realities that never came close to inspiring in her any more than an extreme ambivalence about her life. She clutched Matthew Riggs hard, as if realizing that this might be her last chance. Their bodies gripped each other for a long time before relaxing. They fell into an exhausted sleep safely in each other's arms.

Chapter Fifty-Five

Charlie rubbed the sleep from his eyes and stared over at the phone. It had been a couple of hours since LuAnn had filled him in on all the recent developments and he still couldn't get to sleep. So Jackson was really Peter Crane. That information personally did him no good, but Charlie figured it would help immeasurably the authorities' efforts to track the man down. On the downside, if Jackson knew his identity had been discovered, Charlie figured he would be one pissed-off person. And Charlie wouldn't want anyone he cared for to be in the vicinity of the gentleman if that was the case.

He pulled himself up from the couch. His knees were aching more than usual. All the driving was getting to him. He was very much looking forward to seeing LuAnn. And Riggs too, he supposed. Sounded like the guy had really come through for LuAnn. If he could pull all this off, well, it would be a miracle.

He went into the adjoining room and checked on Lisa. She was still sleeping soundly. He looked at her delicate features, seeing so much of her mother in them. She was going to be tall too. The last ten years had gone by so fast. Where would they all be next week? Where would he be? Maybe with Riggs in the equation, his run was coming to an end. He had no doubt that LuAnn would take care of him financially, but it would never be the same. But what the hell, the whirlwind that represented the last ten years with her and Lisa had been far more than he deserved anyway.

The ringing phone startled him. He checked his watch. Almost two A.M. He snatched up the receiver.

"Charlie?"

Charlie didn't recognize the voice at first. "Who's this?"

"Matt Riggs."

"Riggs? Where's LuAnn? Is she okay?"

"She's more than okay. They caught him. They caught Jackson." His tone was one of unbridled joy.

"Christ Almighty. Hallelujah! Where?"

"In Charlottesville. The FBI had put a team of agents together at the airport and he and his brother walked right into it. I guess he was coming to pay LuAnn back."

"His brother?"

"Roger. The FBI doesn't know if he's involved in all this, but I don't think they care. They've got Peter Crane. They want LuAnn to come to Washington in the morning to give a deposition."

"Tomorrow? What about meeting us down here?"

672

"That's why I called. I want you and Lisa to get packed up right now and meet us in Washington. At the Hoover Building. Ninth Street and Pennsylvania Avenue. They'll be expecting you. I set it all up. If you leave now, you can meet us for breakfast. I personally want to celebrate."

"And the FBI? The murder charge?"

"All taken care of, Charlie. LuAnn's home free."

"That's great, Riggs. That's the most wonderful news I've heard in I can't remember how long. Where's LuAnn?"

"She's on the other phone talking to the FBI. Tell Lisa that her mother loves her and can't wait to see her."

"You got it." He hung up and immediately started to pack. He would've loved to have seen Jackson's face when the FBI busted him. The prick. He figured he'd pack the car before waking Lisa. Might as well let her sleep as long as possible. When she heard the news about her mother Charlie was sure further sleep would not be possible for the little girl. It looked like Riggs had come through after all.

His heart lighter than it had been in years, Charlie, a bag under each arm, opened the front door.

He immediately froze. The man was standing in the doorway, his face covered by a black ski mask, a pistol in his hand. With a scream of rage, Charlie threw the bag at him, knocking the gun free. Next, Charlie grabbed the man by the mask and hurled him into the room, where he slammed against a wall and went down. Before the man could get up, Charlie was on top of him, hammering him with lefts and rights, his old boxing skills coming back as though he had never left the ring.

The piston-like battering took its toll as the man slumped down, groaning from the furious beating, and lay still. Charlie turned his head as he felt the second presence in the room.

"Hello, Charlie." Jackson closed the door behind him.

As soon as he recognized the voice, Charlie leapt for him, surprising Jackson with his quickness. The twin darts from the stun gun hit Charlie in the chest, but not before his massive fist collided with Jackson's chin, knocking him back against the door. However, Jackson continued to squeeze the trigger, sending the massive electrical current into Charlie's body.

Charlie was on his knees using all of his strength to try to rise, to kick the shit out of the man, to beat him into oblivion where he could hurt no one else. He tried to propel himself forward, every mental impulse in his brain craving nothing less than the man's complete destruction. But his body refused to follow his orders. As he slowly sank to the floor, he stared at a terrified Lisa standing in the doorway leading into the bedroom.

He tried to say something, tried to scream to her to run, to run like hell, but all that came out was something that would hardly qualify as a whisper.

He watched in horror as Jackson staggered up, flew over to Lisa, and pressed something against her mouth. The girl struggled valiantly but it was no use. As her nostrils sucked in the chloroform she was soon on the floor next to Charlie.

Jackson wiped the blood from his face and roughly pulled his associate up. "Take her to the car and don't let anyone see you."

The man nodded dully, his entire body one large hurt from Charlie's fists.

Charlie watched helplessly as the man carried the unconscious Lisa out. Then his eyes slid over to Jackson, who knelt down next to him, rubbing his chin gingerly.

Then, speaking in a voice that exactly impersonated Riggs, he said, "They caught Jackson. They caught him. I feel like celebrating." Then Jackson laughed out loud.

Charlie didn't say anything. He just lay there, watching, waiting.

In his own voice, Jackson said, "I knew my phone call would make you drop your guard just enough. Opening the door without checking first, no gun ready. How lax. You were really very diligent about not being followed, though. I knew you would be. That's why on the very first night I was in Charlottesville, I entered the garage at Wicken's Hunt and placed a transmitter inside the wheel well of each vehicle there, including your Range Rover. This particular transmitter was originally designed for military use and employs satellite-tracking technology. I could have followed you around the globe. It was very expensive, but obviously was well worth it.

"I knew after I met with LuAnn that she would send Lisa off with you and I needed to know exactly where you were just in case I needed little Lisa for the final showdown. I love strategic thinking, don't you? It's so rare when someone does it correctly. As it turns out, I do need her. That's why I'm here."

Charlie winced slightly when Jackson pulled the knife from his coat and he flinched again when Jackson pulled up the sleeve of Charlie's shirt.

"I really love this device," Jackson said, looking at the stun gun. "It's one of the few instruments I'm aware of that allows one to have full control over another without seriously injuring them and still leaving them fully conscious."

Jackson packed the stun gun away in his coat. He left the darts in Charlie. He wasn't worried about leaving any evidence behind this time.

"You sided with the wrong person." As Jackson said this he ripped open the shirtsleeve up to Charlie's shoulder to give himself a clear space in which to work. "You were loyal to LuAnn and look where it got you." Jackson shook his head sadly, but the smile on his face betrayed his true feelings of glee.

As slowly as he could, Charlie tried to flex his legs. He grimaced a little, but he could feel something down there. It hurt, but at least he could feel it. What Jackson didn't know was that one of the darts had hit Charlie's thick Crucifix, imbedding completely in it. The other dart had partially hit the medallion before entering his chest, with the result that the voltage that had rocked his body was far less than Jackson had counted on it to be.

"Now, the stun charge will last approximately fifteen minutes," Jackson lectured him. "Unfortunately, the cut I'm about to inflict upon you will only take about ten minutes to cause you to bleed to death. However, you won't feel anything, physically. Mentally, well, it might be rather unnerving watching yourself bleed to death and being absolutely powerless to do anything about it. I could kill you quick, but this way seems far more gratifying to me personally."

As he spoke, Jackson made a precise and deep gash in Charlie's upper arm. Charlie bit the inside of his jaw as he felt the sharp blade slice through his skin. As Charlie's blood started to pour out in a steady flow, Jackson rose.

"Good-bye, Charlie, I'll tell LuAnn you said

hello. Right before I kill her." Jackson snapped this last sentence out, his face a twisted mass of hatred. Then he smiled and closed the door.

Inch by agonizing inch, Charlie managed to roll over onto his back. Then, after an equally hard struggle, he brought his massive hands up, up until they closed around the darts. He was already dizzy from the blood loss. The sweat pouring off his brow, he pulled with all his strength and, little by little, the darts came loose and he tossed them aside. That didn't lessen the numbness of his body, but it felt good nonetheless. With what little control he had over his limbs, he slid over to the wall backward and inched his torso up to a sitting position by levering himself against this solid surface. His legs were on fire, the equivalent of a million burning needles stuck in them, and his body was covered in blood, but he managed to thrust himself upward as though he were squatting weights and his legs held, his knees locked in place. Ironically, the stun gun's impact had made his knees feel better than they had in years. Keeping himself pressed against the wall for support, he made it to the closet, which he managed to throw open. He pushed himself into the closet and gripped a wooden suit hanger with his teeth. All his limbs were on fire now, which was exhilarating because the slow return of his motor functions was becoming evident all over his body. He managed to grip the suit hanger in one hand and rip off the slender stem that normally kept trousers neatly in place. Dropping the rest of the hanger, he pushed off from the wall, propelling himself to the bed. Using his teeth and one of his hands, he shredded the bed sheet into strips. He worked more quickly now as his limbs returned to a semblance of normalcy. He was starting to feel nauseated; the blood loss was taking its toll. He was running out of time. As quickly as he could he wound a long strip directly above the cut and then used the thin piece of wood to torque down on it. The rude tourniquet worked its life-saving magic and the flow of blood finally halted. Charlie knocked the phone receiver off and punched in 911. After giving his location he sat back on the bed, sweat pouring off him, his entire body crimson from his own blood. He was still uncertain whether he was going to live or not, and yet all he could think about was the fact that Jackson had Lisa. He knew exactly what Jackson was going to do with her. The girl was bait. Bait to lure the mother. And when LuAnn went for that bait, Charlie knew exactly what would happen: Jackson would slaughter them both.

This terrifying thought was his last before he lost consciousness.

As the van moved down the highway, Jackson looked over at the unconscious Lisa, finally shining a penlight on her features so he could see them more clearly. "The spitting image of her mother," he said to himself. "She has her fighting spirit too," he added.

Jackson reached over and touched the young girl's face. "You were just an infant when I last saw you." He paused for a moment and looked out into the darkness before returning his gaze to her. "I'm very sorry it had to come to this."

He rubbed her cheek lightly, before slowly withdrawing his hand. Roberta, Donovan, his sister, Alicia, and now the little girl. How many more people was he going to have to kill? After this was all over, he told himself, he would go to the most remote location he possibly could find and do nothing for the next five years. When he had cleansed his mind of the events of this past week, he would go on with his life. But first he had to take care of LuAnn. That was one death he was not going to lose much sleep over.

"I'm coming, LuAnn," he said to the darkness.

LuAnn sat bolt upright in bed feeling as if every nerve were on fire. Her breath came in big chunks, her heart pounding out of control.

"Sweetie, what is it?" Riggs sat up and wrapped an arm around her quivering shoulders.

"Oh, God, Matthew."

680

"What? What is it?"

"Something's happened to Lisa."

"What? LuAnn, you were dreaming. You had a bad dream, that's all."

"He's got her. He's got my baby. Oh, God, he was touching her. I saw it."

Riggs pulled her around to face him. Her eyes were careening all over the room. "LuAnn, there's nothing wrong with Lisa. You had a nightmare. Perfectly natural under the circumstances." He tried to sound as calm as possible, although being wakened out of a dead sleep by this hysterical outburst had certainly unnerved him.

She pushed him off, jumped up, and started tossing things off the table next to the bed.

"Where's the phone?"

"What?"

"Where's the damned phone?" she screamed. As soon as she said it, she uncovered the phone.

"Who are you calling?"

She didn't answer. Her fingers flew across the face of the receiver as she punched in the cell phone number. She was almost vibrating off the ground as she waited for an answer. "They're not answering."

"So? Charlie probably turned off the phone. Do you know what time it is?"

"He wouldn't turn off the phone. He *never* turns off the damned phone." She redialed, with the same result.

681

"Well, if that's the case, maybe the battery's dead. If he didn't plug it in when he got to the motel."

LuAnn was shaking her head. "Something's happened. Something's wrong."

Riggs got up and went over to her. "LuAnn, listen to me." He shook her to the extent his wound would allow him. "Will you listen for a minute?"

She finally calmed down a bit and managed to look at him.

"Lisa is fine. Charlie is fine. You had a nightmare and that's all." He put his arm around her, squeezed her tightly to him. "We're going to see them tomorrow. And everything is going to be fine, okay? If we go tonight and we are being followed, we'll never know it. Don't let a nightmare make you do something that could end up *really* putting Lisa in danger."

She stared at him, terror still in her eyes.

He continued to murmur in her ear and his soothing tones finally reached her. She let him draw her back over to the bed and they climbed in. As he settled back to sleep, however, LuAnn stared at the ceiling, silently praying that it really had only been a nightmare. Something deep within her kept telling her it wasn't. In the darkness she could see what looked to be a hand reaching out for her. Whether in a friendly gesture or not she couldn't tell, because it never fully formed and then it was gone. She put an arm around the sleeping Riggs, holding him protectively. She would have given anything to be doing the same for her daughter.

Chapter Fifty-Six

The two FBI agents sipped hot coffee and enjoyed the late morning calm and beauty of the area. The winds were whipping up, however, as a storm system approached with the promise of even higher winds and a lot of rain, that night and into the next day. Stationed at the road leading up to LuAnn's home, the veteran agents had seen little activity, but they kept alert despite the tedium.

At eleven o'clock a car approached their checkpoint and stopped. The window came down on the driver's side.

Sally Beecham, LuAnn's housekeeper, looked expectantly at one of the agents and he quickly waved her through. She had gone out two hours before to run some errands. When she had passed the checkpoint earlier she had been very nervous. The FBI hadn't explained much to her, but they had made it clear that she wasn't in trouble. They wanted her to go about her normal duties, keep everything the same. They had given her a number to call in case she noticed anything suspicious.

As she passed through the checkpoint this time, she looked more comfortable, perhaps even a touch self-important with all of this official attention.

One of the agents commented to the other, "I don't think Tyler's going to be coming back to eat any of that food." His colleague smirked knowingly.

The next vehicle that came down the road and stopped at the checkpoint drew some special attention. The older man driving the van explained that he was the groundskeeper. The younger man in the passenger seat was his assistant. They produced ID, which the agents checked thoroughly, then made some phone calls to verify. The agents opened the back of the van and it was indeed filled with tools, boxes, and old rolled-up tarps. Just to make sure, one of the agents followed the van up the road.

Sally Beecham's car was parked in front; a shrill beep emanated from the house. The front door was open and the agent could see her just inside the door deactivating the alarm system, he presumed. He was proven correct when the beep stopped. The agent watched the men get out of the van, pull some tools from the back of the vehicle, stack them in a wheelbarrow, and head around to the back of the house. Then the agent got in his car and drove back to the checkpoint.

LuAnn and Riggs were standing in the parking lot of the motel outside Danville, Virginia.

Riggs had talked to the motel manager. The police had been summoned the night before. The man in Room 112 had been attacked and badly injured. Because of the severity of the wound, a medevac helicopter had been called to airlift out the man. The name the man had given was not Charlie's; however, that meant nothing. And the manager was not aware of a young girl being with the man.

"You're sure they were in room one twelve?"

LuAnn whirled around. "Of course I'm sure."

She closed her eyes, stopped pacing, and rocked on her heels. She knew! She knew what had happened. The thought of Jackson touching Lisa, hurting her, all because of what LuAnn had done or hadn't done. It was numbing, absolutely and totally incapacitating.

"Look, how was I supposed to know you have some kind of psychic connection with this guy?" Riggs replied.

"Not him dammit. Her! My daughter."

This statement stopped Riggs dead in his tracks. He looked down and then watched her resume her pacing.

"We need some information, Matthew. Right now."

Riggs agreed, but he didn't want to go to the police. That would entail wasting a lot of time in explanations and the end result might very well be the local cops taking LuAnn into custody.

Finally, Riggs said, "Come on."

They went into the motel office and Riggs walked over to a pay phone. Riggs phoned Masters. The FBI still had no leads on Jackson and Roger Crane still had not surfaced, Riggs was told.

Riggs briefly explained the situation at the motel the night before to Masters.

"Hold on," Masters said.

While Riggs did so he looked over at LuAnn staring at him. She was silently waiting for the worst news she could possibly receive, of that he was certain. He tried to smile reassuringly at her, but then stopped. The last thing he could be right now was reassuring, particularly since he had nothing to base it upon. Why set her up even further for the long fall.

When Masters came back on, his tone was low and nervous. Riggs turned away from LuAnn while he listened.

Masters said, "I just checked with the local police in Danville. Your information is correct, a man was stabbed at that motel on the outskirts of town. The ID found on him gave his name as Robert Charles Thomas."

Charlie? Riggs licked his lips, gripped the phone. "His ID? He couldn't tell the police?"

"He was unconscious. Lost a lot of blood. Damn miracle he's even alive, they tell me.

The wound was professionally administered, designed to slow-bleed the person. They found darts from a stun gun in the room. Guess that was how he was incapacitated. As of early this morning, they weren't sure if he was going to make it."

"What's he look like?" Riggs heard some paper rustling over the line. He was almost certain it was Charlie, but he needed to be absolutely sure.

Masters started speaking again. "Over six feet, in his sixties, strongly built, must be strong as an ox to have survived to this point."

Riggs breathed deeply. No doubt now. It was Charlie. "Where is he now?"

"The medevac took him to the UVA trauma center in Charlottesville."

Riggs felt the presence next to him. He turned to find LuAnn staring at him; the look in her eyes was scary.

"George, was there any mention of a ten-year-old girl being with him?"

"I asked. The report said that the man came to for a few seconds and started shouting a name."

"Lisa?"

Riggs heard Masters clear his throat. "Yes." Riggs remained silent. "It was her daughter, wasn't it? This guy's got her, doesn't he?" Masters asked.

"Looks like it," Riggs managed to get out.

"Where are you?"

"Look, George, I don't think I'm ready to give you that information yet."

Masters started speaking more forcefully. "He's got the little girl. You two could be next, Matt. Think about it. We can protect you both. You have got to come in."

"I don't know."

"Look, you can go back to her house. I've got the entrance under twenty-four-hour guard. If she agrees to go there, I'll fill the place up with agents."

"Hold on, George." Riggs held the phone against his chest and looked at LuAnn. His eyes told her all she needed to know.

"Charlie?"

"Unconscious. They don't know if he's going to make it. The good news is that a medevac helicopter flew him to the trauma center at UVA hospital."

"He's in Charlottesville?" she asked.

Riggs nodded. "It's only a short hop from Danville by air, and the trauma unit there is top-notch. He'll get the best care."

She continued to stare at him, waiting. And he knew exactly what for.

"Jackson probably has Lisa." He moved on quickly. "LuAnn, the FBI wants us to come in. So they can protect us. We can go to Wicken's Hunt if you want. Agents are already guarding the entrance. They think —"

She snatched the phone out of his hand.

She screamed into it. "I don't want protection. I don't need your damned protection. He's got my daughter. And the only thing I'm going to do is find her. I'm going to get her back. You hear me?"

"Ms. Tyler, I'm assuming this is LuAnn Tyler —" Masters started to say.

"You just stay out of the way. He'll kill her sure as hell if he even *thinks* you're around."

Masters tried to remain calm even as he said the awful words. "Ms. Tyler, you can't be sure he hasn't already done something to her."

Her reply was surprising, both for its content and its intensity. "I know he hasn't hurt her. Not yet."

"The man's a psycho. You can't be sure —"

"The hell I can't. I know exactly what he wants. And it's not Lisa. You just stay out of the way, FBI man. If my daughter dies because you got in the way, there won't be any place on this earth that I won't find you."

Sitting at his desk in the heavily guarded Hoover Building, with twenty-five years of high-level criminal detection work behind him, during which he'd confronted more than his share of evil, now surrounded by a thousand superbly trained, hardened FBI special agents, George Masters actually shivered as he listened to those words.

The next sound he heard was the phone slamming down.

Riggs raced after LuAnn as she stormed to the car.

"LuAnn, will you wait a damned minute?" She whirled around, waiting for him to speak. "Look, what George said makes a lot of sense."

LuAnn threw up her hands and started to get in the car.

"LuAnn, you go in to the FBI. Let them protect you from this guy. Let me stay on the outside. Let me track him down."

"Lisa is my daughter. I'm the reason she's in this danger and I'm the one who's going to get her out. Just me. Nobody else. Charlie's almost dead. You were almost killed. Three other people have been slaughtered. I'm not involving anybody else in my screwed up, miserable, sonofabitchin' excuse for a life." She screamed the words at him; when she stopped, both their chests were heaving.

"LuAnn, I'm not letting you go after him alone. If you don't want to go to the FBI, fine. I won't go either. But you're not, repeat not, going after him alone. That way you both die."

"Matthew, did you hear me? Just get out of this. Go to your buddies at the FBI and let them get you a new life somewhere the hell away from all of this. The hell away from me. Do you want to die? Because if you hang around me, you're going to, sure as I'm looking at you." The polished facade had fallen away, shed like a snake's skin in autumn. She was one long, raw muscle standing alone.

"He'll come after me, regardless, LuAnn," Riggs said quietly. "He'll find me and he'll kill me whether I go to the FBI or not." She didn't respond so he continued. "And to tell you the truth, I'm too old, too tired of running and hiding to start it up again. I'd rather go down the cobra's hole and meet him head-on. I'll take my chances with you next to me. I'd rather have you than every agent at the Bureau, than every cop in the country. We're probably only going to have one shot at this, and I'll take that shot with you." He paused for a moment as she stared at him, her eyes wild, her long hair billowing in the wind, her strong hands balling up into fists and then uncurling. Then he said, "If you'll take that shot with me."

The wind was really picking up now. They each stood barely two feet apart from the other. The gap would either swell or diminish with LuAnn's answer. Despite the chill, cold sweat clung to each of their faces. She finally broke the silence.

"Get in."

The room was completely dark. Outside the rain was pouring down and had been for most of the day. Sitting in the very center of the space, her body bound tightly to a chair, Lisa was trying, without much success, to use her nose to inch up the mask that covered her eyes. The intense darkness — being totally and completely blind — was unnerving to her. She had the impression that perilous things were lurking very near her. In that regard she was completely right.

"Are you hungry?" The voice was right at her elbow and her heart nearly stopped.

"Who is it? Who are you?" Her voice quavered.

"I'm an old friend of your mother's." Jackson knelt beside her. "These bindings aren't too tight, are they?"

"Where's Uncle Charlie? What did you do to him?" Lisa's courage suddenly resurfaced.

Jackson quietly chuckled. "Uncle, is it?" He stood back up. "That's good, very good."

"Where is he?"

"Not relevant," Jackson snapped. "If you're hungry, tell me so."

"I'm not."

"Something to drink then?"

Lisa hesitated. "Maybe some water."

She heard some tinkling of glass in the background and then she felt a coldness against her lips and jerked back.

"It's only water. I'm not going to poison you." Jackson said this in such a commanding fashion that Lisa quickly opened her mouth and drank deeply. Jackson patiently held the cup until she was finished.

"If you need anything else, to use the bathroom for instance, then just say so. I'll be right here."

"Where are we?" When Jackson didn't answer, she asked, "Why are you doing this?"

Standing there in the darkness, Jackson considered the question carefully before answering. "Your mother and I have some unfinished business. It has to do with things that occurred a long time ago, although there have been repercussions of a very recent vintage that are motivating me."

"I bet my mom didn't do anything to you."

"On the contrary, while she owes her entire life to me, she has done everything in her power to hurt me."

"I don't believe that," Lisa said hotly.

"I don't expect you to," Jackson said. "You're loyal to your mother, as you should be. Family ties are very important." He crossed his arms and thought for a moment on the status of his own family, of Alicia's sweet, peaceful face. *Sweet and peaceful in death.* With an effort he shrugged the vision off.

"My mom will come and get me."

"I certainly expect her to."

Lisa blinked rapidly as his meaning suddenly dawned upon her. "You're going to hurt her, aren't you? You're going to try and hurt my mom when she comes to get me."

Her voice had risen.

"Call if you need anything. I don't intend to make you suffer unduly."

"Don't hurt my mom, please." The tears materialized behind the mask.

Jackson did his best to ignore the pleas. Finally, the crying turned to bawling and then dissolved into exhausted whimpering. He had first seen Lisa as an eight-month-old infant. She had certainly grown up into a lovely child. Had LuAnn not accepted his offer, the orphaned Lisa would probably be in a foster home somewhere. He looked over at her, suffering terribly inside, her head slumped onto her chest in her private agony. A lot for a ten-year-old to handle. Maybe she would have been better off in that foster home, without ever really having known her mother. The woman Jackson was going to now eliminate from her life. He had no desire to cause pain to the daughter, but such was life. It wasn't fair. He had told LuAnn that the very first day they had met: Life was not fair. If you wanted something you had to take it. Before someone else took from you. Neatly dissected down to its essence, life was one long series of lily pad hoppings. The quick and the resourceful were able to adapt and survive; all others were simply crushed as a more nimble creature landed on the lily pad they had occupied for too long.

He stood completely motionless as though

conserving all his energies for what lay ahead. He stared off into the darkness. Very soon it would all begin. And very soon it would all end.

Chapter Fifty-Seven

The medical facility at the University of Virginia was a teaching component of the medical school as well as a highly regarded public hospital with a level-one trauma center. LuAnn raced down the corridor. Riggs was parking the car and then would follow her in. She reflected briefly on the fact that she had never before been in a hospital. She quickly concluded that she didn't care for either the smell or atmosphere. A lot of that was probably due to the reason she was here: to see Charlie.

He was in a private room. A member of the Charlottesville police force stood guard outside his door. LuAnn shot right past him and started to enter the room.

"Whoa, there, ma'am. No visitors," said the police officer, a solidly built man in his early thirties, holding out a beefy arm for emphasis.

LuAnn had whirled around ready for a fight when Riggs hustled up.

"Hey, Billy."

The officer turned around. "Hey, Matt, how you doing?"

"Not so good. Won't be playing basketball at the Y with you for a while."

Billy looked at his sling. "How'd you do that?"

"Long story. The guy in there is her uncle." He nodded at LuAnn.

Billy looked embarrassed. "I'm sorry, ma'am, I didn't know. They told me no visitors, but I know they didn't mean family. You go on in."

"Thanks, Billy," Riggs said.

LuAnn pushed open the door and went in. Riggs was right behind her.

LuAnn stared across at Charlie lying in the bed. As if he sensed her presence, he looked over and a smile spread across his face. He looked pale but his eyes were quick and active.

"Damn, now that's a real pleasant sight," he said.

LuAnn was next to him in an instant, taking his big hand in hers. "Thank God, you're okay."

Charlie was about to say something when the door opened and a middle-aged man in a white coat popped his head in. "Just making rounds, folks." He opened the door all the way and came in. He carried a clipboard.

"Dr. Reese," he said, introducing himself.

"Matt Riggs. This is Charlie's niece, Catherine." Riggs pointed at LuAnn, who shook the doctor's hand.

Dr. Reese checked Charlie's vital signs while he spoke. "Well, it's very lucky Charlie was so good with a tourniquet. Stopped the blood loss before things got really nasty."

"So he's going to be okay?" LuAnn asked anxiously.

Reese peered at her over his glasses. "Oh, yes. He's in no danger. We replaced the blood he lost, the wound is all stitched up. All he needs is some rest, get his strength back." Reese noted his findings on Charlie's record log.

Charlie half-sat up. "I feel fine. When can I check out?"

"I think we'll give you a couple of more days to get back on your feet."

Charlie was clearly not pleased with that answer.

"I'll be back in the morning," Reese said. "Don't stay too long, folks, let him get some rest."

As soon as Reese was gone, Charlie sat all the way up. "Any word on Lisa?"

LuAnn closed her eyes and looked down. Thick tears slid out from under her eyelids. Charlie looked over at Riggs for the first time.

"We think he has her, Charlie," said Riggs.

"I *know* he has her. I told the cops everything I knew as soon as I came to."

"I'm sure they're working on it," Riggs said lamely.

Charlie banged his fist against the metal sides of the bed. "Dammit, they're not going to catch him. He's long gone. We've got to do something. He hasn't tried to contact you?"

"I'm going to contact him," LuAnn said, opening her eyes. "But I had to come see you first. They said — they said you might not make it." Her voice shook and her hand gripped his tighter.

"It'd take a lot more than one cut to send yours truly into oblivion." He paused, struggling with what he was about to say. "I'm sorry, LuAnn. That bastard's got her and it's my fault. He called in the middle of the night, impersonated Riggs's voice. Said that the FBI had Jackson. That I was to come up to Washington and rendezvous with you at the FBI building. I dropped my guard. I walked right into his trap." Charlie shook his head. "God, I should've suspected something, but he sounded just like Riggs."

LuAnn leaned over and hugged him. "Damn you, Charlie, you almost got yourself killed for her. And for me."

Charlie wrapped his big arms around her while Riggs watched in respectful silence as the two shook and swayed together.

"Lisa will be okay, Charlie." She sounded a lot more confident than she actually felt. However, it would do Lisa no good if LuAnn allowed herself to become hysterical and thus useless.

"LuAnn, you know that guy. He could do anything to her."

"He wants me, Charlie. His whole world is falling apart. The Feds are on to him, he killed

Donovan and Bobbie Jo Reynolds and probably his own sister as well. And I know he thinks I'm the cause for all of it."

"That's nuts."

"It's not nuts if he believes it."

"Well, you can't just walk in there and give yourself to him."

Riggs piped in, "My sentiments exactly. You can't just call the guy up and say 'Don't worry, I'll be right over so you can kill me.' "

LuAnn didn't answer him.

"He's right, LuAnn," Charlie said. He started to get up.

"What the hell are you doing?" she said sharply.

"Getting dressed."

"Excuse me, didn't you hear the doctor?"

"I'm old, my hearing's going. And so am I. Going, that is."

"Charlie —"

"Look," he said angrily as he stumbled trying to get his pants on. LuAnn gripped his good arm, while Riggs steadied him on the other side. "I'm not going to lie here in this bed while that son of a bitch has Lisa. If you don't understand that, I really don't care."

LuAnn nodded in understanding and helped him get his pants on. "You're a big old ornery bear, you know that?"

"I've got one good arm, and just let me get it around that guy's neck."

Riggs held up his own injured arm. "Well,

701

between us we have two good arms. I owe the guy too."

LuAnn put her hands on her hips and looked around. "There's a cop outside."

"I can take care of him," Riggs said.

LuAnn picked up the rest of Charlie's belongings, including the portable cell phone, and put them in a plastic hospital bag.

When Charlie was finished dressing, Riggs stepped out the door and spoke to Billy.

"Billy, you mind going down to the cafeteria and getting a couple of coffees and maybe some stuff to munch on? I'd go but I can't carry anything with this bum arm." He jerked his head toward the room. "And she's pretty hysterical right now. I don't want to leave her."

"I'm really not supposed to leave my post, Matt."

"I'll hang out here, Billy, it'll be okay." Riggs held up some money. "Here, get yourself something too. Last time we played hoops I remember you eating a whole pizza by yourself afterward." He eyed Billy's healthy dimensions. "I don't want you to wilt away to nothing."

Billy took the money and laughed. "You sure know the way to a fella's heart."

As soon as Billy got into the elevator and the doors closed, Charlie, LuAnn, and Riggs left the room and made their way out by the back stairs. With LuAnn and Riggs supporting

Charlie, they quickly walked through the pouring rain to the car. With the thick clouds, it was already dark and the visibility was getting worse every minute.

Shortly, the three of them were in the car heading down Route 29. Charlie used the opportunity to tell them everything that had happened at the motel, including the fact that Jackson had had another man with him. After he finished, Charlie leaned forward from the back seat. "So what's the plan?" He winced as the car bounced over a pothole and jostled his arm.

LuAnn pulled into a gas station. She pulled out a slip of paper from her pocket. "I'm going to call him."

"And then what?" Riggs asked.

"I'll let him tell me," she replied.

"You know what the hell he's going to say," Charlie rejoined. "He's going to set up a meeting, just you and him. And if you go, he's going to kill you."

"And if I don't go, he's going to kill Lisa."

"He'll kill her anyway," Riggs said hotly.

LuAnn looked over at him. "Not if I get him first." She thought back to her last encounter with Jackson, at the cottage. She was stronger than he was. Not by much, but she had the clear advantage there. However, he knew that too. She had seen that in his eyes. That meant he would not go toe-to-toe with her again, at least not physically. She would have to remember that. If he could adapt, so could she.

"LuAnn, I have a lot of confidence in you," Riggs said, "but this guy is something else again."

"He's right, LuAnn," Charlie added.

"Thanks for the vote of confidence, guys." She didn't wait for them to answer. She pulled the portable phone out of the bag and punched in the number. Before it started ringing, she looked at both of them. "But remember, I've got *two* good arms."

Riggs slid his hand down into his coat until it touched the reassuring metal of his pistol. His aim would have to be a lot better this time around. He hoped to not have the painful distraction of a knife sticking out of his arm.

He and Charlie watched as LuAnn spoke into the receiver, leaving the number of the cell phone. She hung up and waited, still not looking at them. Barely three minutes had passed before the phone rang.

Before LuAnn could say anything, Jackson said, "Please know that I have a device attached to my phone that will indicate whether this call is being traced, just in case you happen to be sitting at police headquarters. It will tell me in about five seconds if that is occurring. If you are, I will immediately hang up and slit your daughter's throat."

"I'm not at the police and I'm not tracing your call."

He didn't say anything for five seconds. She

could envision him eyeing his device, perhaps hoping she was lying to him. "I applaud you for avoiding the obvious," he finally said quite pleasantly.

"When and where?" LuAnn said.

"No greeting? No small talk? Where are your manners? Has the expensively constructed princess deteriorated that suddenly? Like a flower without water? Without sunshine?"

"I want to talk to Lisa. Right now."

"Sorry about Uncle Charlie," Jackson said. He was sitting on the floor almost in total darkness. He held the phone close to his mouth, speaking slowly and in as casual a tone as he could muster. He wanted her panic level to rise steadily, he wanted her to feel his absolute control of the situation. When the time came he wanted her to come obediently forward to receive her punishment. He wanted her to come meekly to confront her executioner.

She wasn't about to tell Jackson that Charlie was sitting right behind her wanting nothing more than to wring the life out of him. "I want to talk to Lisa!"

"How can you be sure I haven't killed her already?"

"What?" she gasped.

"You can talk to her, but how will you know it's not me mimicking her voice? 'Mommy, Mommy,' I could say. 'Come help me.' I could say all those things. So if you want to talk to her, you can, but it will prove nothing."

"You son of a bitch!"

"Would you still like to talk to her?"

"Yes," LuAnn said pleadingly.

"Manners now. Yes, what?"

She hesitated for an instant, taking a deep breath, trying to keep her wits and her nerves together. "Yes, please," she said.

"Just a minute. Now where have I put that child?"

Riggs was doing his best to listen in. Exasperated, LuAnn finally opened the door and got out of the car.

She strained to hear any sound in the background.

"Mom, Mom, is that you?"

"Honey, baby, it's Mom. Oh, God, sweetie, I'm so sorry."

"Oh, excuse me, LuAnn, that's still me," Jackson said. "Oh, Mom, Mommy, are you there?" he said again, mimicking Lisa's voice precisely.

LuAnn was too stunned to say anything.

The next voice she heard was Jackson's real one. His tone almost bit into her ear it was said with such forcefulness. "I'll let you talk to her, really talk to her. You can have your mother–daughter emotional exchange. But when you're done I will tell you exactly what you will do. If you deviate in any way from my instructions . . ."

He didn't finish. He didn't have to. They both sat there on the phone, not saying anything, simply listening to each other's breathing, two trains careening out of control, about to slam into each other across the wireless void. LuAnn tried with all her might to hold back the thick gush of air that was ramming against her throat. She knew what he was doing. What he was doing to her mind. But she was equally aware that she could do nothing about it. At least not right now.

"Do you understand?"

"Yes." As soon as she said the word, she heard it. She heard the sound in the background that made her both smile and grimace simultaneously. She looked at her watch. Five o'clock. The smile increased at the same time her eyes took on a gleam. A gleam of hope.

The next minute she was talking to Lisa, quickly asking her questions that only her little girl would know the answer to. They both desperately wanted to reach through the darkness that separated them.

And then Jackson came back on the line and gave her the instructions, the where and the when. None of it surprised her as she focused again on the sounds occurring in the background on his end. He ended the call by saying, with daunting finality, "See you soon."

She clicked off the phone and got back in the car. She spoke with a calmness that astonished the two men, particularly under the circumstances.

"I'm to call him tomorrow at ten A.M. He'll give me the meeting place then. He'll let Lisa go if I come alone. If he even thinks anyone else is around, he'll kill her."

"So it's you for Lisa," Riggs said.

She looked at both of them. "That's the way it's going to be."

"LuAnn —"

"That's the way it's going to be," she said more forcefully.

"How do you know he'll let her go? You can't trust him," Charlie implored.

"On this I can. He just wants me."

"There's got to be another way," Riggs exclaimed.

"There's only one way, Matthew, and you know it." She looked at him sadly before putting the car in gear and driving off.

She had one more card to play. But Charlie and Riggs weren't going to be invited to the game. They had already sacrificed too much for her. Jackson had nearly killed both men, and she wasn't about to give the man another try on either. If Jackson were given an extra shot, she knew what the outcome would be. It was now up to her. It was up to her to save her daughter, and that, she felt, was the way it should be. She had been self-reliant for most of her life, and truth be known, that was the way she liked it. That knowledge was reassuring. And she knew something else.

She knew where Jackson and Lisa were.

Chapter Fifty-Eight

The rain had finally slackened off but the spring showers were far from over. LuAnn had tacked up a blanket over the shattered window of the cottage. Riggs had turned the heat fully on and it was comfortable enough. The remnants of a meal rested on the kitchen sink. Riggs eyed the stains on the dining room floor. His blood. Charlie and Riggs had pulled mattresses down from the upstairs bedroom and laid them out on the floor. They had decided the cottage was the best place to spend the night. Charlie and Riggs had argued with LuAnn for hours trying to change her mind. Finally, she said they could call the FBI in the morning before she called Jackson. It was possible the FBI could trace the call. That had appeased the men enough that they agreed to let LuAnn keep the first watch. Riggs would relieve her in two hours.

Exhausted, both men soon began snoring deeply. LuAnn stood with her back to the window and silently observed them. She looked at her watch; it was after midnight. She made sure her gun was loaded, then she knelt next to Charlie and gave him a light kiss on the cheek. He barely moved.

She moved over to Riggs and watched the even rise and fall of his chest. Brushing the hair out of his eyes, she watched him a while longer. She knew the odds were not good that she would ever see either man again. She kissed him gently on the lips and then rose. For one long moment she leaned back against the wall, taking deep breaths as everything she was confronted with threatened to simply overwhelm her.

Then she was on the move again, climbing through the window to avoid the squeaky front door. She put up her hood against the fine rain falling. Ignoring the car and the unavoidable noise it would make, she went to the shed and opened the door. Joy was still there. LuAnn had forgotten to call anyone to come get the horse; however, the shed was dry and warm and there was still water and hay left. She quickly saddled the animal and swung onto Joy's back. Easing her out of the shed, they made it to the woods with scarcely any noise.

When she reached the edge of her property, she dismounted and led Joy back to the horse barn. She hesitated for a moment and then she took the binoculars off the wall, edged through the thick brush, and set up surveillance in a narrow break in the tree line, exactly where Riggs had earlier. She scanned the rear of the house. She jerked back as a car's headlights glinted off the binoculars. The car pulled around to the garage side, but the garage doors didn't budge. As LuAnn watched, a man got out of the car and walked around the rear of the house as if on patrol. Under the rear floods, LuAnn could see the FBI insignia emblazoned on his windbreaker. Then the man got back in the car and it pulled off.

LuAnn broke from the trees and raced across the open ground. She made it to the side of the house in time to see the car head back down the private drive toward the main road, the one where she had fled from Donovan, the encounter that had started this whole nightmare. The FBI was guarding the entrance to her home. She suddenly remembered that Riggs had mentioned that to her during his conversation with Masters. She would have dearly loved to have enlisted the agents' very able assistance, but they no doubt would have arrested her on the spot. Yet fear of arrest wasn't the chief factor. She simply refused to involve anyone else in her problems. No one else was going to be stabbed or killed because of her. Jackson wanted her and only her. She knew he expected her to walk meekly to him, to receive her punishment in exchange for her daughter's release. Well, in this case, he was going to get more than he wanted. A lot more. She and Lisa were going to survive this. He wasn't.

As she started to head back to the rear of the house, she noticed something else. Sally Beecham's car out front. That puzzled her. She shrugged and went around to the rear door.

The sound she had heard in the background during Jackson's call to her was what had brought her here. The absolutely unique sounds of the old clock, the family heirloom, passed down to her from her mother, the very same one LuAnn had diligently refused ever to part with. It had proved to be the most valuable possession she had because she had heard it in the background during her phone conversation with Jackson.

Jackson had been in her house, had called from her house. And LuAnn was absolutely convinced that Lisa was there now. Jackson was here too, she knew. LuAnn had to admire the man's nerve, to come here, with the FBI waiting just down the road. In a very few minutes, she would come face-to-face with her worst nightmare.

She pressed herself flat against the brick wall and peered in the side door, squinting hard through the pane of glass to see if the alarm light that was visible from this point was red or green. She breathed a quiet sigh of relief when she saw the friendly green. She knew the code to disarm it of course, but disarming it would produce one shrill beep that might jeopardize everything.

LuAnn inserted her key in the lock and slowly opened the door. She paused for a minute; the gun she held made quick, darting movements all around. She heard nothing. It was well past midnight now so that wasn't so surprising. Something was bothering her, however.

Being back in her own house should have brought some comfort to her, but it didn't. If anything it was close to unnerving. Letting her guard down now, letting herself be lulled by the familiarity of the surroundings, could easily result in her and Lisa's not being around to see the sun come up.

She continued down the hallway and then froze. She heard voices clearly. Several people; she recognized none of them. She slowly let out her breath as the music from a commercial came on. Someone was watching TV. A glint of light came from a doorway at the end of the hallway. LuAnn quietly moved forward, stopping right before her shadow would pass across the small opening between door and wall. She listened for a few seconds more. Then she edged open the door with her left hand as she pointed her gun through the opening with her right. The door swung silently inward and LuAnn leaned in. The room was dark, the only light coming from the TV. What she saw next made her freeze once again. The dark hair, cut short around the neck and built high up in the form of a modified beehive, was directly in front of her. Sally Beecham was in her bedroom watching TV. Or was she? She was sitting so still that LuAnn couldn't tell if she was alive or not.

For an instant: the image of LuAnn threading her way through that trailer ten years ago, spotting Duane on the couch. Going toward him, walking right up to him. And seeing him turn, turn so slowly toward her, the blood all over his chest, his face as gray as a Navy ship. And watching him fall off that couch, dying. And then the hand clamping over her mouth from behind. From behind!

She whirled but there was no one there; however, her abrupt movements had made some noise. When she looked back Sally Beecham was staring at her with horror in her eyes. When she recognized LuAnn she seemed to catch her breath. A hand fluttered up to her chest, which was heaving.

She started to say something, but LuAnn put a finger up to her lips and whispered, "Shh."

"There's someone here," LuAnn said. Sally looked confused. "Have you seen anyone here?" Sally shook her head and pointed to herself, the worry lines sprouting all over her ghastly pale face.

And that's when it hit LuAnn, and her own face went pale.

Sally Beecham never parked in front of the house. She always parked in the garage which led directly into the kitchen. LuAnn's hand tightened on the gun. She looked at the face again. It was hard to tell in the dark light, but she wasn't taking any chances. "I'll tell you what, Sally. I want you to get in the kitchen pantry and I'm going to lock you in. Just to be safe."

LuAnn watched as the eyes darted over her face. Then one of the hands started to move behind the woman's back.

LuAnn thrust the gun forward. "And we're going to do it right now or I'll shoot you right here. And pull out the gun, butt-first."

When the pistol emerged, LuAnn motioned to the floor. The gun clunked when it hit the hardwood.

When the person moved in front of LuAnn, LuAnn quickly reached out and jerked the wig off, revealing the man. He had short, dark hair. He jerked around for an instant, but LuAnn shoved the gun in his ear.

"Move, Mr. Jackson! Or should I say, Mr. Crane?" She had no false hopes as to the fate of Sally Beecham, but with everything else confronting her, LuAnn did not have the opportunity to dwell on it. She hoped she would have the chance to grieve for the woman.

When they reached the kitchen, LuAnn shoved him inside the pantry and locked the door from the outside. The door was an original from the house, solid oak, three inches thick with a deadbolt. It would hold him. At least for a while. She didn't need long.

She raced to the end of the hallway and flew up the carpeted stairs. LuAnn made her way from door to door. She was fairly certain that Lisa was in her mother's bedroom but she couldn't take any chances. Her eyes had adjusted well to the darkness and she quickly surveyed room after room. All empty. She went on. There was only one more bedroom left: hers. LuAnn willed her hearing to the highest possible acuity. All she wanted to hear was Lisa sighing, mumbling, breathing, anything to let her mother know she was okay. She couldn't call out, that was too dangerous. She recalled that Jackson now had someone with him. Where was that person?

She reached the door, slid her hand around the doorknob, took a deep breath, and turned it.

A long bolt of lightning cut across the sky, followed by a deafening clap of thunder. At the same instant, the blanket was blown off the window and rain started coming in. The combination of these events finally woke Riggs. He sat up, disoriented for a moment, and then looked around. He saw the open window, the wind and rain coming through. He glanced over at Charlie, who was still sleeping. Then it hit him.

He staggered up. "LuAnn? LuAnn?" His

cries roused Charlie.

"What the hell?" he said.

In a minute they had searched the small cottage.

"She's not here," he screamed to Charlie.

They both raced outside. The car was still there. Riggs looked around bewildered.

"LuAnn," Charlie screamed over the sounds of the storm.

Riggs looked over at the shed. The doors were open. It hit him. He raced over and looked in the empty shed. He looked down at the mud in front of the shed. Even in the darkness, he could make out the hoof prints. He followed the tracks to the edge of the woods. Charlie ran up beside him.

"Joy was in the shed," he told Charlie. "It looks like she's gone back to the house."

"Why would she do that?"

Riggs thought hard for a minute. "Were you surprised she agreed to finally calling the FBI tomorrow?"

"Yes," Charlie said, "but I was too damn tired and too relieved to think much about it."

"Why would she go to the house?" Riggs repeated Charlie's question. "The FBI is guarding the place. What would be there that she'd take that sort of risk?"

Charlie went pale and he staggered slightly.

"What is it, Charlie?"

"LuAnn once told me something Jackson had told her. A rule he lived by."

"What was it?" Riggs demanded.

"If you want to hide something, put it out in plain sight because no one would see it."

Now it was Riggs's turn to go pale as the truth hit him. "Lisa's at the house."

"And so is Jackson."

They raced to the car.

As the sedan flew down the road Riggs picked up the portable phone. He dialed the police and then the local FBI. He was shocked to hear Masters's voice come on the line.

"He's here, George. Crane's at Wicken's Hunt. Bring everything you got." Riggs heard the phone drop to the desk and footsteps running off. Then he clicked off the phone and floored the car.

As the door swung open, LuAnn darted into the room. Smack in the center was a chair and in that chair was Lisa, slumped over, exhausted. The next sound LuAnn heard was the labored ticking of that clock, that wonderful, beautiful clock. She closed the door behind her and ran to her daughter, hugged her. Her face dissolved into a big smile when her daughter's eyes met her mother's.

And then a loop of thick cord was around LuAnn's neck, was pulled tight, and LuAnn's breath was suddenly gone; her gun fell to the floor.

Lisa screamed and screamed in agonizing

silence, the tape still tightly across her mouth. She kicked at her chair, trying to topple it over, trying to reach her mother, help her in some way before this man killed her.

Jackson was fully behind LuAnn now. He had watched from the darkness next to the dresser as LuAnn had sailed toward Lisa, oblivious to his presence in the room. Then he had struck. The cord had a piece of wood attached to it and Jackson was winding it tighter and tighter. LuAnn's face was turning blue, her senses were slipping away as the cord dug deeply into the skin of her neck. She tried to punch him but it was too awkward, her fists flailed helplessly, sapping away what remaining strength she had. She kicked at him, but he was too quick and dodged those blows as well. She dug at the rope with her strong fingers but it was so imbedded in her skin that there was no space left to get a grip.

He whispered into her ear. "Tick-tock, LuAnn. Tick-tock of the little clock. Like a magnet, it led you right to me. I held the phone right next to it so you couldn't help but hear it. I told you I find out everything about someone I do business with. I visited your trailer in good old Rikersville. I listened to the rather unique sounds of that timepiece several times. And then seeing it on the wall of the bedroom the night I first visited you. Your little, cheap family heirloom." He laughed. "I would have loved to have seen your face when you thought you had outsmarted me. Was it a happy face, LuAnn? Was it?"

Jackson's smile deepened as he felt her giving way, her vaunted strength almost gone. "Now don't forget your daughter. There she is." He hit a light switch and swung her around violently so that she could see Lisa reaching for her. "She'll watch you die, LuAnn. And then it will be her turn. You cost me a family member. Someone I loved. How does it feel to be responsible for her death?" He yanked on the cord harder and harder. "Die, LuAnn. Just give in to it. Close your eyes and just stop breathing. Just do it. It's so easy. Just do it. Do it for me. You know you want to," he hissed.

LuAnn's eyes were close to erupting out of their sockets now, her lungs almost dead. She felt like she was deep under water; she would give anything to take one breath, just one long drink of air. As LuAnn listened to those taunting words she was swept back to a graveyard, to a plot of dirt, to a small brass marker in the ground many years ago. Exactly where she was heading. *Do it for Big Daddy, LuAnn. It's so easy. Come and see Big Daddy.* You know you want to.

From the corner of her blood-filled right eye she could barely see Lisa silently screaming for her mother, reaching for her across a chasm that was barely seconds from becoming eternal. At that very moment and from a place so deep that LuAnn never even knew she possessed it, there came a rush of strength so unbelievably powerful that it almost knocked her over. With a shriek, LuAnn jerked upright and then bent forward, lifting an astonished Jackson completely off the floor in the process. She clamped her arms around his legs so that she was carrying him piggyback style. Then she exploded backward, her legs pumping like a long jumper about to erupt into flight until she slammed Jackson violently into the heavy dresser against the wall. The sharp wooden edge caught him dead on the spine.

He screamed in pain but hung on to the cord. LuAnn reached up and dug her fingernails right into the recent wound on his hand — the one from the fight at the cottage — tearing the cut wide open. Jackson screamed again and this time he let go of the cord. Feeling the rope go lax, LuAnn whipped her torso forward and Jackson went flying over her shoulders and crashing into a mirror hanging on the wall.

LuAnn staggered drunkenly around in the middle of the room sucking in huge amounts of air. She reached up to her throat and pulled off the cord. Then her eyes settled dead center on the man.

Jackson grabbed at his injured back and struggled to stand up. It was too little too late, as with a guttural scream LuAnn pounced. She flattened him to the floor and pinned him there. Her legs clamped against his, immobilizing them. Her hands encircled his throat and now *his* face started to turn blue. The grip he felt against his throat was ten times as strong as the one he had battled on the cottage porch. He looked into her blood-filled eyes, red with burst capillaries from her near strangling, and he knew there was no way he could ever break her choke hold. His hands groped the floor as she continued to squeeze the life out of him. A series of visions proceeded across his mind, but there was no rush of strength to accompany it. His body started to go limp. His eyes rolled in their sockets, his neck constricted to the breaking point under the ever increasing pressure. His fingers finally closed around a bit of glass from the shattered mirror and held. He swung it upward, catching her in the arm and cutting through her clothing and into her skin. She didn't release her grip. He cut her again and then again but to no avail. She was beyond pain; she would simply not let go.

Finally, with the last bit of strength he had left, his fingers felt under her arm and he pressed as hard as he could. Suddenly, LuAnn's arms went dead as Jackson found the pressure point and her grip was abruptly broken. In an instant he had pushed her off and sprinted across the room, gasping for breath.

LuAnn watched in horror as he grabbed Lisa's chair and dragged it across the room to the window. She got to her feet, flying toward them. She knew exactly what he was going to do, but damn if she was going to let him do it. He was lifting the chair and Lisa with it, and LuAnn dove for it, her hand closing around her daughter's leg as the chair smashed against the window that overlooked the brick patio almost thirty feet below. LuAnn and Lisa crashed to the floor amid the shattered glass.

Jackson tried to snatch up her gun but LuAnn was one step ahead of him. LuAnn's leg flew up and caught Jackson, who had strayed a little too close, directly in the crotch. He bent down, groaning. She jumped up and landed a powerful right hand squarely against Jackson's chin. He went down to the floor.

In the distance they all heard the police sirens coming. Jackson swore under his breath, picked himself up, and, clutching his privates, raced through the doorway.

LuAnn let him go, slamming and locking the door behind him. Screaming and crying in relief, she gently pulled off the tape and undid the ropes holding Lisa. Mother and daughter held each other tightly. LuAnn clutched at Lisa's body, she pushed her face in Lisa's hair, her nose drank in every wonderful smell of her little girl. Then LuAnn stood and picked up her gun and fired two shots out the window.

Riggs and Charlie and the FBI agents were engaged in an animated discussion at the entrance to the private road when they heard the shots. Riggs threw the car in gear and roared up the road. The FBI agents ran to their car.

Jackson bolted down the hallway, suddenly stopped, and looked in Sally Beecham's bedroom. Empty. He spied the gun on the floor and snatched it up. Then he heard the pounding. He raced to the kitchen and unlocked and threw open the pantry door. Roger Crane, squinting and quivering, stumbled out.

"Thank God, Peter. She had a gun. She put me in here. I . . . I did exactly as you told me."

"Thank you, Roger." He lifted up the pistol. "Tell Alicia I said hello." Then he fired point blank into his brother's face. The next instant he was out the door and racing across the lawn for the woods.

As they jumped out of their car Riggs saw Jackson first and sprinted after him. Charlie, despite his weakened state, was right behind. When the lawmen pulled up seconds later, they ran to the house.

LuAnn met them on the stairs. "Where are Matthew and Charlie?"

The men looked at each other. "I saw somebody running into the woods," one of them answered.

They all ran out onto the front lawn. That's when they heard it, the drone of the helicopter as the blades cut through the rain and wind. It landed on the front lawn. They all saw the FBI insignia on the side. The group raced over; LuAnn and Lisa reached it first.

Several police cars pulled up next to the fountain and a small army of officers poured out.

George Masters climbed out of the helicopter followed by a team of FBI agents. He looked at her. "LuAnn Tyler?" She nodded. Masters looked at Lisa. "Your daughter?"

"Yes," LuAnn said.

"Thank God." He let out a deep sigh of relief and held out his hand. "George Masters, FBI. I came into town to interview Charlie Thomas. When I got to the hospital he was gone."

"We've got to go after Jackson, I mean Peter Crane. He went into the woods," LuAnn said. "Matthew and Charlie went after him. But I want Lisa safe. I can't leave her without knowing she'll be completely safe."

Masters looked between mother and daughter, spitting images of each other. Then he looked at the helicopter.

"We'll transport her to the FBI office here in Charlottesville in this helicopter. I'll put her smack in the center of a room with a half dozen heavily armed FBI agents. That good enough?" He smiled weakly.

A grateful look crossed her face. "Yes. Thanks for understanding."

"I've got children too, LuAnn."

While Masters gave instructions to the pilot, LuAnn gave Lisa one more hug and kiss and then turned and raced for the woods, a swarm of FBI agents and police officers right behind her. As fleet of foot as she was, and knowing the terrain as well as she did, she soon left them far behind.

Riggs could hear the feet flying in front of him. Charlie had dropped back a bit, but Riggs could hear his heavy breathing not far behind. The woods were wreathed in almost complete darkness and the rain continued to pour down. Riggs blinked his eyes rapidly to gain some degree of night vision. He pulled his gun, slipped the safety off with a quick punch of his finger. Then he halted abruptly as the sounds ahead of him stopped. He crouched and swept the area with his eyes, his gun making wide arcs. He heard the sound behind him an instant too late as the foot slammed into his back, sending him lunging forward and then down. He hit the wet ground hard, his face sliding painfully across the grass and dirt, and he ended up slamming against a tree, his gun smacking hard against the trunk. The impact caused his wounded arm to start bleeding again. When he flipped over on his back, he saw the man flying at him, the foot poised to deliver another crunching blow. Then Charlie blindsided Jackson and the two men went sprawling.

An incensed Charlie pounded Jackson with his fists and then cocked his arm back to deliver a knock-out punch. Quick as an eel, Jackson made a direct hit on Charlie's wound, a blow that made him scream and double over. Then, with the same motion employed in striking a cymbal, Jackson smashed both palms against Charlie's ears, forcing a sudden, painful rush of air into his ear canals and rupturing an eardrum. Nauseated and dizzy from the combined blows, Charlie fell off Jackson and lay on the ground groaning.

"I should've slit your throat at the motel," Jackson spat down at him. Jackson was about to deliver a crushing kick to Charlie's head when he heard Riggs scream at him.

"Get the hell away from him before I blow your damn head off."

When Jackson looked over, Riggs's gun was pointed directly at him. Jackson stepped away from Charlie.

"Finally, we meet. Riggs the criminal. How about discussing a financial arrangement that will make you very rich?" Jackson said. His voice was hoarse and weak from his near strangling by LuAnn. He clutched at his torn hand; his face was bleeding from Charlie's blows.

"I'm not a criminal, asshole. I was an FBI agent who testified against a cartel. That's why I was in Witness Protection."

Jackson circled closer to Riggs. "Ex-FBI? Well, then at least I'm certain you won't shoot me down in cold blood." He pointed a warning finger at Riggs. "Understand though, if I go down, so does LuAnn. I'll tell your former employers that she was in on everything, even helped me plan it. I'll paint a picture so dark that she'll be grateful for a life sentence. My attorneys will see to that. But don't worry, I understand you can have yearly conjugal visits in some prisons now."

"You're going to rot in jail."

"I hardly think that. I can only imagine what sort of deal I can cut with the Feds. I would think they'd do anything to avoid public disclosure of all this. When this is all over, I'm sure I'll be seeing you again. In fact, I look forward to it."

Jackson's mocking tones burned through every fiber of Riggs's body. What was even more maddening was the fact that everything Jackson had predicted could very well happen. But it wouldn't, Riggs swore to himself. "That's where you're wrong," Riggs said.

"About what?"

"About killing you in cold blood." Riggs

pulled the trigger. The sound that *didn't* occur seemed to drive all the blood from Riggs's body. The gun didn't fire; the impact with the tree had jammed it. He pulled the trigger again with the same sickening result.

Jackson instantly drew his own gun and pointed it at Riggs.

Riggs dropped the useless pistol and backed up as Jackson advanced. He finally stopped retreating when his foot felt nothing but air. He looked behind him: a sheer drop. Down below, the fast-moving water. He looked back at Jackson, who smiled and then fired.

The bullet hit right in front of Riggs's feet and he stepped back a half inch, teetering on the edge.

"Let's see how well you swim with no arms." The next shot hit Riggs's good arm. He grunted in pain and doubled over, clutching it, trying to maintain his balance. Then he looked up at the sneering face of Jackson.

"Take the bullet or the jump, it's your choice. But do it quick, I don't have much time."

Riggs had only an instant. As he crouched over, the arm that had just been hit slid up the length of his sling — a very natural movement under the circumstances. Jackson had underestimated his resourcefulness. Jackson wasn't the only one who had lived by his wits, who had gotten himself out of tight spots by acting nimbly. What Riggs was about to do had saved his life while working undercover during a drug deal that had gone sour. It would not save his life this time. But it would save several others, including one that he cared more about than his own: LuAnn's.

He locked eyes with Jackson. His anger was so intense that it blocked out the pain in both arms. His hand closed around the butt of the compact gun taped inside his sling, the one he had originally had in his ankle holster. Its muzzle was pointed right at Jackson. Wounded arm and all, his aim was as sharp as ever. And Jackson was only a few feet away. But Riggs had to make the first shot count.

"Riggs!" Charlie screamed.

Jackson didn't take his eyes off Riggs. "You're next, *Uncle Charlie.*"

Matt Riggs would never forget the look on Jackson's face as the first shot Riggs fired erupted through the sling and hit the man flush in the face, tearing first through the powder, putty, and spirit gum, and then slamming a microsecond later into real flesh and bone. The gun fell from an astonished Jackson's hand.

Riggs kept pulling the trigger, sending bullet after bullet slamming into Jackson. Head, torso, leg, arm — there wasn't a piece of him Riggs missed until the firing pin banged empty twelve shots later. And all the time Jackson's countenance held a look of supreme disbelief as blood mixed with fake hair and skin; creams and powders mutated into a dull crimson. The total effect was eerie, as though the man were dissolving. Then Jackson dropped to his knees, blood pouring from a dozen wounds, and then he fell face forward to the ground and did not move again. His last performance.

That's when Riggs went fully over the edge. The multiple kicks from the pistol were enough to completely unsettle his balance, and his feet were unable to counter the slippery red clay. But as he went over, a look of grim satisfaction came over his face even as he stared down at the abyss he was plummeting toward. Two useless arms, both bleeding him to death, deep, fast, icy water, nothing to grab. It was over.

He heard Charlie scream his name one more time, and then he heard nothing else. He felt no pain now, only peace. He hit the water awkwardly and went under.

Charlie scrambled over and was just about to plunge in when a body hurtled by him and went over the edge.

LuAnn broke the surface of the water cleanly and almost instantly reappeared. She scanned the surface of the rapidly moving water that was already pulling her downstream.

From the bank, Charlie stumbled along through the thick trees and heavy underbrush, trying to keep up. The shouts of the FBI agents and police officers were getting louder, but it didn't look as though their help would arrive in time.

"Matthew!" LuAnn screamed. Nothing. She dove under, methodically pushing off from bank to bank searching for him. Twenty seconds later she resurfaced, sucking in air.

"LuAnn!" Charlie yelled at her.

She ignored his cries. As the cold rain pelted her, she sucked in another lungful of air and went under again. Charlie stopped, his eyes darting everywhere, trying to pinpoint where she would come up. He wasn't about to lose both of them.

When LuAnn broke the surface again she wasn't alone. She gripped Riggs tightly around the chest as the current swept them along. He gagged and spit up water as his lungs struggled to function again. She tried to swim cross-current but was making little progress. She was freezing. In another minute hypothermia could well incapacitate her. Riggs was sheer dead weight, and she felt her strength fading. She scissored her legs around his upper torso, angling just enough that his face was above the water's surface. She kept putting pressure on his stomach, making his diaphragm kick up and down, helping him clear his lungs.

She looked desperately behind her, searching for some way out. Her eyes fell upon a fallen tree, and, more important, the thick branch that was suspended partially out over the water. It would be close. She readied herself, gauging the distance and height. She tensed her legs around Riggs and then made her lunge. Her hands closed around the branch and held. She raised herself up. She and Riggs were now partially out of the water. She tried to pull herself up more, but couldn't; Riggs was too heavy. She looked down and saw him staring at her, his breath coming in short gasps. Then she watched horrified as he started to unwrap her legs from around him.

"Matthew, don't! Please!"

Through blue lips that moved in a painfully slow manner he said, "We're not going to both die, LuAnn." He pushed her legs again and she was now fighting him and the current and the weary ache in her limbs as the numbing cold settled deeply within her. Her lips were trembling with both rage and helplessness. She looked down at him again as he tried desperately to free himself, to rid her of the burden. She could simply let go, fall with him, but what about Lisa? She had seconds to make a choice, but then she didn't have to. For the first time in her life, her strength failed, and her grip was broken. She started to plummet downward.

The thick arm that clamped around her body ended her fall and the next thing she felt was herself and Riggs being lifted completely out of the water.

She cocked her head back and her eyes fell upon his face.

Straddling the tree trunk, Charlie, bad arm and all, grunted and grimaced and finally pulled them safely to a narrow dirt bank where they all three collapsed, the water inches from them. LuAnn's legs were still locked in a death grip around Riggs. She lay back, her head on Charlie's chest, which was heaving mightily from his efforts. LuAnn slid her right hand down to Riggs, who took it, laying it against his cheek. Her left hand went up and gripped Charlie's shoulder. He covered her hand with his. None of them said a word.

Chapter Fifty-Nine

"Well, it's all done," Riggs said, gingerly hanging up the phone. They were in his home office, LuAnn, Charlie, and Lisa. A gentle snow was falling outside. Christmas was rapidly closing in.

"So what's the bottom line?" LuAnn asked.

LuAnn and Charlie were healed. Riggs was out of his sling, and the cast he had had to wear to mend the bone Jackson's bullet had broken had recently been removed as well. He still moved slowly, though.

"Not great. The IRS finished its calculations of the back taxes you owed, penalties and interest all compounded for the last eight or so years."

"And?"

"And it came to all the cash you had, all the investments you had, and all the property you had, including Wicken's Hunt." He managed a grin, trying to ease the impact of the depressing news. "You were actually short sixty-five cents so I threw it in for you, no charge."

Charlie snorted. "What a Christmas present. And the other lottery winners get to keep all their money. That's not fair."

"They paid their taxes, Charlie," Riggs replied.

"She's paid taxes."

"Only since coming back to this country and only under the name Catherine Savage."

"Well, she couldn't before. Not without probably going to prison for a crime she didn't commit."

"Well, gee, that's a real winning argument."

"Yeah, but they all won by cheating too," Charlie retorted.

"Well, the government isn't about to announce that to the world. They make billions off the lottery. Telling the truth might just mess that up, don't you think?"

"How about all the millions she gave to charity, doesn't that count for something?" Charlie said angrily.

"The IRS applauded LuAnn's generosity but said they really couldn't help on that because she had never filed a return. I'm telling you it's not a bad deal. She could have gone to prison for a long time over this. Except for that fact, she probably could have kept some of the money. But that was a very real threat over her head. Sheriff Harvey didn't go away very easily."

"I can't believe this crap. After all she's been through. She broke up Crane's worldwide criminal syndicate, the FBI looks like heroes, they confiscated all his property, billions of bucks into the Treasury, and she winds up with nothing. Not even a pat on the back. It's not fair!"

LuAnn put a hand on a seething Charlie's shoulder. "It's okay, Charlie. I didn't deserve any of that money. And I wanted to pay what I owed. I just want to be LuAnn Tyler again. I told Matthew that. But I didn't murder anyone. All the charges against me are gone, right?" She looked at Riggs for confirmation.

"That's right. Federal, state, everything. Free as a bird."

"Yeah, and poor as a church mouse," Charlie added angrily.

"Is that it, Matthew? They can't come back on me later? The IRS, I mean? For more money?"

"All the papers are signed. They dropped everything. It's over. They confiscated all your accounts, they foreclosed on the house. Anyway, even if they came after you, which they can't, you don't have any more money."

Lisa looked at him. "Maybe we can move in here, Mom." She added quickly, "I mean for a little while." She looked between LuAnn and Riggs nervously. LuAnn smiled at Lisa. Telling her daughter the entire truth had been the hardest thing she had ever had to do. But the second she had finished, she had never felt greater relief. Lisa had taken the news admirably. Now at least their relationship could

738

take on a semblance of normalcy.

Riggs looked at LuAnn, a little nervous himself. "I was thinking along those lines myself." He swallowed hard. "Can you excuse us for a minute?" he asked Charlie and Lisa.

He took LuAnn by the arm and they left the room. Charlie and Lisa watched them go and then exchanged smiles.

Riggs sat LuAnn down by the fireplace and stood in front of her. "I'd love for all of you to move in here. There's plenty of room. But —" He looked down.

"But what?" she asked.

"I was thinking about a more permanent arrangement."

"I see."

"I mean, I earn a good living and, well, now that you don't have all that money." She cocked her head at him as he blew out a deep breath. "I just never wanted you to think I was after you because of your wealth. It would've driven me crazy. It was like this big roadblock I couldn't get around. I don't want you to think that I'm happy you're not rich anymore. If there had been some way for you to keep the money, that would've been great. But, now that you don't have it, I just want you to know . . ." Here he stumbled again, unable to continue, suddenly terrified at the deep waters he had ventured into.

"I love you, Matthew," LuAnn said simply.

Riggs's features fully relaxed. He didn't look terrified anymore. In fact, he couldn't remember ever being this happy before. "I love you too, LuAnn Tyler."

"Have you ever been to Switzerland?" she asked.

He looked surprised. "No. Why?"

"I always thought about honeymooning there. It's so romantic, so beautiful. Especially at Christmas time."

Riggs looked troubled. "Well, sweetie, I work hard, but small-town, one-man-shop general contractors don't make enough money to do those sorts of things. I'm sorry." He licked his lips nervously. "I'll understand if you can't accept that, after all these years of being so rich."

In response, LuAnn opened her purse and took out a slip of paper. On it was an account number at a bank in Switzerland. The account had been opened with one hundred million dollars: Jackson's return of her principal. It was all there, just waiting. It cranked out six million a year in interest alone. She would retain her lottery prize after all. And she wasn't feeling any guilt about it this time around. Right now in fact, it seemed like she had earned it. She had spent the last ten years trying to be someone she wasn't. It had been a life of great wealth and great misery. Now she was going to spend the rest of her life being who she really was and enjoying it. She had a beautiful, healthy daughter and *two* men who loved her. No more running, no more hiding for LuAnn Tyler. She was truly blessed.

She smiled at him, stroked his face.

"You know what, Matthew?"

"What?"

Right before she kissed him she said, "I think we'll be just fine."

We hope you have enjoyed this Large Print book. Other Thorndike Press or Chivers Press Large Print books are available at your library or directly from the publishers.

For more information about current and upcoming titles, please call or write, without obligation, to:

Thorndike Press
P.O. Box 159
Thorndike, Maine 04986 USA
Tel. (800) 257-5157

OR

Chivers Press Limited
Windsor Bridge Road
Bath BA2 3AX
England
Tel. (0225) 335336

All our Large Print titles are designed for easy reading, and all our books are made to last.